THE BLANCHARD WITCHES
OF DAIHMLER COUNTY

MICAH HOUSE

This is a work of fiction. All of the characters, organizations and events portrayed in this novel are either products of the author's imagination or used fictitiously.

The Blanchard Witches of Daihmler County

First published 2021

Copyright © 2021 by Micah House

All rights reserved.

Published by Kendrell Publishing, Birmingham, Alabama

Edited by Crystal Castle

Cover design by Paul Palmer-Edwards

Hardback ISBN: 979-8-9887296-0-0

Dedicated to my wonderfully supportive husband Clarke, for allowing me two years to follow my dream of being a writer.

And for listening to me ramble on endlessly over plot points and character development.

You have lived and breathed The Blanchard's almost as much as I have.

CONTENTS

Guess Who's Coming to Dinner. 9
Kitchen Talk. 17
Never the Twain Should Meet 21
Somewhere in Time 30
Where It's Easier 40
Face the Destiny 48
A Little Comfort. 51
The Reason. 55
Healing Hands 58
Madam Zelda 61
Acceptance 66
Fireflies and Cigarettes 71
Salem Laughs Again 76
Practice Makes Perfect. 84
Too Much to Consider 89
A Blanchard in Oleander 93
Working Late 101
Date Night. 105
The Consort 110
The Cremation 116
Pastoria. 121
Salem's Father 125
Demitra's Gift 132
Bad Endings 136
Love and Moonlight 141
Sunday Lunch and Morning News 145
Forgiveness 151
Another Murder 154
The Witch Who Cried Wolf 160

Fable Finds a Man	164
Sherlock Blanchard	167
Empty Nest	170
The Other Blanchards	173
A Sister for Salem	180
Beryl Gets Suspicious	186
Artemis' Birthday	191
Jilted Lovers	194
Dial "P" For Psychic	197
Patric's Hasty Departure	202
Don't Open the Door	205
A Friend at Home	209
The Coven Intervenes	212
Witches Brew	217
Battle with a Werewolf	220
A Fresh Morning	228
Settling In	233
Fable and her Father	236
Sinclair's Request	239
Autumn Leaves	243
Preparing for the Big Day	249
An Obreiggon at Blanchard House	253
The Bachelorette Party	261
Frantic	265
Ties that Bind	269
Beauty and the Beast	272
The Calvary	277
The Light of Morning	280
The Witch Takes a Wife	283

CHAPTER ONE

Guess Who's Coming to Dinner

It was a beautiful Saturday afternoon, her four thousand four hundred and thirty-second Saturday afternoon. Olympia Blanchard was eighty-five, but her mind hadn't slowed down for a second. She was the eldest of her kind in her family, so that made her the wisest. She was sitting on the front porch which wrapped around their large twenty-three room country house. At three stories tall, not including the tower room, the Blanchard house was one of the largest homes in Daihmler County, Alabama. It was on this land where courageous farmers, armed with only their tools and very few rifles, did their best to ambush Yankee soldiers marching their fiery path through Alabama during the Civil War. The ambush did not stop the soldiers whose orders were to burn every landmark and building of prestige, but it is remembered as a courageous endeavor nonetheless. Although if truth be told, the Confederate Blanchard's of the time were running a secret stop on the underground railroad. Jebediah Blanchard and his wife Nancy helped 17 slaves get to the north. And it happened on Blanchard land. Olympia was proud of her home and heritage—most of her heritage.

The soft cushions of the white wicker rocker helped her to relax, as the scents of flowers whiffed by in the quiet breeze. The morning glories climbed high and proud, wrapping around the columns of the porch, displaying a regal shade of blue. Another vine twisted alongside the morning glories, a vine of moonflowers which would open a cascade of white brilliance at nightfall. Around the porch grew her roses, gardenia's, and hydrangeas. A few feet away stood her six tall magnolias, emitting perfume all the way to the pool area beside the house.

She grinned whenever she thought of the pool. The grandchildren had insisted upon that monstrosity. It wasn't natural to dig a hole in the ground and pour concrete and chlorine water in it. Olympia tried to tell them to walk down to the stream if they wanted to swim, but they just had to have a swimming pool. Sinclair had put that dreadful thing in against her wishes. But he'd never been able to say no to the grandchildren, she remembered smiling. He'd loved them as if they'd been his very own. And they'd all adored him.

I should go inside. It's hot and I have been out here too long.

Olympia rolled her eyes. *Will they never learn?*

"Demitra," she whispered into the breeze. "Come here."

Moments later a woman of around forty appeared in the doorway, her raven hair curling gently off her shoulders.

"Yes, Mother?"

"Dear, will you and your sister ever figure out that though I am old, I am still not weak enough for your mind games to work on me."

"Sorry, Mother." Demitra smiled. "But it is too hot out here for you. You should come in where it's cool."

"I know this old body better than you do my Love," Olympia replied. "I want a few more minutes out here in the sunshine with my flowers."

Demitra took a seat in the empty rocker beside her mother and enjoyed a little of the summer's gifts herself. She paused between rocks and asked, "Tell me, mother to mother, how do you differentiate between your own thoughts and implanted ones? I never learned to, and the girls were always doing it to me as teenagers."

"No, they weren't my Love," Olympia chuckled, much too pleased with herself, remembering those long gone days when her daughter's daughters were younger. "That was me. You were much too strict with them. They needed some freedom."

"So, it was you who would plant those thoughts in my head about dropping curfews and letting them date early!" Demitra gasped, but in truth she wasn't a bit surprised by this revelation. "You are unscrupulous Olympia Blanchard!"

Olympia patted her daughter's hand. "It was strenuous on you, Baby. Raising children alone is never easy."

"You managed fine."

"Honey, if I'd managed fine then Artemis might be married with children of her own, and Nacaria might not have ruined her life the way she did."

Demitra smiled consolingly, "You did the best job raising us that anyone ever could do. One single mother with three adolescent witches to raise had to be its own kind of torture. At least I had you and Artemis for help."

The old woman laughed out loud. "Yes, it wasn't easy to remain one step ahead of you three girls. This white hair of mine used to be the loveliest blonde."

"You amaze me everyday, Mother. Always did. Like the mind whisper thing. I could be at a friend's house, and I could hear you speak to me. And you always knew when we were lying to you. I know you're gonna say it's because you're a full witch and we weren't, but I don't buy that. Salem and Seth are full witches, but they can't do all the things you can do."

"Demitra, Demitra, so full of questions. Your mother is old and wise in the ways of the earth and despite your lack of assuredness, so are you."

The tranquility of the moment came to an abrupt end as Seth Blanchard came tearing up the driveway in his white truck. He'd barely stopped the vehicle before he bounded out, bolting up the porch steps to his grandmother and aunt. The sunlight streaming onto the porch accentuated his sandy blonde hair.

"Guess what? Guess what?"

"Slow down Seth," Demitra replied. "What on earth is so important? If this about how much you bench pressed at the gym again, we're not that interested."

"They finally agreed to come to dinner!" Seth exclaimed, lifting the end of his red tank top to wipe a little sweat from his brow. "After all my invitations they finally agreed."

"Who?" Demitra asked.

"His young girl and her father, I am presuming," Olympia answered.

"Yes!" Seth beamed. "Vanessa and her father."

"Oh," Demitra frowned, cutting her eyes to her mother. "The reverend that hates us."

"He doesn't hate us!" Seth cried. "He's just nervous about us. But he's agreed to come for dinner to meet the family. If all goes well and we win him over, he'll stop giving Vanessa a hard time about dating me."

The screen door opened as two women, different in ages, stepped outside to the porch. The first looked very much the same as Demitra, only her raven black hair reached her hips rather than stopping at the shoulders. This was Olympia's eldest daughter, Artemis. The younger woman accompanying Artemis looked like a fresher copy of the sisters with short, wispy hair. This was Demitra's daughter Fable. The sunlight streaming onto the porch cast shadows on the white plank board wall of the house. Artemis and Fable's shadows were not alone. Between them hovered a third shadow but there was no figure on the porch to cast it.

"Seth, are you on fire or something!" Artemis Blanchard scolded, sweeping a bit of flour out of her hair. "I have a cake in the oven."

"Where's Beryl and Yazzy?" Seth asked.

"Beryl is still making her rounds at the hospital," Fable Blanchard answered. "And Yaz is assisting Howard with some depositions."

"Oh, I forgot she took that job at his office," Seth replied. "Well, call them and tell them to be on time for dinner tonight. And everyone is to be on their best behavior. No one is casting, using their powers, or in any way even referencing witchcraft tonight."

"You don't get to order us around Seth Blanchard!" Fable shouted. "I don't care who is coming to dinner, we don't have to change ourselves for anybody."

Olympia waved a hand to shush her granddaughter. "Fable, your cousin is just excited because he wants to make a good impression on his girlfriend's father. You have to admit we Blanchards are a lot to take in. Reverend Collins has certainly heard about us in town since they moved here last winter. I don't think Seth is asking a lot. Simply that we not be too *in their face* about our way of life tonight."

"Thank you, Hecate," Seth grinned. "Now if we can just get *her* to stay upstairs tonight." As he spoke, the third shadow on the wall of the house darted to the open doorway and disappeared into the house.

"Don't speak to her like that!" Demitra snapped.

"Everyone calm down," Artemis said. "Seth- you come with me to the kitchen, and let's figure out what I should feed your sweet Vanessa and her father. If I remember correctly, preachers always used to like fried chicken." They left the porch together as Fable took a seat atop the wooden porch railing.

"This is ridiculous," she said. "Vanessa Collins is not even right for Seth. Why we have to go through the motions with her and her father is beyond me."

"We love Seth," Demitra told her daughter. "He had a very hard time when he lost Susan. It wrecked him. He's done nothing with his life but work out like a fiend and fail college classes. The fact that he appears to care for this Vanessa so much is important. It might put him on the right track. We will do as he asks."

"Yeah, but we all liked Susan," Fable said, remembering her again after so long. "We all went to high school together. Susan was the best."

"And if she hadn't died in that jet skiing accident the summer after graduation, Seth probably would have married her," Demitra pointed out. "It's taken him a while to get over that, and he's dated some doozy mistakes since. This thing with this Vanessa seems different."

"He's too young to get too serious. I sure hope he doesn't plan to marry this girl," Fable scoffed. "Marriages don't work out too well in this family."

"Your father and I had a perfect marriage," Demitra exclaimed. "And Mother and Sinclair were very happy."

"Then I'll restate my comments." Fable sneered. "Spouses don't live a really long time in this family."

"Well, that is certainly the truth," Olympia laughed. "But I've always felt that love, no matter how short-lived, is always worth experiencing."

...

As she shut off the computer, Yasmine Sinclair swept back the same unruly brown curl from her eyes that never seemed to grow out long enough to tuck behind her ear. She glanced around at the tiny little office. It needed a woman's touch. Now that she was working here, she'd make some changes. Plants, pillow cushions on the waiting room sofa. Maybe she'd even give the walls a coat of paint. Howard Caldwell may be a great personal estate manager, but he wasn't the best decorator in the world. Gathering some papers from the printer tray she gave a quick rap on the door to the connecting office before walking inside. Howard was at his desk, busy with the latest mutual fund reports.

"I finished the Carson file. Now I'm hungry and ready for a swim. Wanna come back to the house with me?"

Howard looked up from his work and smiled at his lovely assistant. "Actually, I do. Your grandmother called and invited me to dinner a few minutes ago. My car hasn't come back from being serviced yet, so I'll ride home with you and Uber back later. Now, go down and start the car and I'll be there in a minute."

"Oh goody," she laughed. "I get to sit in the hot sticky car until it cools off enough for you to come down."

"That's what I pay you the big bucks for," Howard winked.

Howard watched her go and then slipped on the blazer which had been hanging on the back of his chair. Yasmine was the best assistant he'd ever had. His office was in shambles after his last assistant quit to marry the FedEx delivery man who knocked her up. Ironic, since he had suspected all along she'd only taken the job in his office to try and meet rich clients whose wealth he managed. It all worked out for the best. He now had Yasmine. She was organized, friendly, smart, and best of all she did not mind working weekends when necessary. Her work ethic was a nice surprise. When she had asked him for a job, he'd only hired her as a favor to her grandmother—or step-grandmother as it were. It was the best favor he'd ever done. If he was not twenty years her senior, he might even allow himself to fall in love with her.

Yasmine drove to Blanchard House while Howard replied to a few urgent emails from his phone. She was a good driver. He'd actually taught her himself just a few years ago when she turned 16. He'd taught her cousin Fable too, a couple of years before that. After Demitra's husband Larry Mariner died, Howard did his best to step in to be the surrogate father figure for all the Blanchard grandchildren.

"I need to speak to your grandmother tonight about her accounts," Howard said once he had sent the final email. "Some of her investments need revisiting."

"Please do not try to talk her into that oil company again," Yasmine laughed.

"Oh, I learned my lesson the last time. It is not easy making sure none of her investments cause any harm to the earth. That is one of the things I need to discuss with her. One of her holdings has just cleared a section of rainforest."

"Uh-oh."

"Uh-oh's right," Howard grimaced. "So of course, now she'll insist on selling. But the worst part is her refusal to do anything with your grandfather's money. It just sits there."

"You'll never get her to spend that money."

"I don't want her to spend it," Howard replied. "I want her to invest it."

"You know Grandmother's reasons," Yasmine answered.

"Yeah, but they are preposterous reasons."

"Maybe so," Yasmine sighed, "But they are her reasons and it's her money. I've lived with her for fifteen years and I've learned a lot. She's a pretty smart cookie. I wouldn't be so quick to scoff at her principals."

"Oh, I'd never be fool enough to scoff at Olympia Blanchard. I admire her. She is a woman of wisdom and substance. But as her financial advisor, it burns me up that she is sitting on a fortune she'll do nothing with. Not to mention the millions she's wasted over the years."

"I wouldn't call it wasted," Yasmine declared. "She's just using it to right the wrongs she feels Granddaddy's company committed to the planet while he was alive."

"That woman has spent years making restitution where none is needed. Your grandfather was a brilliant businessman. But it is her money. At least she set aside a sizable amount for you."

"Not to change the subject," Yasmine said, making the turnoff towards the Blanchard property, "But why did you get invited tonight? Friday night is your typical dinner night at the house."

"Is it so unbearable to have to dine with me two nights in a row?" Howard laughed.

"No, of course not. It just seemed last minute."

"Well, my little sidekick," Howard chuckled, "It seems Seth's girlfriend's father finally agreed to come to dinner to meet the family. I guess I am going to be the conservative normal man to the mix. Imagine a preacher at the table of the Blanchard coven. Should be an interesting night."

"Should be." Yasmine replied softly. She stared down the road as she drove. Her silence was telling.

"How is this sitting with you, Yasmine?"

"What do you mean?"

"You know very well what I mean. You have a thing for Seth. You aren't very good at hiding it."

"I do not have *a thing* for Seth. I'm very happy with the man I'm seeing."

Howard sneered. "Yes, *the man you're seeing*. Do you realize you never describe him any other way?"

"What are you even talking about?"

"Yasmine, you never once have referred to Jake as your boyfriend. Just *the man you're seeing*."

"That's only because we haven't reached that serious a level yet."

"You've been dating for two months!"

"I'm just not quite sure yet how I feel."

"And that's because you are in love with Seth. Always have been, always will be. He's just too dumb to realize he loves you too."

"We are cousins. That's the only way he sees us," Yasmine replied.

"Not blood cousins."

"Doesn't matter," she explained. "When Granddaddy married Olympia, we were all small. They loved him like he was their real grandfather and they love me like a real cousin. Seth has never thought of me any other way. I figured that out when he fell in love with Susan in high school. Then after she died, he wasn't ready for any kind of relationship. I guess now he is, and its Vanessa."

"But if Seth were with you, he could be himself. He can hardly be a Blanchard around that preacher's daughter."

"We will see," Yasmine grinned. "But I'll be honest with you, Howard. If I had any Blanchard blood in me, I'd turn that girl into a lizard faster than you could say 'Abracadabra!'"

CHAPTER TWO

Kitchen Talk

Artemis was busying herself in the kitchen preparing dinner. She loved those rare occasions when company came. It gave her a good opportunity to use the many recipes she learned while in culinary school. It had always been her dream to be a chef, and she might have achieved that dream had her powers not gotten in the way back then. Artemis had the ability to *will* things to happen just by thinking them. It was a strong power which had taken half her life to learn to control.

Once, long ago, when she'd been training with a renowned chef in Birmingham, she'd been undergoing a test—a test which would determine whether or not she'd be awarded a permanent position at the restaurant. She labored hours at home concocting the perfect meal to prepare on test day. When test day came, she was doing pretty well until she overheard two nearby restaurant employees discussing their recent trip to the coast. Their conversation caused Artemis to think about sandy beaches and the taste of salty ocean water. That brief mental flight of fancy ruined her meal. When the chef tasted her food, it was drenched with salt and gritty sand particles.

Whatever her mind thought manifested itself in those days. If she thought of rain, a sprinkler system might activate. If she felt hot, a fire might break out. In her family, Artemis' power was one of the strongest abilities, but it was also the most difficult to master. It caused her much grief over the years. She'd never married. At fifty-one years old she wondered what life might have been like had she not been born a witch. She might have found the right man and settled down. Of course, there was still time. Her face looked like it was in its early thirties. She might still find the right guy one day. As for having children, that wasn't very important. She'd raised her fair share already despite never being a mother. After her brother-in-law Larry died, she helped Demitra bring up Beryl and Fable. And after what happened to her other sister Nacaria, Artemis raised Salem and Seth as if they were her own.

Artemis' life was far from empty, even if some of her dreams may not have come true.

Footsteps clambered on the wooden kitchen stairs as Fable bolted down. "What smells so good?" She lifted the lid on one of the pots atop the stove and breathed in the aroma.

"Get out of that before I smack your behind," Artemis warned.

"Smells great, whatever it is," Fable replied. Hopping up to sit on the kitchen counter, she looked at her aunt with a serious face and asked, "How do you think it'll go tonight?"

"Badly."

"Me too!" Fable confided with a smirk.

The kitchen was well-lit from recessed lighting mixing with the afternoon sun shining through the bank of windows over the large farm sink and counter. But the light infiltrating the room only made the shadow passing over the far wall that much more noticeable.

"How do we explain *that*?" Fable said with an eye roll.

"Maybe they won't notice," Artemis answered.

"Oh, she'll make sure they notice."

Artemis lifted the lid to stir its contents and said, "We'll just have to deal with it. After all, if that girl ends up marrying Seth and comes here to live, she'll have to be told eventually."

The kitchen door swung open as Yasmine and Howard walked inside. "My, my," Howard chuckled. "A witch and her cauldron. I love a woman who cooks. Say, Artemis, why don't you marry me? I'm tired of ordering take-out every night."

Artemis gave him a knowing smile and said, "As I recall, we tried that once and it didn't turn out so well."

"True, true," Howard recalled. "Your mother wasn't on board."

"I didn't know that's why you two broke up back in the day!" Fable exclaimed. "Hecate was against it? That's crazy. Howard, she adores you."

"Maybe so, but she wasn't a fan of your aunt and me getting hitched. But I always felt like it was more as a protection to me. Your aunt was a pretty dangerous witch to be around in her younger days. If I said I thought I had a cold, her wacky power turned it into hypothermia."

"See what agonies you were spared not marrying me!" Artemis laughed, nudging him out of her way so that she could grab a wooden spoon from a drawer.

"Maybe so," Howard smiled, giving his friend a kiss on the forehead as she reached past him for the spoon. "But you still look the same as you did back then, and I am old and bald. Or did you do that to me?"

"Well," Artemis grinned returning to her saucepan, "I may have once thought to myself that your hair was beginning to thin—but I can't be sure."

The laughter from the kitchen brought Seth bounding down the stairs to join them. "Hey Howie! Here to meet my girl tonight?"

Yasmine grimaced. Only Howard noticed.

"Yep, maybe I can keep things on an even keel for you."

The shadow passed across the floor again.

"Damn it!" Seth shouted. "That thing is going to ruin everything tonight."

"*That thing* has a name, Seth," Artemis scolded.

For a moment Seth recoiled in shame, then he said, "I'm sorry, but everything has to go just right tonight. How's it going to look when a phantom shadow hovers along the dining room wall?"

"I'll talk to her," Artemis promised. "You need to relax. But you also should probably face that your girlfriend will need to be told sooner than later if the idea is to see whether or not she is able to join this family."

"Seth," Yasmine said softly, touching his arm, "Granddaddy and I weren't afraid. I'm sure Vanessa won't be either."

Howard watched silently as Yasmine's index finger lightly stroked the bicep of Seth's muscled arm. The way she looked at him made Howard's heart ache for her. She loved Seth and it was obvious to Howard but didn't seem to be to anyone else.

"Don't be so sure, Yazzy," Fable laughed. "We're an awful lot to take on."

Demitra suddenly rushed into the room. "I just had a vision of them! They're almost here. I saw their car coming through town. They'll be here in around ten minutes."

"Damn! They're early," Seth cried. "Where are they now?"

Demitra closed her eyes and let her inner eye run through the streets to find them. "Elm and Madison."

"I have to change," Seth said looking down at his musty tank top and gym shorts. "Can you stall them Aunt Artemis?"

Artemis gave him a quick nod as she poured a jar of broth into a pot of simmering beans. "I'll hold up the traffic light at Elm and Brady. That'll buy you a few minutes. Maybe I'll even roll a stray garbage can into the street. That's always fun."

Seth leapt up the stairs, skipping two at a time. Fable hopped off the kitchen counter to take a look at the bread baking in the oven. "This is going to be quite an evening."

CHAPTER THREE

Never the Twain Should Meet

The Reverend Collins and his daughter Vanessa arrived roughly an hour early after overestimating the amount of time it would take them from their home in Northport to find the Blanchard house. The Blanchards accepted their explanation at face value, all except Olympia, who recognized they had purposefully arrived early in order to see what Seth's family was like when caught off guard. Reverend Collins and Vanessa made concealed inspections of their surroundings as everyone made hurried introductions. From the top of the long straight staircase with its maple railings, across the shiny clean hardwood floors, into the living room just off the entrance way, the Collins' eyes tracked every inch they could see.

Artemis rushed dinner to the table, knowing that Seth didn't want his girlfriend or her father around the family any longer than they had to be. They all took seats around the large dining room table with Olympia taking her place at the head quite ceremoniously with Howard pulling her chair out for her. There was idle conversation, of course. Vanessa complimented the intricacies of the lace tablecloth. Demitra told her she had sewn it herself. Vanessa mentioned that her mother had been an accomplished knitter and tried to pass that skill along to her, but Vanessa had never been very gifted in that regard. Artemis asked the reverend about the traffic conditions on the drive from Northport to Daihmler, and he informed her about new road work being done on McFarland Boulevard. Seth sat nervously fiddling with his fork, nudging the food around his plate without taking many bites. Fable sat and watched with bemused fascination at how anxious everyone seemed to be. Occasionally, she made side glances to Yasmine, but Yasmine appeared to be just as uncomfortable as everyone else. Howard observed his young assistant's discomfort as well and attempted to drive the table talk to less chit-chatty matters.

"Reverend Collins, I suppose you came to Daihmler thinking this would be a nice, quiet little hamlet to take up residence, but I assume you've heard about the two murders in the news."

Vanessa bristled noticeably and sat her forkful of mashed potatoes back down on her plate, "It's scary. The girl they found last week lived not too far from us."

"Did you know her?" Fable asked.

"No," Vanessa replied. "But it still makes me nervous."

Reverend Collins frowned and shook his head in disbelief. "It's disturbing to think about what some human beings are capable of doing to each other. Our church is actually paying for the funeral, once the body is released."

"That's very kind," Olympia said warmly. "What a generous thing to do."

"Yes," Reverend Collins sighed. "The girl's family used to be members of the congregation some years ago I'm told. Of course, this was well before we moved to Daihmler, so I have never met the family personally. I've heard they are a very nice family."

"Daihmler is usually a very quiet place," Olympia said almost apologetically. "I'm sorry it isn't showing you that aspect of its character at present. Typically we are a very safe town."

"Demitra? Has Charlie called you in on the investigation?" Howard asked as he snatched two more fried wings from the large platter in the center of the table. Before the wings had come to a rest on his plate, Yasmine reached over Fable and pulled one back to the platter.

"Your cholesterol is high."

Howard reached back to the platter and took the wing back. "Then I'll get Beryl to heal—"

Seth coughed into his fist and gave Howard a side eye.

"I'll get Beryl to up my medication," Howard corrected.

The Reverend seemed puzzled but turned his attention towards Demitra, who had just begun to answer the question. "No," she said. "I haven't heard from Charlie. But the second murder only just happened. I doubt the police had any idea until then that this was going to be an ongoing situation. The first murder was brutal, but no one would have anticipated there would be another one exactly like the first."

"We may have a serial killer in our midst," Howard said crunching into the crispy skin of the chicken wing.

Vanessa looked pale. "Can we change the subject, please?"

Fable gave off a forced laugh which didn't sound like much of a laugh at all, "Seth, you didn't tell us your girlfriend was so squeamish."

The conversation dwindled back to boring niceties which no one was interested in. But when only the crunch of fried chicken could be heard around the table, the pretenses were dropped, and Reverend Collins got to the heart of the matter.

"All pleasantries aside," he began, "I wanted to come here tonight to meet all of you. It seems things are moving quickly with Vanessa and Seth, and I was eager to learn more about his family and upbringing."

"A reasonable request," Olympia smiled. "Please feel free to ask us anything."

"So, you are Seth's grandmother?" Reverend Collins began.

"Yes," Olympia replied.

"It was my understanding that you are his grandmother from his mother's side of the family. But how is it that your last names are the same?"

Olympia knew what he was intimating. "We Blanchards hold on to our family name regardless of marriage. My married name is Sinclair, but I go by Blanchard."

"Oh, will we be meeting your husband tonight as well?" Collins asked.

"He passed away eleven years ago."

"I'm terribly sorry," Collins blushed. "But you can forgive my nosiness, I hope. I have only the one daughter, and I am afraid I'm very protective of her. It's just that I was trying to make sure that Seth wasn't illegitimate."

Vanessa bristled and elbowed her father in the side. He turned to give her a stern look which made her return her focus to the plate of food and seemingly ignore whatever was being said around her.

"What would that matter?" Yasmine defended, dropping her fork to the table.

Reverend Collins smiled politely, "Well, I suppose in these current times, it doesn't matter very much. Still, I am of an older generation and I am a minister after all. Are you Seth's sister?"

"No. I am Yasmine Sinclair."

"So, you are not a Blanchard?"

"Yasmine is my granddaughter," Olympia explained. "She's the daughter of my late husband's son, who is also deceased."

The shadow passed over the wall. Seth dropped his fork onto his plate nervously. The loud clank startled the table. The shadow lingered a moment, then floated up to the ceiling where it passed over the light fixture and disappeared through the doorway to the kitchen.

"Uh, good meal Aunt Artemis," Seth stammered. "Does everyone have rolls? The rolls are really good."

Howard lifted one and began to butter it. "So fluffy and golden. Butter just melts over it."

"What was that?" Vanessa asked, looking around the room for the weird shadow.

"What was what?" Seth asked without looking up from his plate.

"Something moved across the wall."

"Old houses cast odd shadows," Demitra smiled as she lifted the basket of rolls from the table and offered to their guests. "These are really good rolls."

The sound of the front door opening and a rattle of keys being tossed onto a table announced an arrival. A woman with shoulder length curly honey blonde hair wearing hospital scrubs appeared in the doorway, drawing attention to herself.

"Since when do we eat at 6:30?" she asked, scanning the table and its inhabitants with a puzzled expression. "And this isn't your usual night Howard."

"We have company dear," Demitra told her. "This is the girl Seth's been seeing lately, Vanessa. And her father, *Reverend* Collins. Didn't you get my message at the hospital?"

"No, I didn't go back to my office after I made my rounds."

"I texted you, too," Demitra added.

The woman smiled placatingly and replied, "Well, I guess I didn't look at my texts either, then." She nodded to the guests, "Hello, I am Beryl Blanchard."

"Are you a nurse?" Reverend Collins asked.

"Doctor, actually," Beryl replied. She took her usual seat on the other side of Seth. Giving him a nudge, she whispered, "You look like we all just landed back in Old Salem."

Suddenly Demitra had a strange look on her face. "Salem! Has anyone spoken with Salem today?"

"I talked to her last week. Why?" Fable asked.

"I'm not sure yet," Demitra murmured. She had a bad feeling, but it was not a premonition—those she knew how to handle. This was something else, something she couldn't quite put her finger on.

Vanessa leaned toward Seth and softly asked, "Who's Salem?"

"My sister," Seth replied. "I told you about her, didn't I? She lives in Atlanta with her husband."

"Would you believe Reverend Collins, that I am a great grandmother?" Olympia smiled proudly. "Salem gave birth to a beautiful little boy last year. Michael is my first great-grandchild."

Seth remembered the first time Salem's husband David came to dinner at Blanchard House. Somehow things hadn't felt so awkward that night. But maybe that was because it was all happening to Salem, and this time it was Seth feeling the anxiety. He looked over at his cousin Fable, and for just a second thought maybe he'd enjoyed the tension that night with David just as much as Fable appeared to be enjoying tonight.

Artemis couldn't pull her eyes away from the disturbed look on her sister's face. She elbowed Demitra. "Are you okay?"

"Something is wrong. I can feel it."

By now Olympia too felt something was off in the energy fields around her, although she tried not to show it. There was no point to upsetting their current guests, especially since there was absolutely nothing which could be done right now. She knew all too well from experience that psychic senses cannot be rushed. Visions, premonitions, and the like must come in their own time.

Helping himself to another portion of fried chicken, Reverend Collins continued with his veiled interrogation. "Would it be rude of me to ask what denomination the Blanchard family belongs to?"

"Denomination of what?" Fable asked sarcastically. Seth took a swipe at her leg under the table.

"Church, Miss Blanchard," Reverend Collins replied. "What church is your family affiliated with?"

"We don't go to church," Fable sneered.

"Isn't the world just one big church really?" Seth said.

"I've always thought so," Howard chimed in giving Seth a little help.

Olympia gave Seth and Howard the eye as she returned a polite smile to their guests. "I believe what my grandson is saying, Reverend, is that one only needs to go out into the world at large to find spiritual bonds with the higher powers."

"I, myself, believe in the traditional foundational principles of God's consecrated structures," the minister said mostly to himself.

"Not everyone goes to church, Dad," Vanessa said. "It doesn't mean anything awful."

"Well, Vanessa, I am a representative of the church. I should hope that whomever my daughter chooses to walk through life with would also be of the same religious faith as we."

"Let's just cut to the chase here," Vanessa said to the rest of the table. "I care a lot about Seth, and instead of just being happy about that, my father is concerned because he has heard some talk in Tuscaloosa and Daihmler that the Blanchard family are witches."

"Really?" Seth gasped, feigning surprise.

"Yes," Vanessa replied, swatting Seth's foot under the table with her own. "I've asked Seth about it a time or two, but he dances around the subject."

"I'm glad my daughter cut to the meat of this visit," Collins said. "I have indeed asked around about your family. Of course, here in the south, with families as old as yours seems to be, one can hear any number of things. Please understand that I have heard only positive things about the Blanchard family. I haven't heard a single word spoken negatively about any of you..."

"But you've been told that we are witches," Olympia smiled.

"I do not mean to insult you."

"I'm not insulted," Olympia replied. "Reverend Collins, we *are witches*."

"Hecate!" Seth cried.

"Settle down Seth," Artemis cautioned. "It was bound to come out sooner or later. You didn't really believe you could keep seeing Vanessa without telling her the truth, did you?"

"You admit to this slanderous allegation?" Reverend Collins asked Olympia with a look of bewilderment.

"I don't consider facts to be slanderous, if they are indeed facts," Olympia nodded. "I am a witch. My father was a witch. My mother was a witch. My grandfather, great-grandmother...and all of my children and grandchildren are witches."

"Well..." Yasmine blushed.

"Yes," Olympia grinned, patting her youngest granddaughter's hand. "Almost all of my grandchildren. Basically, if you have Blanchard blood coursing through your veins, you are a witch."

"I cannot believe how readily you admit this."

"It's not a crime Reverend Collins," Olympia explained. "It's also not a secret. Everyone around here knows about the Blanchard witches. People of Daihmler and as far as Tuscaloosa, frequently come to us for help on certain matters in their lives.

Our own Demitra here often works with the police department on some of their most puzzling cases. Our Beryl is a prominent doctor. Fable is one of Alabama's leading veterinarians. Our being witches is simply one part of our identity, just as your being a Reverend is only a part of yours."

"My Christianity is the totality of me. I give myself wholly to the Lord. I am afraid there is no way my daughter can be associated with practitioners of witchcraft. It would be the equivalent of allowing her to worship the devil."

Fable leaned into the table. Everyone knew that when Fable Blanchard leans forward and makes direct eye contact, she's about to school someone. "Reverend Collins," she began, "you might be surprised to know that being a witch has nothing to do with the devil. In fact, I don't even believe in the devil, because I don't believe in God."

Seth smacked his hands into his forehead. *Why did Reverend Collins have to rile Fable?* Getting Fable agitated was always a recipe for disaster. All you had to do was ask the mailman who tore her copy of Vogue last month, or the poor Starbucks guy who gave her foam last week when she didn't want foam, or anyone at the gym who tries to superset exercises by taking up more than one piece of equipment. Fable's greatest gift was going off on people.

"I'm not surprised to hear you don't believe in God, young lady," the Reverend huffed.

"Well, listen to my next one and perhaps you will be. It is true, I don't believe in God. I find the entire concept to be a childish holdover from the Dark Ages because unfortunately mankind is still too frightened to admit that the things that happen to us in life are all by chance. Most need some ethereal finger to guide their life because they do not have courage enough to guide their own. You need God. I, personally, do not.

"But it may interest you to know that many witches do believe in God. Many witches believe they are God's chosen ones--set a rung up on the ladder above other humans in order to protect and enrich them in this life. Earthly angels so to speak. How else would a man of faith be able to rationalize the powers a witch might possess. Wouldn't it seem more likely that your God gave them their abilities, much the way you would believe in the power he gave to angels."

"But angels weren't burned at the stake a few hundred years ago by Christian people. Witches were," Collins countered.

"And from that statement alone, who sounds like the bigger monster?" Fable said with a searing look. "Another fun fact for you," she went on, "none of the men and women ever killed during those times was truly a witch. Because quite frankly, a real witch would easily have gotten away if they had wanted to. Just like if I wanted to right now, I could bring down a swarm of blue birds to shit on your head—or peck your eyes out."

"Fable!" Beryl shouted at her sister.

"I don't like this man!" Fable shouted back.

Seth barked across the table at his cousin, "Stop being a bitch Fable!"

"Children, stop this now," Olympia warned.

"We are getting off point." Artemis interrupted, turning her attention back to the reverend. "Reverend Collins, I fully understand that you have a faith which makes it difficult for you to understand our ways. My niece was—rather rudely—trying to make a point. Like with everyone else in the world, some people subscribe to certain religious faiths and others do not. My niece is an atheist. Militantly so. I myself am more agnostic. It matters very little to me if there is a God or not. My mother, however, is a Christian and a follower of Christ's teachings, as is Seth's sister Salem. Also, my niece Beryl here. Even within our own family we differ. But regardless of religious affiliations, we are in fact witches. The two things have nothing to do with one another."

"I disagree emphatically," the Reverend stated. "In my faith it is abhorrent for one to assign themselves to witchcraft."

"I don't think we so much chose it, as it chose us," Beryl quipped.

"You have no idea what devilry you are playing with!" Rev. Collins warned.

"Meaning no disrespect, Sir." Olympia smiled. "You have no idea the things I have seen and the evils I have battled to protect this great earth God has given us. You sit in the very solemnity in which my kind have fought to protect for you. So, let us simply end the frictions of this conversation. You are welcomed guests in our home, and we are glad you are here sharing our meal with us. We will naturally disagree on this fact because we have both been raised with a different set of teachings. But in no way should this affect Seth and Vanessa's courtship."

Seth looked to his Aunt Artemis as if to say "Help". He could always count on Artemis to run to his rescue. She'd been doing it all of his life. Every mess he'd ever gotten himself into she had gotten him out of—If anyone could reel this thing back on course, it would be she.

"The bottom line," Artemis said calmly after giving her nephew a reassuring wink, "Seth cares for Vanessa. I can see that Vanessa also cares for Seth. At the end of the day, if they want to be together none of us can stop them. Our jobs as their families is to love and support them, whatever they decide."

"Normally I'd agree with you, Miss Blanchard," Reverend Collins said. "But your family's unique situation gives me great pause."

Artemis nodded her head in understanding. Holding direct eye contact with their guest she did her best to calm his worries. "If you are concerned about our way of life, you needn't be. The Blanchards are good people. Loving people. And as you have already done, you may ask anyone in our community. We are kind people. I get the sense you and your daughter are probably kind as well. I hope so. If Vanessa ever joins our family, she will join it with love and welcoming hearts, but that is really up to her and Seth to decide- not you, not me, not any of us."

Vanessa grabbed Seth's hand in her own and squeezed it. He smiled at her and gave her a peck on the cheek. Howard was watching Yasmine, and his heart felt a little like it did all those years ago when Artemis let him go.

CHAPTER FOUR

Somewhere in Time

The sweet scent of the gardenias encasing the porch drowsed Olympia like a lullaby. She rocked back and forth in her rocking chair, listening to the summery sounds of nature's tenants chirping in the trees and buzzing in the grass. On her porch stood several potted hibiscus plants, each sporting blooms of yellow, orange, and pink. Along the balustrades of the porch the sun shone over several overflowing planters of zinnias, brightly colored like the day itself. The potted dahlias in red, yellow, and tangerine sprinkled down the wide front steps. Olympia glanced down from the porch to a patch of lawn where butterfly bushes in high bloom seemed to be attracting far more bumblebees than butterflies.

She leaned back and thought of the night before when Reverend Collins and his daughter made their hasty retreat from the house shortly after dinner. She thought of the poor girl. Vanessa seemed nice. She appeared to genuinely care for Seth. Olympia understood the child would have quite a battle with her father if she pursued the relationship. Olympia hoped she would. In her own youth, she'd had quite a few rounds with her sister when Olympia chose to marry John Windham. But in the end her sister accepted John. Or pretended to at least. Looking back now, Olympia had to admit that her sister Pastoria was probably right about that union. It had been fraught with conflict. But she acquired three beautiful children from those days which made it all worthwhile.

In the oak tree by the driveway, a squirrel was being chased away from a nest by a protective mother bird. Olympia smiled as she continued to rock. She thought of her own brood. Her children, her grandchildren, and little Michael. Her first great grandson. She stopped rocking. The feeling which had begun last night was growing now. Salem. Something was terribly off regarding Salem.

"Artemis! Demitra!"

"Mother, what's wrong?" Demitra cried rushing outside.

"Salem!" Olympia shouted. "Demitra, do you *feel* Salem?"

Demitra closed her eyes. "I don't."

"I don't either," Olympia said.

Artemis came outside now, dish towel in hand from the morning wash. "What's happening?"

"We need to do a thread," Olympia said. "Right now."

...

It only took a few minutes to rouse Seth out of bed and get him downstairs to the kitchen table. The other Blanchard's were at work, but they didn't need to be physically present for a thread. It would reach them wherever they were.

"What's going on?" Seth asked as his aunts clasped his hands in their own and then took Olympia's.

"I'm not certain," his grandmother replied. "Something is off. The balance is off."

"I felt it, too, last night," Demitra said. "I've been waiting for a premonition, but it hasn't come."

Olympia closed her eyes. She forced her concentration into the task. As head of the Blanchard coven and the matriarch of her family line, she was the only one who could begin the thread. It was not something she enjoyed doing, for it always left her feeling temporarily drained. Old age made that even more tiring. But there was no other means of discovering what she needed to discover. It must be done.

Focusing on herself first, reaching deep into her mind's eye and finding her own spirit within her body, she visualized herself as the first link in the chain. Next, she pictured Artemis as she squeezed her daughter's hand, allowing her spirit to flow directly into her eldest daughter's. Olympia could feel Artemis within her, almost as if their two souls had merged for a moment into one being. Artemis felt the connection in the same way as she and her mother became one single entity. The moment their two souls touched it felt as if a radiant light swelled within them. Their bloodline was turning on. Olympia moved to Demitra next, mentally envisioning her second daughter's spirit linking to Artemis and her own. Within seconds all three of their souls were aligned. There was a break in the flow now--a missing component, like a gap in a road. Nacaria. But Olympia understood that break in the chain. That was not a mystery. She moved on to Seth next. Though he was not the next chronologically in the bloodline—that would be Beryl—he was the closest in proximity, and Olympia needed the strength of the chain to power its ability to travel the distances to everyone else. It only took a moment to connect with Seth's soul and attach it to her own and his aunts'. Olympia focused on Beryl now. This link would take longer. Beryl was miles away at Daihmler County Hospital, forcing the thread to travel to reach her.

. . .

"I need Mr. Blake's test results from the lab before I meet with his wife," Dr. Beryl Blanchard told the nurse as she shuffled the charts clutched to her chest. It had already been a busy morning, but she was nearing the end of her rounds and preparing for her in-office consultations.

"Here it is Dr. Blanchard," the nurse said, handing over the file. "Dr. Blanchard. Dr. Blanchard?"

Dr. Blanchard wasn't listening. She had her eyes closed. All focus now turned inside herself as she felt the tendrils of her family's conjoined energy flowing into and through her. Beryl felt the wave hit and invade her body. Her family was connecting to her soul and that was the only thing she could feel at the moment. *Why are they performing a thread?*

Olympia found Beryl and passed through her; she was now on her way to Fable. This would take a little longer. Fable's practice was nearly on the other side of town, but the combined force of her spirit, mixed with Artemis, Demitra, Seth, and now Beryl made the thread move faster now.

. . .

"All right Spritzie," Fable smiled at the white schnauzer standing on her examination table. "Tell me what hurts."

Mrs. Renlap, Spritzie's owner, always thought it was cute the way Dr. Blanchard would speak to her patients as if they were human. It showed clients a sign of respect for the pets they loved. Mrs. Renlap appreciated that small nicety from her vet.

"This started after your granddaughter visited yesterday, correct?" Fable said.

"How did you know my granddaughter came over yesterday afternoon?" Mrs. Renlap gasped.

Fable was listening to Mrs. Renlap now, and she was no longer speaking mentally with the dog on her table.

"I'm afraid she fed Spritzie some fruit that isn't agreeing with her stomach," Fable told Mrs. Renlap. "That's why she won't eat anything today and why she keeps yelping. Spritzie's stomach is very upset."

"How do you—"

Now Fable's attentions were turned inward. She did not hear the rest of Mrs. Renlap's question. She could only feel her sister Beryl's spirit touch her own. Behind Beryl was her cousin Seth, then her mother and her aunt, Artemis. And at the end of the chain, her grandmother Olympia.

...

Olympia continued to move through her family, using their souls like conduit, or perhaps like a vehicle—driving their bloodline as if it were a highway. The next stop would be Salem Blanchard. Olympia pictured her granddaughter in her mind. Salem's large green eyes and beautiful flowing auburn hair. This connection would take the longest, but not too long. Threading from Alabama to Georgia would normally require a few minutes, but the addition of Fable was speeding things up. She continued to grip her daughter's hands at the kitchen table, as they held Seth's. Each of them in full concentration, just as elsewhere Beryl and Fable were doing the same. They were one entity now. One chain flowing through one another, trying to reach the next link. But there was nothing. *Nothing*. No Salem. Olympia concentrated harder but the thread simply broke where Salem should have been. Just then something small came through. Weaker, tinier, not fully formed yet. Michael. Baby Michael. But something wasn't right with that connection. It was far too weak, even considering he was merely a baby. His force should have been clearer. Olympia unclasped hands with her daughters. The chain was ended. The surge they'd all been feeling disintegrated, leaving everyone with a feeling of exhaustion. Across town both Beryl and Fable grabbed at a nearby piece of furniture to stabilize themselves as the link broke and rendered them a little wobbly. Olympia opened her eyes at the kitchen table.

"Salem's gone," she said. "It skipped her and found the baby, but Salem is missing."

"No!" Seth screamed. "Salem isn't dead. She can't be dead!"

"She's not dead," Demitra reassured. "David would have called us."

"We should call David," Seth suggested.

A few minutes later there was no answer when Seth tried calling his brother-in-law.

"Hecate?" Seth whispered after hanging up the phone. "Could something have happened to all three of them?"

"I would have felt it if Salem were dead," Olympia answered. "I can't explain why I can't sense her, but I'm sure she's alive."

"But Michael," Artemis noted. "Didn't that feel off? I know he's a baby, but still it was.."

"Muted," Demitra interjected.

"Static," Artemis corrected. "Frozen!"

Olympia stood up from the table. "Frozen."

"Oh my God," Artemis cried. "But why? What's going on?"

Olympia turned to stare at the kitchen stairs. "Artemis go down to the vault and get me the book labeled *Time*.

Demitra jumped up from her chair, fully understanding what her mother's intentions were by retrieving that specific book. "No, Mother. You are too old. I'll go."

"No Dear, I'm going," Olympia insisted. "Besides, I've done this before. I know the way."

"You were a lot younger back then," Artemis pointed out. "Back then when you were active in the Witches Association affairs you were a young woman. And you had Zelda and Aunt Pastoria with you. I'm the next in line as head of this family. I'll go figure out what's happened to Salem."

Olympia placed her hand on Artemis' shoulder. "I know you raised her. I know you love her as your own. But you are not her mother. And since her mother isn't here, it's going to have to be me."

None of them had thought of that. A grandmother was the next best thing to a mother in the bloodline. An aunt wasn't a direct enough tether.

"I can go," Seth offered. "We share the same mother and father. I'll go find my sister."

"Again," Olympia smiled, "I have done this kind of thing before. Seth, I'm afraid you aren't skilled enough yet to see this out."

"I still say no, Mother," Artemis replied. "You are far too old to jump through time anymore."

"When it comes to legal matters my dear, for instance if and when I should go to a nursing home, you and your sister are in charge of me," her mother countered. "But in matters of witch business, I am still the leader of this Coven and my word is law. I will go find Salem. Artemis, get the book."

Artemis left the table and walked to the kitchen staircase. This was the only way to enter the secret room in Blanchard House known by the family as *the vault*. The vault was accessed by a secret door hidden under the kitchen stairs. From the kitchen floor there were three stair treads rising up to a small landing whereupon another set of stairs stretched upward behind the kitchen wall leading to the floor above. Standing on the landing and reaching down to grasp the first step of the staircase to the second floor, Artemis lifted the entire tread of stairs—hinged by a rod and piston system. As the staircase rose pivoted into the air, another staircase—leading down—was revealed. She descended the secret staircase down into a basement no one knew Blanchard House had.

The room under the kitchen was where the Blanchard family kept generations of materials. Books, spells, histories, herbs, talismans— everything needed for their magic. Artemis and Demitra's father installed this room and its secret entrance when he added the kitchen onto the house right before he married their mother and moved in. It was his bargain with Olympia. If she could keep her supernatural world separate from their marriage, he could manage being married to such a powerful being.

The vault was not a very large room. Not really any larger than the kitchen itself. It was sparsely furnished with only a wooden table and a couple of matching chairs. All along the walls were shelves housing various volumes of books, diaries, and potion making ingredients. Artemis scanned the shelves for the book labeled *Time*. She found it on one of the shelves whose contents Olympia forbid the family to touch. The things on those shelves were much too powerful, and the misuse of such items could prove too consequential. The family had learned that lesson the hard way many years ago.

Artemis returned to the kitchen with the book in hand. It was the first time in her life she had ever touched it. Though the book itself was only a bound collection of notes and spells scrawled by the hand by long-dead ancestors, Artemis could almost feel the power contained within its yellowed, fragile pages.

It took a little while to get things started. Beryl and Fable had to be called home, as was Yasmine. Such a spell required the whole of the coven. Demitra assembled

Seth, Fable, Yasmine, and Beryl on either side of the kitchen table while Artemis withdrew a large pot from the pantry. From the sounds of the clanging, she was busy removing several smaller pots she'd been storing inside it.

"Seth, you and Fable go out to the garden. Bring me back sprigs of oleander, bloodroot, rosemary, nightshade—here just take the book and grab everything it needs. Beryl, go down to the vault and bring back the jar of bone dust."

"Whose?"

"Grandfather Blanchard's is probably best. He's the closest tie to Salem."

While Fable and Seth took a large basket outdoors to collect the living ingredients, Beryl went downstairs to a set of shelves near the back of the room. These shelves contained jars of the crushed, ashy remains of cremated Blanchard ancestors. The jars were almost never used in spells. Most spells did not require such potency. Only the most powerful magic required the remnants of a long dead blood-related witch. Beryl could not remember a single time from her life when she'd been aware of anyone using any of these. Perhaps when Aunt Nacaria got into all that trouble years ago with the infamous spell she'd cast, but Beryl wasn't certain. She'd been a little girl when Nacaria went away. But for Olympia to be using the ashes of her own father in this spell to find Salem, Beryl knew this was serious business.

"There is still tomato sauce stuck to the sides of this thing!" Demitra yelled when Artemis presented her with the family cauldron.

"We used it last week when we had spaghetti," Artemis noted. "I'm sure it's fine."

"Who washed this pot last time?" Demitra shouted to her relatives.

"Give it rest Demitra!" Artemis said rolling her eyes. "It's fine."

"Yes, I doubt a little spaghetti sauce will hurt the spell," Olympia reassured.

As everyone regrouped around the table, placing their various collections around the pot, a shadowy specter ran rampant back and forth across the walls and ceiling. There was a franticness to its movement. It seemed to be as concerned as everyone else in the kitchen.

"You are not helping matters!" Seth shouted to the air.

"Seth!" Artemis scolded. "Be kind."

"It's a distraction," he huffed.

"Stay to the far wall," Demitra commanded the entity. "You may watch from there." The ghostly thing moved to the wall adjacent to the living room and hovered against it, an opaque shadow obscuring the wallpaper.

"Maybe I should leave too," Yasmine offered. "I can't do anything to help."

"You are family, and this is a family problem," Fable said grasping her cousin's hand. "Besides, we need someone to hold the book open."

"Can we please hurry up and find out what has happened to my sister?" Seth groaned.

Olympia placed the book on the table and began perusing the pages, pausing every so often in thought. Once or twice she smiled to herself, as if recalling some memory from her glory days when she, her sister, and their best friend would have used this book on one of their adventures. Olympia continued to scan the frail pages, one after the other, searching for something. The rest of the family watched quietly, although none of them quite understood what she was looking for.

"Hecate, what is it exactly that you are trying to find in that book?" Beryl asked. "We don't even know what has happened to Salem."

"I'm afraid we do," Artemis said. "Salem isn't dead. Mother would have felt that when she performed the thread."

"How can we be sure she would?" pressed Beryl.

Olympia looked pensive for a moment, lost in an ancient memory. "I know what it feels like to thread into someone who has died. It's how my sister and I learned of our father's passing. It is a cold blackness that seeps into your soul and doesn't let go." She looked as if she might cry, but she steeled herself from it and shook the painful memory away. "I did not feel that with Salem."

"But Salem doesn't appear to be in this world either," Demitra noted. "And if little Michael has actually been frozen…"

"Salem has the power to freeze time," Fable noted.

"So, are we assuming that Salem froze Michael and then disappeared?" Seth asked.

"I think she's left this plane of existence." Olympia explained. "The spell she must have used is this *Withdrawal* spell. It removes a person from this plane and places them on another."

"But there are a zillion planes, Grandmother!" Yasmine cried. "How are you to know which one she went to?"

"I don't," Olympia admitted. "She could be anywhere. The past, the future, another dimension? I will only be able to find her with the *Tether* spell. And let us hope my blood tie to her is strong enough to pull me to wherever she is."

"It works best if it's a parent, doesn't it?" Beryl asked. "You are a generation removed. If we had Salem's mother here…"

"Yes, that would have been preferable," Olympia sighed.

"Just one more thing my mother fucked up!" Seth snapped.

"We don't have time for that now," Artemis said, smacking the back of his head lightly with the palm of her hand.

"My tie is enough," Olympia assured. "My connection to Salem will work."

"Let's do this," Demitra announced, lifting the large pot to the kitchen fireplace.

Artemis closed her eyes, envisioning a fire which immediately ignited within the logs under the pot. Fable poured a pitcher of water into the pot as Yasmine lifted the book and held it open-faced towards her family.

Olympia read from the book...

"Gone from this world, gone from this life

Here is the mother, where is the child?

Across the oceans and winds of time

Carry this mother to the arms of her child."

Demitra dropped several ingredients from the basket into the pot as Olympia continued her recitation...

"Bloodroot is my tie, my blood and my child.

Rosemary is my love, my blood and my child.

Oleander is my escape, my blood and my child.

These blossoms are my awakening,

These bones are my kindred.

Cast to the ages where time is unlimited.

Take my blood to the place of my child."

"Earth is my element. Communication is my power," Fable said as she sliced her finger with a dagger and dropped her blood into the pot.

"Fire is my element. Action is my power," Artemis said as she sliced her finger as well, dropping the blood into the pot.

"Air is my element. Prophecy is my power," Demitra said following suit.

"Water is my element. Healing is my power," Beryl said, doing the same.

"Air is my element. The elements are my power," Seth said, placing his own blood into the pot.

"Earth is my element. Time is my power," Olympia said inserting her own.

Seth and his grandmother clasped hands. Everyone knew why this final part of the spell required only the two of them. It wasn't because they were Salem's nearest blood relations—that part was a coincidence. For Olympia and Seth Blanchard were the only Blanchard witches, besides Salem, who were full witches—undiluted by regular blood.

Olympia took the large wooden spoon from the table. Still holding her grandson's hand, she stepped closer to the cauldron and recited...

"Hecate, Demeter, Artemis, the three.

Take Hecate to Artemis, over time and sea.

Blood to blood, time to time,

Mother and Child

Take me to mine!"

"Drink quickly," Artemis said as her mother dipped the spoon into the pot and drank down the contents.

Olympia felt the scalding burn to her lips as the liquid touched them. The broth scorched her throat as it ran down. She wanted to scream from the pain, but then it was gone. Everything was gone. She was gone. Olympia was no longer in her body. Seth caught his grandmother's empty shell before it hit the floor.

"Is she?" Yasmine couldn't bring herself to say the words. She knew they all knew what they were doing even if she didn't quite understand herself what it was like to be a witch. Despite the number of years she'd been with them, she still didn't understand everything.

"She's dead," Demitra said. "In a manner of sorts, and just for the time being."

"Dead?" Yasmine sobbed.

"Not exactly dead," Artemis explained as she comforted her niece with a side hug. "Her soul has just left her body and gone to find Salem's. She will come back to her body once the potion wears off. In the meantime, Beryl will keep her body alive."

Seth carried his grandmother upstairs to her bedroom where Beryl had already set up everything she'd need to keep Olympia Blanchard's lungs breathing and heart pumping. It was handy to have a doctor in the house, especially one who was a witch.

CHAPTER FIVE

Where It's Easier

Salem couldn't figure out where that horrible screech was coming from. It sounded like a scream. It sounded like her scream. She opened her eyes and realized it was no scream at all, only the horribly irritating shriek of their alarm clock. She rolled over and slammed her hand down on the snooze button to silence the beeps until her sleepy hands fumbled for the off switch.

"I hate that sound," she said.

"I don't know why you have that archaic machine," David growled beside her.

"A clock?"

"Why do you not just use the alarm on your phone?"

"Because I always forget to charge it," she replied.

"Plug it in on your nightstand every night before you fall asleep."

"No room. The alarm clock and lamp are plugged into that outlet."

"You are so ridiculous," David grinned rolling over and stroking her hair. "You getting up first or me?"

"You are," Salem yawned. "And throw the clothes in the dryer please."

"If you feed Michael," David whispered into her ear.

She rolled over to look her husband in the eyes. "Why do I always get the big jobs?"

He laughed and kissed her nose. "Well, if you weren't so bossy throwing laundry duty in with my shower you might not get saddled with the large jobs."

"Next time I'll remember to volunteer for the small jobs and let you tackle the big ones."

He pulled her on top of him and gave her a real kiss. "You, my love, are not quick enough to think of that this early in the morning." He rolled over on top of her now and kissed her again, longer this time. Then he hopped off the bed and went into the bathroom to turn the shower on.

"Hey!" Salem called from the bed. "What about the clothes in the washer?"

David poked his head out of the bathroom and grinned, "Oh I forgot. Since you're gonna be up anyway feeding the baby, you won't mind."

Salem threw a pillow at his head, which he quickly dodged. She crawled out of bed, swatting her unruly auburn hair out of her face. Walking into the bathroom she reached into the shower and slapped his bare bottom before she flushed the toilet needlessly and walked out.

"Hey!" he called out, cringing from the change in water temperature.

"You had it coming."

Salem was in her fluffy white bathrobe sitting at the small kitchen table looking out of the window onto Piedmont Park while she drank her coffee. Michael was in his highchair playing with his cereal more than he was eating it. David came into the kitchen wrapped in a towel, dripping water all over the floor. She didn't say anything. What was the price of a few puddles when she could see her amazingly handsome husband wrapped in a towel? He still had a great body, despite their recent laziness. There'd once been a time when they'd already be out with the other morning joggers on the park paths or playing afternoon tennis on the park courts. All that changed with Michael. After working all day and chasing a one-year-old around all night, neither of them had the energy to exercise anymore. Salem glanced down at her own stomach.

"I need to lose weight."

"Here we go again," David sighed, pouring himself some coffee.

"What's that supposed to mean?"

"Every couple of days you look at yourself and say you need to lose weight," he said.

"Well, I do. I'm fat."

"Yes, honey you are."

"What!" Salem shrieked. "I'll have you know, David Lane, that I only went up two sizes when I was pregnant with Michael, and I am almost back down to my original size. I think I look pretty damn good for a 28-year-old mother."

"Then stop bitching about it," David said kissing her forehead and starting back down the hall, pausing only to yell behind him, "And you're 30!"

Damn, she thought. *I walked right into that one.*

Salem carried Michael into the nursery to dress him for the day. He was such a happy baby, most of the time. As she laid him down on the ottoman to remove his pajamas he laughed and shook his arms playfully at her. David came in already suited up for his day at the office.

"I'll get the baby ready," he said. "You get ready for work."

"Are you taking him to daycare today, or am I?" Salem asked her husband.

"I can take him," David said, holding his son. "You have that big meeting this morning. I'm gonna go on and leave as soon as I get him dressed. Kiss me."

She did. It lasted seconds longer than most couples probably kiss goodbye because their kisses always lasted longer than most. In the years they'd been together, their passion for one another had not diminished—not even after the baby. Whatever fueled their love showed no signs of ever burning out, and Salem was very grateful for that gift. Most of her friends already found their husbands to be a nuisance or talked about them as if they were the dumbest creatures God ever placed on earth. Salem still adored David, and he her. They felt profoundly lucky to be as much in love as the day they married.

"Don't forget you have those notes you made last night on the nightstand," David shouted as Salem disappeared into the bathroom. "Love you!"

"Love you too!" she yelled from behind the door.

...

After battling the ever-congested roadways of Atlanta and only swearing at three people along the drive in to work, Salem rushed into the office, almost knocking over her assistant as she came in the door.

"You're late. They've already started," Cindy whispered.

"I know," Salem whispered. "David took Michael for me this morning but somehow that always makes me later. I guess I keep thinking I have more time, and then somehow I end up without any at all."

She rushed down the hall to the conference room. She could hear the voices from the other side. The meeting was already in progress. She wasn't too worried about it; they couldn't get very far without her in on things. She whisked open the door and found her seat.

"So sorry guys. Working motherhood and all."

"Quite all right Salem," her boss Travis Dandridge nodded, pouring her a cup of coffee from the pot in the center of the table.

"We were just discussing the layouts for the Mitchell job. I'm meeting with him at lunch," said Ray Conners, the head of the concept department.

"So, Salem," Travis began, "As our art department head, do you have any ideas for the Mitchell campaign?"

"Several," Salem nodded. "I'm not sure what direction he wants to take his ads, so I ventured out into different directions. I have them all for you to present to him on this thumb drive and there are materials and mockups at Cindy's desk. Once we get input from him as to which he prefers, I can flesh his picks out more."

"Fine. Fine. What about the Louden layouts?"

Salem reached into her satchel and withdrew her sketches. "Right here. Exactly as he wanted them. But I also made another set with changes which I think are even better than what he asked for. I thought Neil might want to present them as well when they meet."

Neil Thompson, the rep for the Louden account, flipped through Salem's sketches. "Salem these are really fantastic. Way better than what he asked for. I love these. Thank you. I'll make sure he considers them as well."

"You know we really need to promote Salem and give her her own client accounts. She's wasted in the art department," Ray smiled.

"No thanks," Salem laughed. "I'm good where I am. If I had to meet with the clients personally, I'd never see my husband and son. And with that, I need to go. I have an art department meeting at 10 o'clock, and I need to get my notes ready for the staff. Things were so much easier when *I was* the art department."

"Progress my dear, progress. This company has grown a lot over the last few years," Travis said, walking her to the door. "By the way, Molly has a blanket she crocheted for Michael. It is in a bag in my office by my desk. Grab that before you leave today. And speaking of Michael, how is my great nephew? Haven't seen that boy in a while."

"He's growing and growing," Salem said proudly. "If you'd leave the office some time you and Molly could come over for dinner the way you used to. And you could go fishing with David again. You need to remember you have family that misses you. I'm the only one that ever sees you anymore."

"Well, tell that nephew of mine that I promise we will get out on the lake before summer is over. Maybe next weekend."

"Can't next weekend. I'm hoping we can sneak home to Daihmler and see the family."

"Well if you do, please let your aunt know that cream she made for me worked. My arthritis is completely gone now!"

Salem went to her meeting and handed off the necessary assignments to her staff. The remainder of her day was spent sketching layouts and approving sketches made by her underlings. She was so immersed in her work that she didn't hear the knock at the door. Looking up she saw Travis holding baby Michael.

"Say hello to Mommy," Travis said in baby talk to his great nephew.

"What's my big boy doing here?" Salem beamed.

"Hey, Red," David said, stepping inside her office himself.

"I called David after we chatted this morning and asked him to drop by after work. You were right, it has been way too long since our little family was together. I called Molly and she made a reservation at the Laurence. I'll pick her up in a few minutes and we can all have a family dinner."

"Just leave your car here," David suggested. "Ride with us and I'll bring you to work in the morning."

"Actually, I still have about a half hour left on this," Salem said. "David why don't you take Michael to go pick up Molly, and I'll ride to the restaurant with Travis."

David walked over to her desk and kissed his wife on the cheek before leaving, and whispered in her ear, "Michael has been moving toys around again with his thoughts. The daycare lady thinks she's going crazy."

Travis hadn't overheard their exchange. As close as Salem and David were to David's aunt and uncle, they'd never confided in them that Salem and Michael were witches. It wouldn't have made any difference to them, but Salem preferred to keep some things private. Back home in Daihmler there was no escaping the label in a town where everyone knew everything about her family. Everyone knew Salem Blanchard was a witch. But in Atlanta, she enjoyed the obscurity and anonymity of simply being Salem Lane.

Travis was a great man. She respected him immensely. She'd been working for him about a year when he introduced her to his only nephew—his only living relative—at his annual Christmas party. Salem and David were married by the following Christmas. It was a good marriage. More ups than downs and always laughter and love. David was never afraid of her powers. He wasn't frightened by a family of witches. In fact, he rather enjoyed having a wife who could stop time itself when necessary. Or a wife who could levitate furniture so that he never had to lift anything heavy around the house. He didn't even mind very much when she froze him during sex. Although he preferred to think that she didn't have to resort to that very often. He learned over the years to save his pride and not look at the clock.

Travis and Molly practically raised David after his parents died. The situation was very similar to how Artemis had raised Salem and Seth. It was just one of the many areas Salem had in common with her husband. She felt lucky to belong to two very close, even if very different, families.

Salem finished her sketches and set everything aside for tomorrow. Travis was waiting in his office for her. She found the crocheted blanket Aunt Molly had made for Michael. It was truly beautiful. She couldn't wait to cover her son with it that night at bedtime. They locked up the office and soon Salem and Travis were driving down the streets of Midtown Atlanta towards The Laurence.

...

She was just beginning to realize the screech she heard sounded an awful lot like a scream when she awoke to discover the sound was actually the alarm clock. She had only been dreaming. Salem rolled over and slammed her hand down on the snooze button to silence the beeps until her sleepy hands fumbled for the off switch.

"I hate that sound," she said.

"I don't know why you have that archaic machine," David growled beside her.

"A clock?"

"Why do you not just use the alarm on your phone?"

"Because I always forget to charge it," Salem replied. *Wow. I'm having Deja veux.*

David rolled over and gently patted her head. "Because this is how things go every morning. So, are you getting up first, or me?"

"You are," Salem yawned. "And throw the clothes in the dryer please."

"If you feed Michael," David whispered into her ear.

She rolled over to look her husband in the eyes. This had all happened before. As he got out of bed, she already knew he was going straight into the shower.

"Hey!" Salem called from the bed. "What about the clothes in the washer?"

David poked his head out of the bathroom and grinned, "Oh I forgot. Since you're gonna be up anyway feeding the baby, you won't mind."

This has happened before. I think it's happened two or three times already. This is when I throw the pillow at him.

She threw the pillow at his head and he dodged it. She walked into the bathroom. She slapped his rear end as he stood in the shower, then she flushed the toilet on him. *Just like last time.*

Salem fed Michael in the kitchen and then had a pointless conversation about her weight where she was actually fishing for a compliment, but David turned the tables and didn't give her one. He offered to drive Michael to daycare. Salem knew he would. She also somehow knew that Michael was going to move toys around the room with his powers while at daycare that day. But how could she know that? He hadn't even gone to daycare yet. *What is going on?*

Salem went to the shower to get ready for work. She heard David caution her to not forget the notes she'd made for work and set on her nightstand. Then he called out "I love you." She was just about to say, "I love you too", but instead she bolted from the bathroom and ran stark naked down the hall towards her exiting husband.

"Wait!" she shouted.

"What's gotten into you?" David smirked.

"I love you, that's all," she said.

"Well, don't you think you need to put some clothes on in front of our son?"

"Please," she sneered. "He's dined on these."

He kissed her lips. "I love you too, you know."

"David? When was the last time we made love?"

"I don't know?" David said. "A few days ago. Yeah. In the kitchen, remember?"

"A few days is too long ago," Salem wrapped her arms around him. "Come to the bedroom with me."

"Salem," David gasped. "We have to go to work."

"Work can wait," Salem replied, kissing him passionately. "Daycare can wait. The world can wait."

"What about our son?" David asked. He stared into his wife's eyes. Slowly they were changing from dutiful mother to the lover he so enjoyed spending time with.

He sat his son down on the floor. "Do it," he said with a coy grin.

Salem waved her hand over their son. Michael froze in place, completely still. His eyes didn't move, his breath didn't inhale or exhale. He was paused in time and space. David heard the clock in the hall stop ticking. All time everywhere had halted in place.

"A witch should do little things like this sometimes for her husband," she smiled.

David pressed her against the wall, kissing down her neck to her chin. He continued moving downward inch by inch. Salem peeled off his jacket, shirt and tie, then his pants. Soon they were entwined in each other's arms on the living room floor. The passion between them was just as intense as the first time they'd ever made love.

Salem showered after David and Michael left the house. She was definitely going to be late to her meeting, but she didn't care. She only knew that for some inexplicable reason, she and her husband had needed that moment together this morning.

She stepped out of the shower and reached for her towel. She grabbed it from her grandmother's outstretched hand. It startled her. She jumped backwards, nearly falling into the shower.

"Hecate!" she cried. "What in the world are you doing here?"

Olympia stood solemnly before her granddaughter and placed her hands on Salem's wet shoulders. "Child, the real question is, what are *you* doing here?"

CHAPTER SIX

Face the Destiny

Olympia waited in the living room while Salem dressed. She glanced over the little house her granddaughter and husband occupied, delighted in its homey feel. She didn't often leave Blanchard House and had only been to Salem's home twice before. It had been painted since her last visit, which was right around the time Michael had been born. The walls had been light blue then. Now they were beige. *Salem really oughtn't have painted the house with a baby in it. Paint fumes are not good for little ones to inhale.* Olympia dismissed the thought and continued looking around. She smiled warmly at all the photos of her little great-grandson, some of which she'd not yet seen. Toys lay on the sofa and coffee table. An empty jar of Gerber baby food laid on its side on an end table with a tiny spoon still inside. Olympia noticed an empty mini bag of Cheez-Its discarded clumsily under the ottoman of David's favorite chair. Anyone else might have assumed that bag would have belonged to baby Michael, but Olympia knew her grandson-in-law's favorite snack quite well. She always stocked up on Cheez-Its whenever David and Salem came to Daihmler. And that old chair—David's chair. A holdover from his college apartment which Salem had been unsuccessful in convincing him to shed. Olympia smiled as she looked around. This was a home. Salem's home. A place where no doubt the happiest years of her granddaughter's life were being spent. Salem, now dressed, joined her grandmother in the living room.

"Hecate," she began. "It's great to see you, but why are you here? You should have called me. I could have come out to the airport to get you."

Olympia stood silent a moment, grasping the reality before her. Salem had no idea what was going on. She was just as lost as everyone else.

"Or did you drive in? Who drove you? Is Seth here too?" Salem asked peering through the living room curtain.

Olympia was even more concerned now than she was before, "Salem, dear…"

Salem continued talking as she looked out to the street for her brother or her cousin's car, "You don't drive. Somebody had to drive you. Is Seth outside? Or did Fable bring you?"

"Salem!" Olympia commanded silence. "I did not fly here. I did not drive here. I could not have possibly done either because there is no *here* to fly or drive to."

"Hecate, what are you talking about?"

Salem was now beginning to feel apprehension of her own. It was not like her grandmother to just show up in Atlanta unannounced. And to see that she had come alone, especially considering Salem had never known her grandmother to drive. Something was terribly wrong, and Salem felt almost too afraid to give Olympia time to tell her.

"Salem, I came here by *casting*. The entire family cast a spell and sent me here. Here to the past."

The answer flabbergasted Salem. "The past? What are you talking about? This isn't the past."

Olympia took a seat on the plump sofa nearby. "Salem, this is the past. Judging from the newspaper on your coffee table, this is the past of about three days ago."

Salem walked to the coffee table and lifted yesterday's paper. It looked just as it had last night. She then grabbed her phone from her purse. "Hecate, I think something is wrong with you. I don't know how you got here, but I'm calling the family." Salem knew this wasn't the case. Olympia Blanchard was not the type to suffer from dementia. No one had a more level head on their shoulders. But Salem had to make herself believe Olympia was the one wrong here because to admit otherwise was much too frightening a possibility. "I think Beryl needs to heal you," Salem continued. "Maybe your mind is starting to drift. I'll call the landline. Someone will be home. They're probably worried sick about you."

Olympia didn't try to stop her. She waited as her granddaughter made the call. She could hear the phone ring twice before it was answered. Salem said nothing to the person who answered. Her face was pale, confused. She hung her cell phone up and dropped it back into her purse.

"*You* answered."

"I am in *your* past Salem. Not my own. In my past, three days ago, I was home in Alabama."

"I don't understand this," Salem said sitting down beside her grandmother on the sofa.

"Neither do I," admitted Olympia. "All I can tell you is that for some reason we don't yet know, you sent yourself backwards in time three days. I am here to take you back. Of course, the only way to get back is to get you to understand why you did this in the first place. And since you do not yet know why you are in the past, we are stuck here until you figure it out."

"Well, what do we do?"

"Go on about your day and I'll pop in and out to check on you."

"How are you going to pop in and out?" Salem asked.

"My body is physically at home. Only my astral body is here in Atlanta right now. I can move around here to anyplace I need to with a mere thought."

Salem didn't understand. She was not as versed in these things as her grandmother. Olympia Blanchard had lived a life filled with things such as this which her children and grandchildren had been largely shielded from. Salem could not wrap her head around any of this, but she did as she was told and went to work just as she would have any normal day.

CHAPTER SEVEN

A Little Comfort

Yasmine stepped off the front porch of Blanchard House and started walking across the lawn towards the back of the house. She passed by her grandmother's rose garden. The sweet air wafted over her as she made her way along the footworn path past the chicken houses and through the apple orchard. Moving through the trees she came to the row of fencing with the grapevines twinning around the pickets and stretching up overhead onto the arched arbor. Just beyond that came the slight downhill path to the stream. The clear water was running slowly, probably from lack of rain, but she sat down on the bank and slipped off her shoes to dip her toes into the crisp, cool water. Things out here seemed so peaceful, despite the events currently happening within the family. A brown dove winged by for a moment as if contemplating whether Yasmine was safe to perch beside. Deciding not to risk it, the dove flew away.

"That ugly mug of yours will scare anything off," Seth remarked coming across the meadow. "Maybe we should stand you in the garden instead of the scarecrow."

She feigned a laugh mostly out of politeness, understanding Seth's need to make jokes so that he never had to face anything too serious for too long. Yasmine knew he was scared. Seth had always been close to his older sister Salem. Despite having Yasmine, Fable, and Beryl to grow up with, Seth and Salem often felt like they only had each other. Both basically orphaned early due to the selfish choices of their parents. The uncertainty right now regarding Salem's whereabouts and safety was scaring Seth more than he wanted to let on.

"Grandmother will find her, you know."

"Yeah," he replied breathing in the warm air. "Let's talk about something else."

"Okay..." Yasmine said searching her mind for something—anything—to talk about.

"Can't think of a thing, can you?" he smirked.

"Yes, I can," she began. "Ever wonder why products become suddenly new and improved? Are they finally admitting to us that their old formula was always inferior? Doesn't exactly instill shopper confidence that the company was perfectly happy to give us a product they didn't originally believe in."

"You are so lame."

"At least I don't date cranky preacher's daughters," Yasmine scoffed.

"That might actually be kind of fun to observe," Seth said devilishly. "I'd watch that show."

She rammed her shoulder into his as punishment for his lewd brain. She scooted a little closer to him. Her hands wrapped around her knees as she wiggled her toes in the water. He was leaning back, braced by his thick arms stretched behind him with his feet propped up on a rock by the water.

"I'm worried, you know?" he admitted. Yasmine noticed his leg was shaking a little--fidgeting--as if the stress inside him was trying to release itself whichever way it could.

"I know."

"Salem's all I have left," Seth confided. "I mean, I know I have family. Grandmother, the aunts, Beryl and Fable...even irritating little you. But Salem's different. My sister, you know?"

Yasmine sighed and slid herself under his arm. "I do. I love this family with all my heart, but I still miss my own sometimes."

"We *are* your own," Seth corrected.

"Oh, I didn't mean that the way it sounded. But in the way you mean with Salem. I feel part of the Blanchard family, but I miss my parents a lot. And I miss my brother Ollie. And especially Grandad."

"We all miss Granddad," Seth smiled. "He was the best. The only grandfather I ever knew. But I know what you mean about your parents. I miss mine sometimes too—at least the idea of them. Whatever the case may be."

"But you do remember your mother a little, don't you?" Yasmine asked.

"Not really," Seth admitted. "I know she looked something like Aunt Demitra and Aunt Artemis—or at least what someone would look like if they both looked more like each other. Make sense?"

Yasmine nodded. "I've seen pictures of Nacaria. She does look like a cross between them, just with blonde hair. The aunts share similarities, but when you see pictures of them with your mother, you know right away they were all sisters."

"Yep," Seth's tone turned bitter, "But she had to be selfish. Thoughtless. And now we will never see her again."

"Don't say that Seth," Yasmine replied. "You don't really know that. She might come back one day."

"She's dead Yazzy. Good as well as, at least."

"I don't believe that's true."

"I don't feel like talking about her, either," Seth grumbled.

Yasmine leaned forward to toss a daisy from the water's edge into the stream. It floated downstream a few feet until a rock caught it in place. She leaned her head back onto her cousin's shoulder again. He'd been to the gym again. She could smell it. She thought about saying something but figured it probably was not an appropriate time to tell him he was ripe. She really didn't mind it though. She liked the way he smelled when he'd been sweaty.

"The other day I went to the movies with Jake. I was uncomfortable in my seat, so I bent my leg up under me and sat on it. After a while I shifted some and my leg popped through the back of the seat. So, there I am straddling the movie theater chair, one leg in front and one wedged in back. I was stuck. When the movie went off and everyone got up to leave, there was no hiding the fact that I was caught in the chair. Jake looked at me like I was crazy. It took him quite a while to get my leg out. I was so embarrassed."

Seth started laughing. "You know those things only happen to you. No one else ever gets in the predicaments you do."

"I know."

"Jake got to be your hero, I guess."

"I guess."

Seth looked at Yasmine and tilted his head slightly to the side. "So, do you, like… love him or something?"

"Jake?!" she exclaimed. "No. I don't love him. I think he's nice… I like him."

"Are you two…"

"Are we two *what*?" she repeated.

"You know."

"No, I don't know. What are you asking me Seth?"

"Are you two collecting antique pottery! Yazzy you know very well what I am asking you. Are you two having sex?"

"That's not any of your business!" she cried.

"Okay," Seth huffed. "Nevermind then. It's not my business."

His demeanor changed. He pulled away and sat singularly by the water, staring out at the stream. Yasmine scooted closer to him. She looked up at him and tried to force a smile on his face.

"It may be *a little your business,* I guess. If it's something you need to know."

"I'd like to know."

"We are not having sex. I've only been dating him a month."

"People have sex within a month, Yaz."

"Well, I haven't."

"Okay," Seth seemed friendlier again. He nudged her back with his shoulder. "Okay."

"What about you and Vanessa?" she asked.

"That's none of your business," he answered.

CHAPTER EIGHT

The Reason

Salem had her meeting with Travis and the department heads. When she had wrapped up the meeting with her own department, she retreated to her office. Everything felt redundant. Every word, every step, everything she witnessed felt like it had all happened before. *Hecate must be right.*

"Of course, I am," Olympia announced standing by Salem's office door, closing it for privacy.

"Any clues about why we're in the past yet?"

"Not yet. But go on about your day. I'll be around," Olympia said before disappearing from sight again.

Salem's day proceeded. She was finishing her work when David bounded into her office with Travis and baby Michael. The men went through a speech about meeting Molly for dinner. Salem already knew they'd say *at The Laurence* before they'd even said it.

David left with Michael to pick up Aunt Molly, while Salem wrapped up her work before driving with Travis to the restaurant. It was at the restaurant, before David arrived, when suddenly Salem observed everything around her freeze completely still. The waiter walking past stopped in mid-step—his leg suspended in air as if just about to complete his next step. Travis's hand was as if a piece of stone gripping his cocktail to his lips, mid sip. Salem herself had the power to stop time in motion, but she hadn't done this. Only Olympia also possessed that power. Salem turned to glance around her, trying to spot her grandmother.

"I'm here, my dear," Olympia said over the still quiet as she glided around the figures stopped from their motion around the room. "This is it, Salem. This is the precise moment when you go back to the beginning of the day. Obviously, you are not trying to change something, but to avoid it."

"I don't understand Hecate."

"Neither do I, Baby," the old woman said clasping her granddaughter's hand. "But this time you are going to face it. Remember, even though you won't see me when I unfreeze everyone, I'll still be here watching. You'll be alright. Hecate is here. I will not leave you."

"I'm afraid Hecate," Salem admitted. Even saying the words felt like an admittance of weakness to someone as strong as her grandmother.

"I know, Baby. Fear is normal, do not run from it. Stay and face it. You are a Blanchard. There is nothing a Blanchard cannot survive." Olympia faded like a mist into the air as the hustle and bustle of The Laurence resumed.

Travis sipped his drink and pulled out his phone. "They should be here by now. I'll call Molly and see what's the holdup." He phoned his wife as Salem sat and listened to his end of the conversation.

"Are you guys almost here yet?

What?

He hasn't?

But he left an hour ago.

Yeah, traffic is rough, but he still should have been there.

We only live a few miles from the office.

Yeah, wait there and we'll come home."

"David hasn't shown up yet," Travis told Salem as he hung up the phone. "Molly has been waiting this whole time."

What could have happened? Salem's mind immediately rushed to the worst of possibilities, but she quickly dismissed those. That would never happen. *David's a great driver. He just stopped off for gas or ran into an old friend somewhere and got distracted talking.* But Salem knew deep down this was it. This was the reason she'd hurled herself backward in time, and it had nothing to do with her husband running into an old friend. Whatever happened was exactly why she was stuck in the past.

Travis broke every traffic law on his way to his house, but they never made it there. The flashing blue and red lights on the side of the road, along with the dozens of cars stopped in place between the lights and Travis' car, told Salem all she needed to know. David had been in a crash.

"Salem wait!" Travis shouted as his niece bolted from his car and began darting around stopped vehicles in the chaotic maze of the traffic jam.

She ran as fast as she could towards the flashing lights. Five cars away. Four cars away. Three. Two. Then she saw the pileup. Two sedans and one transfer truck lay mangled across all four lanes of traffic. There was also a fourth car. David's car.

She knew the moment she approached that her husband was dead. She could see his body being loaded onto a stretcher by two medics. His face was covered in blood and unrecognizable. One of his arms was missing but she recognized his suit. The suit was all that was recognizable about him.

"Ma'am, get back," a policeman told her, pushing her backward away from the scene.

"That's my husband!" she screamed. "Leave me alone!"

"Ma'am, you have to step back. You cannot go up there."

"Where's my baby?! That's my husband! Get away from me!!!"

Salem waved her arm across the officer's head. Suddenly the officer, as well as the two others now running forward to block her way, were sent hurdling backwards over the hood of the closest vehicle involved in the wreckage. Her path was cleared as she sprinted forward toward her husband. David was dead. Undeniably dead. She stood staring at the carnage which had once been the man she loved. Somewhere beneath the torn flesh and bloodied face was her husband. The missing arm, his left arm, was where he wore their wedding ring. Salem suddenly found herself wondering where the arm—where the ring—could be. But another thought flashed into her mind making the visage of David's decimated body fade away. *Where is my baby?*

"Out of the way!" shouted another medical professional rushing forward with a gurney. Strapped to it was the tiny form of baby Michael. "We're losing the baby!"

Salem stood stunned, almost out of body as she witnessed her infant child being rushed towards the back of the ambulance. Instinctively she shoved her hand forward into his direction and froze the scene. Everything stopped.

CHAPTER NINE

Healing Hands

Beryl Blanchard was one of the finest doctors Daihmler County Hospital ever had the privilege of employing, and they all knew it there. Despite her young age, she already carried quite a reputation. Staff called her The Miracle Worker. No one knew exactly what she did or how she did it, but Dr. Blanchard's patients rarely ever died. More than that, her patients seemed to share a common habit of somehow miraculously healing from their ailments. Of course, rumors being as common as houseflies, gossip flew to all reaches of the hospital. Everyone in Daihmler knew about the Blanchards. People knew Beryl was a witch—a fact that kept some citizens reluctant to become her patient, while others begged for the honor. But there was no denying, Dr. Blanchard was a very sought-after physician.

She made her rounds quickly that morning. Her grandmother had been in a coma for two solid days back at home, and she wanted to hurry home to check on her. As she made her way to Room 251, she was glad to know this was the last patient she needed to see today. She gave a short knock at the door before entering. Her patient was asleep, but his wife was sitting uncomfortably in the chair beside the bed.

"Dr. Blanchard!" the woman exclaimed hopping up from her seat.

"How is our patient today?" Beryl smiled.

"Not much better," his wife replied. "I'm afraid the operation wasn't a total success. They could only clear two arteries."

Beryl smiled kindly at the man's wife. "Well then, let's try another approach."

"Please," the lady pleaded. "Dr. Matthews is a wonderful doctor. He did all he could for my husband. But it wasn't enough. I've heard about you, Dr. Blanchard. Will you please help us?"

"That's why I'm here," Beryl nodded. "Dr. Matthews asked me to consult."

"He did?" the woman said in disbelief.

"Dr. Matthews and I are good friends. I'm happy to take a look at your husband."

"When I was your age," the woman began. "I was told I was barren. My doctor said I was never gonna have any kids. Then I heard about your mother. She helped a friend of mine with a rash none of her doctors could rid of. Your momma made a salve for her and it went away."

Beryl smiled. This wasn't the first time she'd heard similar stories from patients. "And did she help you?"

"She did. I went to see her, and she told me I wasn't barren. She told me exactly what my husband and I needed to do to get pregnant. I got me three children now, teenagers. All because of your momma. So, you have my full faith, Dr. Blanchard."

Beryl smiled again. "Thank you. Now let's see what we can do for your husband, however I need to be alone to examine him. I can't promise you anything, but I will see if I can help him."

"I understand. I thank you for even trying."

The patient's wife left the room, giving Beryl privacy with her spouse. Beryl placed her hands on the patient's chest. Almost the exact moment her hands connected to his body, Beryl felt the familiar warm sensation begin to swell within her. As if some radiant light hidden away deep in her soul turned on and grew brighter and brighter beneath her flesh. Closing her eyes, she allowed her now fully charged senses to scan his body. Her physical contact allowed her to evaluate his body's frailties as if her hands possessed the power of a CAT scan. All the while her hands inspected his physicality, her inner eye looked more deeply into the totality of this man's life and worth. She could see him walking through a field, possibly a farm on the outskirts of town. She saw him at work; he was a hard worker. Long hours, little income. She saw him at the dinner table at night, laughing with his family. She saw him helping his children with their math homework. She saw him giving his wife a coy wink when she passed by—his little way of telling her he loved her. This was a good man, a good father, a provider. Beryl liked him. This man deserved more years of life. He was younger than he looked, but country life ages a body fast. His body was overweight, his heart was worn out, but he deserved to live.

Beryl felt the familiar tremor in her soul, that reliable power she had come to master over the years. The tremor began to course through her arms and into her fingertips. It was as if some inner Light, borrowed from something bigger than her--filled her hands and entered the patient. Beryl never quite understood where this power came from. Was it inside her all the time or was she merely a conduit able to channel some outside force through her extremities? But it never failed her. And it never taxed her—which made her sometimes wonder if she were just the director of the force rather than the generator of it. Either way, she visualized the man healthy, growing older with his family. The tingle in her fingers felt almost like sparks ready to ignite. She moved over his heart and down his legs where the blockage was worsening. She could feel his passageways clearing as she touched him.

"You are going to recover, Mr. Reed," she whispered into his ear. "You've worked too hard to be robbed of your golden years now."

...

Later in her office, gathering her belongings before heading home, a knock came at her office door. Dr. Matthews entered. In his hand were new scans of Mr. Reed's heart. He presented them to Dr. Blanchard.

"You've done it again. He's clear."

"That's really great," Beryl said. "You did that in surgery you know?"

"You're generous to say that, but we both know it wasn't all me," Dr. Matthews said.

"Mr. Reed would have died hours before I walked into his room had you not saved his life in emergency surgery. You gave him life. I just added a few more years."

"Well, whatever you did, I thank you."

"You're welcome."

"Can I thank you more properly? Say, perhaps dinner tonight? Nothing fancy, just a couple steaks at Nicks in the Sticks?"

"Raincheck?" Beryl asked. "I'm needed at home. Family emergency."

"Have anything to do with that medical equipment Dr. Herring helped you sneak out?"

Beryl raised a brow, "You know about that?"

Dr. Matthews gave a little chuckle and winked to his colleague, "Don't worry Beryl, too many doctors around here owe you so many favors…I don't think anyone is going to turn you in for borrowing a few pieces of equipment. If you need my help for whatever it is you have going on at home, I'm on call for you."

Beryl smirked at her friend. "I have it under control. But I will take that steak dinner down the road."

"You got it."

CHAPTER TEN

Madam Zelda

Zelda came up the driveway like a race car driver. Dust and dirt spewing out from under her car as she went. Jumping out of her old Ford Taurus, she stomped up the porch steps and flung open the door to Blanchard House.

"Where is Lympy!"

Demitra had been upstairs with her mother when she saw Zelda's car coming down the road from the window. She rushed down the stairs to meet the old woman. *Zelda.* Leave it to her mother's best friend to pick the most inopportune time to visit.

"I just had a vibration!" Zelda announced as she slammed the front door behind her.

"Good for you," Demitra remarked. "I hope you turned it off before you left home."

"Don't be flippant, girl!" Zelda snapped as she pranced into the living room and nestled her rather large bottom onto the sofa. Her loud purple and yellow blouse stood out against the sage green sofa like grape juice on a white carpet. Zelda spread her pink skirt out over her legs. With her slightly maroon hair, she looked like a clown had dressed her.

"Come on in, will you?" Demitra said sarcastically, joining her in the living room.

"Where's your mother?" Zelda demanded. "I'm worried. I was doin' a reading for Mrs. Winthrope when I had this horrible feeling sum'thing is wrong with Lympy."

"I assure you mother is fine, but we are quite busy around here today. I'll be sure to tell Mother you dropped by."

"I'm not going anywhere, Demmy," Zelda asserted. "Not till I see Lympy."

They heard the front door open and close as Artemis came in holding a basket of vegetables. "Hello Zelda," Artemis called. "I thought that was your car tearing up the road while I was in the garden." Artemis paused in the doorway to the living room and stared at the old woman. "Zelda, your hair."

"You like it? It's called *Grandly Garnet*. I dyed it myself yesterday."

"Well, it certainly is fascinating."

"Those tomatoes look marvelous Arty," Zelda said spying the basket. "I believe I'll grab me some from the garden before I leave."

"Help yourself," Artemis smiled.

"Got any Purple Hulls out there?"

"A few," Artemis answered. "Help yourself to anything you want."

"Zelda just popped in to see Mother," Demitra said with a wink to her sister.

"Oh, didn't you tell her?" Artemis replied.

"Tell me what?"

"I thought it was best to keep it in the family," Demitra snapped.

"Zelda is family," Artemis countered.

"Demmy seems to forget that I'm your mother's closest friend in the world," said Zelda.

"Oh, don't you two start bickering," Artemis scolded. "Zelda, we've had a bit of trouble around here. For some unknown reason, Salem sent herself into another time. We don't know why or when. Mother has gone after her."

Zelda pondered the thought a moment before replying, "When did all this happen?"

"A few days ago," answered Demitra.

"It's all going to be fine though," Artemis added. "Beryl has Mother hooked to machines to keep her body going while she's gone after Salem. Although we did expect her to be back by now."

"Naw," Zelda scoffed. "Takes longer than you'd think—something like that. Back when we was girls, your Aunt Pastoria went off in time for about six days before she came back. I forget why she went though. But your mama and me was plenty scared till she got back. Ya'll got any idea why Salem went?"

"None at all."

"Well, I hope Lympy gets back before the Consort Meeting."

Artemis replied, "Is it time for that again already?"

"Sure is. Every three months. Can set your watch by it. You know there's talk of a new Queen in the works."

"Has something happened to Ursula?" Demitra asked, a little embarrassed to even be interested. For the most part the Blanchards didn't participate in the Witches Consort business, except of course when election time came.

"Ursula just wants out," Zelda explained. "Too many obligations involved. You know she only ran for it cause her Daddy was so well liked as King, and she felt like she owed it to his memory. But she's been Queen of the Consort for years, and she's just tuckered out."

"I suppose," Demitra scoffed.

"You don't like Ursula much do you, Demmy?"

"Zelda, I hate when you call me Demmy. You know I hate that. And yes, I do like Ursula. Or at least I used to."

Artemis clasped her sister's hand in solidarity. "Demitra and Ursula were very good friends before Nacaria got in trouble."

Zelda huffed and slapped her hand on her leg. "You certainly can't blame Ursula for any of that! She wasn't even Queen back then."

"But she didn't have to side with the ones opposing our sister!" Demitra blasted. "She only did it because she had ambitions to be Queen one day."

"Now don't get all snippy with me Demmy," Zelda warned. "I was on your family's side as you recall. Just like I always am."

Relaxing her bristled demeanor, Demitra smiled weakly at the old woman and said, "Yes, you did. You always have our back."

"Well, it just wasn't fair," Zelda said, half to herself. "He was as much to blame as Nacaria. And the Council never even gave Niki a chance to defend herself. Anyway, it is in the past. But back to Salem and Lympy…do ya'll think we should ask the Consort for help bringing them back?"

"No," Artemis said sternly. "I don't think it's that serious a matter to involve the Council. Besides, we don't even associate with them that much. Mother goes to the Consort meetings and that is the extent of it. The rest of us pretty much keep to ourselves. This is a family matter. We will handle it."

Zelda moved the conversation along to other topics. Zelda was the pipeline to all the gossip in town, and the Blanchards usually got the lowdown on the various people they knew from Zelda. Zelda also usually caught them up on the goings on of her own two daughters, Melinda and Sarah. Sarah, always dieting, was also always being reminded by Zelda that she was fat. Sarah lived in the shadow of the prettier Melinda, but unfortunately, Zelda did not seem to care much more for Melinda than she did Sarah. This visit Zelda told them all about the recent car accident Sarah was involved in when she'd been ordering dinner on Postmates while driving. No one had been hurt in the accident, but Sarah's car was pretty smashed up.

"Those two girls are gonna be the death a' me some day. I swear I shoulda bopped them both in the head with a frying pan when they was little," Zelda confided. "Well, I better go. I gotta do a reading on Laura Hartley that owns the flower shop in a little bit. She don't know that I already know she's having an affair with that new pharmacist at Grady Drugs. She never was more than a slut anyway. Didn't Seth used to run around with her?"

"I'll be sure to tell Mother to call you for all the gossip when she wakes up," Artemis said escorting Zelda to the door.

"And don't forget to remind her about the Consort meeting next week. And, Arty, if sum'thing bad has happened with Salem, let me know—all right?"

"You know I will."

"Oh, and ya'll be careful 'round here. Did you see the paper this morning?" Zelda warned.

"No, we haven't had a chance to look at it," Artemis said. "There hasn't been another killing has there?"

"Yep, last night," Zelda replied. "That makes three in the last couple months. Terrible. Terrible. You heard anything from your detective friend, Demmy?"

Demitra shook her head. "No, I haven't been called in on it. I assume the two deaths before were considered coincidence. Did the paper say this third death resembled the other two?"

"Yep," said Zelda. "Throat cut. Body torn up. Looks like Daihmler's got a serial killer runnin' loose. So ya'll be on the lookout way out here. You gotta lot a land, real secluded."

"Well, I think we are pretty well fixed for taking care of ourselves around here," Demitra smirked. "And we will let Mother know you stopped by." Zelda took the cue that it was time to leave.

Zelda left out as fast as she had come in, forgetting to stop by the garden for the peas and tomatoes she'd wanted. But Artemis knew she'd be back again in a few days. Demitra gave a sigh of relief once the house was empty of Zelda's presence.

"It's always like a big wind blows out after she leaves."

"She's been a good friend of this family since before we were born. Don't forget that, Demitra."

"I just don't like the way she sells her gifts. Running a business selling psychic readings and fortune-telling to customers. It's not right, using your gifts for profit," Demitra noted.

"Oh, get real Demitra Blanchard," Artemis laughed out loud. "Beryl became a doctor because she has the power to heal. Fable became a vet because she can communicate with animals. You work for the police department sometimes because you have psychic abilities. Zelda isn't doing anything wrong."

"Let's drop it," Demitra huffed. "But she does bring up a good point about the murders. We do need to be cautious--especially the girls. Beryl and Fable do not have the most active powers. If faced with danger they aren't well equipped to fight. And then there's Yasmine, she has no power at all."

Demitra was interrupted by the ringing on the landline phone in the entranceway. She reached to grab the receiver and noticed the caller I.D.

"It's Travis Dandridge, David's uncle."

CHAPTER ELEVEN

Acceptance

Pain was just a word, an adjective, Salem had used to describe many things before; a headache, a stomped toe, tax time, her brother when he was at his most irritating. The word took on a new depth and meaning now. It seemed absurd that such a small, four-letter word like pain could carry such a punch to her heart as it did now. David was dead. Torn from her life by a tragic car accident. She didn't even know what caused the accident. Was someone texting while driving? Did someone not see another car in the blindspot? She had no answers, but even if she had, they would have provided no comfort. Her husband—her best friend—was dead. And Baby Michael was clinging to the last seconds of life when she'd used her powers to freeze him in time. Had she been home in Daihmler, she might have been able to keep Michael frozen until Beryl could heal him. But that probably would not have been possible, she realized now. She had arrived too late to the scene. In the very second Salem lifted Michael's suspended state for the paramedic, poor Michael passed away. It was much too much for her. At some point standing among the swirling red and blue lights at the crash scene, she lost consciousness.

When she awoke, she was in the passenger side of Travis' car as he drove her home. He'd wanted to take her home to Molly, wanted for them to look after her. But Salem insisted on returning to her own home. Only in her own home could she still feel the spirit of her husband and son. Within those walls and those walls alone lived all of her memories of being a wife and mother. Travis tried to come inside with her, but she refused. In the driveway, Salem rushed him away. Travis didn't want to go, but she needed him to. She knew what she needed to do, and she had to be alone to do it. She had to save her family.

Once, as a child, she watched from the crack in the door of her mother's bedroom as she had cast a spell. This spell. The spell that would undo things. Salem never forgot what she saw that day or what all the spell required. She'd written it down and kept it always in her own personal spell book. Nacaria Blanchard was a master spell maker in her time, and Salem knew whatever her mother was doing in that bedroom was important and should be recorded. It was almost as if somehow her soul knew she might need that knowledge one day. Today. With this spell she could go back in time and change the day's events. She could rid her life of this terrible tragedy—steal it from time completely—and restore her family.

Salem located her book of spells from the fireproof box under the bed where she kept things of this sort. Her own miniature *vault*. She even had bone dust, swiped as a teenager from her grandmother's stash. Kneeling beside the bed with the box safely in her hands, her eyes lifted to the top of the bed. Their bed. She felt her heart sink further. Lifting her hands up to pull back the comforter cover, she felt the sheets beneath--this was David's side of the bed. This is where his body had lain the last night they'd had together. He would never again lay here. He would never share this space with her again. Tears welled up in her eyes but she pushed them away with defiant fingers.

I will not cry. I am not in mourning. I am not a widow. My husband is coming back. He will be laying here again tonight.

She pulled the box from the floor as she rose and moved to the kitchen table. Carefully she pulled out the contents: her notebook, her herb jars. *I don't have any white oleander.* That was going to be a problem. *Wait. I can go to Pike's nursery. They will have it. I can break into the garden area easily.* She had everything else she'd need—if not in her box, she had it in her kitchen or her own garden in the backyard. She just had to go to Pike's and then come back to start the spell.

"No, Salem," Olympia said, materializing beside her.

Salem had all but forgotten about her grandmother since the wreck. "Get out of my way, Hecate," she said angrily. "I have something important to do."

"You cannot do this, Salem."

"Watch me," Salem scoffed pushing past and grabbing her keys from the counter. *My car is at work. I'll get an Uber.*

"You cannot resurrect the dead Salem."

"I'm not going to resurrect them. I am going to stop this from happening to them."

"It will not work," Olympia cautioned.

"Yes, it will Hecate. All I have to do is stop them from getting in that car. Stop them from leaving at that precise time. Suggest we have dinner with Travis and Molly a different night. There are a hundred different ways to stop this."

Olympia reached out her hands and pulled Salem into an embrace. Salem tried to pull away, but she couldn't. An urgency surged within her—she had to cast this spell and save her family. But the comfort she felt inside her grandmother's arms was much too needed to pull away from. She gave into it, allowing herself to be a child again and be consoled by those loving arms. *I'll let her hold me for just a minute, and then I'll call the Uber. Then I'll fix all of this. I just need a moment to breath and someone to hold me while I plan.*

"Salem, listen to me please," pleaded Olympia.

"You aren't going to stop me from doing it, Hecate. I have to do it."

"That is my point, Salem. It isn't going to work. Honey, you have already done it. If it would have worked it, they would be here. You are in the past already. You already cast the spell. It did not save them. All you have done is relive this horrific day over and over again."

"No."

"You didn't bring them back to life, you only stopped moving forward after the accident. It cycles over and over from the beginning of this day and always ends with casting the spell. It never brings them back to life."

"But I can stop them from driving!" Salem shrieked.

"Then why haven't you?" Olympia challenged, contradicting her granddaughter's logic. "You don't stop them from driving because when they go to leave you aren't aware they are going to die. When someone goes backwards, nothing changes in *their* experience. They just re-experience it. You were present in this reality. Your soul simply merges with your past self. You can't recall a future that has not happened yet, and you cannot be in two places at once."

"Then *you* can go back and save them," Salem announced with a new fervor in her eyes.

"No. I can't."

"Yes. Yes, actually I think you can Hecate!" Salem said excitedly. "You weren't anywhere around when all this happened. You're the perfect person!"

"You cannot change death Salem. You cannot change death. There are a million things that can go wrong and destroy reality. There are reasons for our laws. Reasons your delirious mind cannot comprehend right now during this tragedy."

"But—"

"But nothing!" Olympia shouted. "This is the reason I never taught you children about time travel. Too much can go wrong. Your mother tried to change history and look what happened to her. Your husband is dead. Your son is dead. It is agony. And it is unstoppable. And it must be faced."

"You don't understand."

"I understand all too well, Salem. I have watched this three times already," revealed Olympia. "I have allowed this cycle to continue because *I needed time*. Time to think. Time to gather myself so that I could be strong for you. I loved David, too. And baby Michael was my only great grandchild. So much hope for the family rested in his little life. I too needed time to adjust. And now you are going to face this like an adult."

Salem wept into her hands and when lowering them, Olympia shuddered at the anguish on her poor granddaughter's face. "Hecate, something has to work. Surely there is a way. We just have to find it."

Olympia paced the room wringing her aged hands, "This is my fault really, Salem. After your mother tried to alter fate by going back in time, I was certain that teaching you kids anything about that kind of magic was a mistake. We avoided the subject completely in our lessons when you were growing up. It is the responsibility of the witch to protect the Natural Order. If bending time at our whim to make our lives easier were possible, then no witch would ever know tragedy or sadness or even run late to work. The power to travel time does not work that way for a reason. I'm sorry I never taught you that, but you cannot change death."

"What do we do then?" Salem whispered hopelessly to the air.

"You face it. Accept what has happened, and we pick up our pieces and try to go forward. I am going home. I will awaken in my bed and tell the family what has happened. I will send Seth to get you. He will be here in a few hours. In the meantime, you will mourn, and you will pack. Your brother is coming to bring you back home to your family."

...

Demitra and Beryl were there in Olympia's bedroom at her bedside as Olympia awoke from her coma. Beryl gave her an injection as Demitra removed the oxygen mask from her mother's face.

"Mother? Do you recognize me?"

"Yes, Demitra. I am all right."

"Rest, Hecate," Beryl advised. "I know that you are mentally intact, but your body has been lying still in this bed for several days. Before you attempt to get up, I need to heal you. I have to make sure your muscles and joints are stabilized before you stand up."

Olympia did as she was told but asked, "Did Travis call?"

"Yes. He told us about David and Michael. He said he found Salem on her kitchen floor unconscious. We presume from her spell. He says she is coming around now. Seth and Fable left out already to bring her home."

"Good."

"They're really dead?" Demitra asked her mother.

"Yes. He told us about the accident. He told us about David and Michael. He said he found Salem unconscious on her kitchen floor this morning when he went to check on her."

"Yes, that would make sense," Olympia explained. "Salem's soul was out of her body and lost in her own past. I was with her there, in her past. Travis must have found her before her spirit returned to the present. Was he very concerned?"

"At first," Demitra replied. "But he was able to rouse her back awake."

"Then her spirit is back where it should be, in the proper time," Olympia sighed.

"Seth and Fable are on their way to Atlanta now to get her," Beryl added. "I need to heal you now, Hecate."

Demitra left Beryl with Olympia and started downstairs. Passing through the upstairs hallway she stopped to take a moment to look at the photographs on the wall. Pictures of all those lost to the family over the years. Her father. Nacaria. Sinclair. Now David and Michael. And of course, Larry. Her precious Larry.

Demitra knew how painful losing a husband can be. She had never recovered from losing Larry. To this day she missed him. It had taken her a long time to be able to move on and face each new day without him. Salem would be in for a very rough time dealing with her losses. To lose a husband and a child at the same time. Demitra could not imagine. She only hoped Salem would be stronger than she had been. She had fallen apart. The family always referred to it as when Demitra was in mourning, but Demitra knew it was worse than that. She had been insane. She had fallen completely apart, and it took years before she was back to her old self again. She knew how grief can drive you mad if you've loved deeply enough.

CHAPTER TWELVE

Fireflies and Cigarettes

For the first time since she pulled up in the driveway with Seth and Fable that afternoon, Salem was experiencing some quiet. She had spent the drive home from Atlanta drowning in her brother and cousins' sympathy. Then walking into Blanchard House she'd had the rest of the family to endure with their consoling hugs and declarations of love. It had been exhausting. Added to her own family's suffocating support came an influx of phone calls, voicemails, texts, and Facebook messages from everyone she and David knew in Atlanta. Salem stopped even looking at her phone. She was now experiencing the solitude of Blanchard House land. She sat on the wooden bench in the garden. She'd painted that bench its pale blue hue herself, years ago. Now only flakes of chipped paint revealing gray weathered wood gave any indication how much time had come and gone.

She heard the screen door to the kitchen slam shut as someone came outside. Secretly, Salem hoped no one would find her in the garden. She had been through enough comforting for one day. A strange calm came over her once she saw it was her brother. Seth had stepped out to the lawn for a breath of fresh air, or perhaps just to step out of the heaviness inside. He did not see Salem at first, and she didn't alert him to her presence when she saw him squat down in the grass and cry. He was hurting too. They all were. It had not really occurred to her that everyone else was suffering a loss as well. Her own pain was consuming her, and she had overlooked how much all the family loved David and Michael. She watched Seth for a few minutes. Her own anguish seemed to pause as she observed someone else's. When he eventually stood back on his feet, she called out to him.

"Sit with me."

Seth scanned the yard for the voice until he saw her across the lawn in the garden. Wiping his eyes on his shirt tail, he walked slowly toward her. "I didn't know you were out here."

"I needed a break from everyone's sympathy. I swear if one more person tells me how sorry they are or asks me if I'm okay, I am going to slap them. I know what they are all thinking. That I am going to lose my mind. But I'm not. David hated drama. And for some reason I don't feel sad right now. I'm just angry. I'm so fucking angry."

"I know," Seth said, placing his arm around her. "No, I don't know. I don't know anything about what you're feeling. I know what it's like to lose the person you love, but Susan and I were kids still when she died. Not like you and David." He paused and a tear fell from his eye. "Man, I loved David. It was nice having a brother. Another guy in the family. And Michael—I barely even had any time with my only nephew. I feel robbed of something, and I don't even know what it is. And none of that, none of it, can possibly compare with how you feel."

Salem looked into her brother's eyes—green like her own. "It's just not fair," she said angrily. "It isn't fucking fair. We've lost too much in our lives already. The bullshit with our mother, then being left alone. You lost Susan. We have a father we never see."

Seth could feel the rage swelling inside her as she began talking. It almost vibrated from her.

"Then I grew up and made something or myself. I educated myself. Found a good job. Found a good man. David was perfect for me! And he loved me. Finally, someone loved me!" she was shouting now. The anger seeping out of her every pore. "We had a baby. A beautiful boy who filled my heart with things I've never felt before. And all this gets snatched away from me. Why? I don't understand why. Why would God be such an asshole to me? Why take everything from me all at once? Why not kill some abusive asshole in that crash? Or some geeked out drug addict? Why my husband and our innocent baby?! I want to know why God did this to me! Where the fuck does He get off doing this to us!"

She couldn't control the rage. It was bigger than she was. It was an entity with its own life and mind. There was just too much anger—too much power—surging through her body. The force inside her had to escape. Involuntarily, Salem found herself thrusting her arms outward as though let loose from a cannon. Fire exploded before her onto the lawn. It wasn't enough. There was still more anger swelling inside her. Without a moment's pause or reaction, she swiped her hand to the right and blew up the fence post. Seth fell backward off the bench. He had never seen his sister so powerful. She was shaking from that much energy. Suddenly she slapped her hands together with a force she'd never before demonstrated. Seth watched in utter disbelief as the earth in the meadow before them rose up in right and left sections, rising vertically as if being unhinged from the ground. The two sections, roughly 20 feet each, smashed together in the air with such intensity that it made a sound resembling a sonic boom. In its aftermath, dust, dirt, and little blades of grass filled the air. As it all settled to the now marred ground, it looked as if a bomb had exploded on that patch of land. One small pine trunk remained, stripped of bark, limbs, and needles—an empty shaft tilting to the side like a flagpole staking some obliterated battlefield.

The family heard the commotion from inside and rushed out to see. Artemis ran over to the garden to restrain Salem. Her niece was still shaking. Her power was still growing. Artemis could feel the surge like a tidal wave about to make landfall.

"Stop, Salem! Stop!" Artemis screamed. "You're going to hurt someone."

Salem was trembling. She looked at the lawn, now a misshapen crater. Shards of broken limbs, disintegrated plants, broken soil, and falling dust covered the patch of ground. In a moment of recognition, she fell into her aunt's arms and wept.

"It's all right, baby," Artemis soothed her. "Everyone go back inside, and leave us alone out here."

The family, shocked from what they had witnessed, returned indoors. Artemis said nothing to Salem. She simply laid her niece's head upon her chest and rocked her. She rocked her as she had when Salem was a little girl. Whenever Salem had felt frightened or alone, Artemis had rocked her in her arms. She never thought she would be doing it again. The garden fence was still burning from the explosion Salem sent it. Artemis closed her eyes and envisioned a tiny rain cloud over the rail. It doused the flame.

"I didn't know you could start fires," Artemis remarked while still holding Salem. "And what was that thing with the yard? You just lifted up two patches of land and smacked them together! I've never seen anything like that."

Salem glanced up. A mildly astonished smile broke the facade of emptiness in her expression. "That's never happened before. David would have enjoyed seeing that."

"It's your emotional state. We can do a lot of things we don't know we can do when our emotions are high. I used to get the hiccups when I was nervous and every time I hiccupped; a window shattered."

Artemis reached her hand down under the bench and lifted a loose clump of grass. Under the grass was a small plastic box. She lifted the box and opened it. Inside were a pack of cigarettes and a lighter.

"Thought you quit a long time ago," Salem remarked.

"So does Demitra and Mother. But you won't tell on me, will you?"

"No," Salem smiled. "Give me one."

The two of them sat together in silence, smoking their cigarettes and listening to an orchestra of crickets playing their well-rehearsed symphony. A small cluster of fireflies hovered a few feet away, the light from their tails diluted amid the haze of smoke from the cigarettes and the still-smoldering fence.

"You see Salem, grief is like a firefly. It burns and burns, and then it looks as if it stops. But if you wait long enough, it fires up again. Like the smoke, time passes and passes and builds up a fog to slowly cover the pain. The pain will still be there, but it won't burn so brightly anymore."

"Bad analogy," Salem quipped.

"Okay, then look at the cigarette," Artemis directed her niece. "Think of life like a cigarette. As soon as you light it, it begins to fade. You can smoke it fast, taking all you can get from it, but using it up sooner. Or you can leave it to stand and burn its course slowly, never enjoying or savoring it—trying to make it last a little bit longer. Or you can just put the cigarette out early, wasting all that is unused because you've just had enough of it."

"You lost me."

"Every object has meaning if we want to attribute any to it. And every event carries a lesson or a purpose if we need it to have one. But then we spend our time trying to figure out what that purpose was—and that is just too much room to go crazy in. You can smoke fast, or slow, or extinguish it all together, but while you are waiting to figure out the meaning, just inhale. Sometimes just inhaling is all there is."

"My two cigarettes are gone. I don't have anything left," Salem said.

"No, they aren't gone," Artemis said. "Like with your cigarette, there will be ash left, and a little stub. The memories. And those aren't nothing Salem."

"It's not enough," Salem said resentfully. Her face hardened, obscuring some of its delicate beauty.

"Sometimes 'not enough' is all we have to hold onto."

"But it isn't fair, Aunt Artemis."

"No, it isn't," Artemis said as she kissed the top of her head. "There is nothing about any of this that is fair. You deserve to have many more years with David. You deserve to see your son grow up, fall in love, give you grandchildren. Life has a crazy way of being very unfair to the ones who deserve fairness most. And there's nothing we can do about it, except deal with it however we can. It sucks, and it hurts like hell sometimes. But no one gets promised *fair*. Not even a witch."

Salem sat quietly. She felt like crying again, but tears didn't come. Only a sense of loss and burgeoning desire to understand why it was that she was destined to endure as much loss in her lifetime as she had.

"I just want to see them again."

Artemis held Salem close to her, giving her arms a gentle squeeze. "Their energy is still out there, you know. Maybe it'll be reborn, maybe it won't. Maybe it will mix with the energies of someone loved and lost by others. Maybe it stays one whole, but simply moves on to Heaven or some other plane of existence. I don't know how it works exactly, but I do know you will cross their energy again one day."

"How will I know when that happens?"

Artemis sighed and looked skyward as if searching the clouds for answers. "I don't know. I like to think it's when we are remembering them. Perhaps you'll be walking through a park—or maybe a store--and suddenly they'll cross your mind for no reason at all. I like to think at those times maybe they entered my mind because I just passed a little piece of their essence inhabiting someone else now."

Salem liked the idea. If she could know for sure that somewhere out there in that great big world a piece of her little boy or her husband might end up a part of someone else—someone she might one day encounter—maybe she'd feel it. Maybe for a solitary second she might sense them again. For now, that was the only thought she could take comfort in.

"Give me another cigarette."

CHAPTER THIRTEEN

Salem Laughs Again

Everyone who knew the Blanchards sent condolence cards or flowers. Many also brought food to Blanchard House. The family had many friends in Daihmler-people they'd helped in various ways over the years, and when the townspeople heard the news of a death in the family, they showed their support with baked and fried love. The funeral was held on the Blanchard property, as was custom in the family. It was a double funeral, officiated by Travis Dandridge. As he stood before the family—and being a private funeral, it was family only—he was completely unaware that the little coffin beside David's was empty.

He spoke lovingly of his nephew and grandnephew. He told stories about David's childhood and the joy he had brought Travis and Molly through the years. He told the story of how he'd been the one to rush Salem to the hospital the day she gave birth to Michael. He talked about how close he came to being in the delivery room holding her hand until, in the final hour, David was tracked down at work and made it just in time. Travis spoke with a mixture of laughter and tears for his nephews. At one point, he placed his hands on each coffin and stood in silent prayer. He had no idea baby Michael's remains were not in the box before him.

A sorrowful sky sat overhead that afternoon—a greenish gray horizon carrying a still, hot air all around. Tornado weather, but thankfully none developed. Travis and Molly were invited to stay for dinner and overnight if they so desired, but declined. They said their goodbyes to the family, and to a numb and silent Salem. Travis assured her that her job would be waiting for her whenever she was ready to return. He reminded her that David's death did not end the fact that she was family to he and Molly and always would be. She was now their last relative on earth. Olympia made a point to let the Dandridges know they were also part of the Blanchard family and were welcome anytime.

After the Dandridges drove away, Olympia sat down in the living room to contemplate the day. Salem was already sitting in one of the winged-back chairs by the fireplace, her legs pulled up to her chest like armor. Silently, she sunk her face into her knees. Olympia watched her, wishing there was something she could do to ease her pain. There was nothing Olympia Blanchard hated more than seeing one of her babies hurting. She understood all too well the pain Salem was feeling. She had lost three husbands in her time. First John Windham, then Martin Caswell, and lastly her sweet Sinclair. She also understood the pain of losing a child. She had gone through that torment with Nacaria. Olympia knew the fine line between grief and madness. Salem was holding it together much too strongly. Olympia knew her granddaughter well enough to know Salem would never release the pent-up emotion with tears. Since the crash, she had only cried once the swell became too much to contain, and then she cried only the amount needed to release the overflow—the rest she locked inside behind the dam. She had learned to do that after her mother was taken. Olympia regretted now having allowed that child to cope with pain by stoically suppressing it. Adult Salem was not equipped for releasing grief because the child she'd once been refused to succumb to it. What Salem needed was a laugh. Laughter could release the pressure just as well as giving into tears. And a release was needed to empty out everything her granddaughter was holding in. No one wanted her to blow anything up again.

Olympia noticed that the rest of the family were busying themselves in their own way. Fable was in the living room with them, sitting on the sofa, glancing through family photo albums. She had paused at the pictures of Salem and David's wedding, staring blankly at the happy snapshots of the day. Olympia could hear noise in the kitchen where Demitra and Beryl were helping Artemis wash up the coffee cups and saucers. Seth was out in the graveyard, covering David's grave. And Olympia could hear the faint voice of Yasmine from the porch. It sounded as if she were greeting, and stopping, her new boyfriend from coming inside.

...

"It's just not a good time to come in, Jake," Yasmine said uncomfortably. "I'm sorry. It's just family right now."

Jake ran his hand clumsily through his dark, curly hair and broke eye contact. He felt a little embarrassed to have barged in on such a private moment. He didn't know the Blanchards. Only Yasmine. He realized it had been presumptuous to drive out there.

"I understand," Jake replied. "I didn't exactly know what I should do. I know I don't really know your family, but I felt like I couldn't stay home, not without at least driving by a minute to tell you in person how sorry I am for your family's loss."

"I appreciate it. That was really kind of you. It's just a hard day. My cousin isn't very responsive. She just sits there."

Jake looked away a moment out into the meadow. Just beyond a cluster of trees he was able to make out the figure of a man shoveling earth. It seemed out of place for a moment until it dawned on him the man with the shovel was burying something. "Is that where they are being buried?"

"Yes," Yasmine answered. "Seth dug the grave and is now covering it."

"Grave?" Jake noted. "I thought there were two losses."

"Sorry, graves," Yasmine corrected.

"Isn't it a little strange to bury people in your yard?" Jake questioned.

"Not here," Yasmine explained. "Blanchard relatives are always buried here. Out where Seth is, is the family graveyard. My grandmother's three husbands are there. My grandfather being one of them. One day that's where I'll be too, I guess."

"Not if someone marries you and takes you away from here to start a life of your own."

Yasmine gave him a gentle look, but firmly said, "I would never go away from here."

Their conversation was interrupted by a car pulling up in the gravel driveway. Vanessa Collins stepped out and shut the door behind her. She began walking towards the porch until she spied Seth in the distance. She glanced up to Yasmine as if to ask permission.

"Go ahead," Yasmine said. "He is having a hard time. It might help if he sees you."

Vanessa walked the distance across the meadow to the patch of trees sprinkled with headstones. Seth was shoveling the final layers of dirt as she came up. Sweat covered his brow and had soaked through the back of his shirt and under his arms. He wiped his brow with the back of his dirt-stained hand, leaving a smudge on his forehead.

"How are you holding up?" she asked.

Sticking the shovel in the ground over David's grave, he lifted a water bottle from a nearby headstone and took a sip. "It's not easy."

"Why are you digging the grave?" Vanessa asked. "Your grandmother is loaded. Couldn't she have hired someone to do this?"

"We bury our own," Seth said as if the tradition gave him a sense of family pride. "I would never let anyone else bury David. He was my brother."

Vanessa looked around at the graves. There were several. Each had a tall headstone etched with the names and dates of the beloved Blanchard relatives. It was an odd practice from her experience in the church. She had never known anyone to be buried on a family property before. She was certain her father would not approve. Then again, he would not even have approved of her drive out there to see Seth today. She'd made that excursion in secret.

"Are your parents buried here?" she asked.

"No. My father is still alive." His jaw tensed, betraying a rage boiling beneath the surface. It was a rage he was adept at hiding, but in the moment he slipped, opening a crack allowing her to glimpse inside. "I've just never met him."

Vanessa nervously retracted her lips into a pursed expression, "I'm sorry, Seth. I didn't know. You've never told me that. I assumed both of your parents were dead. Is your mother's grave here?"

"No," Seth answered flatly, without further explanation. "My mother isn't buried here."

A long pause passed between them. Seth picked the shovel back up and smoothed out the clumps of dirt and grass over the grave he had dug. Vanessa watched him in silence. There was so much she did not know about his life. He'd been through things in his life--hard things. It wasn't difficult to figure that out. But what they were remained a mystery. Seth wasn't the type to dwell in uncomfortable places. Vanessa knew him well enough to know that whatever pains he carried inside he considered private. He never shared them. In fact, he avoided them at all cost, usually masking them with humor. She realized now that the characteristics she found most endearing about him—his sense of humor and his almost religious dedication to fitness were only shields to distract from whatever wounds he was trying to hide.

With the job completed, he rested the shovel along the edge of the waist-high iron fence nearby. Vanessa pushed a strand of hair out of her face which the gentle breeze was blowing into her eyes. Birds were chirping in the trees as the sun was beginning to set beyond the woods across the meadow. Seth was unusually quiet. Pensive. Vanessa wasn't sure what to say or do for him. He'd never been this way before.

Exhausting all other possible things to say, she simply said, "I wish I could have been with you at the funeral."

Seth looked at her and made a bad attempt at a smile, "I know. I appreciate that."

"I suppose coming inside to pay my respects to your sister isn't a good idea either?" Vanessa asked. "I see Yasmine has porch-blocked her boyfriend."

"Jake is here?" Seth shrieked, turning to look towards the house. It was the first bit of real emotion he'd displayed since she had approached. "Why is he here? He isn't her boyfriend. They are barely even dating."

"Does he bother you?" Vanessa asked.

"No," Seth replied. "I don't even know him. I can't see him well from here. Kind of short, isn't he?"

"I didn't think he was particularly short," Vanessa said looking again.

"Well, hopefully he's leaving. He shouldn't be here."

Vanessa bristled, "Like me, too, I suppose."

"I didn't mean it that way." Warmth was returning to Seth's eyes now. He felt bad at how his remark had come off. "You are my girlfriend; Jake is nothing to Yasmine."

Vanessa eyed Seth for a moment and then said what she was thinking, "Do I need to point out the fact that she is your cousin?"

"What are you talking about?"

"Nothing," Vanessa said concernedly. "You just seem to have a noticeable aversion to your cousin's boyfriend."

"I don't care either way," Seth snapped. "But he's not her boyfriend. Like I said, they barely date. It just seems pretty presumptuous of him to drive out here—today of all days."

...

Back in the house, Salem had not stirred from her place in the chair. Fable tried offering her some tea, but she did not look up. Yasmine came back into the house. As she passed Salem's chair, she reached her hand out and caressed her cousin's soft red hair. Words were useless now. The simple gesture was all she could think of to show she was there and she cared. Salem took no notice of that either. Olympia was worried. The air around was heavy and solemn, deafened by the sound of loss. The old woman had rarely felt powerless in her life, and when she had, she hated the feeling. She felt powerless again now. Part of her job as a grandmother was to protect her offspring. And her sole job as Hecate of their family coven was to guide and protect her witches. There was nothing she could do with this situation except wait it out and watch her granddaughter mourn. Suddenly the front door swung open as Zelda stomped inside. With her swept in a wave of chatter and life, infiltrating the somber air.

"Hey kiddies!" she yelled slamming the door behind her. In her arms were bottles of Pepsi and two buckets of fried chicken. "I know you all want to be alone, but hey—you're not gonna be."

Salem looked up for the first time in a half hour. It surprised her that she felt like giggling at the sight of Zelda in her chartreuse moo-moo juggling chicken and soft drinks. And that magenta hair! Salem had not seen Zelda's new dye job since she'd been home.

"Zelda," she said, rising from the hold the chair had on her. "I haven't seen you in a year or more."

"I know, Kiddo," Zelda winked. "I'm sorry about everything. But I bet you're sick of people saying they're sorry for you, so I'm not going to say it again. But I had to say it at least the once otherwise I'm just some old, silly bitch. Now grab some of this chicken. I remembered how you liked it."

"Thank you, Zelda," Salem said, taking the chicken from her and grabbing a drumstick off the top.

"Zelda, Mrs. McKenzie brought us some of her homemade fried chicken an hour ago. We were just about to heat it up in a little while," Fable said.

"Throw that mess away!" Zelda cried. "Delma McKenzie is about the worst cook in Daihmler. I bet you she brought that crap over cause her family wouldn't eat it. She just acted like she made it for ya'll."

"Good old Zelda," Olympia said to herself as she joined her friend.

"Lympy, you remember how sick ever'body got after that book club meeting she hosted when she served her sausage balls. That woman is a terrible cook." Zelda carried the Pepsi bottles to the dining room table setting them down amid the spread of food from the community. "Oh, Lord. I recognize Buella Crowly's flowerdy casserole dish with the chip in the handle. Toss that out, too. She just throws together whatever cans of shit she has in the cabinet and pours some mushroom soup over it and calls it a casserole. You're better off eating out of the garbage."

Salem laughed. A real, genuine laugh. It felt good and she felt guilty from it. Yet she found herself laughing again. What right did she have to laugh? This was not a day for laughter. She scolded herself, but within seconds she found herself smiling again as Zelda paraded around the table making commentary.

"Oh, and look," Zelda snorted. "Inez Dillingham made macaroni and cheese. Filthiest kitchen in town and she's gonna bring this mess? Mac and cheese! What's she think, ever'body here is ten years old? Bet this stuff came out of a box. And of course, she labeled her pan with a piece of tape and her name in Sharpie. I've seen the bottoms of her pans before. They're all rusted. Ain't nobody tryin' to keep her nasty ass pan! Toss this crap out."

Artemis came out of the kitchen, "What's going on out here?"

Salem reached for her aunt's hand and whispered, "Zelda just gave me a cigarette." Artemis put her arm around Salem and hugged her tight.

"Anyway," Zelda could be heard saying from the living room—already midway into another story, "I don't care if your feet do dry out and crack open when you walk across my carpet barefooted, I'm not ripping up my rug just cause you're allergic to Scotchguard."

"What are talking about now Zelda?" Salem asked, coming into the living room with another chicken leg.

"I was just telling your Hecate 'bout how my Sarah says she's allergic to my new carpet. Says her feet crack open. If you ask me, those feet a' hern crack open cause the sheer pressure of carrying that big fat ass of hers around."

"That's awful to say," Olympia scolded.

"How is that diet of hers going Zelda?" Artemis asked. "I gave her several good recipes for low carb cooking."

"Arty, you won't believe what that fool gal did. Made all that stuff you told her and poured gravy all over it, then made a chocolate cake. The girl is gone need her own area code 'fore too long."

Olympia patted Zelda's hand as they both sat down on the living room sofa. Zelda understood the meaning and opened her mind to her friend's mental wavelength, like tuning to her favorite radio station through all the fuzz. *Thank you*, Olympia mindspoke to her. *You always know just what is needed at just the right time.* Zelda, being as well versed in mindspeaking as her friend, replied back to Olympia, *Old Death can snatch up who he likes but he ain't gonna break our Salem. Not as long as I got a say.*

Olympia and her family often used mindspeaking to convey private messages to one another, but she and Zelda had been mindspeaking together all of their lives.

Back in the old days when the world had been much less safe than it is now, the two of them and Olympia's sister, Pastoria, had avoided much peril using the ability to silently communicate with one another.

"Zelda you really should be more supportive of your daughters," Beryl commented coming into the living room by way of the dining room, where she had scored herself a piece of chicken.

"Nah," Zelda scoffed. "I never really liked them very much. Lympy here had the good kids, the whole lot of you. I got shafted. Nothing but lazy stupid girls, the both of them. Course Melinda was pretty at least. Ain't so much now, but she used to be. I wanted boys. Didn't get any. Now my girls are so ugly, doubt I'll ever even get son-in-laws."

"You're awful," Demitra said.

"Used to look at them when they was little and wonder how in the world it was those two sperms that made it through out of all the other'ns."

The shadow passed across the floor, then onto the wall and hovered a moment. No one said anything. Salem stared blankly at the shadow. Her face contorted a little, as if in anger towards it.

"Salem, acknowledge her," Zelda said.

Salem did not say anything.

"Salem, dear, you haven't even spoken to her since you came home," Olympia said. "He was her grandson after all."

"Go away, Mother!" Salem shouted at the wall. "You are the last thing I need to be reminded of right now."

The shadow moved quickly out of the room.

CHAPTER FOURTEEN

Practice Makes Perfect

Here and there throughout the room, various items were scattered about. Jars lined the windowsills on all sides of the room. A table of books and feathers and bricks sat in one corner. A fire extinguisher sat alone in another corner, and many other peculiar items could be seen in various odd places. This was *the magic room*. More appropriately, the training room. Once a week, for as long as anyone could remember, the Blanchard's would gather together in the large square room at the top of Blanchard House. Only accessible from a twisting wooden staircase on the third floor, the room was actually the tower which crowned the front of the house. The tower was a very special and ornate adornment to the house. More like a fourth-floor room than an actual tower, but the family always referred to it as *the tower* to outsiders and *the magic room* within the family. The walls came up only halfway, about three feet from the floor, and from there wooden square frames held a multitude of window panes finishing the wall to the ceiling. From the tower room almost all of the Blanchard land could be seen. Historians would say this was where the old plantation master would have purveyed his lands and slaves, however if a historian did proper research, they would know that there was never a slave owned by a Blanchard.

It was in this room where all Blanchard children first learned to exercise and control their powers. Salem moved her first object in that room—quite by accident when she was frustrated that she couldn't keep Beryl successfully frozen for more than a few seconds. Seth first altered the weather outside standing at the windows of this room. He had been trying to provide Daihmler with a white Christmas that year but only succeeded in summoning snow clouds over Blanchard House. The mailman had been quite stunned on his delivery that day. And Beryl healed her very first patient in this room when she was seven years old, it was her hamster Ricco who'd been attacked by Fable's cat Mr. Ice Cream.

Many memories of struggle and triumph had been made in the magic room. Every Blanchard succeeded in cultivating their own special gifts here, and as time passed and the young witches grew, they found training still an important part of growth as they tried to master new abilities.

"What am I working on today, Hecate?" Fable asked. "There's pretty much nothing else to master with my animal communication."

"Try astral projection today," Olympia suggested.

"Why bother?" Fable remarked. "It never works. I can only do the one thing. No matter what else I try, I can't do anything but talk to animals."

"You are the laziest witch I've ever seen," Demitra scolded her daughter. "You can keep trying, you know."

"Why bother? I'm only half witch. I think I've peaked at my talents."

"Artemis and I are only half, too, but we still practice new things. You never know what could develop."

"Well, I can use the distraction," admitted Salem. "I haven't been in the magic room for years. I have so many fun memories here. It'll be good for me to get my mind off things. At least I hope it does."

"Yeah, well you are a whole witch. It's easy for you," Fable sneered.

"Not necessarily," Salem replied. "Seth is, too, and he can't do much of anything but control the weather."

"That's because Seth is just as lazy as Fable," Demitra chuckled. "I myself need to practice mind speaking."

Olympia cautioned her daughter, "Be sure not to lapse into mind reading, they are two separate things. You are so gifted at the latter it may cloud your ability for the former."

"I think that's the problem," Demitra nodded. "I am so used to using my psychic abilities to read minds or pick up trace memories from locations that I end up reading minds rather than speaking to them. I can't seem to find that specific wavelength."

With a reassuring pat on the back, Olympia said, "It just takes more practice."

"What do I do, Hecate?" Seth asked.

Olympia looked at her grandson for a moment, contemplating ideas. She went over to a small cabinet and withdrew a pendulum. She placed it on a nearby table and said, "Use this and attempt to stop it by freezing it in motion. Salem can do this, and so you could be able to do it as well."

"Uh, is anyone gonna mention the fact that Salem can also lift up our lawn and smash it together in the air?" Seth cried. "Why is no one addressing that little feat since it happened?"

"What Salem did the other day was achieve a very potent levitation ability," Olympia explained. "An ability she needs to hone. That is what I am expecting her to focus on today, by lifting those bricks in the corner and placing them on this table in the center of the room."

Within minutes the Blanchard's were all working on their various assignments, with the exception of Beryl and Artemis, who were not there. Beryl had rounds at the hospital and Artemis was running late from doing the grocery shopping in town. When she finally arrived and walked into the magic room she saw the kids struggling with their lessons. Seth was trying to halt time, but it looked more like he was swatting at invisible gnats. No matter how many swipes his hands took at the air, nothing manifested. Artemis thought to herself for a brief moment, *maybe the boy should study orchestra conducting*. Fable was attempting to exit her body and manifest her spirit across the room. She was having about as much luck as her cousin. Artemis suppressed the urge to comment, but if she had she would have asked Fable if she were trying to force herself to go to the bathroom--because that's about what it looked like. Salem was trying to levitate bricks. She had more luck with her lesson. The bricks were not exactly levitating, but every now and then one shook a little. Demitra appeared to be working on something of her own which she was not sharing with the rest of the class. Artemis was pretending to work on telekinesis, but in fact she was trying to figure out what her sister was up to. Demitra was lost in concentration and every so often her closed lids opened and Artemis thought she saw her eyes darting from left to right at such a frequency it made Artemis think of a copying machine--scanning something.

"Hecate, I can't get the bricks to move very far," Salem admitted after half an hour. "I just can't focus."

"Try harder."

"I am, but it's not working," Salem huffed.

"Demitra," Olympia beckoned. "Stop what you're doing for a moment, and look into Salem's mind and tell me what is clouding it."

"Michael," Salem said tearfully; she didn't need her aunt's power to figure that out for her. "I can't stop thinking of him. I can't pretend my heart isn't in pieces while I work on magic. I don't even know what the purpose of having powers is if I can't save my family with them!"

Suddenly the bricks jumped into the air and splintered off in all directions, crashing through the windows. Seth had to duck to keep one from smashing into his head.

"Well, I'm glad now I didn't get around to washing those windows this week," Artemis chuckled as she swept her long black hair behind her shoulder. "I'll call the window guy tomorrow."

"Take some time my dear," Olympia said rubbing Salem's back gently with her palm. "It has only been a week. Your grief is as powerful as you are. Channel it, use it. It will help you."

"Nothing can help me," Salem said, collapsing into her grandmother's arms.

The day's lesson ended after that as Olympia took Salem downstairs for a rest. Seth and Fable left the magic room too, neither one feeling much like working on anything with Salem in so much anguish. Only Demitra and Artemis remained, tidying up the room after lessons.

"I wish I could do something, anything, for her," Artemis said. "My heart is broken seeing her in so much pain. Especially when I know she still hasn't allowed herself to feel the breadth of it yet. Most days she is coasting until she has one or two tiny breakdowns. Then it's back to the steely face and acting like she's just here for a visit."

"I know what you mean," Demitra agreed. "Once or twice I've tried to tap into her mind to gauge where she is, and it's just too much for me to feel. The intensity of what she is hiding from us is so great. I know what that feels like."

"She's been like my own daughter since Nacaria became that thing on the wall," Artemis frowned. "I have raised that child. I've doctored her scrapes and bruises. Held her in my arms when boys broke her heart. Rejoiced with her when she married and had a baby. But I can't do anything with this. I can't fix anguish of this magnitude."

"Maybe we can," Demitra said with a glint in her eye which disturbed Artemis. "Maybe we could do a *summoning* spell."

Artemis was astounded. "I cannot believe my ears. You seriously are not suggesting this."

"Just temporarily," Demitra explained. "Just long enough for her to say goodbye."

"No, Demitra. No. It isn't a good idea to try to regroup old energy. Think of the people and things that now contain David and Michael's energy. Stealing that out of them is dangerous. We can't deplete another entity's ethereal composition."

"They've only been dead a week, Artemis. Who knows if their energy has even joined anything else yet? And even if it has, that person will just feel disoriented for a while. It would just be a little piece of them removed for a very short time. They'll chalk it up to bad equilibrium."

"You know as well as I do it gets way more serious than that, Demitra. No. Summoning their energy back is not the answer," Artemis declared emphatically. "We don't mess with that."

CHAPTER FIFTEEN

Too Much to Consider

No witch ever knew ahead of time where the Consort meeting of the Southeastern Witches Association would be held, not until the letter arrived revealing the location. This was a holdover tradition from the days gone by when witches had to exist in secret to escape danger from *regulars* that didn't understand their ways. In the current era, keeping private wasn't so important anymore, but the tradition had been set and no one knew where they'd be expected to meet until the mail brought them the invitation. Much like a convention would arrange things, the Witches Association met at various locations in their district four times a year. Though no meeting was considered mandatory, it was strongly suggested over the years that the Autumn meeting should not be missed by any coven leader. Coven members could attend, or not attend meetings at their own convenience, but coven leaders usually came to as many Consorts as they could. Olympia, as head of the Blanchard coven, was the only witch in her brood who usually attended meetings, although sometimes Artemis and Demitra would attend an occasional Consort. Salem, however, was required to attend this Summer meeting of the Witches Association because she was the witch with business on the agenda…the cremation of her child.

"I am not going!" Salem bellowed when she looked at the letter from the Consort.

"Yes, Child, you are," Olympia said decidedly.

"No, I will not go to the home of those people."

Olympia could hardly blame her, but Salem was allowing her emotions to cloud her better judgement. It unfortunately mattered very little how difficult this particular meeting—this particular location—would be, Salem had no choice but to attend because Michael's remains had to be disposed of in the proper ways.

"We will just cremate Michael here," Salem suggested. "I don't want the others involved anyway. Especially there!"

"Salem," started Olympia, "Michael will be given the ceremony all witches are given. The ceremony all Blanchards have been given. And he will be given it by the Council. Our family has been a member of the Consort for one hundred and eighty-six years. We are not about to start going it alone now. You never know when you'll need the help of others."

"But Hecate, I don't want to see *them*."

"I know you don't. I don't especially want to see them either, but we are just as much a part of the Witches Association as they or anyone else."

"But they hate me!" Salem cried. "They hate all of us."

Olympia smiled reassuringly at her granddaughter and said, "You must remember Salem, that it was the Consort as a whole that brought down the verdict on your mother, not just the Obreiggons."

"Is *he* going to be there?"

"I rarely see him at any of the meetings. Atheidrelle heads their family coven. She is usually alone."

"But the summer meeting will be at their home. He's bound to be there."

"Oleander is a big place. Even larger than our property. I assure you if he wants to be invisible, he can be."

...

The laughter and loud jabbering of Fable, Yasmine, and Seth filled the third floor and reached down the stairs to Beryl's bedroom on the second floor. She was trying to nap from a long day at the hospital. Their voices were so loud that she had to get up to close her bedroom's door.

They were in the little den on the third floor which Grandfather Sinclair designated during his time at Blanchard House to be the kids' den. Since most of the children had their bedrooms on the third floor, he felt they might just as well stay up there for their roughhousing and hijinks. As the years passed, the kids' den became more of a television watching room than anything else. Seth, Yasmine, and Fable were watching old reruns on T.V. and laughing hysterically at an episode of *The Andy Griffith Show* when Barney Fife had made a jack-ass out of himself.

"Ya'll ever notice how mean Andy treated Opie once the show started airing in color?" Fable asked during a commercial.

"Not just Opie, but the whole town," Yasmine pointed out. "When it was black and white, he was like, *oh what a charming town with all these wonderful, zany citizens,* but the second it aired in color he was just *over it.*"

"*Frasier* did that too," Seth noted. "Like around the time Niles and Daphne fell in love, Frasier acted a little more put out with everyone—especially his Dad."

"I got one," Fable declared. "Remember how on *I Love Lucy,* Lucy's maiden name was McGillicuddy? Then when they went to Europe and were going to Scotland, Lucy wanted to look up her mother's family, the McGillicuddys."

"So?" Seth replied.

"Well, if Lucy's mother's family were the McGillicuddys and Lucy's maiden name was McGillicuddy, then Lucy was illegitimate."

"Oh my God, I never thought of that!" Yasmine exclaimed.

"Lucy was not illegitimate!" Seth said. "Not that there's anything wrong with that. Hell, I am! But they wouldn't have put that on television back in the 50's. They couldn't even use the word pregnant when she was pregnant on the show."

"Then explain how McGillicuddy is her maiden name and her mother's family's name, and they never once mention Lucy's father."

"We watch way too much TV," decided Seth.

"Hey, let's go pull Beryl out of bed and throw her in the pool!" Yasmine suggested.

"Yes!" Fabled gasped. "We haven't done anything like that in ages. She will be livid!"

"Yeah, we usually did that to Yazzy anyway," Seth reminded. "It'll be funny to do it to Beryl."

The three of them sneaked downstairs as quietly as possible. Fable and Yasmine giggled as they went. They all remembered to step over the squeaky fifth tread on the stair—the one which was always the reason they got caught sneaking in late as teenagers. When they reached the second-floor hallway they walked very slowly—single file--until they reached Beryl's door. Opening it ever so gently so that the natural creak of the wood was not quite so audible, Seth entered first, followed by Yasmine, then Fable. They could see Beryl's form laying under the quilted bedspread. All at once they leapt atop her and pinned her down. Seth tossed back the covers and jolted back. It was only pillows! Laughter rang out behind them, laughter from Salem and Beryl in the doorway. Suddenly the devious trio were lifted into the air as Salem raised her hands.

"Salem stop it!" Fable pleaded. "It was just a prank."

"I know," Salem grinned, Beryl's arm around her shoulder in camaraderie. "So is this."

"Come on, Sis!" Seth cried. "Put us down."

"Oh, she will," Beryl grinned.

Downstairs, Artemis and Demitra were sitting in the living room reading the afternoon paper when Beryl and Salem came down the foyer stairs backwards, Salem's arms still mid-air with the trio of pranksters hovering above the staircase, still caught in her trap.

"Dinner will be ready soon," Artemis called out. "Don't be long."

"They're all crazy, you know," Demitra told her sister, barely looking up from her section of the paper.

Outside now, Salem held her focus on her brother and two cousins as she slowly backed her way across the lawn to the pool area. Seth, Fable, and Yasmine were still screaming for her to stop as she levitated them directly over the cool clear water of the swimming pool and released them. The collective splash reached all the way to the potted shrubs on the tiled pool deck.

Beryl and Salem stood laughing at the sight of the three fools swimming back to the side of the pool. Suddenly the wind kicked up. The treetops were bending in the breeze. The pool chairs began to slide around from the force.

"Seth, are you doing this?" Fable asked as she gripped her cousin's shoulder with one hand and clung to the pool deck with the other.

"It's not me," he said.

The wind was really kicking up harder now. All of the sudden, Beryl and Salem were sent toppling into the pool themselves, drenched from head to toe. They looked around in disbelief, as did Seth, Fable, and Yasmine who now clung to the pool's edge as the wind slapped water into their faces. Artemis and Demitra stood on the lawn several yards away, laughing themselves now at the sight of the prank *they* had just pulled.

"The Aunts!" Salem shouted.

Demitra wrapped her own arm around her sister's shoulder and replied, "Now *that* is funny."

CHAPTER SIXTEEN

A Blanchard in Oleander

The drive from Daihmler to Charleston took just over six hours. It was quite a long trek to make for a Consort meeting, but since the ancestral home of the Obreiggon family was the site chosen to host this quarter's meeting, the trip was unavoidable. Salem, Zelda, and Olympia decided to stop by the hotel in downtown Charleston to rest before dressing for the meeting. Salem had never been to Charleston before. The streets downtown were narrow and tight to maneuver through depending on how much traffic was on that particular street. Modernization of roadways and buildings had not tarnished the historic roads of Charleston. The storefronts, churches, and homes which Salem drove past had been there for more than two hundred years. Because city ordinances mandated that no new construction and no tearing down of any building was allowed within the historic district, everything the trio saw was just the way it had been in antebellum times.

"Everything is so cute," Salem remarked as she turned onto the street where the Frances Marion Hotel stood. "Nothing is over three stories."

"That's so you can see the church steeples," Olympia explained. "No building can be higher than the church. It's the law."

"How do you know so much about it?" Salem asked with a raised brow.

"Girl, your Hecate and me wasn't always two old biddies!" Zelda shot back. "We been here a few times. Hey, Lympy, remember when we wiped out that rogue coven that was tryin' to zombify people? I think their house was over there off the Battery."

"I remember," Olympia winked.

"Zombies!" Salem cried. "What?"

"It's not important, Dear," Olympia replied with a pat to Salem's hand on the wheel. "Just get us to the hotel."

...

After a short nap and a shower, the trio dressed for the Consort meeting. Olympia didn't often dress up, but when she did she looked like a regal diplomat. Wearing her light blue silk dress with the delicate pearl beads along the skirt, Olympia looked impressive. Salem marveled at her grandmother for a second and hoped that she might be that beautiful when she was that age. Zelda wore an electric pink top with a fluorescent green skirt. She looked like she'd been dressed in neon markers. Her magenta hair did not help matters, either.

Salem did not want to be there. She did not want to go to this meeting, but she knew she had to—it was required. After all, it was her son who would be cremated that night. Salem glanced over to a desk in front of the hotel room window. The box sitting on top of the desk—that was why she was there. Her little boy's remains were in that box. She could feel the pain swell inside. She wanted to cry, but she swallowed the feeling down. She would not break, not tonight. And she found herself dressing as if there was a point to be made that night. She chose her mid length, floral-print gown with intertwined flowers on a white background. She looked like a breath of spring in the middle of autumn. Her waist-length, auburn hair looked great against that dress. Standing back to look at herself in the mirror she told herself, *If I have to see those people, then at least I look fantastic.* She felt guilty for having the thought. This wasn't about her. It was about her son. She was going to lay him to rest tonight. A second glance to the mirror made her less arrogant. She could see now in the reflection that a broken woman indeed stood before her no matter how strong she liked to believe herself to be. She wondered about herself. What is the line between strength and coldness? She'd always been a strong person—she'd had to be from the moment they'd taken her mother away. She would have to be careful to ensure that losing her family did not make her cold moving forward.

The drive out to the Obreiggon estate was a long and confusing one, but the maps app on Salem's phone helped. What she really wanted to do was skip the Consort altogether and drive to Folly Beach. Walking the sandy shoreline under the sunset seemed far more attractive a way to spend her evening. She wanted to forget the Witches Association meeting and her purpose for being there tonight, but she couldn't. She made the turn to James Island and resigned herself to her duty. She did not have the luxury tonight to be a child; she had one final responsibility as a mother.

The Obreiggon's lived on Wadmalaw Island, only accessible by passing over James Island, then John's Island. The acrid stench of the marsh infiltrated the car through the air conditioning system. It was off-putting. It didn't match the serenity of the landscape as the setting sun glowed like red embers of a fire disappearing behind the tall reeds in the river. The reeds created small channels, like water highways through the marsh. The tide was coming in, and the shrimp boats who had fished the brackish waters were slowly returning from their day's work.

The oaks lining either side of the road reached their long fingers toward each other as if to clasp hands. It had taken hundreds of years for them to reach to the other side, in maybe another hundred years their fingers might finally touch. The massive limbs bent toward the car allowing the Spanish moss to lightly stroke the top and sides of Salem's SUV. Long-abandoned houses with their sinking roofs and broken porches were half eaten by brush and vine. Sprinkled along the road among them were new builds, beautiful homes not hindered by the decay of their neighbors.

In the distance, the glow of light broke the canopy of the road's darkness. Electric lanterns lining a long wall led the way to the open gates welcoming Consort members. Arching over the gate was the word "Oleander." Turning into the estate, white oleander trees lined the way, shielding eyes from the dense thicket of trees and scrub behind them. Oleander as an estate had once been a tea plantation. In the fields beyond the road, tea plants still grew— long untended and wild now.

As Salem drove down the driveway, she saw the small guest house ahead where drivers were stopping to hand off their keys to parking attendants. From there, guests appeared to be making their way across the lawn to the pavilion where Consort members were gathering. In the distance stood the great plantation house. As she exited the car, Salem looked down the road towards it. It rose like some forbidden kingdom, off-limits to everyone, but there to show them it was always watching. From what her vantage point offered, it appeared to be mammoth. Three stories tall, with white columns standing like sentries flanking the façade of the house. Elongated capitals gave the sense that the house towered over everything around. Iron banisters ran across the long front porch and the balconies above and stretched around the curved bay wings on either side.

An Obreiggon servant guided Olympia, Zelda, and Salem beneath the bright moonlight to the open courtyard and meadow by the pavilion. At least two hundred people were mingling and sipping from crystal wine glasses and brass goblets. Salem was less interested in the people around her and more interested in that great house in the distance. Oleander. She thought the name fit, beautiful yet somehow poisonous. The courtyard they were standing in was connected by an arbor to a rather large Victorian structure which looked like a cross between a portico and an open-sided cathedral.

"It is beautiful," Salem admired. "I have to hand them that."

"The Obreiggon's always were stylish," Olympia said. "This estate has belonged to the Obreiggon family for generations."

Salem was taking it all in.

"Are you all right?" Olympia asked.

"Yes. I'm just surprised at my own morbid curiosity."

Salem caught sight of a fountain along the high wall of the courtyard. Leaving Zelda and Olympia chatting with someone they knew, Salem walked over to admire it, but as she grew closer, she realized it wasn't very beautiful. Time had weathered the stone, but she could still tell it was a statue of a woman. Moss obscured some of the face, but what was visible was unnerving. She had harsh, threatening features. The face was probably supposed to be beautiful, but something sinister about the smile unnerved Salem. Suddenly there was a tap on her shoulder.

"Admiring my statue?"

Salem whirled around to see the very image from the fountain looking back at her in flesh and blood. Everything beautiful yet threatening about the sculpture was just as evident in the inspiration for it.

"Welcome to my estate," the woman said arrogantly. "I am Atheidrelle Obreiggon. I do not believe I have ever seen you at one of our meetings before. Are you a new member? Perhaps you've recently relocated from up north? I confess I do not know many members of the Northern Witches Association." There was something condescending in the way Atheidrelle Obreiggon was speaking to her.

"No," Salem forced a pained, gritted smile. She hated this woman with every fiber of her soul. "No, I am not, Mrs. Obreiggon."

"Oh, then who exactly are you?"

She really doesn't know who I am. She has absolutely no idea.

It then occurred to Salem that the woman wouldn't have had any reason to have known who she was. Salem had never been to a Consort meeting in her life and no one at the Consort, except select friends like Zelda, would have had any way of knowing she'd be there or why.

Before Salem could open her mouth to reply to the woman, Olympia walked up to the fountain and stood next to her granddaughter. "Good evening, Atheidrelle."

"Olympia."

Salem could feel the tension between the two of them. Mortal enemies, face to face. It was palpable. Never in her life had Salem ever known Olympia to possess hatred in heart for anyone, but standing by the fountain now Salem could feel the animosity in her grandmother's heart for Atheidrelle Obreiggon. *I think Hecate despises her even more than I do.*

"I was just about to introduce myself to our hostess," Salem told Olympia.

"That isn't necessary," Olympia replied. "Come, the meeting is about to start. We should say hello to Ursula before it begins."

"No, not yet," Atheidrelle demanded. She had an inquisitive look upon her steely face. "I wish to know my guest's identity."

"I am a Blanchard," Salem replied.

"I rather gathered that," Atheidrelle said coldly. "Judging from your youth, I must assume you are a granddaughter. One of Demitra's I presume."

"You presume wrong," Salem sneered. Taking one small, defiant step closer to her hostess, Salem stood eye to eye and said, "Nacaria."

Olympia took Salem by the arm, gave a generous yet disingenuous nod to her hostess, and led her granddaughter away. Atheidrelle stood by the fountain watching as they withdrew. She trembled with a fury which she took great care to conceal from anyone who might be watching. And they were watching— she could feel their eyes. She knew the entire Consort would be engrossed in spying on their interaction. Atheidrelle wished she could kill that girl. She had the power to do it swiftly anytime she wanted, but she could not give in to such base emotions. Time would handle everything. And time was on Atheidrelle's side. A young woman, possibly nearing 30 years old, scurried up to her. She looked very much like Atheidrelle, only not quite as hardened.

"Mother, are you alright? You have a very strange look about you."

"Guess who has come to Oleander, Daughter?"

"Who?"

"A child of Nacaria Blanchard."

The girl gasped. "Why? What on earth would bring one of her bastards here of all places?"

"I don't know, Cassandra." All at once a wicked smile crossed Atheidrelle's face. "Unless..."

"Unless what, Mother?"

"It doesn't concern you," Atheidrelle replied. "There is only one reason I can imagine which might demand Salem Blanchard's presence here tonight. We shall see if I am right."

"He's still away though, isn't he?" Cassandra asked.

"Yes. He could not make the meeting tonight. He returns tomorrow. Therefore, if that is what she came for, she will not get the satisfaction."

"Then everything is alright then, isn't it Mother?"

"No, everything isn't alright, Cassandra. Not as long as those Blanchard women are on my property."

A man who had been standing in the shadows, eavesdropping, stepped forward now. He was on the shorter side, with a bushy grey mustache above his trimmed beard. He looked displeased.

"Excuse my overhearing, Atheidrelle, but is it not the sign of a good hostess to extend hospitality to all her guests?"

"Brimford Uding," Atheidrelle addressed him. "You would yourself admit that these circumstances are extenuating."

"The Blanchards are members of the Witches Association," the stalwartly man said, rubbing his wispy sideburns. "They have every right to attend any meeting they so choose. I sympathize with your position, but as a member of the governing Council, I must suggest to you that if you find it distasteful to show grace to some of your guests, perhaps you should remove your home from the lottery of meeting locations."

...

Olympia guided Salem to a small group of people talking. Salem was both uneasy and excited to finally take part in one of the meetings. She was mesmerized by the woman speaking to the little group. She was a breathtaking woman. Tall, slender, strong with years of wisdom yet her face seemed as fresh and youthful as if she were a woman of thirty. Salem imagined that if the Statue of Liberty came to life, she might look a lot like this woman.

"...so you see my dear," the woman was saying to a much younger, but nearly as striking, woman, "though Wiccans may not be all powerful, your very ability to respect the earth can deliver you much power. Teach your coven to listen. Listen to the trees, the flowers, the rocks. There is energy all around us and everything is alive in some way. Through a deep connection to the world around you and every particle in it, you can achieve an enlightenment to rival any power of action a birth-witch might possess."

"I understand," the other woman replied.

"And not just the pretty things, child," the wise woman continued. "Even the ugliest insect, the peskiest weed, and the filthiest body of water are our brothers and sisters made by the earth or if you believe, by the hand of God. There is no rank or importance. We all carry an equal importance in the Natural Order."

The young woman thanked her for the advice and walked away. She looked to Salem to be in awe of the wiser, older witch. The regal woman turned now to Olympia and Salem.

"Olympia Blanchard. It is so good to see you."

"Ernestine Craven," Olympia began. "This is Salem, my—"

"You do not have to tell me who this person is!" Ernestine said breaking her air of austerity and embracing Salem warmly. "Salem you have your mother's beauty!"

"You knew my mother?"

"I knew your mother very well indeed. Most people here will only recall her from seeing her at The Judgement, but I knew her very well before all that ugliness occurred. Your mother was my daughter Ursula's very dearest friend."

"The Queen?" Salem gasped.

"Yes, she is Queen now. And I must say a rather good one. Of course— not quite as good a leader as her father, in my opinion, but I'm rather prejudiced. I loved my husband very much and no one, not even my own daughter, can rival him in my mind when it comes to Consort leadership."

"I agree with you on Brustius," Olympia nodded. "A fine King. And though Ursula was among those who convicted Nacaria, she was also one of the few who spoke out against a harsher punishment."

"Speaking of that mess," Ernestine replied, "Has Atheidrelle seen Salem yet?"

"Yes," Salem smirked proudly. "I don't think she likes me very much."

"I'm sure she's seething with hatred as we speak," Ernestine quipped. "But don't you worry about the Obreiggon's, my dear. They have only one seat on the Council. Your Hecate here has many friends filling most of the others, myself among them."

CHAPTER SEVENTEEN

Working Late

Nine o'clock, Fable noticed looking at her phone. *Time to go home.* She didn't often stay so late at the animal clinic, but she couldn't bring herself to leave, not with Scooter so afraid. He was lying on her lap while she sat at her desk going over the month's statements. Fable owned the clinic, which gave her the opportunity to indulge her greatest passion, caring for animals, but it offered her little monetary means to afford adequate staff. This meant that sometimes Fable was forced to stay late to catch up on the paperwork. With the lion share of her daytime spent seeing patients, the invoices, monthly bills, and tax payments tended to stack up. This month she also had the unpleasant task of writing the newly increased rent check for the space she occupied. Many times, her grandmother had offered to purchase a building for her practice, but Fable could never find the exact one she wanted. Every month when she would write out the lease check, she kicked herself for allowing another year to go by without accepting her grandmother's generous offer.

She did not mind staying late tonight. There wasn't a whole lot to go home to that night anyway. Olympia and Salem were away in Charleston. The Consort meeting was tonight. Fable wondered how that was going. She knew it was a difficult trip for her cousin. Seth and Yazzy both had dates. Seth would be off with Vanessa, and Yasmine had plans with Jake. Beryl was doing whatever it was Beryl did when she was not at work, which was rarely. Fable could have gone home and spent time with her mother and aunt, but they never seemed to be doing anything that interested her. Passing her night by keeping Scooter company after his surgery was the best way she could think of spending her time. He was a sweet dog and needed her more than anyone else in her life did right now. But another glance at her phone told her it was time to go home. Especially since she had to be right back in the office by 9am tomorrow.

"You're gonna be fine tonight, Scoots," Fable said kissing his soft, gray fur. "I want you to take this medicine in this dropper before I leave. It will help you sleep tonight. I'd take you home with me, but I don't have permission from your owner."

They wouldn't mind, Scooter told her.

"I'm not so sure about that," Fable replied. "But I have a deal for you. I won't put you back in the kennel tonight, if you promise to stay here on my couch and not wander around the office. I know you don't like it back there with the other dogs. Will you make me that deal?"

Yes!

Scooter licked her face several times as a thank you for the consideration. She locked up, turning out all the lights except for a desk lamp in her office for Scooter. There were a few stops she needed to make before returning home. Artemis had requested she pick up a large roast for Friday's dinner, and she needed to drop the checks and cash in the bank's night deposit drawer.

The bank was well lit at night, which made Fable feel safer on the nights she worked late. The only other car in the lot was pulling away from the ATM stall when Fable pulled up to the night deposit drawer. She leaned out of her vintage white Jeep to place the client checks in the pull-out drawer but had not leaned in far enough. The heavy drawer snapped back shut sending her checks scattering across the drive-through lanes beside her.

"Damn."

The slight breeze began rolling her checks into the parking lot. She could have chased them down one by one, but luckily being Fable Blanchard, she did not have to. She closed her eyes momentarily and sent out a beacon, a message for assistance from her friends. Within seconds a couple of squirrels ran down from nearby trees and pitter-patted their way across the parking lot, each collecting a check in their tiny paws. Several birds winged down from their perches and lifted the few remaining checks in their beaks, flapping their wings and gliding towards Fable's Jeep. The birds obligingly dropped the checks into her lap as the two helpful squirrels scurried up Fable's front bumper, across the hood, and presented the checks back to her.

"Thank you so much," Fable smiled at them.

She had a little bag of peanuts and a small box of birdseed in her glove compartment and spread it all out on the pavement beside her car. As she deposited her funds in the drawer, the happy animals ate her thank you with gusto.

There weren't too many shoppers at the grocery store that late at night. Fable took her time through the store, picking up a few extra things she realized they needed back at home. On the coffee aisle, she spotted a rather large woman with a rather large little girl meandering along the aisle. The woman stopped to compare the various coffee flavors, completely unaware that behind her back her daughter was opening the boxes of cereal from the opposite shelves. Fable watched as the chubby little girl dug her dirty hands into multiple boxes, scooping out a handful to taste before moving to the next brand. Fable left them on the aisle and proceeded to the back of the store to the meat department.

She encountered an old woman and her blind husband on the meat aisle. The woman was comparing expiration dates on the packages of ground chuck. Fable was almost in reach of the pot roasts, but the woman was blocking her access by mere inches. Fable waited patiently, taking the time to admire the blind man's dog with them. He was a gray German Shepherd. Fable spoke to him and patted him on the head.

"Well, ain't that nice, Trigger," the blind man laughed. "You must be a pretty lady if he let you touch him. He's a good ole dog, big help to me, but he ain't much for people."

The woman moved her buggy further down the meat aisle and called for her husband and Trigger to follow. Fable picked out two extra-large roasts that would please her aunt. Friday nights were typically Howard's nights for dinner, and he had an enormous appetite. As she was pushing her cart away, she observed a rather good-looking man pass her. For a second, she thought she heard him speak to her, but when she whirled around to look, she saw that he hadn't. He was however, filling his cart with every meat product he could get his hands on. *Big family I guess*, she thought.

She felt it again. *Had* he said something? It seemed as though he had, although she couldn't clearly make out the words. It was more of a feeling than a spoken word. It was the same kind of feeling as when Scooter or one of the other animals at the clinic spoke to her. But it also was a little like when her grandmother would mindspeak to Fable. *Was he a witch?* She almost walked right up to him and asked but thought better of the idea. Still, he was very attractive. She found herself unable to look at much else in the store but his physique. He had a terrific body, a swimmer's body, lean and taunt. His skin was slightly pale, but smooth. His curly brown hair accented his chesnutt eyes, and she could faintly smell the aroma of cologne.

He turned to look at her after becoming aware she was staring at him. Embarrassed, Fable ducked down behind her buggy. While doing so, she accidentally rammed the cart into the McCormick Seasoning rack. The tower rack and all its contents spilled out over the aisle. Further down the aisle, the chubby little cereal muncher stood crunching on an open box of uncooked macaroni noodles. Her mother was nowhere in sight. Undoubtedly the hungry girl had wandered off in search for more snacks. Upon seeing Fable's mishap, the little girl began to laugh hysterically at Fable, drawing even more attention from the attractive man. Fable was mortified. She closed her eyes and sent out a silent message to the air.

Suddenly the blind man's gray German Shepherd came charging, leash flapping behind him. He took off after the little girl, who was now screaming like a banshee down every aisle trying to find her mother—Trigger was aggressively, but not dangerously, hard at her heels. Fable whispered a "thank you" as he ran by.

CHAPTER EIGHTEEN

Date Night

The gym was busy for a Thursday night, at least Vanessa thought so. Not being a gym rat like her boyfriend, she never expected so many people would be working out at this time of night. Of course Seth was a regular two-a-dayer, so this wasn't uncommon for him. Typically he'd have already completed his second workout for the day, but once Vanessa had agreed to start going to the gym with him after work, he pushed his 4pm workout until after dinner so that they could go together.

Vanessa Collins was a student teacher at Cottondale Elementary School in Tuscaloosa. Her future plan was to be an elementary school teacher and she only had a year left until graduation. She had very little time in her life for a gym routine, but dating a man like Seth required some sacrifice if she hoped to be able to connect with him on any meaningful level. Seth's whole life seemed to revolve around half-attended college classes and gym visits.

"I like to break my workouts into certain days for certain muscle groups," Seth told her as they walked to a mirrored wall with a cable rack in front of it. "Chest day, back day, arm day, leg day, abs, cardio."

"I don't think I have that much time every day, Seth."

"Then we can break it down into combined sessions. Chest and Tri's, Back and Bi's—"

"Can't we just work out?" Vanessa sighed.

Seth blushed, a little embarrassed at his own enthusiasm, and showed her how to use the cable rack. He set the handles to level ten height and the weight load at 15 pounds, then he stood on the left side of the rack holding a handle in his right hand as he braced himself by gripping the left side of the rack with his left hand. He began pulling the handle towards his cheek, engaging the bicep of his right arm.

"Do ten of these, then move over to the right and hold onto the machine while you workout your left arm."

"Do you usually do 15 pounds?" Vanessa asked.

Seth grinned proudly, "No, I do a lot more weight but you'll need to work up to that."

Vanessa positioned herself exactly the way Seth had been standing and engaged the pulley to curl her bicep. She pulled very hard, and the weights flew up smashing into the top. Seth looked surprised.

"Wow! You are a lot stronger than you look. Maybe 15 pounds is too light for you."

He raised the weight to 30 pounds and watched as Vanessa exercised her muscles in a smoother, more even rhythm. Next he took her to the bench press and began to show her how to safely lift a barbell without causing injury to one's self. He'd loaded the bar with heavy weight, and Vanessa knew he was less interested in teaching her and more interested in showing off how much he could bench press. Once he'd completed his first set, he began to unload some of the weight to make it lighter for her set. He grabbed a 45-pound disk from one side and replaced it on the hook rack beside the bench. Vanessa grabbed the other one with one hand and carried it without strain to the rack herself.

"Damn, Vanessa! How strong are you?"

She gave a sly smile and replied, "I'm not the weakling you seem to think I am."

Vanessa completed four sets of reps and waited for Seth to finish his. While waiting she glanced around the gym floor at the number of hard muscular bodies strolling around in stringer tank tops and tight workout shorts. It was only natural for her to peek, but she had to admit that of all the good looking guys there tonight, her man was by far the hottest. Seth's body was amazing, and Seth knew it, which created both an unattractive arrogance and a sexy swagger that turned her on.

"Blanchard!" shouted a man from a nearby leg press machine. "This isn't your usual time. You changing routines on me?"

"Hey, Zeke," Seth called back. "No, I'm still doing my usual times. Just have my girlfriend with me tonight so we came later. Vanessa, this is Zeke, he's a trainer here."

"Nice to meet you," Vanessa said.

"So you're Seth's lady!" Zeke replied. "Nice. You did good Blanchard; she's a keeper."

Seth was reracking weight and didn't reply. Zeke didn't seem to care, he just went on talking.

"I been trying to get this boyfriend of yours to go through the course to become a personal trainer, but he doesn't seem interested."

"I'm going to school for accounting," Seth reminded his friend.

"When?" Zeke guffawed. "You're always here. When does all this school shit take place? I'm telling you man, three months of studying for the test and bam! You're a trainer. This gym would hire you in a second."

"Seth, that sounds like a job you'd love," Vanessa commented.

"I don't know," Seth said with a pursed mouth. "I doubt Aunt Artemis would be okay with that. She wants me to be all white collar."

"Well, with the kind of money your family's got you could open your own gym," Zeke pointed out. "Hell—you and me could go in together, and I'd run the joint, if you'd just front the money."

"It's a thought," Seth said. "But for now, I'm on a date Zeke."

"Some date," Zeke snarked. "A smelly gym."

"I'll take what I can get," Vanessa laughed.

...

The ice cream shop was just about to close when Jake yanked Yasmine through the door and dashed to the counter. The poor counter boy, barely 18, was not happy about the last-minute customers. But Jake ordered quickly—two scoop chocolate mint for Yasmine and two scoops of Brambleberry for him. The pair at least had the courtesy to eat their ice cream outside on the picnic table and allow the teenager to lock up the shop and begin his nightly cleaning.

"This is nice," Jake said looking up at the stars. "It's been such a great summer so far. Probably because I met you."

"I am something special," Yasmine laughed as she tried to lick the piece of chocolate which had fallen off her cone and stuck to the side of her lip. "I love summer, too, but fall is the best. It's not too cold, and it has Halloween and Thanksgiving and then runs right into Christmas."

"I guess Thanksgiving is a pretty big deal at your house," Jake remarked. "All that family."

"Oh, it gets even bigger sometimes. We have relatives in Mobile that come up some years. I can remember holidays where we had twenty people or more all staying at the house."

"Man, that's a big family."

Yasmine noticed a sadness in the way Jake said that. Almost an envy. She knew very little about the man she was seeing. He wasn't very talkative about his life. Most of their conversations revolved around their jobs or whatever it was they happened to be doing on their date. Nothing ever went very deep or in any way revealing.

"You don't have much family, do you?" she asked.

"Just my sister."

"I'm sorry."

"It's okay," Jake said. "I'm used to the solitude. I've been alone pretty much all of my life. It's not so bad."

Yasmine stared up to the sky, unsure how to reply to such a melancholy statement. She decided to focus on what lay above instead. "I think we have a full moon coming up next week. I read it's supposed to be a blue moon or a blood moon or something rare. Maybe we should make a picnic in the park that night and enjoy it?"

Jake shook his head. "Sorry, I can't. I gotta do something."

"You don't even know which night!"

"I'm busy a few days next week helping my sister clear out a storage unit."

"Need help? I'd love to meet your sister."

"She and I can handle it. When you meet her, I want it to be more special than cleaning out old boxes."

The door to the ice cream shop opened, signaled by the irritating bell tied to its handle. They turned to see the teenager locking the door and walking away. He paused by the picnic table and said goodnight to them, thanking them for the generous tip.

"Ya'll don't hang out here too long by yourselves," he cautioned. "Not with that crazy killer on the loose."

Jake gave him a thankful nod for the concern and watched him walk to his car and drive away. Yasmine seemed a little nervous now after being reminded about the new situation in town—a town that had always been so peaceful up until now.

"You getting all fraidy cat on me now?" Jake joked.

"I just feel so creepy knowing somebody out there is killing people here in our own town."

"People kill people in every town," Jake argued. "Why should this one be any different?"

"I've lived here most of my life," Yasmine replied. "Nothing like this has ever happened here."

Jake shook his head in slight disbelief. "I've been around a lot and lived in a lot of places. Things like this happen everywhere. Don't worry, you're safe with me."

"Are we still on for tomorrow night?" Yasmine asked.

"Yeah," Jake replied. "I'm open until next week."

For a moment Yasmine thought about the picnic idea again. She was a little disappointed he was unavailable, but not because of any longing to see him--quite the opposite. The setting of a romantic full moon and a basket full of food and wine sounded like a good idea to try and see if she might spark an ember between them that she hadn't yet felt. She liked Jake well enough, and he was certainly attainable, but there was no chemistry on her part toward him. No matter how much she tried to create flames out of soggy timber, it came up short every time. She wondered if Seth felt that way about Vanessa. They certainly seemed to have no troubles in the dry wood department. She resigned herself to keep trying. Perhaps Jake couldn't enjoy the full moon with her, but she would think of something else. Surely she could find something about him to excite her eventually.

CHAPTER NINETEEN

The Consort

Candles from hundreds of sconces atop the rafters lit up the cathedral-like structure on the lawn of Oleander. The shimmering light cast wavering shadows on the arches of the ceiling, sending amber reflections onto the stone floor below. The members of the Consort sat in circular rows around a center circle housing the round table of Council members. Salem thought it odd for the seating to be arranged in this way until Olympia explained that the arrangement made it possible for the Consort members to be closer to the Council than had it been staged in a more traditional auditorium style. She also pointed out that the seating circles reflected their strong belief in infinity and how everything in nature is connected with no apparent beginning or end—like energy. Salem thought of her husband and son when her grandmother said this, it comforted her somewhat to know that they might still go on somehow.

Olympia and Salem were seated in the fourth row, facing three Council members straight on. Salem felt strange to be looking at side views or the back of the head of several other Council members. They were not exactly sure where Zelda had wandered off to, but knowing Zelda's penchant for gossip, she was probably off collecting stories for later telling.

The Council identified themselves for all of the first-time Consort members: Brimford Uding, Ernestine Craven, Millicent Davis, Jason'te Barstow, the despicable Atheidrelle Obreiggon (who was standing in as proxy to her husband, the actual Council member), Amory Vendell, and of course Ursula Craven the Queen of the Consort. All voices were quietened as Ursula began her speech.

"Welcome all of you to the Summer Consort. I am pleased to see many new faces here tonight. I would like to welcome you to our association, and I would also like to thank the Obreiggon family for offering their magnificent home for our gathering."

A round of applause went out from those gathered as Atheidrelle rose from her chair and bowed. Salem and Olympia sat motionless through the ovation.

"We will begin tonight," Ursula continued, "with current business. We have many in our congregation tonight from our new charter Wiccan organization. Millicent will later be giving a lecture on proper conduct and enlightenment. I realize your covens primarily center around earth magic, and a great deal of our association business revolves around witches born as magical beings, so we have added several lectures to the docket to reflect your individual needs."

Salem observed some of the members seated in the audience smirk to one another and a few even made eye rolls. Salem always knew that in the witching world Birth Witches tended to look down upon Regulars who took up the arts of witchcraft. Typically, they were thought of as "playing with magic" rather than magic being a part of the makeup of their beings. Even she had to admit there was quite a difference between a normal person who chose to take up the practice of witchcraft and someone who was born with actual powers they had to learn to control. Salem had seen the Wiccan fad grow and decline depending on what was happening in popular culture at the time. Movies like The Craft and Harry Potter always spurred interest in the occult. Some witches found that offensive, but Salem was not among them. To Salem, it was an honor that regular people wanted to learn about their beliefs and their world. It also had made life much easier over the last generation because Salem didn't seem so unhinged if she confided to someone close that she was a witch. Of course, no one ever really understood that when she said "witch" she meant WITCH. Frankly, watching the condescending looks from the Consort members as Ursula talked about the Wiccans in the room made Salem embarrassed that her own people could feel so prejudiced and intolerant when they'd spent centuries hoping for acceptance themselves.

Ursula finished whatever it was she was saying that Salem had stopped listening to and moved on to other topics. The first item caught Salem's immediate attention because it seemed to be directly aimed at her and those also possessing her unique gift. "The next thing I wish to discuss strictly concerns such magical beings, particularly witches gifted in the ways of time intervention. Too many witches are halting time for one reason or another, and it has got to stop. Consider the rest of mankind for a moment. Witches are not the only living beings on this planet. The Earth rotates around the sun at its natural pace whether you freeze time or not. When you unfreeze the time you halted, clocks jump forward, and all the people without your gifts have lost part of their day. It doesn't always go unnoticed. A few minutes here and there can be explained by the mind as losing track of the time, but hours are a lot harder to justify. Remember that people have jobs to fulfill and lives to lead. It is grossly inconsiderate to halt time unless absolutely necessary for some kind of life and death situation. Please respect the rest of Earth's creatures by not shrinking their day. Your power is great and should only be used in emergency situations. Not to keep stores from closing until you have made all your purchases or to direct revenge on a rude member of a restaurant waitstaff or to wedge your car in to the front of school pickup lines. Powers are for bigger uses than making your personal lives more convenient."

"I feel awful," Salem whispered to her grandmother. "I have done all three of those things." She didn't, however, feel any guilt over the last time she used her gift—that morning with David, when she'd frozen time to have one last moment with her husband. She would never regret that.

Brimford Uding signaled Ursula. She stepped away from her seat and approached the old man, who passed a piece of information in her ear. Ursula stifled a grin and returned to her place before continuing.

"It has been also brought to my attention that one among you has been reported to be donning some sort of superhero costume, assigned yourself a persona, and has been crime fighting in your community lately."

The members of the association all chuckled in unison. They looked around the audience trying to see if anybody was blushing or ducking enough to reveal the identity of the culprit. The very idea that someone was trying to play Superman or Wonder Woman with their powers was pretty amusing.

"It is commendable for one to use their powers to help people. I applaud the effort. After all what are witches for in the Natural Order if not to assist those who cannot help themselves. However, I caution you that such theatrical performances place a magnifying glass on our kind and puts us all in harm's way. Please cease your comic book escapades. Leave the crime fighting to our community's brave men and women in blue."

The crowd gave another laugh as Ursula continued.

"Next on the agenda will be our upcoming election. As many of you may know already, I have not opted to run for re-election as Leader of this Consort. It has been a glorious six years as your queen, but I am ready to step down and allow someone new to take the helm. To all newcomers tonight, let me explain our governing process. We, the members of the Council, are similar to a Supreme Court. There are six members to the Council and the King or Queen fills the seventh chair as a kind of president."

A woman raised her hand from the second row facing Ursula. "Yes?" Ursula said, pointing to her.

"I have a question," the woman began. "My name is Jana Cummings. I am the head of the southeast order of the Wiccan Association. This is my first meeting."

"Welcome to the Consort, my dear," Ursula replied. "You may ask your question."

"I was wondering how a person becomes a member of the Council, or how you can run for Queen."

"Good question, Jana. For those of you who are new to our organization or haven't belonged to the Consort since the last election, a King or Queen is elected every three years by the entire Witches Association. Each member casts one vote. Many witches that belong to the Association but do not attend our meetings will have their vote cast by their Coven leader.

Council members are a different matter. A Council member is appointed by a ruling King or Queen and serves for life, or until retirement."

Jana sat back down, and Ursula moved on with her speech. "As I said, I shall not be running for re-election as Queen. Therefore, anyone who wishes to throw their hat into the ring should do so by the Autumn gathering where the nominees' names will be presented. This will give Association members three months to consider the choices before we vote at the Winter Consort. Any man or woman interested in being the Consort's next King or Queen should contact Jason'te Barstow. He resides in Birmingham, Alabama. Cards containing his contact information—phone number, email, and social media accounts—will be at the sign-in table upon your leaving here tonight. Now I pass the meeting over to my mother, Ernestine."

The striking lady Salem met earlier in the evening stood from her chair. "Thank you, Ursula. I would like to talk about finances tonight. As most of you are aware, the Consort has been attempting to remove pollution from Junction Lake in Butler County, Tennessee. Thanks to many generous contributions we were actually able to purchase the lake before it was completely ravaged by the industries dumping their waste. We have acquired the land with the donated funds but are running short for our detoxification plans. I ask anyone who can afford it to donate to our cause of water restoration. I know some of you have more than others, but anything is appreciated. See me after the meeting if you wish to make a donation."

Ernestine sat down, and Brimford Uding stood to face the congregation. "Hello friends," he began. "I will now call for any members of the Consort who have personal business to stand and be recognized."

A woman stood.

"Yes, Mrs. Connelly."

"Mr. Uding, I have had the unfortunate situation of having to place my mother into a nursing home due to her advancing Alzheimer's." The woman was almost in tears.

"I am terribly sorry, Mrs. Connelly," Brimford said compassionately. "Your mother was a wonderful friend to many of us and has been an honored Consort member all of her life."

"My first request is to have Mama's membership to the Association relinquished. I would also like for her sister Clara to be registered as the new head of our family Coven. I work as a nurse in the nursing home where my mother is a patient, and I plan to be spending more of my time there with her. That will eliminate me from taking over the coven. My aunt is the better option at this time."

"Certainly, certainly," Brimford replied. "The Consort will make the changes, and we wish you well as you traverse these uneasy waters. May the strength of Demeter be with you."

"Also," Mrs. Connelly added, "I request that the Council bind Mama's powers. She is no longer able to control her actions, and her powers can be dangerous if left in her unstable hands."

"We understand," Brimford said. "As law dictates, an investigation must be completed to confirm your mother's condition." He faced Ursula. "As a long-standing friend to the Connelly family, I will personally conduct the investigation into Jewel Connelly's mental state and report back to the Council. We will remove her powers once a confirmation is made."

The Council members nodded in agreement.

"Next order of business?" Brimford asked the congregation.

Olympia nudged Salem. "Don't be afraid, dear. It must be done."

Salem raised her hand and stood. Voices gasped from around the rows of seats. Whispers of "that's her" and "Nacaria's daughter" were heard in every direction. Atheidrelle glared at Salem from her seat on the Council.

"Yes, Ms. Blanchard," Brimford acknowledged. "What is your business?"

"My son," she said timidly. "The cremation of my son."

The crowd collectively gasped again; this time it was one of sympathy.

"I am profoundly sorry for your loss, Salem," Brimford frowned. Olympia noticed a smirk of satisfaction come over Atheidrelle's wicked face.

"We brought the child with us," Olympia spoke up. "The attendant at the gate said he would bring him to us once the ceremony is ready to commence."

Ursula stood up. "Olympia, you and your granddaughter—your entire family—have the whole of the Consort's sympathy. If there is no further business, I move we adjourn and proceed directly with the cremation."

CHAPTER TWENTY

The Cremation

When a witch dies, it is the duty of the Supreme Council of the Consort to preside over and deliver the cremation of the deceased. Only the Council and the family of the deceased are allowed to attend. It had been this way since the beginning, and it would always be that way. Far from the crowd of the other witches, across the meadow almost hidden from sight, the Council stood alongside Salem and Olympia. Michael's tiny body was laid on a bed of kindling and pitch. All of the sounds of the night seemed to go mute in Salem's mind. The muffled sounds of the Consort party across the lawn were imperceptible to her now. She didn't even notice the sounds of nightbirds chirping overhead or the gentle rustling of the limbs in the breeze. The chorus of crickets lost her as an audience, and only her heart beat could be heard in her ears. Everything else was solemnly quiet. All she noticed was that tiny body of her son laying still atop the pile of wood. That body had been her son. It had been a giggling face when she'd make silly sounds. It had been a long, high-pitched cry when he was hungry, wet, or mad. It had been the bond which had forever tied her and David together. Salem never once thought that bond might die. But there he was, Michael—lifeless, unmoving, pale, and dead on a stack of wood on a lawn she would never see again. Though Salem knew intellectually he wasn't inside the body any longer, she still couldn't help but feel protective of his corpse. She didn't want the others to see her son like this. If only they had been able to see him run to the TV to smack the screen when he saw a dog appear. Or if they'd heard the lilt of his laugh. Or seen him try to master walking and always falling back on his diaper-padded bottom. She knew that Michael. They only knew this empty shell.

Ursula approached Salem with a torch. Lighting it with a match, she passed it to Salem and took several steps back to stand with the Council. Salem stood alone before the pyre. To be the one to toss the torch was more than she could stand, but tradition was tradition…even if it seemed much too tribal and insensitive—or was that only because it was now happening to her? She felt Olympia step forward and place her gentle hand on Salem's shoulder. She placed her hand on the torch with Salem's, and together they tossed it onto the piled wood at their feet. It ignited immediately.

His body burned for a long time. Salem stood alone, unblinking as she stared into the flames of blue, red, orange, and yellow. To some the smell might have been putrid, but to her it was necessary to experience. These were the last scents of her son she would ever know. She thought back on her short time with him. The way his baby skin smelled in her arms after a bath. The aroma of the baby food he used to spit back out the second she fed him. When he moved onto real food, the way he had spread his dinner all over his highchair tray at every meal—smashing it with his hand before lifting it to his mouth.

The scent of his burning flesh and bone were now all she had, and it too was waning. She would not cry. Salem vowed only to weep in private—not even in front of her family anymore. Only at night when the moon was growing tired and everyone in Blanchard House was sleeping. That was her designated time to cry. Then and only then would she allow her heart to split open. But here and now, as the last crackle of fire began to burn out, and the form of what had once been her son was melted away, Salem thought of David and hoped his spirit had joined with Michael now. *He's too young to be alone. Even in death, he is still just a baby.* She knew better than this of course. Her son was in Heaven now with God, for whatever inexplicable selfish reason He'd have taken him so early. Or if there wasn't really a God, she knew Michael would be only mindless energy now. She was comforted by either outcome. Her child with his father in Heaven, or the two of them merely joined energy. Either way she liked to think of David and Michael together, holding hands in the adventure of uncovering Death's other worlds.

"I suppose you don't care what we do with the bones," Atheidrelle said coldly, approaching the smoldering pile and bursting through Salem's solemn thoughts.

"What?" Salem said looking up from the ash, startled.

"He was just a child, after all," Atheidrelle pointed out. "A baby witch. His power was not yet strong enough, nor cognizant enough to be of any future use. I don't suppose you'll be requiring the bone dust."

Olympia, who had followed Atheidrelle once she saw her moving towards Salem, heard what Atheidrelle just said. "As tactful as always, I see," Olympia said glaring at Atheidrelle as she took her place beside her granddaughter.

"I am only being practical," Atheidrelle replied, eyes glimmering as though they were smiling even though her mouth was not. "I only wanted to know what we should do with the remains. I suppose I will have to dispose of them myself."

"That's enough," Ursula said, approaching with Brimford. "I have heard this entire exchange, and I am appalled at your insensitivity, Atheidrelle Obreiggon."

"I'm afraid you have misconstrued my intentions," Atheidrelle smiled cunningly. "I was simply offering to remove the boy's ashes. This young woman should not have to deal with such matters at a grievous time as this. I can have one of the servants bag it all up and place with the rest of the trash to be hauled away."

Olympia stepped into Atheidrelle's personal space, looking her directly in the eye. "You are coming dangerously close to awakening my anger. You know how unwise that would be."

Ursula intervened between them. "I will not have this. Atheidrelle, you are behaving badly—unbecoming to a Council member, even if you are only seated in that chair as your husband's proxy. This will cease now."

Salem looked directly towards Atheidrelle as she spoke to the two genuine Council members. "As his mother, I have final say as to what happens to his remains."

"Yes, dear," Ursula stated. "That's the law."

"Then I wish him to be buried here, on this very spot...at Oleander."

"I will not allow it!" Atheidrelle shouted.

"No, Salem," Olympia gasped. "He belongs at Blanchard House."

"I want him here," Salem grinned. "That is within my rights according to Association law. Isn't that right your majesty?"

"That is correct." Ursula stated. "But I think it unwise, Salem. Wouldn't you prefer him to be buried at home where you can be near him?"

"I want him here at Oleander."

Atheidrelle folded her arms in a standoff. "I refuse."

"Then you break one of our Association covenants," Brimford alerted. "That is a violation with severe ramifications. You'd forfeit your husband's seat on the Council."

Atheidrelle had no choice if she wanted to protect her position in the Consort. "You will live to regret this action, Salem."

THE CREMATION

Salem took another bold step towards Atheidrelle, standing so close their noses were almost touching. Atheidrelle's black eyes bulged in a mixture of fury and apprehension. "My son," Salem asserted, "has more of a right to be here than you do."

Olympia walked alone back to the courtyard. Salem wanted time alone in the meadow. She sat on a grassy hill watching two Oleander servants burying Michael's remains on the spot where he'd been cremated. She wondered if she was doing the right thing leaving him there or if she had just been so filled with spite that she'd made a hasty decision. Suddenly Salem felt a meek tap on her shoulder. A young woman, barely twenty, stood beside her. The girl's hair was as long as Salem's but redder--almost crimson. She also had Salem's green eyes.

"My name is Arielle Obreiggon," she said.

Salem met her with resentment. "I suppose you have come to harass me for my decision to bury my son on your property. Your sister Cassandra has already been by to tell me what she thinks of it."

"Oh no," the girl smiled brightly. "I think it is a lovely idea. I think he has every right to be here. Was he a beautiful boy? I wish I'd known him."

Salem was at a loss for words. This was not the reaction she'd expected from anyone named Obreiggon.

"I would have loved to have seen him," Arielle continued. "You're so very pretty. Did he look like you?"

Salem was flabbergasted. She didn't know what to say. An Obreiggon showing her kindness? Or was this a trick? Everything inside her was telling her this girl was genuinely kind, but then again, she was an Obreiggon.

"He's here you know." Arielle said. "He was out of town on business, but he made a special trip back once he learned you were here."

"He's here?" Salem gasped. "How could he have known I was here?"

"I called him."

"But how could he get here so quickly?" Salem asked.

"Didn't you know he can *leap*?"

Salem had never known that about him. She had never really known much of anything about him, but this was especially interesting to learn. It was a rare gift for a witch to possess the power to move across great distances in the blink of an eye with mere thought. The idea that you could disperse your body's own molecules and reconstruct them elsewhere was mind boggling to her. A witch with that gift never need deal with the frustrations of an airport or five o'clock traffic. Salem was not aware *he* held the ability.

"I didn't know he could do that," Salem answered honestly. "He's really here tonight, at Oleander?" Her voice betrayed her. It was noticeably clear the idea of seeing him excited her.

"He asked me if I would find you and bring you to him. He's back at the house," Arielle smiled again. "Salem, would you like to meet our father?"

CHAPTER TWENTY-ONE

Pastoria

Olympia saw Zelda in the distance on the lawn talking to a woman Olympia had never met before. The woman had the familiar deer-in-headlights look that many people experience in Zelda's presence.

"So anyway..." Zelda jabbered on to the woman as Olympia came closer. "You whack your husband uptop the head with something ever' once in a while, and he won't be such an ass to you anymore. I used to hit my husband with shoe once or twice a week back before he died."

"Zelda!" Olympia interrupted as she approached. "I have been looking for you."

The woman who had been trapped by Zelda used the opportunity to back away slowly, then bolted for another group of women standing across the lawn. Zelda never seemed to notice that her companion had gone, nor did she ever return her attention back toward the empty space where her companion had previously been.

"Lympy! You know I gotta make the rounds! That's how you get all the good gossip. And I got some doozies! Erma Fendlebreyer switched covens and is now part of the Corwin clan. Joyce Frickie has left her husband and done become a total lesbian. And Jakeb Vernon has opened up his own law practice in Shreveport and withdrew from the Association altogether. He's joinin' up with the northern branch."

"Did you miss the meeting while getting all the news?"

"Nah, I sat in the back when I saw it'd already started. How's Salem holdin' up? Ya'll already done the cremation I guess."

"Yes, and Atheidrelle was a horror. I'm really worried about Salem. Do you know what she did, Zelda?"

"Lord, yes!" Zelda exclaimed. "It's all anybody is talking about now. You know I had a vision she was gonna do sum'thin stupid like that. Should'a warned you."

"I wish she would reconsider burying him here. Michael belongs at Blanchard House with the family."

Zelda huffed to the wind. "It's poetic justice if you ask me. I kinda like her gumption. It is stupid, but it's gumption. That bitch Atheidrelle wanted Nacaria executed all those years ago, and she made it impossible for her husband to even see his kids. She even takes his seat on the Council ever' chance she gets. I think it's a kind of justice for Michael to be buried here. Let her walk past him every day. Besides, he's an Obreiggon ain't he?"

Zelda had a point. Olympia had to admit that. But her fear of Salem's decision being one of impromptu spite rather than a well-considered sentimental choice bothered her. It also was not a good idea to resurrect old feuds, and interring Michael in Atheidrelle's backyard was going to do nothing but bring wrath.

"I been look'in for Pastoria," Zelda said, changing the subject.

"I'm sure she's here somewhere," Olympia said. "Although I haven't seen her either. But I have been rather occupied with Salem. I have not made the rounds yet."

"You talk to her lately?"

"Not lately," Olympia admitted. "We've been so wrapped up with the death of David and Michael, I haven't had a chance. I know that Demitra spoke with my nephew Seneca, so they do know about what happened."

"Lympy, when did you last talk to your baby sister yourself?"

"I guess about two months ago. Why? Has something happened to her?"

"She's stone broke, Lympy," Zelda confided. "Shirley Fielding told me all about it earlier. She wondered if you knew. Shirley works at an insurance office in Mobile, you know. Well, she told me Pastoria's house and auto insurance lapsed. She called her herself. Pastoria told her she was having money problems and would have to let it lapse till she can get on her feet and reinstate it."

"Oh, my!" Olympia sighed. "Is it as bad as all that?"

"It sure looks that way. I say you call that bank president down in Mobile. Your stepson. Martin's son, you know?"

Olympia smiled. "Yes, Zelda, I am very well aware of my second husband's son."

"Well—he lives there, and he's her banker. I think you need to call him and see what's going on. You ain't got but one sister. You need to figure out how to help her out."

Suddenly a deep voice interrupted the two friends' private conversation, "She won't let you. I wouldn't even try."

Olympia and Zelda whirled around to find a dashing man in his late forties standing behind them. Olympia's surprised face turned into a smile as she embraced her handsome nephew.

"Drake Blanchard!" she cried. "You seem to have determined to stay good looking no matter how old you get."

"Aunt Olympia," he grinned. "And Madame Zelda, I see you've changed your hair since I saw you last Consort. It was kind of orange then, I believe."

"Yeah, I darkened it a bit for the summer."

"We were just discussing some gossip Zelda heard about your mother," Olympia explained.

"Yes, I overheard. I saw you and was coming over to say hi when I picked up on the tail end of your conversation."

"Drake, are things really that bad for her?" Olympia asked.

"Yes," Drake admitted. "Dad's hardware stores are going under. They've been a bit mismanaged since his death, I think. Mom put too much faith in the manager's abilities. She should have let Seneca and me run things, but she didn't want us disrupting our own careers."

"Do you think the business can be saved?" Olympia asked.

"I doubt it. We just can't compete with the big box stores like Lowe's and Home Depot. Even though we've been around forever, customer loyalty doesn't outweigh cheaper prices," Drake mused.

"What can I do?"

"Aunt Olympia, I wish you could do something," Drake sighed. "But you know your sister as well as I do. If she will not let her sons help, she's not going to let you. Seneca made some payments for her behind her back, and she hit the ceiling."

"My sister has always been a stubborn woman."

Zelda chuckled, "Yeah. It ain't a *family trait* at all."

"Is Pastoria here with you Drake?"

"No ma'am. I represent the Blanchard family tonight—well, the Mobile Blanchards that is."

"You tell Seneca that your aunt will handle everything. You boys stop worrying," Olympia promised.

"I told you, Mom isn't going to accept any help from you or anyone."

"Drake, I have my ways of handling my baby sister. Half the decisions in her life

I made for her without her ever knowing they were not her own idea. I will find a way to help her, and she won't even know she's been helped. You boys leave it to Aunt Olympia."

CHAPTER TWENTY-TWO

Salem's Father

Victorious in every step, Salem followed Arielle across the meadow, far out of range of the party. They took a detour through a wooded area and emerged before the house. The white behemoth structure, complete with its triglyph cornices and iron railings looked like something out of an antebellum book of architecture. Arielle clutched Salem's hand in her own as she guided her around back and through the side door of a smaller two-story wing.

Arielle paused at the door and cautioned, "We mustn't let any of the servants see us. They tell Mother everything."

Salem couldn't help but think to herself as she held Arielle's hand, *this girl is my sister*. The idea was strange. Never before had Salem wished for a sister because she'd always had Beryl, Fable, and Yasmine. But this felt different—more different than she might have expected it would. Because this girl—this sister—shared her father. That exclusive club to which before only Seth and she had belonged, now had another member. Not only did Arielle share their father, she *knew* their father. She'd grown up with him. Traversing Oleander land hand in hand with this girl who, so far, seemed so kind, made Salem feel special. Cassandra, during their very brief exchange, was purely *Atheidrelle's daughter*. Salem felt nothing in her which seemed remotely sisterly. But Arielle didn't appear to have any of Cassandra or Atheidrelle's cruelty.

Salem was unsettled by what the house looked like on the inside. It felt suffocating. The openness which the outside promised had been bastardized inside. Dark curtains, bleak tapestries, and heavy gothic furnishings made the inside of the plantation house look like something medieval. The rugs, though no doubt expensive, were equally grim with their moody colors and frayed edges.

Arielle seemed to pick up on her apprehension, pausing to say, "I know. My mother decorated to reflect her childhood home nearby. It's depressing."

They maneuvered through a passage of rooms and came to the front entrance hall. Arielle motioned for Salem to wait as she poked her head around the corner, ensuring no servants were around. When the coast was clear, they dashed up the grand, rising staircase to a landing which split into two separate runs. The left side reached to what must have been the second floor. The right side went higher, perhaps to the third. Salem had to pause a moment to take it all in. There was something disturbing about the design—an architectural feat, no doubt, but the off-balance symmetry made her apprehensive. The archaic furnishings of the rooms they passed seemed to be waiting for Lady Macbeth. It was a sinister house, befitting Atheidrelle Obreiggon, but somehow Salem could not picture her father living there. A sudden pity for him came into Salem's mind, as to what his life must be like in this dreadful house with that dreadful woman. Was he as despicable? She had always assumed so. Always hated him. But now, just moments from his presence, Salem didn't think she felt that way anymore. Besides, Arielle seemed so nice.

Soon Arielle stopped at a door down one of the corridors. She opened it and pulled Salem inside. The room was dimly lit, but far more appealing than the rest of the house. The large chamber was furnished with oversized chairs and a couple of sofas. Cheery art clung to the white plastered walls, lessening the severity of the rest of the house. A series of bookcases lined one side of the room and on the other side stood a tall bank of windows. This was *his* room. A haven in a sea of darkness.

As her eyes adjusted to the dim lights, Salem caught sight of a figure standing in the shadows of the window's heavy drapes. She couldn't make him out. For a fleeting moment she thought to herself *are both my parents shadows*? Only once he stepped out enough for the overhead light to hit his face could she at last see what he looked like. He was tall and handsome. He looked exactly like Seth, or rather what Seth was sure to look like in another 25 years.

"Daddy," Arielle beamed, "this is Salem."

"You are exquisite," he said. "More beautiful than I ever imagined." He came closer toward her, examining every inch of her face as he approached. "You are your mother, in all her splendor. Please—sit down."

Salem took a seat on the nearest sofa. He sat down beside her—close, but not too close. A respectful distance considering the fact that they were strangers.

"I'll go," said Arielle. "I know you two must want to be alone. Salem?" she asked timidly. "In case we do not see each other again tonight, may I call you sometime?

I'd like the chance to get to know you."

"I'd like that," Salem smiled as Arielle closed the door behind her.

A thick silence huddled around Salem and her father once Arielle left. Each of them intensely ready to say all the things they had individually imagined they would say if presented with the other's company. But now the words they had rehearsed a thousand times were lost to the stale, shadowy room.

A couple of times one of them seemed on the brink of beginning to say something, but each stopped before anything more than a breath escaped their lips. What can you say after a lifetime of nothing? No interactions had taken place between them since Nacaria was cursed into the shadows by the Witches Council. Salem vaguely remembered her father from early childhood. Her mother had taken her to see him clandestinely a few times, but she'd been far too young to remember very much about it. She had so many questions. Too many. There was so much to know that finding a starting point was impossible. This man was her father, but was also the man who had allowed her mother to become damned for an affair he never should have begun. Yet Salem knew her mother was not an innocent victim—far from it. She'd tried to kill Atheidrelle Obreiggon and failed—thus ruining everyone's life in the aftermath. How could Salem find the words to address all that needed to be said?

Her father broke the silence first, making things a little easier to begin. "I am Xander Obreiggon. I know you know that, but I am at a loss for any other way to begin a conversation with you. I have wanted to see you very much over the years, but especially now. I am so deeply sorry for the loss of your son."

Her son. Michael was dead. For a second that had slipped her mind as her own childhood's sadness over never knowing her father flooded back to her. Xander's words reminded her that she was a grown woman now and not a frightened little lonely girl. She had been a mother...for a time.

"Thank you. It's been...difficult."

He took a deep breath, as if to fill the time during the newest onset of awkwardness. Then he spoke again. "There must be so many questions you want to ask me. And I you. However, first I must let you know that I am profoundly apologetic for never having contacted you. But under the circumstances..."

"My grandmother has told me that you cared for my mother very much."

"No," Xander interjected quickly. "No, not cared. Loved. I loved your mother immensely. In fact, I worshipped Nacaria. I have never loved another creature as much as I have loved, still in fact, love your mother."

The statement shocked Salem for some reason. She had not expected to hear such passion from this man—this man she'd hated all of her life. It had been he and his wife who destroyed her mother and took her away from Salem and Seth.

"Then why didn't—No. I don't want to do this," she said. "This is my father sitting beside me. I do not need answers now. I just want to savor this moment and remember it in every detail for the rest of my life."

"Salem," Xander started. "We haven't much time. There are things I have always needed to say to you and your brother. Things I want to say now."

"Then say them."

"Firstly, I do not want you to blame your mother for what happened. The fault was not hers alone. I could have stopped it, but perhaps I secretly wished for her to succeed."

"Don't you love your wife?" Salem asked.

"No." He took no time in answering. His candor came as somewhat of a shock. For the first time ever in her life, Salem realized that Xander Obreiggon loathed his wife. Just sitting beside him on the sofa she could physically feel the intensity of his hate when he said her name.

"But if you loved Nacaria, then why?"

"Why?" he repeated. "Why did I advocate her being banished? Why did I join the Council in her condemnation? It is rather simplistic, my dear. I would much rather your mother be cursed than be killed. They were all pushing for that, you know. Pushing to execute her. It was I who convinced them to punish her rather than crucify her. Brimford Uding helped me to convince the Council."

"Why didn't you help her?"

"I did help her. Better to be cursed into shadows than be delivered into death. The affair was my fault. I loved her so much. I knew I should have ended it, and after you were born, I knew that I could not abandon her. We saw each other in secret. I saw you when I could. Then when Seth was born, I knew that my duty to Atheidrelle did not outweigh my love for your mother or you and your brother. I wanted to leave my wife, but she also had my child. My choices were clear—abandon Atheidrelle and Cassandra or reject Nacaria, you, and Seth. My choice was made, not too many people know that. I had decided to leave my wife. I say *decided* now, but at the time it was not even that much of a decision. I adored your mother. I would have left even if you had not been born. But there are rather complicated ties which bind me to Atheidrelle. Ties made by our fathers before we were married. Unknotting those knots took longer than I had expected. But I was in the process of freeing myself to be with Nacaria. I had made the choice. But Nacaria made one as well, without consulting me."

Salem found herself tearing up a little. Instinctively she moved closer to Xander on the sofa. She reached out her hand and clasped his. The moment her skin touched his, tears fell from both their eyes. *After all these years, I am holding my father's hand.*

"I didn't know you were planning to leave to be with us. If mother had just held out, trusted in the love you shared, none of this would have happened. But she turned greedy and wanted you all for her very own."

"Had she waited even two days, she'd have found me on her doorstep," Xander said. "Unfortunately, she took it into her own hands to undo Atheidrelle's life. After that, it all came down to a question of your mother's life or death. I swayed the Council, and she was cursed instead."

"It was Atheidrelle who pushed for my mother's death," Salem realized, bitterly. "She hated her because you loved her, so she tried to have my mother killed."

Xander shook his head. "Atheidrelle was the victim, Salem. You must understand that. I understand your contempt for her. She can be a very contemptible woman at times, but technically she was the victim. Nacaria had no right to do what she did. You *do* understand that don't you, Salem? Your mother attempted to murder Atheidrelle by casting a spell and propelling herself back in time to undo Atheidrelle's birth. She tried to erase her from time completely, as well as our children together. You do understand that your mother had no right to do that, don't you?"

"What she did, she did out of love for you. It was blind of her, but she wasn't thinking clearly. I understand that far better now more than I did when I was growing up. I too have been recently blinded by love and attempted to alter the Natural Order."

"It was a crime, what she did," Xander stated. "But I confessed our affair to the Consort, and I told Atheidrelle if Nacaria was executed I would bring you and Seth to live with us at Oleander. I struck a deal with her. I promised to leave you where you were. I promised to remain married to her. I promised to share my seat on the Council with her. And I relinquished all my rights to you and your brother, vowing never to see you again, all in exchange for her agreeing to the banishment."

Salem was silent. Taking it all in. She gave his hand a light squeeze and looked into his teary eyes. Salem went silent—considering everything she had just heard. Patting his hand as she rose, she walked to the window to stare down and out to the party still going on in the distance. She ran her hands through her hair and lifted it up slightly from her back, wringing her long locks in her hands.

"Mother died anyway," she said from the window. "It doesn't matter whether she is a jar of dust on a shelf or a shadow on a wall. Either way she is still out of our lives. I see no difference than if they had hanged her."

Xander fidgeted with his hands on the sofa. His instinct was to go to his daughter and embrace her, but he had lost that right years ago. "Please believe me when I tell you that I had no idea her punishment would be so cruel. To be banished to the shadows of the very home her children had to grow up in--for you and your brother to have to see her silhouette every day yet never be able to talk with it, to hold it, to be comforted by it. It was a cruel punishment, not only to her, but to you children as well."

"It has been a kind of hell for all of us," Salem revealed. "Over the years, Seth and I have taught ourselves to largely ignore her because it is far too painful to think of that ghost on the wall as our mother. I'd rather she had died."

Xander stood up shaking his head, "No, you mustn't say that Salem. She will be released one day."

"When?" Salem screeched, whipping her hair around her back angrily as she turned to face him.

"I-I-I don't have that answer, Salem," he stuttered. "No one knows when. That's part of the punishment. Only the King knew when, and he is long dead now. But one day her punishment will be over."

"Does that matter anymore?" Salem asked. "I grew up. Seth grew up. She wasn't there when we needed her to be. We never had our mother. Or our father!"

"I am so terribly sorry, Salem."

Salem's eyes carried a deep hurt in them that only now Xander could truly see. She had been through too much in her young life, and a lot of that was his fault. Maybe all of it.

"I got married," Salem continued. "I fell in love, got married and had a child. A child my mother never held. And now that child is gone. My husband is gone. I have lived and lost an entire life while my mother is still merely a shadow on a wall.

It's worse than had she died."

"Then it was all for nothing." Xander said sadly. "All my pleading. My deal with Atheidrelle. If my bargain spared no grief for your life, then it was all for nothing."

"'I'm afraid it was."

CHAPTER TWENTY-THREE

Demitra's Gift

Gas torches mounted on the brick walls cast a dim and romantic light over the diners at The Cobblestone. Couples, mostly, filled the tables of lace cloths and linen napkins. Soft votive candles sat in the center of each table with clean, clear glass shades over them as ceiling fans turned slowly overhead. Little trickles of smoke escaped the tops of the candle holders to dissipate into the air of soft music. Demitra stared out from the tableside window over the water. A long black barge moved like a turtle down the Black Warrior River.

"Okay, we've finished off two glasses of merlot, ordered our filet mignons, and picked over our salads," her dinner companion, Howard, said. "Are you now going to tell me why we're here?"

"Look around this place, Howard," Demitra began. "Oak beams, cobblestone floors. During the winter, they light the three stone fireplaces and string lanterns all along the overhangs of the outdoor porch. In the summer, the patio has lanterns where customers can dine with the river flowing past them. There are five separate dining rooms, two bars, and an upstairs banquet hall for parties. It's sitting here like a haven on the riverbanks."

Howard was confused. "Yes, Demitra. It's a nice restaurant."

"It is for sale," Demitra said as the light from overhead glistened on the inky blackness of her shoulder-length hair.

"I see."

"How much money would you say I have Howard?" She was in business mode now. He didn't often catch Demitra in business mode.

"You have enough to last you, I'd say," Howard answered.

"You know, I never keep up with those things. That is why I rely on you. I know that mother is loaded with Sinclair money, but I know there was a substantial amount of Windham money, too, that my father left us girls. Not to mention Larry's insurance and savings. I should be pretty well fixed, right?"

"I'd say you're worth a few hundred thousand."

"Wonderful," Demitra said, folding her arms and leaning closer to the table. "I want you to try and get this place at a good price for me. You know all the ins and outs."

Howard made the face he was known for making whenever he heard a bad idea. "You want to buy The Cobblestone. Why? Why buy the most expensive restaurant in Daihmler when you don't know the first thing about running a restaurant."

"It's not for me," Demitra said with a glint in her eye.

Howard leaned back in his chair and wiped the corners of his mouth with his napkin. He looked at Demitra with a knowing gaze.

"Oh, well now I am beginning to see the picture a little more clearly," Howard grinned. "You want to buy this for Artemis."

"Precisely."

"Expensive gift," Howard scoffed. "Wish you were my sister."

Demitra looked as though she were about to reply, but the waitress came to the table with the steaks. The filets looked tasty, but as Howard carved into his and took a bite, his face revealed the mediocrity of the cook's ability. Demitra seemed to read his very thoughts, and perhaps she had.

"Wouldn't Artemis create the most marvelous dishes if she owned this place? All her life she dreamed of being a chef. Now she can be. Even if her powers manifested in some way and caused a little problem, she would be the boss. She wouldn't fire herself."

"But Demitra, buying this place would drastically reduce your accounts to *very* little."

"What do I need money for?" Demitra laughed. "I live in a huge house which has long been paid for. Mother's household account pays for all household costs and food. I never go anywhere because I dislike traveling. Clothes and gasoline for my car—what else do I need money for? And I receive the occasional income from the Sheriff's department when I help with a case. Surely I will have enough money left to keep living the way I live."

"I see your point," Howard nodded. "But Demitra, a place this size. It's still a great deal of money for a present."

Demitra's face turned more serious. "Howard, you know as well as I do how much Artemis has sacrificed her life for the greater good of the family. After the two of you broke up, she devoted her life to the rest of us. She has never pursued a life of her own. There hasn't been a day gone by when she hasn't fed us, cleaned up after us, shouldered most of the day-to-day responsibilities. When Nacaria was cursed, she took over raising Salem and Seth. When Larry died and I had my breakdown, she took care of my girls as well as me. My sister has spent every one of life's moments in service to our family. It's time for her to have something for herself. A place to pour her creativity. She's earned this."

Howard was quiet for a while. He didn't disagree in the least with the argument Demitra made. No, he was remembering a time long ago when he was supposed to be the one who'd make Artemis' dreams come true. But he didn't. He was afraid to marry a witch. It was different just being friends with the Blanchards, but taking one as his wife had carried with it too much baggage with her powers so hard for her to control. Olympia had helped him realize that. Still, there had come a day many years later once Artemis had mastered—or practically mastered—her powers. Howard had looked back in regret at having let her go before. But by that time Nacaria was gone, and the family needed her much too much for him to selfishly try and rekindle the flame. Artemis deserved something special all for her very own.

"I'll see what I can work out," Howard said.

"Howard Caldwell," Demitra beamed. "You are just as sentimental as the rest of us."

"Maybe, or maybe I still have a special place inside me for your sister. I want to see her happy."

Demitra was about to comment—about to ask why Howard had never tried again with her sister when it was still so painfully clear that he loved Artemis. Just as she was about to say something, a man approached their table.

"This saves me a phone call," said the man. "Hello, Howard."

"Chief Bennet. Nice to see you."

"I hope you don't mind if I interrupt your dinner for a quick word with Demitra."

"Not at all."

The Chief of Daihmler police extended his hand to help Demitra rise from her chair. The two of them stepped outside onto one of the side porches of the restaurant. Howard could see them through the glass windows but could not hear the conversation.

"Charlie," Demitra began. "I had a feeling you'd be reaching out to me soon. It's about the murders?"

"Yeah," Chief Bennet replied. "At first we just thought it was a regular murder. Kinda gruesome though, but nothing crazy. Then the second happened. Same kind of thing. But this third one makes me think we have a lunatic running around town. People are starting to get panicky."

"Any leads at all?"

"Not a one. Some in the department think it may be a satanic thing. Like those killings Tuscaloosa had at Maxwell Crossings a decade ago. But I don't think so. These don't look to be ritualistic in any way."

"What were the circumstances with the victims?" Demitra asked.

"Pretty basic. Attacked. Battered a bit. Scratches. Throat cut with something jagged enough to really leave quite a tear. But this is where it gets creepy, Dee."

"Creepy?"

Chief Bennet lowered his voice even though no one else was in earshot. "Examiner says there was animal hair on two of the victims that struggled the hardest. I'm wondering if this lunatic is using trained dogs to attack them first."

"Using dogs?" Demitra gasped. "That'd be very unusual."

"Yeah, but two of these victims were men, big strong men. If the killer is a singular person, how else would he be able to subdue a guy like that? I really am just guessing here. I have no leads whatsoever. Could really use you on this one. We solved that missing boy case in two days with the clues you gave us. And that meth lab ring that started up two years ago. We'd never have found those guys without your assistance."

"I'm glad to help Charlie," Demitra said. "If you will email me the locations of where the bodies were discovered, I'll go out and see what I can pick up."

"I'm afraid the victims' clothing is locked up in evidence. Contamination risk, you know. But—"

"Don't worry about that right now," Demitra said. "Let's wait and see what I can learn from walking around the discovery sites first. If that doesn't give me any visions, then we'll see what we can do about my holding their possessions."

"You are the greatest, Dee," Charlie said, hugging her. "I take a great amount of credit for cases you've solved for me. I am the master at tracing leads, determining motivation, and finding evidence no one else thinks to look for—but you. You just close your eyes and see the whole thing. Sure has kept me from arresting the wrong suspect a time or two. And no telling how many lives you've helped me save over the years. Wish we didn't have to work in secret, but nobody on the force would believe I solved cases with the help of a psychic."

"The important thing is finding this killer."

CHAPTER TWENTY-FOUR

Bad Endings

Yasmine patted her mouth with the napkin and placed it by the empty plate on the coffee table in front of her. Jake finished the last of his burger and sat his plate beside hers. He steeled back against the couch in his apartment and guided Yasmine back into his chest, his arm around her shoulders.

"Pretty good wasn't it?" he said. "I told you I make a mean burger."

"It was a great burger," Yasmine replied. "The fries were good, too. Homemade fries are not easy to get right. I'm not that great of a cook myself."

"It's nice to be here at home," Jake said. "No crowded movie or restaurant. You know we are hardly ever alone."

Yasmine laughed the thought away, "Oh, we are by ourselves plenty of times. I've always had fun on our dates."

Jake leaned in with a mischievous look in his eye, "I have too. But here, by ourselves, we can have new kinds of fun."

He kissed her- softly at first—a kiss she felt comfortable returning. It was the deepening of that kiss as he knit his fingers into her hair and pulled her body closer to his that made her bristle and pull away from him. After a moment, she realized she was looking at him with a stern, quizzical expression. She relaxed her face into a sweet smile and leaned up to grab the remote.

"Want to cuddle up and watch a movie?"

"Cuddling up is more what I had in mind—minus the movie," Jake said with a grin.

He leaned forward again and planted another kiss. She politely returned it although he didn't seem to be aware, or perhaps didn't care, that it was a kiss empty of any genuine feeling.

"Slow down, big boy," she said making light of the situation. "You know I like taking things slowly."

"How slowly do you plan to take it?" Jake remarked with an impatient tone. "We've been practically at a standstill since day one."

"That isn't true, Jake. We've had lots of fun."

"Movies, dinners, going to the fair—that's not my idea of fun, Yasmine. I'm ready for more. It's time we got this relationship advanced to the next level."

Yasmine pulled away and put some space between them on the sofa. "I'm not ready for that yet."

"Not ready?" Jake cried. "We've been dating over a month, Yasmine! It's time we explored more physical sides to this romance."

"I am not ready for sex, Jake."

"Well, it's time you started getting ready because we've waited longer than anyone has a reason to expect."

"I don't owe you sex simply because we've gone out a few times," Yasmine huffed, standing up.

"Sit down!" Jake yelled. "I'm not finished talking to you yet. You've been yanking me around like a dog on a leash for weeks. It's time we got this show on the road."

Yasmine grabbed her purse from the end table. "I think it's time we just called this off. It's clear we want different things."

"I'm beginning to realize what it is you do want," Jake snapped. "I think his name is Seth."

"Seth?" Yasmine cried.

"Yes. Your cousin, Seth," Jake sneered. "I have been going out with you all this time, but I've never seen you once look at me the way you do the two times I've seen you around him. And the way you talk about him all the time. I think I'm getting the real picture here."

"I think you are ridiculous," Yasmine said. "Don't bother calling me again. I'm going home."

Jake grabbed her by the arm and slung her back to the couch forcibly. "You'll leave when I am ready for you to leave." He began kissing her again, this time against her will. She fought and pushed against him, but he held her too tightly for her to get any leverage on him. "You owe me something for time served."

He pinned her to the sofa and crawled on top of her. While he was pressing his lips onto hers and smearing across to her face, his right hand was grabbing at her while his left arm was pinning her down. Yasmine screamed for him to stop. He wouldn't. He was like an animal unleashed. As she lay under him, she wondered how she could have ever been so wrong about a person. She could not believe this was Jake treating her like this. *Is he going to rape me?* The thought made her sick to her stomach. Was she going to be a statistic? Was this how all date rapes started? She had begun this evening so innocently and now it was going to end like this. *He is. He is going to rape me.* In a brief flash of a second, she imagined having Salem's powers. The ability to freeze him in place and escape. Or the power to lift him up in the air and slam him back-first into the ceiling above. But she had no powers like her cousins had. *I'm not a witch.* Then suddenly another thought occurred to her at the exact moment Jake began trying to tear off her shirt. *But I'm not a victim either.*

Yasmine slid her hand out from underneath her back and fumbled for the coffee table. Her arm wasn't long enough. She placed her arm on Jake's back and began to rub his back, as if she were finally giving in and starting to enjoy this scenario. He liked it. He pulled back and stared into her eyes. She smiled coyishly. He pushed his lips into hers again devouring her with his kiss. Yasmine wrapped her legs around his waist and scooted herself a few inches across the cushions, inching a little closer to the coffee table. Jake removed his hands from her shirt and began fumbling around at his pants, unzipping them and pulling them down. He then moved to Yasmine's shorts. While he grabbed at the waist to pull them down, Yasmine's free hand found the coffee table. With one swift swipe she grabbed the fork from her plate and stabbed into the back of Jake's thigh!

"What the fuck?!" he shrieked, jerking upright and falling to the floor. He reached around and felt the fork sunk all the way into his hamstring.

"You stay away from me!" Yasmine screamed, jumping up from the sofa, grabbing her purse and running towards the door. "You come near me again, and I swear my next wound will be in a place you won't heal from any time soon."

...

Across town, Seth pulled his car into Reverend Collins' driveway with Vanessa seated beside him. He could tell from the movement behind the living room curtain that her father had seen them pull up.

"He knows we've been out," Seth told her. "I just saw him peeking."

"I don't care if he knows or not," Vanessa said. "I have bigger concerns."

"Such as?" Seth asked.

"Do I really have to tell you?" she replied. "Seth Blanchard we just spent the evening in virtual silence. You have barely spoken to me. Things have changed between us."

"My brother-in-law just died, Vanessa," Seth explained. "My family is going through a lot right now. My mind is not in the game."

"The game?"

"You know what I mean."

"No, I really don't. I thought our relationship was important. It was to me at least. But ever since that dinner at your house, I feel like we're growing apart."

"It's just a difficult period," Seth said. "Don't read too much into it."

"And what about your cousin?" Vanessa asked. "Yasmine. What should I read into that?"

Seth rolled his eyes and shook his head before turning to face Vanessa with a look of exasperation. "Please don't start up with all that shit again. She's like my little sister. I don't know why you're so jealous of her."

"I'm not jealous of anyone," Vanessa clarified. "But I also am not stupid. I thought it was cute at first, how close you were with your sister and your cousins. Not a lot of guys bond so closely with female relatives. But as time went on, I started to notice how your face is different when you talk about Yasmine. It is not the same as your other cousins or your sister. Then the other day when her boyfriend was at the house, and I was with you in the cemetery—Seth you couldn't take your eyes off them."

"Vanessa, this is really stupid."

"Then tell me, Seth," she confronted. "Before I move one more step into this relationship with you. Before I alienate my father even more for being with you. Look me in my eyes and tell me that Yasmine is not in your heart. Tell me you don't love her."

"Of course, I love her," Seth countered. "She's my cousin. I remember being very young when Granddaddy left the house one night, really upset. He came back the next morning holding the hand of this little girl. She was so little and scared. Me, my sister, my cousins, my aunts, my grandmother—we were this big group of strangers that met her at the door. This scared little girl who had just lost both her parents and her brother. Right away I wanted to protect her and look out for her. Then as we grew up, I used to tease her. I shot bottle rockets at her one 4th of July. Boy, she was so mad at me. I remember that one Christmas when she and Fable and I all figured out there was no such thing as Santa. Yasmine cried and cried. So, I put on the old suit my Uncle Larry used to wear and snuck into her room that night, trying to show her Santa was real after all. You should have seen this suit, Vanessa. It was just dragging on me. Hell, I was maybe 10. She was 8. I wanted to make her believe again. I didn't want to see her cry anymore. She'd already lost so much in her life."

Vanessa sat silent, watching Seth's face lighting up in all the ways she'd just described. She didn't interrupt. There was no need to. She had been provided her answer already. Now she waited for this to play out until Seth finally saw the plain truth as well as she could.

"Then when Granddaddy died," Seth continued. "Oh my God, Vanessa it almost killed us all...but Yaz. Little Yaz—he was her whole world. Her only living blood relation. Of course, by then she was as much a part of us as we were of her, so none of us really thought much about that really being her only relative. But the way she grieved for him...I couldn't take it. Half my crying over his death was from watching her cry. I used to go into her room at night and sleep on her floor, just so she could hold my hand until she fell asleep. So, she wouldn't feel alone."

Seth stopped talking. He sat in the driver's seat staring at the wheel, as the world dawned on him for the first time. Vanessa leaned over and kissed his cheek. She withdrew her purse from the floorboard and opened her door.

"It's all right," Vanessa said. "Goodbye, Seth."

CHAPTER TWENTY-FIVE

Love and Moonlight

Yasmine was sitting by the pool when Seth came to the archway in the wall of the pool area. Though he already had on his swim trunks and a towel in his hand, he didn't go in. She looked deep in thought. For a moment, he felt like he shouldn't disturb her. He held back before alerting her to his presence. Maybe it was the moonlight above, or the scent of the confederate jasmine hanging over the wall of the pool deck, or maybe it was simply the sight of her splashing her toes in the water under the moonlight, but he felt hypnotized watching her. His breath caught in his chest, and he had to process what that meant. He had to process what he felt earlier in the car with Vanessa when he was reflecting on Yasmine. *Did he love her?* Really truly love her, the way a man loves a woman, not a cousin.

He finally felt ready to approach her. She looked distressed, and he was concerned. "You okay?" he asked, walking up and tossing his towel down on a nearby chaise lounge.

"Had a rough night."

"Wanna talk about it?" he asked sitting down beside her.

She did want to talk about it. She wanted to tell someone how frightened Jake had made her, but she also knew if she told Seth he'd go after Jake. She just wanted to forget the matter. "No," she said.

"I had a pretty bad night myself," Seth admitted. "Vanessa and I are done."

"Really?" Yasmine exclaimed in surprise and hoped she hadn't sounded as happy as she felt. "What happened?"

Seth didn't say anything. He just kicked the water with his feet, trying to splash to the other side of the pool. He wanted to tell her, but it was embarrassing. This was not something he could tell her. Was it?

Leaving Seth his privacy, since he clearly wasn't going to divulge anything further, Yasmine decided to share a little of her tale as well. "It's over with me and Jake too."

Seth's heart thumped in his chest. "Really?"

"Jake turned out to be pretty awful. Not the guy for me."

"Same. Except the awful part," Seth replied. "Vanessa's pretty great. Just not the one for me."

Yasmine was confused. "What's wrong with her?"

He hadn't meant to, and he could have kicked himself the second it left his lips, but his heart betrayed his better sense and Seth replied, "She's not you." Then he dove into the pool.

Yasmine's heart nearly stopped. She could not believe what she just heard. Seth was swimming underwater now as she sat there questioning whether or not he'd actually said the words she thought she'd heard. His head popped up on the other side of the pool, and slowly he began walking back towards her, moonlight glistening off his smooth chest.

"What did you just say?"

Seth faced her from a few feet away. He sighed, then swept his hair back out of his eyes. "Yaz, there's a moment, just one little moment, when one word can change things forever," He was nervous now. Unsure. "But if we let that moment go without saying it, then life won't change. Things will just go on as they always have. I don't want things to go on the way they always have. But I also don't want to change the way things have always been."

"You are not making sense, Seth. Say it."

"One little word though, Yaz. It can ruin everything. Or it can make everything. What if it all changes and nothing is ever the same? What if it gets even better? But what if it doesn't?"

"Seth!" Yasmine exclaimed. Then she smiled. It was a safe smile. A reassuring smile. A requited smile. "Seth. *Say it.*"

He moved even closer. Her legs now dangling at the sides of his chest. He rested his arms on her knees. She shivered from the cold drops running off his arms. "I love you, Yaz. I guess I have always loved you. You're the only person on earth I can never live without."

She slid off the edge of the pool into his embrace. They kissed. It was gentle. It was tender. It told everything. Seth placed his hands on her head and pulled her lips closer. The kiss turned more passionate, more electric than either of them had ever felt in their lives. When it was over, she laid her head against his wet shoulder. He could feel her heart beating against his chest. Her soft hair tickled his nose in the summer breeze. She smelled of jasmine. Or maybe it was the vine. He didn't know. All Seth Blanchard knew was that he had never known such peace in all of his life as he stood in the pool holding Yasmine in his arms.

"Aren't you forgetting to say something?" he grinned tilting his head to stare one eye into hers below him.

"Oh," she laughed. "I love you, too, Seth. I have loved you all my life. I remember two things from the first night I came to live here. I remember how kind Grandmother was to me when Granddaddy brought me into the house. And I remember the grubby little boy with dirt on his face and a leaf still stuck in his wooly sweater. He looked after me. He also picked on me and put gum in my hair. But he still looked out for me. I knew that night I loved that little boy."

Seth grinned. "I wonder whatever happened to that little boy."

"Well, from the feel of it," she smirked looking down at the water where their waists were pressed against each other. "He's not so *little* anymore."

Seth blushed.

Upstairs, hours later, Seth held her in his arms as they rested in his bed. Her cheek was pressed to his chest, and she ran her fingers lightly up and down his forearm into the open palm of his hand. It was a familiar caress, from a long time ago—but somehow different when she did it now. He moaned at her touch.

"I like that; I remember that," he whispered.

"Granddaddy used to soothe us like that when we were little and he'd be reading to us before bed," Yasmine reminded him. "It was so soft. It always put us right to sleep."

"I had forgotten about that 'till now."

Yasmine suddenly changed the subject with a timid laugh and the blurting out of, "I can't believe you've seen me naked now."

"I know!" Seth chuckled. "I thought the same thing when you stripped me down and jumped on me."

"Seth Blanchard that is not at all what happened, and you know it."

"I distinctly remember you being unable to control yourself," Seth smirked. "And I never would have thought in a million years you'd do the things to me you did tonight."

Yasmine gently punched him in the side. He pulled her closer to his chest and kissed the top of her head. She still smelled like jasmine. Or maybe that wasn't her or the vine after all, maybe that's simply what love smells like.

"You know you wanted me," he teased.

"You are so vain, Seth Blanchard."

"It's okay," he kissed her hand as he clutched it to his chest. "I wanted you just as much. I guess I always have."

"What do we do now?" Yasmine asked. "Do we keep this quiet? How will the family take this?"

"There's no way to keep it quiet," Seth started as he sat up. He looked serious now. He wasn't playing anymore. "This isn't a fling, Yaz. This isn't a one-night stand. This isn't even the beginning of a relationship. We've been having a relationship for years; we just wouldn't admit it until tonight."

"You're right, Seth."

She liked that he had been the one to say it. She liked that he was recognizing now the thing she'd hoped for years he would see. Yasmine and Seth had spent their entire lives teasing each other, confiding in each other. They'd been one another's rock during the hard times and a soft place to land in the desperate times. Yasmine Sinclair had always wondered how Seth could receive all of those things from her yet always searched out some other girl when it came to falling in love. Why couldn't he see that was under his nose all along. Now he did.

"So we tell the family?"

"Are you asking me or telling me?" she replied.

"I don't know," he blushed. "As for me, I say we tell them--but if we are together now then we are partners. I can't just decide. You have to weigh in on what you want, too."

Partners. He gets it, she thought. *He finally gets it.*

"Well, partner," she quipped. "We will tell them tomorrow."

CHAPTER TWENTY-SIX

Sunday Lunch and Morning News

Birdseed was thrown into the backyard every morning, and by eight o'clock every bird nesting in the surrounding trees was gathered on the lawn for its breakfast. Artemis had already walked down the road to the mailbox, retrieved the morning paper and laid it at Olympia's place at the table, even though Olympia was not yet home from Charleston. Artemis usually read her news from her phone in the wee hours while having her coffee, but Olympia was old school and preferred her news to come folded and in thin white paper form. It would be there for her whenever she and Salem came in from their long drive home. When she had awakened that morning, Artemis saw a text from Salem saying they'd left out around 5am in the hopes of getting back to Daihmler by noon.

By lunchtime the large table in the dining room was ready for the hungry whenever the lazy Blanchard's at home and the road-weary Blanchard's driving back made it to the table. Being a Sunday morning, everyone was sleeping in it seemed. The smell of the country fried steak and gravy was appearing to rouse a few. Demitra was down now, helping load the peas and potatoes into bowls as Artemis put biscuits onto a platter. By 11:45 everyone in the house stumbled their way down the kitchen stairs to take their prospective seats around the table. Seth and Yasmine looked to have just woken up and thrown something on just to be presentable. Fable commented on their slovenly appearances. Beryl was ignoring everyone as she flipped through emails from her phone. Artemis and Demitra took their seats at the precise moment Salem and Olympia came through the door—both very pleased to see they'd made it in time for lunch. They were starved.

Over lunch, Olympia gave the family a condensed summary of how the Consort meeting had gone. Salem remained quiet about meeting her father. She was not quite ready to talk about that experience yet. She suspected Olympia knew—Olympia always knew everything—but since her grandmother had not mentioned it, Salem assumed she was respecting her privacy.

"What did everybody else do last night?" Fable asked, cutting into a piece of fried steak. "Yaz, didn't you have a date with Jake? Looks like you got in awfully late. What did ya'll do last night?"

"Broke up." Yasmine smiled.

"What?" Beryl exclaimed.

"Wow." Fable gasped. "Well you don't seem very upset up about it."

"I'm not."

"Wanna share any details?" Fable asked.

"Not really."

"Okay," Fable continued. "Seth, how was your evening with the preacher's daughter?"

"We broke up." Seth grinned.

"Geez!" Beryl said. "It was a bad night for Blanchard romance."

"Not necessarily." Yasmine giggled. Seth blushed, and nodded permission to her.

"What is going on with you two?" Demitra asked.

"Oh my God, you two had sex last night didn't you!" Fable exclaimed.

Yasmine and Seth both turned beet red. "Fable!" Yasmine cried.

The older Blanchards were not prepared for this declaration. Artemis nearly choked on her coffee while Demitra dropped her fork onto her plate with a loud clank. Olympia appeared to be almost on the verge of laughing—something in her wise old eyes was perhaps not as surprised by Fable's outburst as her daughters.

"I thought I heard noises coming from your room last night Seth." Fable continued. "That bedframe of your needs some grease if you two plan on doing that again."

All eyes turned to look at Seth Blanchard. He found himself, the only male in the family, being stared down by every set of female eyes in the household. He gave an uneasy shrug and tried to look back down at his plate but continued to feel all the women's eyes burning into him.

"Seth what games have you been playing with this child?" Artemis scolded.

"No, no no!" Seth stuttered. "You don't understand. Yaz and me love each other."

"I am thoroughly confused here." Beryl said.

Olympia clasped her hands together and beamed from across the table. "I for one am thrilled. I have felt for some time there was something between the two of you. I had given up hope you two would ever become smart enough to figure it out."

Beryl pressed her hands on the table before her and tried to get some clarification, "Let me get this straight. You and Yaz are in love now?"

"I don't think *now* is the right word," Seth replied, looking directly into Yasmine's eyes. "Yaz, you and I have been doing this thing since we were teenagers. I don't need time to know if it's right or not. Tonight—or last night rather—when I was talking about you and the way I feel about you to Vanessa, I realized you've been my girlfriend all these years."

Everyone around the table were now looking directly at Yasmine and all could see the mammoth tears welling in her eyes.

"Seth," she whispered.

"I thought about it all the rest of the night," Seth continued. "You know, after you acted like a big slut and then went back to your room."

Yasmine kicked him under the table as Fable simultaneously slapped his arm as hard as she could.

"You are the one Yaz. The only one."

Yasmine grabbed his hand and asked, "What are you trying to say?"

Seth jumped from the table and popped down on one knee before her—and the entire family. "It's you Yazzy. You. The only one for me. I do not need time to figure that out. I want you now, as my wife."

A collective gasp of shock and disbelief erupted from the throat of every Blanchard seated.

Yasmine, too, was startled by the proclamation. "Wife?"

Seth grimaced, "Well, you don't have to vomit in the back of your throat over the idea."

"No, no Baby, that's not what I meant," she said taking his face in her hands and kissing him gently. "It's just--wouldn't you like more time to make sure this is what you really want? We don't have to get married to be together."

Seth looked up at the others, all staring down at him. Little beads of embarrassed sweat began to form on his brow and run down behind his ears. Was Yaz really turning him down in front of everyone?

"I don't need or want time," Seth stammered. "I just want you at my side as my wife till the day I die. Are you saying you aren't ready? Do you not want to get married?"

Yasmine's brilliant blue eyes widened as she grasped his hands tight, "I would love to be your wife. I have dreamed about it for as long as I can remember, but I pushed the thoughts away because I didn't think you felt the same. But Seth I love you so much. I'll marry you anytime anyplace."

"Am I the only one that thinks everyone has gone insane during the night?" Demitra said.

"I feel like I have whiplash now." Artemis said to her sister. "I did not see this coming."

Salem grabbed her brother's hand and Yasmine's. "I am stunned," she said. "But in a mind-blown, happy way. Little brother, you know how I feel about you and Yaz has always been like a sister to me. Now she's actually going to be!"

Artemis cleared her throat in that authoritarian way she had just before handing down an opinion to the children. "May I ask a question? Is there a reason for this rush to marry?"

"No, Aunt Artemis. Yaz isn't pregnant." Seth rolled his eyes. Then suddenly he paused and turned to look at Yasmine. "Oh my God, we didn't use—I mean, are you on the—"

"Seth, please shut up." Yasmine grumbled, turning redder.

Seth turned back to his aunt. "As of up until last night, Yasmine wasn't pregnant. We are not getting married because we have to. We are getting married because we finally realized we've loved each other for years. Why waste any more time? We know this is right."

Olympia clapped her hands together ringing out a sound that garnered everyone's attention. "This is an exciting day! I am exceedingly pleased with this development. There is no woman on earth better suited to put up with Seth than our sweet Yasmine. And I think Yasmine is quite fortunate to have found a man willing to look as foolish as Seth has looked at this lunch today, just to declare his love for her. I can feel it in my heart that the two of you are soulmates. You always have been."

"Mother, don't you think this whole thing is going just a little too fast?" Artemis pointed out.

"Let it go, Sister." Demitra cautioned. "Just let them do them."

Artemis shook her head in frustration and pushed her plate aside. "I'll start the dishes."

"Have a wedding date in mind?" Fable asked.

Yasmine and Seth looked at each other. "Today?" Seth asked.

"No." Yasmine said, shaking her head. "How about October. That gives us time."

"Oh, Halloween!" Fable suggested.

"Fine by me," agreed Seth.

"Excellent." Olympia smiled. "I think that will be a perfect day and plenty of time to make this a perfect wedding. And Yasmine, your grandfather kept a couple of things I was to give you on your wedding day. I can't wait to get them out of storage."

As the children all left the table to begin their various days. Olympia scanned the headlines of her newspaper as she sipped her coffee. Artemis and Demitra were clearing the table and putting away the breakfast things. They'd ended any discussion of the engagement because arguing over whether it seemed too soon or not was pointless. Seth and Yasmine appeared to be happy and in the end that was all that counted. Topics moved on to more mundane things—the dishwasher was acting up again. Someone left a fork in the disposal. It was only when Olympia spoke up, reading a headline, that their attention turned to more important things.

"There's been another murder in Daihmler." Olympia announced. "Last night. A girl in the park."

"Which park?" Demitra asked.

"Yerby Park," Artemis answered. "I read about it this morning online. Why? Are you on the case now?"

"Yes." Demitra answered. "Charlie Bennet asked me to start working on the case. I have to go check out the crime scenes. I guess I'll drive out to Yerby Park this afternoon."

"Let me go with you. Just in case it's not safe."

...

The section of the park was blocked off by police tape, although no officers still lingered from the day's investigation. Demitra and Artemis canvassed the area, unsure what they were expecting to find. Demitra touched a few things. A tree, the ground, a nearby trash can lid. She could feel something but nothing definite. Whatever it was, was faint.

"Sense anything?" Artemis asked.

"Not really." Demitra said. "There is something here, but I can't zero in on it."

"You're not getting images?"

"No, it's hard to explain. It's like there's a definite impression here but I'm not connecting to it yet." Demitra explained. "There was a mother and her little girl here. I am honed into their imprint. They had ice cream. The little spilled some on her new dress and was terribly upset. The mother used Wet Wipes. The stain was still there. I see them very clearly. The little girl was so upset. She loved her dress."

"Funny that would be the overlaying emotion left at a murder scene." Artemis observed.

"Unless this isn't the murder scene." Demitra considered. "Maybe it is just where the body was left."

"If the murder didn't take place here," Artemis said now understanding. "Then there's no real emotion or energy imprinted here."

"Except the killer." Demitra said. "I should be able to connect to him. People, no matter how good or bad, leave a trace of their feelings lingering for a while. But I'm getting nothing."

Artemis walked over to the chalk outline of where the body was found. It disturbed her to know this was where an innocent person had been so monstrously discarded, as if their life hadn't counted. The victim deserved better.

"Try touching the ground here," she suggested to her sister.

Demitra placed her hand where the victim had been discovered, but no impressions came to her at all. It was no different than any other spot she had laid her hands. This was unusual for Demitra Blanchard. Usually she picked up on trace elements of a scene rather quickly. But there was nothing here to absorb.

"I don't feel anything, Artemis."

"What if we go to one of the other crime scenes?"

"We can try." Demitra said. "But this was the most recent. It has the best chance. The field around the others has probably faded by now. I just don't understand why I'm not getting any kind of residue from the killer."

"Maybe he's just that cold." Artemis replied. "Maybe he has no emotion at all. Nothing you can read."

"I can't imagine a person who could be that cold."

CHAPTER TWENTY-SEVEN

Forgiveness

Fable pulled up to the house around 6 o'clock after a hard day at work. Salem was sitting in Olympia's front porch rocker, picking petals off an orange daisy in her lap. The summer sun was not yet ready to close up shop for the day, but it was showing signs of exhaustion by casting its reds and orange hues all around. Salem looked troubled, Fable thought. *Of course, she's troubled. She's been through more than anyone else could bear.*

"You okay?" Fable asked, taking the seat beside her.

"I called Travis today," Salem said. "I'm going back to Atlanta. I need to get back to work."

Fable didn't understand. "Why? You should just stay here. This is your home. You shouldn't be alone right now. You just lost your husband and son. The last thing you need is to go back to Atlanta, to the place where you lived with them. The thought of you in that house alone..."

"If I sit around here anymore, I'll go crazy," Salem said. "I need to join my life again. It's too easy to sit back in this chair and sink back into my old life."

"What's wrong with that?" Fable asked. "Here with your family. Maybe that's what you need."

"It's the last thing I need," Salem snapped. "Fable, if I stay here and fall back into the old dynamics of our life here, I will lose myself. I am not Salem Blanchard of Daihmler anymore. That was a whole world ago. I am Salem Lane, art director...widow. I have to go back. Staying here would be like erasing everything I built in Atlanta."

"But Salem, back there, especially in your house, you'll be surrounded by memories. The pain of everything you lost will be everywhere. Here, you won't be reminded at every corner of what is missing."

"I want to be reminded of what is missing, Fable. I know it will hurt but I'm too numb here. This was another life—a life without David and Michael. Back home was our world. I need to be there, in that world, no matter how hard it will be. If I do not go home, it's like I am erasing them."

Fable leaned her head onto Salem's shoulder and grabbed her hands with her own. They sat quietly for several minutes as a family of squirrels raced back and forth between two of the oak trees by the driveway.

"I guess I just don't understand," admitted Fable. "I think you're leaving behind the very thing that will help you heal right now. But I trust you know what's best for you."

"I do," Salem said. "I can't heal here. This is a dream world. The mysterious Blanchards. The people in town coming here for help with their problems. Walking through the shops of Daihmler and hearing whispers. People treating us like we are something they are simultaneously afraid of and grateful for. In Atlanta, I am just Salem. No magic, no ghostly parents on the wall. I liked being Salem Lane. I liked who she was. I am not ready to give her up yet. And if I stay here, I lose her. And that life, the one with my husband and my baby, will start to feel less and less real. I can't let that happen. For now, at least, I need to go home and feel everything no matter how hard it will be."

She didn't agree with Salem's decision, but it was Salem's decision to make. She couldn't understand why Salem would want to remain separated from the Blanchards when there was nothing left in Atlanta for her but work. Then again, Fable had never really left Blanchard House to go anywhere except the few times she'd driven to Birmingham to visit her father's family. She had no concept of what life on her own could be like. Sensing Salem wanted to be alone, Fable went inside, leaving her cousin on the porch.

Salem continued to sit in the rocker listening to the orchestra of crickets and katydids. In the distance, she saw the late afternoon fireflies filling the garden. She sat there for quite a while. So long in fact, that the bats came out for their evening swoop over the pool water to dine on mosquitoes and bugs—the last of the fading day's creatures arising before night took over. Nacaria's shadow passed over the wall of the house beside the rocking chair, just under the now lit porch lamp.

"I saw him, Mother," Salem said aloud, hardly believing herself that she was speaking to her. But she felt like speaking to her. In her loneliness and grief, she had lost some of the resentment she'd long held towards her.

The shadow lingered under the light, as if waiting to be confided in, or perhaps even *forgiven*. It had all but given up hope of that. Or perhaps it was simply whatever remained of a mother's love, sensing that her baby needed her.

"He is still very handsome," Salem went on. "I liked him. I didn't want to, but I did. I won't be seeing him again. He belongs where he is, with his family. He always did. And he still loves you, Mother."

Salem paused, wondering if she should continue. Were her words only causing more pain? She thought it funny she would now be concerned with how her mother might feel. Never before had she regarded the shadow as having feelings. Now as she looked more closely at it, she was reminded of something she had only really noticed when she was little. The shadow had form and shape. Her mother's shape. Salem could almost make out the hair curling at the shoulders, her long legs and arms. She began to feel empathy for the shadow. Somewhere in that opaque silhouette was a heart. She may not be able to see it or hear it, but it was there.

"I'm leaving soon, Mother. Going back to my own house. I have a lot of issues to deal with, and it is too complicated here. I hope—" she stopped. Tears filled her eyes. She decided to say it, to say what her heart had long refused to let her say for years. "I hope one day I will see you in the flesh again. I forgive you, Mother."

The shadow inched closer to the chair. Hopeful.

"I think I understand a little why you were driven to do what you did. I did something wrong, too. I tried to tamper with the Natural Order. I tried to play with fate. I have learned love will stop at nothing to save itself. So, I do forgive you, Mother. And...I love you."

A black hand reached from its shadowy form and outstretched one-dimensionally across the plank-board wall of the house. Salem stood up and placed her hand flat against the cold board atop the shadowy hand of her mother. For one fleeting moment, she felt warmth emanating from the spot. She felt her mother's love.

CHAPTER TWENTY-EIGHT

Another Murder

Clicking off the downstairs lights and about to go to bed, Demitra faintly heard her phone ringing from the kitchen outlet where it had been charging. She rushed to answer it without tripping over things in the dark. She managed to navigate everything but Seth's shoes he had kicked off after dinner. *Boys*, she huffed to herself as she snatched the phone, last ring, from the charging cord. She saw from the screen it was Charlie Bennet calling.

"Charlie?"

"There's been another murder tonight."

"Oh, no!" Demitra gasped.

"Can you meet me here at the scene? I warn you, it's very graphic, but if you can stand it you might pick up something while it's fresh."

"Where are you?" she asked.

"Back in Yerby Park again. This time it's near the picnic table pavilions."

"I'm on my way."

Demitra hadn't been to Yerby Park since the days when Seth played little league. Now she was there for the second time in two days. She couldn't help but smile at the memories of days gone by in that park as she passed the baseball field. Larry had been one of the coaches for Seth's team. Seth had been a pretty decent ball player—when he wasn't benched by his Uncle Larry for using his powers during a game. Those other little boys never had any idea why they would suddenly lose control of their bats or have a ball they'd intentionally pitched with a specific spin suddenly right itself and land smack into Seth's bat. But Larry knew, and he would punish Seth for the infraction. *"You can't manipulate the wind during a game, Seth!"*

Demitra had no trouble finding the crime scene. The flashing red and blue lights of the many police cars could be seen almost a half mile away in all directions. Walking across the dewy grass toward the cluster of dumbfounded professionals, Demitra was confronted by one particularly obstinate officer.

"Ma'am, you can't be out here. This is police business."

"Let her through, Johnny," Charlie called out from nearby as he made his way to greet her.

"This is Miss Blanchard," Charlie said. "She has my permission to go anywhere she likes around the scene."

Johnny rolled his eyes, "Oh. You're *that* woman. 'Course I don't buy any of that psychic shit."

"Of course, you don't," Demitra replied. "Just like your wife doesn't buy your explanation of why she found those gay porn sites on your computer."

Demitra clasped on to Charlie's arm as he guided her through the crumpled grass where moments before, investigators, coroners, and officials had been standing. Everyone cleared back as Demitra came through.

"You've never called me out to a scene with this many people around," she told him. "Won't you get flack for this?"

"I don't care at this point. I need something to go on," Charlie said. "You told me earlier that when you were here today, you couldn't pick up on anything. I thought a fresher crime scene might help."

"We'll see."

"It's bad, Demmy," Charlie warned. "Brace yourself for it. I'm sorry you have to see this."

Nothing could have prepared Demitra for the sight she would see. Blood was splattered everywhere, across the grass, against the trees, onto the nearby picnic table and bench. And the body looked almost as if someone had dipped it in blood. She shielded her eyes for a moment to steady her stomach. When she was ready, she looked back at the victim.

It was a man. His head was twisted to the side, turned that way so ferociously by the killer that it looked to be partially torn off. He had one eye missing and deep gashes in his face underneath the bloody, hollow socket. His left leg was snapped backward into an angle it would have never bent naturally. There were bits of bone revealed through the torn flesh. He laid on the grass, the bent leg underneath him. Two of his fingers were missing from his right hand.

Charlie gently guided Demitra aside when he suspected she was about to vomit. She didn't. She dry-heaved a moment, then composed herself.

"It's okay," he consoled. "It's the most gruesome slaying yet. I'm sorry you have to see it."

"I'll be alright. Just tell me what you know."

"We think the killer, or killers, cut his eye out with a switchblade. Those marks are deep. We haven't found the eye yet. Maybe it was taken as some kind of keepsake of the kill—a trophy."

"Were any body parts missing from the other victims?" she asked. "What about this man's missing fingers? Have they been located?"

"He's never taken any body parts from a victim before," Charlie said. "We found this guy's fingers nearby. They are bagged already."

Demitra was still feeling a little shaky and nauseous from the gruesome scene. Feeling a swirl of unsteadiness coming on, she automatically reached for Charlie's arm. He helped her to a nearby tree she could lean against for a moment. Taking a series of short breaths to calm her nerves, she closed her eyes in hopes to clear her mind of the sight she had just witnessed so that her focus could move more to her other senses. Suddenly she shuddered, Charlie gripped her arms. She clutched his wrist for stabilization.

"He was in this tree!"

"Who?" Charlie cried. "Can you see him?"

"No," she answered. "I don't have any sense of the killer. But the victim was under this tree. He'd been jogging."

"Yes!" Charlie confirmed. "It looks that way. We found headphones and his cell phone on the ground a few feet from here."

"The man stopped to send a text," Demitra recounted, staring off into the distance at the nothingness of the dark night in order to let her mind see inward. "He heard rustling above. He started to look up, but before he could something jumped him from above."

"From the tree?"

Demitra focused harder. "Yes, I think so. It came from the air. He didn't have time to look up, so I cannot see what he saw. They wrestled. Rolled on the ground. There was a terrible noise, then pain as his neck ripped. He was losing consciousness when his body was flung to the ground. His leg snapped behind him from the impact. Oh Charlie, I can feel his fear. His agony…then nothing. He was dead."

"Demitra, can you tell me anything about the man at all? The killer, I mean."

"Nothing," Demitra shook her head. "Charlie—I cannot connect to him. Or them. I can feel the energy all around from the victim. I am tapped into him. But there's nothing around the killer. No feeling at all."

...

Demitra did not sleep that night. The things she witnessed and felt disturbed her far too greatly. She came down for breakfast with the family but could not bring herself to eat anything. She gave a brief report to the members of her family without descriptions of the things she saw.

"It's really strange that you are unable to get a link to the killer," Artemis remarked. "That's really a first for you."

"I know," Demitra agreed. "I can't understand it myself. But I am going back out there when I get dressed. I have to see if maybe there's something I missed."

"I'll go with you if you want, Mama," Fable offered. "Yerby is just a few streets from my clinic. I can go with you before I go in to work."

Mother and daughter hurried to dress and drove out in separate cars to the picnic area of Yerby Park. The blood was still clinging to the grass where the body had been discovered. Demitra walked around quite a bit, pacing the crime scene, still unable to pick up on anything regarding the killer's identity or emotional state.

"It's obvious this was the site of the murder," Fable remarked, "unlike the other one you and Aunt Artemis went to yesterday. There is no denying this was where this one occurred. I wonder if the other took place somewhere else in the park and the killer just dumped her body in the other location."

"It's possible," Demitra replied.

"Can you try to get a feel for that lady in this spot?" Fable suggested. "Maybe she was killed right here, too, the night before, and for some reason just got moved."

"Worth a try," Demitra said.

She closed her eyes and focused her brain on the location she had been to the day before with Artemis. She wasn't rewarded for her effort. There were no traces of the girl. She had not been killed at this same location. But that man...that poor jogger. Demitra was being swept up in it all again. The fear, the pain. He hadn't known what hit him. The memory of his mangled body invaded her thoughts again. The image of him was forever burned into her mind.

"Mama, you okay?" Fable asked.

"It was so awful, Fable," Demitra confessed to her daughter. "I don't think I'll ever forget what I saw last night. And I am not being any help to Charlie at all. I cannot tell him a single thing about this murderer. I just don't know why I can't get a trace of him."

Fable opened her arms and took her mother in for a much-needed hug. Her mother wanted to be of help so much and the fact that all these killings were going on in Daihmler and Demitra—for the first time ever—wasn't able to assist the police, was weighing on her. Fable held her for a few moments. Demitra rested her chin on her youngest child's shoulder.

Suddenly she tensed. Her head darted up as she looked around. Fable looked into Demitra's eyes but didn't see her mother looking back at her. Demitra was in trance. She was having a vision. Fable let go of her and stepped back to give her room. Demitra instantly returned to her normal state of being. Her eyes no longer glazed over in psychic state.

"I saw it!" Demitra cried. "Felt it... but it's gone now."

"Surely you can tap back into it, Mama," Fable urged. "Try."

Demitra did try. But failed. It was gone. Gone before she could even see what it was, she was connecting to.

"I can't get it back."

"Relax a second," Fable advised giving Demitra's shoulder a squeeze. "Give it a minute and try again."

Suddenly Demitra seized up again. Her eyes went clear as her mental powers surged. *It was dark, the wind was blowing. The moon was bright in a cloudless sky. The jogger was tired, but still had one more half mile in him. He stopped by the tree to check the time. 8:45. He had promised to pick Linda up from work at 9. He was running late. He started to text her. Then that sound. That horrible growl rang out even with the headphones in his ears. Suddenly something hit him from above, knocking him to the ground.* Demitra jumped from the impact of the force she felt.

"Mama!" Fable cried as her mother stumbled backwards. "What happened?"

"You," Demitra said in disbelief. "You let go and it's gone."

"What?"

"Fable, I can't see anything. Except when you hugged me and then just now when you touched my shoulder. Give me your hand."

"I don't get it?"

"Just give your hand, Honey. Trust me."

Fable placed her hand in her mother's.

The killer pushed him to the ground, digging his claws into the joggers back. The jogger fought back, taking a blind swing behind him in an attempt to knock the killer off. The killer snapped his jaws down on the man's hand, severing two fingers in his powerful bite. He lifted his claws to the man's neck and separated his head from the shoulder. Then he lowered his mouth to drink. Demitra saw the snout. The teeth. The dark, dark fur. She released her daughter's hand.

"Oh, dear God!" Demitra exclaimed.

"Mama, what is it?"

"I know why I couldn't locate him now—why I could only feel the victim and not the killer," Demitra said.

"Why?"

"Because I have to be touching you in order to tap into the animal kingdom."

"I don't understand," Fable replied.

"The killer isn't human."

CHAPTER TWENTY-NINE

The Witch Who Cried Wolf

Wordless disbelief hovered in the air as Demitra Blanchard told Chief Bennet what she had seen. Charlie got up from his desk at the station and closed the door to his office where no one else outside could overhear.

"Demitra, how can I be expected to buy this story of yours?"

"Charlie, it's a wolf. I think it's a werewolf."

He raised a brow and shook his head.

"You asked for my opinion, and that is what I saw. You have known me long enough to know that I am not prone to exaggeration. I do not make up outlandish tales. I saw an animal. A big animal."

"Okay, an animal maybe. But a werewolf?" Charlie scoffed.

"It was different from an animal's mental capacity. It was humanoid. Purposeful. It was not simply a wolf or a coyote. This thing was big and powerful and cunning. A killer's mind. But hungry."

"I cannot do anything with this, Demmy."

"I am rarely wrong in these circumstances, Charlie. And you've known my family long enough to believe in the unbelievable."

"Look Demmy," Charlie said. "You helped me out a lot in the past, and I am grateful for that. But information like this…I'd be laughed out of my job if I told my guys to be on the lookout for a werewolf."

"Then I'm afraid they will remain on the lookout for someone they are never going to find if they think this is just a man."

Charlie scratched his head and shook it again. He went back to his seat and placed his hands palms up on his desk. "I don't want to ridicule your beliefs or your gifts, but there are no such things as werewolves. Next thing I know you'll be talking about vampires or mummies."

Demitra was becoming frustrated. "I believe I know a little more about what is possible in the world than you do, Charlie Bennet. I have seen people move objects with their minds. I have seen people speak in depth with animals. I have seen time stopped completely and a woman turned into a shadow. There are people out there who can morph into objects, people who can revive the dead—and yes Charlie, there are such things as werewolves and vampires. Do not try to tell a witch about what's possible in the world. You'd be like a newborn in a room with Nobel Prize winners."

"Okay, okay, calm down Demitra," he said. "Regardless of what you're saying, I cannot tell the police department to be on the lookout for a freakin' werewolf."

"Then don't. You keep looking for a man, and I'll keep searching for a monster."

Demitra stood to leave, but Charlie asked her to wait. He walked over to the front of the desk and sat down on the edge facing her more closely. He reached over beside him and turned around a photograph from his desk which had been facing the side he usually worked from. The photo was of four people. Two men, two women. Demitra was one of the women. Charlie was one of the men.

"We've known each other a long time Demmy," he began. "When Peggy died, I was all over the place. It was Larry that kicked my butt back into life. I will never forget him coming into the house and smashing every bottle of whiskey I had and snatching me up by the neck. He pulled me to the mirror and made me confront what I was becoming. He told me I owed Peggy something. I owed our kids something and that something wasn't gonna be found in the bottom of a goddamned bottle."

"Larry was one of a kind," Demitra smiled. "They both were."

"Best friend I ever had in this world," Charlie said. "And you were there right along with him. Sometimes I think they are both up there in Heaven watching you and me, yelling at us when we get frustrated with each other. Look, Demmy, I can't say I believe this shit you're selling. But I do know I believe in you. And I know Larry believed in you and all this crazy shit that happens in your family. We had many a conversation about it back in the day. If you say this is so, I have to—on some small level—be open to it. But my hands are tied with the department. You give me any information you come up with privately, and I'll investigate it on my own time. In the meantime, this department will be looking for a regular two-legged madman."

"I'll do whatever I can."

"But explain this to me," Charlie said. "I don't even know what a werewolf is, outside the movies. Do I need a silver bullet or something if I find him?"

Demitra laughed. "No. No silver bullets. You can't kill the wolf. But you can kill him in human form, just as you would any other man."

"Is this like in Hollywood where if he bites someone, I'm looking at two were-wolves now?"

"That isn't his goal. Or *her* goal," Demitra said. "It could be a woman. But it isn't trying to make more of its kind. That would be too much competition for prey. Let me give you the brief *Witch-opedia* version of what this is.

"A long time ago, in Europe, near the old Celtic lands, there was a coven of witches living in one of the many fiefdoms—I couldn't tell you which one specifically. Back in those days it was as if every territory had its own king—until the time of William the Conqueror, who united the kingdoms under his rule. Anyway, these kingdoms were always at war with each other. During one of these wars when a king was off on some sort of Crusade or campaign against another king, the witches of that land—who had always kept their powers quiet, living among the people as though they were normal—decided to unite together to take over the land in the king's absence. They demonstrated their powers to the people and sent fear into their hearts should they defy the coven.

"When the king returned, he found his people enslaved to the witches, being used by them for their own unmentionable purposes. The king and his army set out to free the people and strike the witches down with his sword. One witch, the leader of the coven who had set himself upon the king's throne, had the power to transform into any animal he desired. He also held the power to transform others.

"Under attack by the true king of the land, the king witch changed all the remaining members of his coven into beasts. Wolves, panthers, leopards, and some beasts even more terrifying. Their plan was to hide in the mountains, blending with the other animals of the mountain forest until they could formulate a new attack. The King Witch transformed many in his coven to animals, but just before he could transform himself, the Celtic King found him and struck him down. With the King Witch dead, all of the others who had been transformed into animals, were unable to change back."

"This sounds like a child's fairy tale," Charlie remarked.

"Most children's fairy tales have a basis in fact," Demitra continued. "Legend has it that these animals, who still possessed the minds of human beings despite their animal form, mated together in the mountains, only to be shocked when their offspring were born in human form. But these offspring were not fully human. During certain times of the moon cycle, these humans changed back into the animal forms of their parents."

"Werewolves," Charlie snorted.

"Werewolves. Wendigos. Cat People. Who knows?" Demitra replied. "That's the legend anyway."

"That's pretty preposterous."

"I wasn't there," Demitra smiled. "I'm just telling you the story I grew up with."

Charlie got off the desk and escorted his friend to the door.

"Whatever this killer is," Charlie said before he sent her on her way, "we're going to catch him. Man, or beast."

CHAPTER THIRTY

Fable Finds a Man

Fable took the afternoon off. There were no patients scheduled at the clinic for the rest of the day, and she decided to take one of the dogs in her care for a walk. His name, he told her, was Buster. Buster lived in a neighborhood near Yerby Park. He had been turned into her clinic after being found, starving on a road nowhere near the park. Once she had fixed his dehydration and filled his empty belly, he'd told her how he had accidentally jumped into a neighbor's car one day because he'd smelled food in the back seat. He'd found a bag of hot dogs. He was munching on them when the angry neighbor discovered him in the car and stopped the car on the highway. Buster was afraid and ran off. He tried to find his way back home, but never found it. With him now fully recovered, Fable decided to drive him around the streets near the park to see if he could recognize his home.

It was only when Buster alerted her that he needed to relieve himself, that she pulled into the park and took him for a walk. She saw the picnic area where she'd been with her mother the day before. It was no longer roped off, but news of the murder had spread through town and there was absolutely no one anywhere near the pavilions. Fable parked her car in the general parking area and led Buster off on a leash. He didn't need one. She knew he had no intentions of running away again, but leash laws required it.

As they walked, she hoped some of the very attractive male joggers running shirtless on the path might take notice of her and stop to say hello. It had been months since she had a decent date with a man.

As she and Buster turned down a path between a canopy of shady trees, she noticed a guy approaching her walking his own dog, a gorgeous brown Great Dane. The man was equally as gorgeous. She thoroughly inspected him behind her sunglasses. Tall, lean, muscular with almost white blonde hair. Typically, she did not like blonde men. A blonde man was either outdoors playing sports way too often to be any use to a woman, or he chemically highlighted it—which posed its own set of issues. A vain man, or an overly stylish one, didn't appeal too much to Fable. However, it had been such a long time since she'd enjoyed the company of a man she decided if this man showed her even the slightest bit of attention, she'd go out with him.

She maneuvered herself, and Buster, closer to the man's side of the walking path so that he had to notice her. "You have a beautiful dog."

"Thanks," he grinned. "He's not as cuddly as the little guy you're with, though." As he gestured to Buster, Buster took it upon himself to pick this inopportune time to relieve himself on a nearby bush.

Good. We're talking, Fable thought to herself. *I hope he's not gay. With that hair, you never know.*

"What's your dog's name?" she asked the man.

"Tank."

Doubt he's gay then.

"And yours?"

"Buster," Fable smiled. "But he's not my dog. He's my patient. I'm a vet. We are just out for a stroll before I take him home."

Before the guy could speak again, Buster and Tank began barking ferociously at something near their feet. Fable glanced down and discovered a copperhead slithering between she and the man. The man jumped backwards and screamed a high pitched, almost glass shattering, cry.

He's gay.

The man bolted with Tank, leaving Fable standing in his dust as he escaped the slithering snake. *My Lancelot,* Fable thought to herself. Buster was still barking, and the snake appeared to be curling up ready to strike. It raised its head, gearing up for action. Its forky tongue fluttered out, tasting the air--feeling it's strike zone. As its body coiled more tightly and its head reared back on the ready, Fable looked down to the snake.

"Do not bite us. We are just passing by. We are not your enemy or your prey. And you are in danger here. There are dogs everywhere. One of them is going to hurt you."

The snake relaxed its body and responded to her with a slithery tongue.

Fable knelt down to it and cooed, "Of course I worry about your safety, too. I'm a friend to all creatures, not just fluffy pets."

The snake backed away and slithered back into the woods. Almost at once she caught sight of a man a few feet behind her. He had been watching the exchange. Normally she wouldn't have spoken aloud. She hadn't been aware anyone was around. She had not heard him walking up. She quickly got to her feet.

"You are gifted," the man said. "A lovely thing like you, able to converse with the beasts of the world. You must be a remarkable lady."

Fable was surprised by his nonchalant reaction. There was something remarkably familiar about him. She couldn't quite place it. She wracked her brain to figure it out. He wasn't a client. He wasn't an old schoolmate. He wasn't a fellow witch—at least not one she'd ever met.

"You're wondering why I look familiar," he said grinning and blushing.

"Yes. I am."

"We've never met," he said. "But we were in the same grocery store several nights ago. I think you'd just knocked down a spice display."

Now Fable was the one blushing.

"I'm Patric."

"Hi. I'm Fable."

"Fable," the man replied. "Quite fitting. Even the animals appear to be aware you are their princess."

CHAPTER THIRTY-ONE

Sherlock Blanchard

Knowledge was perhaps the greatest gift age had bestowed to Olympia. She knew most everything about everything. *Old eyes see much*, she would say many times as she quoted her father whom she believed to have been the wisest and strongest witch she'd ever known. Then again, most families think that of those that came before them. Olympia suspected her children and grandchildren thought *her* to be the wisest and most powerful witch that ever lived—which was flatteringly untrue. This was why Demitra came into her room at the break of morning to sit on the edge of her mother's bed.

"Tell me child," Olympia said, adjusting her eyes to the morning light penetrating the window sheers. "What has you stirring so early?"

"Does anything have to be wrong for me to come sit with my mother?"

"Frankly, yes," Olympia yawned. "Morning only finds you in here when you are troubled."

Demitra pushed a few strands of her mother's hair out of her face and said, "You are right as always."

Olympia moved over in the bed and patted the covers for Demitra to sit down beside her. Demitra did so as Olympia took her by the hand.

"Tell Mother what has you so unsettled?"

Demitra climbed under the covers to nestle into the other pillow beside Olympia. She looked into her mother's ancient eyes which were contrasted by her nearly ageless face.

"The killer who has been in the news. Charlie Bennet asked me to meet him at the latest crime scene the other day. It was awful."

"You're working on another case for the police department?"

"Mother, his face was torn. His leg was broken. His head almost ripped off. I still can't shake the images."

Olympia kissed her head. "Have you had any visions that might help solve the case?"

"I did. But Charlie doesn't believe me. It's a werewolf, I think."

Olympia did not act surprised or skeptical. She knew her daughter too well to doubt her opinions and her old eyes had seen much in their day—too much to question the validity of Demitra's findings.

"Can you describe his human form?" Olympia asked.

"I haven't seen his human form. I don't really know how to help. And the police can't really go on what I say. They're looking for a man, not a monster."

"You can't force anyone to believe you. Most people are blind to what is really out there in this world which is why it takes people like us to protect the rest. Nothing happens without a reason. You are supposed to stop this."

"How?"

Olympia squeezed her arm around her daughter's shoulder. She felt sympathy for Demitra's situation. Olympia knew all too well how frustrating it is when you know a truth no one else can understand. "The *how* I cannot help you with, Demitra. But other people are going to die until this beast is caught."

Demitra sighed, "I don't even know where to begin."

"Begin at the beginning," Olympia advised.

Demitra shot her a challenging glance, "I went to one of the prior crime scenes, but the trace was faded or nonexistent."

"Ask yourself this my dear," Olympia smiled. "Where did this wolf come from? Was Daihmler the true beginning?"

Demitra sat up. "Oh my God, you're right. It's so clear. He had to originate somewhere. If he had been here all along, we would have far more murders. He is not from here. I just have to find the trail."

...

Demitra spent the entire day at the computer in the den. First, she checked databases, with the use of Charlie's passcodes. She found writeups of a similar killing from Florence, Alabama the month before. *North. He came from the north.* She checked databases in Louisiana but found nothing resembling the Daihmler and Florence killings. Next, she checked Tennessee and discovered two murders fitting the profile in Chattanooga. She found evidence by day's end of a dozen killings stretching across the map. She found Charlie Bennet at his desk midafternoon eating a turkey on rye when she barged through his door unannounced. She slammed her papers on his desk beside the sandwich.

"Eight murders before these four in Daihmler. All during nights with a full moon." she said pointing to the map where she'd circled the cities. "In Kentucky they called it a mountain lion. In Indiana it was a bear. In Iowa, they called it a Devil Cult. In Wisconsin, they dismissed it as a brutal robbery. But it is all the same guy. The same circumstances."

"How did you—"

"By beginning at the beginning. This is not a local Daihmlerian who just snapped and started killing people. He's from out of state."

"That's not much help," Charlie scoffed.

"Really?" Demitra snapped. "Because I think I just eliminated the entire natural population of this town as suspects. Check credit card records and see who has been passing through all these towns. Even a werewolf needs a hotel room and a square meal on nights when the moon isn't full."

"So, he's moving south," Charlie said looking at her map.

"Wrong," Demitra said. "He's already where he wanted to go. Four murders in Daihmler. That is at least two more than anywhere else. He has been here for two months. He is already where he set out to get to. He meant to come to Daihmler. We just need to find out why."

CHAPTER THIRTY-TWO

Empty Nest

Salem got out of the Uber and stepped onto the sidewalk in front of the row of houses facing Piedmont Park. The park was the draw when she and David purchased the house. Ready to start a family, Salem could think of no better place to raise children than across the street from the park. Her childhood at Blanchard House had been spent roaming hillsides, flying kites in meadows, lazing under a shade tree with a book. Piedmont Park was about the closest thing there was to that in Midtown Atlanta. Pulling her bag behind her up the steps to her door, she guessed that didn't matter so much now. She had no children to run free there.

The house was like a tomb inside. Hollow silence confronted her at the threshold and filled every corner of the living room. The moment she entered, she felt the absence of her husband and son in the house. It used to be when she came home, she'd have been struggling to unlock the door balancing Michael on her hip. Most days she would give up on entering the house the normal way and just used her powers to unlock and open the door. David always cautioned her that people strolled up and down the sidewalk in the front of the house all the time and it was risky to use her powers. But then he never had to juggle a kid, a purse, a briefcase, and several bags of groceries all at once.

Slowly she walked through the rooms of her house on her way to the kitchen. The remnants of the potion she had used to propel herself back in time were still scattered across the kitchen counter. She would clean that up later. For now, she needed to look around, to feel. To try and get some sense of David, or Michael. She did not know what she'd expected exactly when she had decided to return home. But whatever she'd thought she'd find waiting there, wasn't there. There was no warm blanket of memories to comfort her. She wasn't met at the threshold with some sudden release from her feelings of loss. Salem had genuinely thought coming home would provide something tangible which might alter the emptiness in her heart. But this was just an empty house. Hauntingly empty. Any life which once roamed here had faded away.

There had been dirty dishes in the sink from the previous night's dinner, she remembered. But the sink was clean. No dishes in sight. And there had been laundry in the washer and some in the dryer. Salem went into the laundry room; certain mildew had ruined whatever clothes had been in the wash. But both the appliances were empty. *Molly. Molly and Travis probably came over here while I was gone and tended to things.* She glanced back at the counter where the ingredients to her spell still lay along with her notebook of spells. *I bet they didn't touch those. I'm sure they have a lot of questions after seeing that.*

Salem was now wishing she had not come back to Atlanta after all. Though everything she had said to Fable on the porch yesterday was true, she just hadn't expected home to offer no solace. This house was a shell now. A sad memory of a life which was over. And Salem was all alone with it.

The phone rang from her purse, breaking into her thoughts like a siren. At first, she thought to let it ring, but something inside made her answer. She did not recognize the number.

"Hello?"

"Salem?" called a meek female voice.

"Yes. Who is this?"

A pause came after Salem spoke.

"Hello?" Salem said again. "Who is this?"

"Arielle. Arielle Obreiggon. Is it alright that I called?"

Salem was unprepared.

"Salem? Hello? This is a bad time isn't it? I am so sorry I bothered you."

"No, wait!" Salem cried. "Yes, it is a bad time. I just got back to my house in Atlanta for the first time since—but I am glad you called."

"I telephoned your family home in Daihmler, and they said you'd gone home. I didn't tell them who I was. Anyway...when they said you had gone home, I just thought it might be difficult. I wondered if maybe you could use a friend?"

"That's very sweet of you Arielle," Salem answered. "It was thoughtful."

"I'm actually going to be in Atlanta tomorrow," Arielle announced. "If you feel like getting together...but if you don't it's totally cool. It was just a thought."

Salem paused momentarily. This was the last conversation she expected to be having, especially right now. Part of her felt as if she were being placed on the spot, but Salem could not help but also feel endeared to the innocent clumsiness of the girl.

"Arielle," she began. "Why are you going to be in Atlanta?"

"I—I, eh, have a friend that lives there," Arielle fumbled.

Salem grinned. "What is your friend's name?"

"Uh...Betty."

"Betty?" Salem laughed. "You are how old? Twenty? I didn't know too many young girls were named Betty anymore."

"Yes," Arielle replied. "Her name is Betty...Ford."

Salem could almost hear Arielle's hand slap her own face as she said that. "Betty Ford?" Salem repeated. "Interesting."

"All right!" Arielle confessed. "I don't have any friends in Atlanta. I just wanted to get to know you a little, and I thought that coming home by yourself might be really, really hard on you. I thought you might could use a friend. I know I'm being presumptuous. Now that I hear all this coming out of mouth, it was a really stupid idea. You want to be alone right now, and you don't even know me."

"Call me when you get into town," Salem smiled to herself and to the nervous girl over the phone. "I'll see you tomorrow."

CHAPTER THIRTY-THREE

The Other Blanchards

Howard found Demitra sitting by the pool when he arrived. The sun was beginning to set and there was an amber glow to the sky. A rumbling thunder rolled from miles away, and sharp displays of heat lightning crackled above. The timers to the landscape lighting clicked on to illuminate the pots along the pool deck wall.

"Summer's ending soon," Howard observed. "It's getting darker earlier now."

"Yes, it is," Demitra said, patting a chaise lounge chair for her friend to accompany her. "It must be Friday dinner again."

"Yep, been looking forward to it all week," Howard said, taking a seat on the chair opposite. "Guess I better get all I can while I can. Soon Artemis will have a restaurant to look after. Doubt we'll get too many Friday dinners."

Demitra stood up, unable to contain her excitement. Her hand flew to her mouth, covering her smile until she heard him actually say it. "Does that mean you have news for me?"

"Not much," Howard teased. "Just that I bought a restaurant for you this afternoon."

Demitra was ecstatic. "Oh, Howard that's wonderful! Artemis will have the best birthday ever!"

"It wasn't easy keeping this from Yasmine. She handles all the contracts for me you know. I had to tend to this one myself. I figured you didn't want her to know."

Demitra sat back down on the lounge chair, scooting closer to Howard, "Not until Artemis' birthday. It's in a few days, so this is perfect timing."

Howard smiled. "And I hear Yasmine has big news of her own. It's all she talked about at work. She and Seth. I have known for a while how crazy she is over him. Glad to see he feels the same. She'll have her hands full now, working for me, going to school, and a husband at home."

"I'm sure she'll still find plenty of time to loaf around the house with Fable and Seth."

Howard kicked his feet up on the lounge chair and crossed them as he put his hands behind his head. "Aren't you going to ask me how much you paid for The Cobblestone?" Howard asked Demitra.

"Did I have enough?"

"Plenty," he said. "I managed to get a pretty sweet deal on account of the previous owners having to sell quickly to expedite their divorce."

Demitra frowned. "I hate to profit from someone else's misfortune."

He leaned up in exasperation, "Demitra, if it weren't for other people's misfortune no one would ever profit from anything at all."

When Howard and Demitra went inside for dinner they took their respective chairs at the large dining table. Both were a little surprised to see a newcomer seated with the family. Fable had a guest. The table was brimming over with food: pot roast with creamy gravy, garlic mashed potatoes, field peas, squash casserole, fried green tomatoes, and freshly baked cornbread.

Fable introduced her guest, Patric, to everyone at the table. He nodded graciously and complemented the delicious looking spread laid out before them.

"We are glad to have you, Patric," Artemis acknowledged with a nod.

The family dove into the meal placing spoonfuls of food onto their plates. For a few moments the only sounds around the table was the clanking of serving spoons, plates, and utensils.

"Are from Daihmler, Patric?" Howard asked. "I thought I knew practically everybody around here, but I don't believe I know you. What is your family name?"

"I don't have any family," Patric answered. "Only a sister."

Silence fell over the table in response to the bizarre answer. Howard was just about to say *But you do have a last name don't you?* when Yasmine accidentally dropped the serving spoon from the pot roast into the mashed potato bowl, splattering Howard with gravy droplets. He wiped them off and forgot to ask.

"Patric and I met in the park the other day," Fable told the family.

"Which park?" Demitra asked.

"Yerby," Patric answered. Suddenly Demitra felt a chill down her spine.

"He helped me find a lost dog's home, and afterward we spent the rest of the day together, and the day after that as well," Fable informed them.

"That was kind of you to help find a poor lost dog's home," Olympia said with an approving smile. She shifted into interrogation mode. "Patric, what is it that you do?"

"At the moment, I am not working. I moved here to be close to my sister."

"Do you have any plans?" Demitra asked. "Do you have any hobbies?"

"I hunt."

Demitra did not like the way he said it. He seemed to be saying something else beneath every question he answered. It frightened her a little. *He* frightened her a little. Yasmine broke the awkwardness by informing Howard that she expected him to give her away at her wedding on Halloween. Howard was truly touched by the request and immediately agreed.

"Should I be searching for a new assistant after the ceremony?" he asked.

"Hell, no!" Seth blurted. "This girl is gonna work. I'm still in school, and it's already hard enough getting any pocket money out of the aunts. I need a wife bringing home some dough. Besides, sitting around here all day eating Aunt Artemis' cooking isn't a good idea. She's got a wedding dress to fit into."

Yasmine elbowed him in the ribs, "Are you calling me fat?"

"No! Of course not," Seth answered. "You look great. Seriously. I'll love you no matter how big you get."

"Seth!" Beryl exclaimed.

"I can't imagine your bride-to-be could ever be anything other than beautiful," Patric said smiling at Yasmine. She smiled back.

"You'll have to excuse these two, Patric," Artemis explained. "I'm afraid they've been cousins a lot longer than they've been a couple, so old habits die hard."

Demitra wasn't paying much attention to the banter going on between Yasmine and Seth. She'd heard these same kind of playful insults from all of the children their whole lives. Her mind was focused more on Patric. There was something not quite right about him. She couldn't shake the feeling.

"I suppose it's a little disturbing, Patric, to have come here to visit your sister just at the time we have a serial killer roaming around town," Demitra said.

"Frankly, I haven't thought much about it."

"Really?" Artemis questioned. "It's all Daihmler is talking about."

"People are killed every day," Patric noted. "I suppose in a small town it's shocking."

"My ex boyfriend said the same thing recently," Yasmine noted. "But it still frightens me. I bet your sister is a little afraid too."

"My sister has nothing to worry about," Patric remarked. "Not with me around."

Fable clutched his arm and pressed her cheek to it, "I hope that includes me too?"

Patric gave her a small kiss atop her head, but said nothing.

...

After dinner, Beryl, Yasmine, and Seth decided to take an evening swim while Fable and her guest went off by themselves. Olympia asked Howard to discuss something privately with her in the study, so Demitra helped Artemis with the dishes.

Artemis attempted to make conversation, but it fell on deaf ears. Her sister was much too preoccupied, spying through the window on her youngest daughter as she and Patric sat under a tree in the meadow—he, stroking her hair as she laid in his lap.

"Look Dee, Fable has brought home losers before. Don't worry about this guy. He's a little weird, but still an improvement from that guitarist she dated in the spring. Remember him? The one that smelled like he bathed in patchouli. Patric sounds like he is pretty transient anyway. Doubt he'll be around long."

"It is more than that, Artemis," Demitra confided. She kept staring at them through the window as she mechanically dried the same dish twice. "Something about him... something I can't put my finger on. Or maybe I can. Maybe that's what scares me."

"All right then, over-protective-momma. Use your powers to peep inside his head and see what he's about."

"I tried," Demitra confessed. "All through dinner I tried. I couldn't do it. He is like a steel vault. Very guarded. What's more, I think he could tell I was trying. I think he knew the entire time."

Meaning it to be a lighthearted poke at her sister's overprotection, Artemis suggested, "Maybe he's a witch."

Demitra continued staring outside. "Or something much, much darker."

...

Inside the study, just off the foyer, Howard nestled into the comfy leather chair opposite his client. Olympia sat at the desk. The chair was much too tall for her small frame and she squirmed a little in the chair before speaking.

"I always feel ridiculous at this desk," she said. "I've thought about changing out the chair or the desk itself, but I can't bring myself to do it."

"Understandable," Howard replied. "After all this was Sinclair's office. House wouldn't seem right if you changed it."

"Did you bring the papers I asked for?" Olympia requested.

"I did," Howard said, opening his briefcase. "And as you requested, I didn't say anything to anyone, and I didn't let Yasmine see these. I've been doing a lot of that lately it seems."

Olympia took the papers from Howard and looked them over for a moment. She seemed to approve everything she read and began initialing and signing the proper lines.

"If I am perfectly frank, Olympia," Howard began, "I'm more than a little surprised by this transaction. You are actually using some of Sinclair's estate after all these years, for some personal use. You've never done that before."

"A little out of character for me, is it?"

"Frankly, yes. I've spent years trying to get you to enjoy your fortune—ever since I took over your accounts after Dad died. And you've remained adamant that Sinclair's money and his lands only be used for conservation and charitable purposes."

Olympia gave a great smile across her face, "My, your father was a great man. And a great friend to me."

"He thought a great deal of you, Olympia," Howard admitted.

"I almost married him once," Olympia revealed, startling Howard. "You never knew that, did you?"

"No," he replied. "When?"

"Oh, it was before he met your mother and you were born."

"I never knew you two were once in love," Howard said.

Olympia laughed to herself, as if remembering something personal and private, but dear. "I don't think you could have called us *in love*. We were familiar. Friends. It seemed as though we should have been in love, and perhaps at the time we may have assumed we were."

"What happened?" Howard asked.

"Your mother happened," Olympia smiled. "Your mother came along, and Nate Caldwell was head over heels."

"Did you resent my mother for that?"

"Your mother?" Olympia scoffed. "Oh Heavens, no. Howard, your mother was one of the most radiant and giving people I have ever known. I am truly sorry she died before you had a chance to know her. She loved you very much." Olympia gave a slight sniffle and wiped a stray tear from her eye.

"You okay?"

The old woman nodded her head and said, "Yes. I am fine. It was a heartbreaking time. You can't understand what pain it caused her to know she wouldn't be around to see you grow up."

"It's still painful for you, isn't it?" Howard asked, appreciating how much the old woman must have regarded his mother. He liked having someone remember his parents. They'd been gone so long that most people had forgotten he ever had any. But Howard thought of his father quite often, and he always felt a pang of sadness over not knowing his mother.

"Lost friends are always difficult," Olympia replied. "Lost family you think of practically every day. Your heart has all the time necessary to mourn and heal. But lost friends are different. You tend to forget about them more easily. Days go by. Then months. Sometimes years. And when they creep back into your mind, it surprises you. And you can't believe you almost forgot to keep remembering them."

"Why didn't you and Dad rekindle things after Mom died?"

"No, by then I held too much respect for your mother to marry her husband. Besides, I was in love with John Windham by then."

"Well," Howard said. "Let's get back to the business at hand, shall we?"

"Let's."

"So, tell me Olympia, why after all this time have you chosen to do something with this Butler County land?"

"You recall my sister, don't you Howard?"

Howard thought for a moment. He did, actually. It had been some time since he had heard anything about her, and he'd only met her once or twice in his youth. It seemed odd to him now to have put her completely out of his mind. He always just sort of thought of Olympia as some kind of perpetually old sage, guiding her family through life. It took him a moment to stop and remember that she'd been young once, and there was another Blanchard of her generation still alive.

"Her name is Patricia?"

"Pastoria."

"Well, what does she have to do with land in Butler County?"

"Nothing, yet," Olympia said. "Pastoria lives in Mobile with her family. Her husband is deceased now, but he was a fine hard-working man in his day. They lived here at Blanchard House for the first two years of their marriage. He wanted to open a hardware store. I tried to give him the money, but he refused. Proud. He said he and Pastoria would earn their own way. He planned to open a chain of stores, but only ever succeeded in opening a few in Mobile."

"I am not following what this has to do with anything."

"I'm getting there my boy," Olympia cautioned. "Pastoria had three boys, of course they are all grown now—just like my girls. Poor Henry left the hardware store in debt when he died and the meager amount of money he left his family has long been used up. It has been brought to my attention that my sister is struggling.

"I want you to move the Butler land into one of Sinclair's minor corporations that will not be tied to me. Its natural gas land—very profitable. Then I would like you to manipulate some documents which make it appear as though my brother-in-law...his name was Henry Dorance, owned the mineral rights to the land. Contact whichever energy company would want to drill for the resource and they will approach my sister's sons for the rights to drill. That should provide quite an income for my struggling sister and her boys."

"Why can't you just give your sister some money?" Howard suggested.

"No, she would never take it. This must give every appearance of being something her husband invested in long ago and has only recently come to light."

"I cannot believe you would allow drilling on any of your land. It's so unlike you."

Olympia mused a moment and smiled. "I suppose I am breaking one of my own rules. But if you sell the land, and then they drill, it's not really as though I'm doing anything against my principles. What happens to the land after I sell it is out of my control? Besides, I'd do anything for my baby sister."

CHAPTER THIRTY-FOUR

A Sister for Salem

Arielle was just as lovely as Salem remembered. Seeing the girl standing at her front door, Salem rid herself of any misgivings she might have had in inviting her. Arielle rushed into her arms as if they'd been lifelong friends. By the afternoon, Salem felt as comfortable with Arielle as she would have one of her cousins. And the house no longer seemed so threateningly empty.

"Daddy was so pleased you gave him the chance to talk with you," Arielle told her as she peeked into Salem's freezer and suddenly removed a package of frozen chicken while they talked in the kitchen. "He told me that he finally got to tell you about how much he cared for your mother." She began rummaging through Salem's cabinet until she found a skillet. Placing it on the stove she turned to Salem and said, "You don't mind if I make us dinner, do you? I'm kind of hungry."

"Knock yourself out," Salem smirked, both surprised and amused at the girl's complete forwardness.

Arielle placed the chicken pieces, still frozen, in the skillet and placed it atop the stove. "I hope you don't mind that I'm talking about your mother and their relationship. Daddy has always confided in me—even when I was little. We tell each other everything." She fumbled for a minute in the pantry until she found a bottle of vegetable oil and poured it over the chicken. "He knows I came here, but I told my mother that I was visiting a friend in Connecticut who I went to boarding school with."

Salem was listening to the words, but the sight taking place before her eyes held the majority of her attention. Arielle began opening drawers, then more cabinet doors, then back to the pantry where she found what she was looking for. She withdrew a bag of flour and opened it. She dumped half the bag on top of the oiled chicken. The flour dust swirled into her nostrils and she winced.

"My mother and my sister are awful people," Arielle continued. "Mother doesn't like me very much. Never has. I used to think it was because I always felt closer to Daddy and her sister, my Aunt Blackie, but Cassandra told me once that I reminded our mother of the fact our father doesn't love her."

"How so?" Salem asked as she further observed the cooking catastrophe before her. Arielle was now cracking an egg and dropping it over the pile of flour, which was sitting atop the oiled frozen chicken. Salem continued to watch as Arielle then poured a little milk on top of that.

"You see," Arielle explained, "my mother tried to seduce him once after the whole trial with your mother was over. She cast a spell on him to get him to come to her bed one night." Arielle paused her story and began inexplicably beating the chicken with a wooden spoon. "This batter doesn't seem to be sticking very well." Salem snickered as Arielle picked back up with her tale. "Anyway, the spell worked, but not the way Mother wanted. She meant for it to make him love the woman he saw—meaning her. Instead, he saw the woman he loved—meaning Nacaria. Daddy thought he was making love to Nacaria and even called out her name. Mother was furious. And that was how I was conceived. As a result, Mother doesn't like me a whole lot."

Surveying the contents of the skillet, Arielle rubbed her forehead a moment, then added more oil. She began smacking the chicken with the spoon again after which she pulled a lid from the cabinet of pans and covered the dish, turning the burner up to high.

"Arielle?" Salem said softly. "You don't know how to cook, do you?"

"Not at all," Arielle said. "But I think I did everything right. It just needs to simmer." Suddenly the oil boiled over from under the lid and the skillet became wrapped in flames. "Is that supposed to happen?"

It was all too much for Salem. She had been doing her utmost to remain silent and not hurt her guest's feelings, but it was impossible to hold back now. She burst into laughter at the ridiculousness of it all as well as Arielle's sheer innocence during the whole thing.

Arielle began trying to beat back the flames with the wooden spoon, but to no avail. Salem took charge. She grabbed the fire extinguisher off the wall and was about to put out the flame, when she witnessed something extraordinary. Arielle pointed her finger at the skillet, gesturing towards the sink whereupon the skillet—as if obeying orders, lifted into the air and floated across the room to the sink and lowered itself into the basin. With a mid-air flick of Arielle's wrist, the water faucet cut itself on, dousing the flaming chicken. As for the grease fire taking place on the stovetop, Arielle simply blew a small puff of air from her lips in the direction of the fire, and it evaporated. She turned back around to Salem's astonished expression.

"What?" Arielle asked, "Can't you do that?"

...

She hadn't been aware she had put on one of David's shirts—the red tee with his team number from office softball league. She crawled into bed beside Arielle, who was sitting Indian style as if she were at a slumber party.

"You sure you don't mind me sleeping with you?" Arielle asked. "The couch is totally fine."

"No," Salem smiled. "I don't want to sleep in here alone. Last night was really difficult."

They were quiet for a while as Salem tied her hair in a ponytail and Arielle picked lint from the toes of her knit socks. Salem broke the silence, perhaps in need of words to fill the stillness of that room.

"Thanks for driving up here," she told Arielle. She wanted to say more but couldn't find the words. The feelings were all present, but the words would not come. Looking into the eyes of this girl, this sister she had never known, the dam broke inside her releasing a torrent of complicated tears. Tears for David. Tears for Michael. Tears for a father's presence that she was denied growing up. There was so much to feel. Too much to sort through now. Salem didn't try. She simply let it flow and hoped she'd feel the better for it after.

Arielle was not experienced in grief counseling nor was she particularly adept at comforting anyone other than herself. Yet, instinctively, she knew that the best thing she could possibly do for Salem was to simply sit and hold her. It was enough. Salem snuggled in under the safety and sympathy of Arielle's arms and remained there until the pain began to loosen its grip and let her breathe again. As the pain began to ease, Salem's thoughts drifted for some reason back to the image of Arielle attempting to fix dinner. A sound rang out from within Salem which surprised them both, laughter.

"What's so funny?"

Salem rubbed her tear-stained face with the palm of her hand and snorted, "You frying chicken. I can't stop thinking about it."

Arielle laughed now too as she looked into her sister's eyes, red and irritated from crying. "Well, I may not have been able to feed you, but at least I made you laugh."

Salem sighed and rubbed her eyes again. She exhaled a deep breath as if expelling away the feelings of sadness she'd allowed herself to succumb to. "Thanks for making me laugh. Thanks for taking what would have been an unbearable time and making me remember there are still some good times to be had. New memories to make. Last night here alone was very painful."

"My pleasure," Arielle grinned. "I'm having fun. I know that sounds horrible with all you are going through...but I've never had a real sister before. Sorry I almost burned down your house."

"That was the funniest thing I have seen in a long time," Salem said, slapping her knees. "And I grew up with ditzy cousins, so I've seen a lot of funny things."

"You're lucky. Oleander is not a very fun place to grow up."

Salem now felt sorry for Arielle. How the girl had managed to retain such a warm personality was remarkable. The few minutes Salem spent in the presence of Atheidrelle and Cassandra Obreiggon were miserable. She imagined Arielle's life could not have been very pleasant. Salem may have been knee deep in grief but at least she had known love. She'd known family and the joy having people who love you in your life can bring. Arielle was a stranger to these things.

"When you moved that pan, and took out that fire," Salem said, changing the subject, "that was remarkable. I can do *some* things. Freeze time, move objects. But it requires major concentration or a high emotional state. You just blew out a fire like it was nothing."

"My Dad—excuse me, *our* Dad, is full-blooded by six generations. My Mother even longer. I guess using the power comes easier for me. But it is a very simple concept. You don't really have to think about it that much."

"It takes a lot for me to focus on an object to get it to move."

"Oh!" Arielle exclaimed. "That's the problem! You're doing it the really hard way. Don't worry about the object, just focus on the air under it."

Arielle settled against the headboard and pointed to a picture of David on the dresser across the room. It lifted into the air and floated towards the bed, hovering before Salem.

"Touch the air underneath," Arielle instructed.

Salem ran her hand beneath the floating frame. "Wind?" she asked. "I can feel a current."

"That's right," Arielle said confidently. "Air is everywhere. And so easy to manipulate. Objects are too complicated, and you have to zone in on every one. But if you master moving air around, then that's all you have to think about. No matter how heavy the object, just focus on the microscopic spaces between the object and what it's touching—the empty space—the air. Then once you have zoned into that, expand it, direct more air from other places around the room to merge into it, and soon you have a current strong enough to move anything. There's always air."

"That's brilliant."

Arielle took the picture out of the air and held in her hands. "Your husband was very handsome."

"He always was," reflected Salem. "I keep expecting him to walk in. Realizing he's never going to walk in again…" Her voice trailed off.

Arielle set the picture aside and clutched Salem's hand.

"I still haven't been into my son's room yet."

"When you're ready," Arielle whispered. "You'll be able to."

Salem looked at Arielle sitting beside her. She felt safe with her around. Stable. Not so alone after all. It was a different kind of companionship than if a Blanchard had been with her. As much as she loved the family, they were not very distracting. They pitied her too much. Or they worried too much when she appeared too strong. But Arielle was a stranger, yet didn't seem like one at all. Salem felt free to feel or not feel whatever came to her at the time.

"Arielle, will you stay a while?" Salem asked. "I think I'd like you here with me when this all sinks in. Right now, it is still so surreal. But I have a feeling once the surreal wears off and the real takes hold, I'm going to need you."

"I'll stay as long as you want," Arielle replied. "Do you want to talk about how you feel tonight?"

"Not, now. Let's just get some sleep. Tomorrow I'll take you in to see my office, and you can meet my boss."

The baby. He's crying. "David, wake up," Salem moaned groggily. She pushed the body beside her. "It's your turn." *He always does this, pretends to be asleep so he doesn't have to get up.* She stood and shuffled through the bedroom and down the hall. "I'm coming, baby. Mama's coming."

She opened the door to Michael's room and went over to his crib. She placed her hand down to grab him. He wasn't there. "Michael?!" she screamed. "David where's Michael?!" And she remembered. *But that was just a dream, wasn't it?* Footsteps sounded behind her in the doorway. "David?"

Salem collapsed to the floor in tears, anguish sweeping across the nursery like an ocean wave. Arielle rushed to her side and held her in her arms. Salem's guttural cries softened into soft sobbing after a few minutes. Arielle said nothing, simply held her until the crying subsided. Then silence fell. A long silence, probably much needed, giving Salem time to process. Time to let some of her sorrow go.

"This room has Michael's scent everywhere," Salem finally whispered. "And David, he's in this shirt. He's on the couch. In the bed. They are everywhere. What will it be like when I can't smell them anymore?"

"I don't know, honey."

"Every day that comes is going to steal away a little bit more of their scent from me. My Aunt Demitra said something years ago after my Uncle Larry died. She called it *the hollow moment*. It is the moment when the last tangible thing is gone and all you have are memories and photos. Their favorite drink isn't in the fridge anymore. The last post-it they wrote on has been tossed out or put away. The last bottle of shaving cream they'd used is used up. When everything in the house is new since they left."

"Nothing has to go, Salem," Arielle said. "You don't have to toss out anything you don't want to."

"But to hold onto everything would be standing still…Fireflies and cigarettes."

"What does that mean?" asked Arielle.

"Nothing. Just advice from another aunt."

CHAPTER THIRTY-FIVE

Beryl Gets Suspicious

Daihmler County Hospital was hectic on a usual day, but Beryl was finding today doubly so. Dr. Hawkins had come down with the flu, leaving his patients in her charge. Her morning was extremely busy with the addition of his patients added to her own, but she was checking everyone off the list in decent fashion. Walking into the room of the next patient on Hawkin's list, she thought she might still be finished by her usual time that afternoon.

"Good morning Miss Leighton," she said approaching the bedside of the young woman. "I'm Dr. Blanchard. Dr. Hawkins is sick, so I'll be looking out for you today."

The young woman had been turned towards the window. As she turned to face Beryl, Beryl was not prepared for what she saw. Yes, the chart had informed her about Lana Leighton's condition, but it hadn't prepared her for Miss Leighton's appearance. *She must have been very pretty once,* Beryl lamented silently to herself. The gauze covering her neck and most of her face was becoming discolored and did little to hide the gashes across her face and left eye. Her hair had a very noticeable bald patch with scabbing where it looked as if some of her hair had been ripped out—perhaps in struggle.

"Who did this to you?" Beryl asked.

"I was attacked," Lana answered. "The police think it was the killer they're all looking for."

"You are very lucky to be alive," Beryl noted. She flipped through the chart and read more details of her injuries. "Says here your neck was partially torn open. Required a lot of stitching. One more centimeter and you might have bled to death."

"I know," the patient sighed.

"How is your pain level today?"

"Bad," the girl replied. "But I don't care about that. No one will tell me the truth about how I am going to look. Doctor, you're a woman. You know what I mean. These men just tell me to be patient. That there's no way to know until I start healing. But Doctor, please tell me—will I look horrible?"

She could not have been more than 21 or 22, Beryl observed. Her whole life was ahead of her and to go through that life disfigured, or with such noticeable scars across her face...Beryl knew she had to help if she could.

"I'm going to freshen up your bandages for you, Miss Leighton. It might burn a little."

Beryl very carefully unwrapped the gauze from the wound. Dried blood made the layers cling a little to each other. As she removed the final layer of gauze and pulled away the cotton padding from the incision, Beryl saw beads of blood still secreting from the wound. She placed her hands on the girl's neck, trying to summon that familiar surge of power she had used time and time again to heal countless people. Nothing happened. Beryl tried again, forcing her mind to rid itself of all thoughts except the healing of this girl. Still nothing. Surely, she hadn't lost the power to heal. That wasn't possible. Blanchard's kept their gifts all their lives. The only way to lose one's powers were if the Council bound them. Still, nothing was happening. No sign of Beryl's abilities. She took fresh gauze from the rolling table nearby and redressed the wound, disposing of the old wrappings in the plastic bin mounted to the wall.

"I'll be back to check on you a little while later," Beryl said softly.

To be certain she had not lost her skills, Beryl ducked into the room of another patient. It was not a patient of her own, or of Dr. Hawkins. The patient was a Mr. Wyatt. Beryl had heard the nurses discussing him yesterday. He had been in a serious car accident earlier in the week. Dr. Gillis noted paralysis in his chart.

Mr. Wyatt was on a good deal of pain killers and was fast asleep as Beryl crept in. She quickly placed her hands on his legs and summoned the power she was not able to find for her last patient. She visualized Mr. Wyatt walking again, slowly at first—taking baby steps on his own with a walker. Then she pictured him moving without aid but taking things slowly. She envisioned him climbing stairs. The power was surging and by the time she'd finished she had him jogging marathons in her mind. His legs were healing. The paralysis would not be permanent. She felt so pleased for him. But it arose again the question as to why she could not heal that poor girl down the hall.

...

"...And you say her throat was slashed?" Demitra asked her daughter late that night when they were having iced tea on the porch, just the two of them.

"Yes," Beryl replied. "And for some reason I couldn't heal her wounds. I know that sometimes with outsiders it's more difficult because I have to put a slow heal in place, which is trickier. They can't very well just have no wounds anymore the next day or the hospital would start to ask questions. But when I couldn't manage a slow healing for Lana Leighton, I got desperate and even tried to do an instant and complete heal on her—which is very easy for me to do because it requires little thought. But even that didn't work."

"Curious."

"I've never had this happen before," Beryl said. "Can we sometimes not be able to heal others?"

"I don't know Beryl," Demitra told her eldest. "You are the only member of the family with that power. No Blanchard has held that particular ability since your great grandfather's brother." Demitra sipped her tea. Tiny sweat droplets from the glass fell onto her knee. She wiped them off with her sleeve. "And you say there were gashes in her face?"

"Yes."

"Did they look like claw marks?"

"I guess they kinda did," Beryl reflected. "Three of them right in a row."

"I want to confide something into you, Beryl," her mother told her. "Charlie Bennet asked for my help with this serial killer case in town. I went to a crime scene and had a vision. I think it's a werewolf."

"A werewolf!" Beryl cried. "Mother, you can't be serious."

"Beryl Marie Blanchard!" Demitra exclaimed. "Are you going to sit there like a little hypocrite and tell me there is no such thing after we've just been discussing your power to miraculously heal people?"

"But Mother, a werewolf? That's a bit hard to swallow."

"Is it? In this family?"

"Okay. Okay. I believe you," Beryl acquiesced. "Did you tell Mr. Bennet?"

"Yes," Demitra said. "He is barely tolerating my notion. But I researched and discovered this killer has a long path stretching from the Carolinas to Daihmler. Perhaps this is why you can't cure that girl."

"Why should that matter?"

"Because," Demitra noted, "*whoever is bitten by a werewolf and lives, becomes a werewolf himself.*"

Beryl looked confused. "Mother, that's just in movies."

"It's also the truth."

Their talk was suddenly disrupted by the startling presence of Patric standing on the top step of the porch. He smiled at them and gave a short laugh.

"Sorry to interrupt what appears to be a deep conversation, but I am here to collect Fable. We have a date tonight."

"At this hour?" Demitra remarked. "It's past nine."

"We have a date regardless," he replied.

Demitra excused herself inside to go alert Fable that her date was there. She felt apprehensive leaving Beryl alone on the porch with him. She felt even more disturbed that her other daughter had plans to leave with him, but she knew from experience there was no way to stop Fable from doing anything Fable wanted to do.

Outside on the porch, Beryl made an effort toward conversation with Patric. "So where are you two off to tonight?"

Patric ignored her question, or perhaps he hadn't heard it. He had stepped back down the porch steps a few treads and was staring up at the house towards a window on a higher floor. Beryl tried again to make small talk.

"Don't worry. She'll be right down. That's not her room up there, anyway. Her room faces the back."

"I know which room belongs to your sister," Patric said rather rudely, still holding his gaze above.

"You know, a kind word every so often could take you far in this world," Beryl said, unable to excuse his continual rudeness.

He brought his gaze back down to meet her own and replied, "I've traveled far enough for one lifetime."

Fable sprang through the door, slamming the screen and causing Beryl to jump. "Hey cutie!" she cried to her date. "Ready to go?"

"Yes."

"See ya, sis!" Fable waved as they climbed into her car to leave.

They were already down the gravel driveway headed to the main road when Beryl felt a terrible urge to go after them, to stop her sister from leaving. On top of that, Lana Leighton's battered face came across her mind. Beryl wondered why Patric perplexed her so. Why did she have a distinct dislike for him? True, he had no manners it seemed, but Fable had dated worse for sure. Something else was going on with Patric. The word *dastardly* popped into her mind. Something about the way he was staring up to the house unnerved her. He looked as if he had been planning something. Maybe just a secret liaison with Fable in the night, but he'd said he already knew Fable's room was in back. Yasmine's room was the only window that looked out over the roof of the porch.

Then Beryl's mind drifted away from Patric and the window and moved toward another puzzling question. Where was Patric's car? They left in Fable's. How had he come to Blanchard House? On foot? She and her mother certainly had not heard a car pull up, otherwise they wouldn't have been so startled from their conversation. Had Patric walked to Blanchard House?

CHAPTER THIRTY-SIX

Artemis' Birthday

Zookeepers have better luck keeping their animals quiet than Olympia and Demitra had in keeping their brood from snickering at the amount of candles Fable was placing on the cake. The first ones lit were already burning down to the middle before Fable ever got the last few lighted.

"We don't want to make her cry," Seth commented. "Just put a candle in the middle. She knows she's old."

"Hey!" snapped Demitra. "She's only three years older than I am."

"Yeah, well, you're old too," Seth teased.

"Ssshh. She's coming!" Olympia cautioned.

Artemis came down the stairs, ready to begin her daily routine of breakfast for her family when everyone screamed, "Surprise!!!!" She was startled at first, then deeply touched. Her family were all gathered in the kitchen with an enormous cake which appeared to be lit by way more candles than years she'd lived.

"I don't believe it!" she exclaimed. "This is so sweet. But my birthday isn't even until the 14th. Leave it to you all to surprise me early."

"Arty," bellowed a tardy Zelda now coming through the back door. "It's the 14th!"

"Well, I guess it is," Artemis grinned. "I should have known something was up when I didn't hear Fable and Yasmine fighting over the bathroom. Oh everyone, thank you so much!"

Yasmine gave her aunt a big hug and a kiss. "Happy Birthday, Aunt Artemis! And guess what? I made breakfast."

"Oh," Artemis smiled. "That should be quite...bad for our health."

"Come on," Yasmine cried. "I think I did pretty well."

"Don't listen to her," Seth laughed. "She whisked up the shells with the eggs and burned all the toast."

"Laugh if you want," Beryl advised, "but remember you're marrying that girl. I guess you'll stop making fun of her when she's cooking your breakfast every morning."

"Who says I'm cooking that fool breakfast after we get married?" Yasmine guffawed. "I work. He doesn't. He will be making me breakfast."

"I go to school," Seth retorted. "I have college classes all day."

"You do?" Yasmine laughed. "When do you go to them?"

"I don't have to go to them." Seth said. "I have online classes. Besides, Aunt Artemis will still be here to make us breakfast."

Demitra beamed. She had been waiting for this moment. The moment of surprise to pay her sister back for all the love and generosity she had shown them all over the years.

"That is where you are wrong, Seth Blanchard!" she cried. "My sister will not be making our breakfasts, or our lunches, or our dinners anymore after today!"

"Are ya'll throwing me out on my birthday or something?" Artemis asked.

"In a way," Demitra smiled. "Happy Birthday, Sis!"

Demitra handed an envelope to her sister. Artemis opened it hesitantly. Her eyes scanned the pages of the document, her mouth dropping open as she read. She couldn't believe what she held in her hands.

"What is it?" Fable asked. "Grandmother, what have you and Mother done?"

"I am just as ignorant of this as the rest of you," Olympia admitted. "Demitra, what is that?"

Artemis' eyes welled up in tears and gratitude. "Dee, you didn't? I can't believe this. Is this for real?" Artemis looked at the document again.

Suddenly all of her childhood dreams rushed back to her. Years she had spent concocting recipes from scratch in the kitchen and forcing her sisters to sit at the kitchen table as her guinea pigs. So many awful failures mixed with a lot of triumphant successes. Artemis knew she'd wanted to be a chef from age twelve and not becoming one was one of the bigger disappointments of her life. Now her sister had handed her the opportunity in a cluster of paperwork. Artemis owned a restaurant. She looked from the document back to her sister, her eyes swelling with humble gratitude.

Demitra walked over to her sister and held out her arms. The two women hugged for a long time, Artemis crying happy tears on Demitra's shoulder. The rest of the family waited, wondering. What had Demitra given her that brought about this much joy?

"It's too extravagant," Artemis said. "I can't accept this."

"The hell you can't!" Demitra cried. "You've taken care of us so many years, given up on your dreams or a life of your own. It's your turn now. I only ask that I eat free."

"What are you two talking about?" Beryl demanded.

"The Cobblestone," Artemis said, showing them the paperwork. "Your mother has bought me The Cobblestone!"

"You're kidding!" Yasmine cried.

"What a terrific idea!" Fable exclaimed. "Aunt Artemis you are the best cook I know!"

"Might have to start going out to eat myself now," Zelda added.

"Tomorrow Artemis starts getting to know her new staff, planning new menus, ordering food and liquor. Your Aunt is going to be a terribly busy lady from now on," Demitra informed the group. "Obviously, I'll help you get started in any way you need, but once you're up and running, this is solely your baby."

Artemis fell into her sister's arms again. "This is just too much. This is the happiest day of my life. Thank you, Dee, thank you!"

Seth stood expressionless for a moment. Then he reached over to the table and lifted a brightly wrapped package and handed over in Artemis' general direction. "Mine's just a blouse."

"Mine's a scarf," Beryl said meekly, following suit.

"Shoes," Fable said.

"Book of the Month Club," Yasmine shrugged.

Demitra laughed. "I guess I really should have gone last."

CHAPTER THIRTY-SEVEN

Jilted Lovers

Vanessa Collins hadn't been sitting very long at the little coffee shop on the corner of Hackberry and Vista, when her coffee date came in and took the seat opposite her. She'd only ever actually seen Jake once or twice before and always in the company of Yasmine Sinclair. It felt strange seeing him without her and it felt equally strange not having Seth with her in his company. When he'd phoned to ask her to meet him, she had a pretty good idea what it was going to be about.

"Yasmine dumped you, I'm assuming?" she said the moment he took a seat in front of her.

"Yes," Jake grimaced. "I have tried to call her, but she's blocked my number. Then I saw on Facebook that she has now marked her status *engaged*."

"She didn't block you on social media?"

"She has now. I sent her a DM after I saw that. She never answered."

"Seth and I broke up too," Vanessa acknowledged. "His status notes the same change. *Engaged*."

Jake began tapping his fingers rapidly, and firmly on the table. The motion began to slightly slosh Vanessa's coffee. She watched his fingers as he bopped them up and down. His nails were in need of a trim, longer than most men's and a little pointy.

"The best thing to do is to just move forward," Vanessa advised. "I'm hurt, too. I actually thought Seth and I might get married down the road."

Tap, tap, tap of the fingers. Jake was agitated. "You never suspected they were messing around on us?"

"Oh, I don't believe for a second they were messing around," Vanessa argued. "In fact, I'm quite sure that it came as a complete surprise to Seth when he realized it was Yasmine he was actually in love with."

Jakes nails dug in and scratched down the tabletop two inches. Vanessa noticed the marks they left in the grain. She glanced up at his eyes. He was furious. Almost crazed. It seemed to her to be an outsized reaction considering he and Yasmine Sinclair had not been that serious.

"Jake," she contemplated, "surely you had signs."

"That my girlfriend was in love with her cousin?!" he roared. Heads at nearby tables turned to see.

"Was she your girlfriend?" Vanessa asked. "I know that Seth and I were exclusive with each other. We've been seeing each other a while. But it was my understanding that you and Yasmine had only recently begun dating."

"She was mine," he growled. "I was hers."

"I see," Vanessa said, feeling a little apprehensive at the animosity brimming from him.

For days she'd been wallowing in her own resentment towards Seth and Yasmine, but now she found herself feeling oddly defensive of them. Almost rooting for them and happy Yasmine had gotten away from this volatile man sitting before her now.

"I know for a fact that Seth and she never at any time behaved inappropriately behind our backs," Vanessa informed him. "I began to suspect Seth held some deeper feelings for Yasmine, and when I finally confronted him about them—you should have seen his face—the thought had never occurred to him until I mentioned it. Then it all became quite clear in his mind. He did have feelings for her. Feelings he had never allowed himself to admit. I don't think he meant to hurt me or lead me on."

"Why didn't you fight for him?" Jake challenged. "Sounds to me like you just gave up."

"Fight for what? A man who prefers to be with someone else?" Vanessa scoffed. "I am not the kind of woman who hangs around waiting for a man to choose me. You either want me or you don't. I am worth more than that."

"But you love him."

"So what?" Vanessa said. "I love me more. No man on earth is worth debasing myself for by begging him to stay. Love isn't enough, not if it isn't returned. That sort of love is worse than never feeling anything for anyone at all."

Vanessa was more than a little surprised at Jake's mindframe. Was he really so insecure—or controlling—that he'd prefer Yasmine stay with him even knowing she wanted someone else? The look in his eyes was disturbing. A refusal to accept defeat lurked there, and it frightened her. Vanessa had more pride than that. Yes, she loved Seth, but all it took for her to move on was knowing Seth didn't love her back.

"It was clear that Seth wants Yasmine, so I set him free. I hope he and Yasmine find happiness. I intend to find some myself."

"I'm not that forgiving." Jake snapped. "I offered myself to her, and she threw it back in my face. I didn't know why at first, but now I do. She was just stringing me along waiting for Seth."

"I don't know Yasmine well," Vanessa offered, "but she doesn't seem that manipulative."

"You don't know what she is!" he bellowed. "She's that and a lot more. Do you know that she came on to me the other night? Hot and heavy. Then playing some sick twisted game, she rejected me. Even hurt me physically. She's not going to get away with this either."

Vanessa was flabbergasted. Jake was infuriated and it was clear that he felt he had reason to be. And maybe Yasmine Sinclair was all the things he was saying, but Vanessa had never held that impression of her. But what she *was* getting, was the impression that Jake was unstable. She wanted to leave. She stood up and placed a couple of dollars on the table for the tip.

"I hope you find some peace with this and let it go," Vanessa advised. "Seething over it isn't healthy. And it will not change anything. Go out with friends. Spend time with family. I promise you'll feel better."

Jake glared up from the table into Vanessa's eyes and replied, "I have no friends or family here. Yasmine was the first person I met here."

Vanessa wanted to leave, but curiosity got the better of her. She wanted to know something. "What brought you to Daihmler then? If it wasn't family, or friends. Work?"

"I moved here with a girlfriend. We broke up. Then I met Yasmine."

"Any chance of reuniting with your ex?"

"I don't think so. The last time Lana and I got together it didn't end well."

CHAPTER THIRTY-EIGHT

Dial "P" For Psychic

Readings were an everyday activity for Madame Zelda. She spent most of her days going from one house to another, giving detailed descriptions of past, present, and future events to her clients. Her clientele was as varied as imaginable; from the mayor's wife and her suspicions of his adultery, to the struggling single mother of four living in Tuscaloosa's Deer Lick trailer park who wondered when she'd ever get her head above water financially. Zelda always told people the unglorified truth, even when it was dreary, which was exactly the reason people kept coming to her for guidance. Zelda learned one great truth from her many years as a professional psychic— Everyone has a challenging life, according to them, and everyone is looking for a magical fix for it.

As Zelda was getting ready to go to bed after another long day of readings, she went through her usual routine to clear her mind of other people's problems. It was a taxing endeavor to see the dark places of other people's lives. Joys were few and agonies always outweighed them. It stood to reason—no one seeks advice when they are happy. Cleansing her clients' woes from her mind took some doing if she ever wanted to sleep. Chamomile tea, a chapter from a trashy novel, and a little Michael Buble on Spotify. The latter always worked—once Seth had shown her how to use the app. Zelda was just winding down when a knock came at the door.

She was more than a little surprised to find Beryl Blanchard standing on her doorstep seeking information. Beryl was a witch, but a scientist as well. Facts and faith are usually bitter enemies, and Beryl had the difficult burden of having to reconcile both because she belonged to both worlds. Zelda liked to call people such as Beryl, "tritches" because some witches were never satisfied with *believing*, they wanted *truth*. The quest for logical explanations for things that could not be explained was a hard road to wander. Zelda always felt like the world is better when left a mystery.

Zelda led Beryl to the living room where they both sat down at the little round table where Zelda performed at-home readings for clients who came to her rather than the other way around.

"What brings you here, Beryl?"

"I need your help. I couldn't talk to you at the house yesterday morning with everyone around. Then tonight, I decided to just come to you."

"Well, you know I'll do anythin' I can to help you. What's it all about?" Zelda asked.

Beryl hesitated before speaking. Zelda could see how difficult it was for someone like Beryl to bring herself to someone like Zelda for assistance. The Beryl Blanchards of the world rarely asked for help and almost never asked for guidance. "I need you to try and see Fable's future for me," Beryl requested. "Or her present."

"I don't think I'm a'followin' you, Beryl."

"You see, Fable is seeing this man we know absolutely nothing about."

"Ain't she always?" Zelda laughed. "You know I love me some Fable, but she is kind of a tramp. You ain't ever meddled in her life before. Why you doin' it now?"

"There is something very wrong about this one," Beryl confessed. "Mother feels it too, and you know Mother is never wrong about her feelings."

"Why don't *your momma* try to look into Fable's head or this guy's?"

"She has tried. He is a steel trap. And you know Mother can't see the future, just the past and the here and now. Zelda, you are the strongest psychic witch I know. I've come to you for some peace of mind."

Zelda rose up a little in her chair, puffing her chest. It wasn't everyday she got such a compliment from the most reasonable and humorless Blanchard. She patted Beryl's hand and nodded. She settled herself comfortably in her chair and dimmed the overhead lights with a switch attached to the top of her table. She closed her eyes to begin, but quickly opened them and raised a brow towards Beryl.

"You know, when I open up and do my visions, I don't just see what you come here for. I see it all. My clients' secrets all pour into my stream. Lying, cheating... kinky stuff too. If I open the wavelength..."

"I understand," Beryl exhaled. "I have nothing to hide. No kinky secrets. Wish I did."

"Then let's start," Zelda said.

Beryl reached into her purse and removed a hairbrush. "This is Fable's. I swiped it from her bathroom. I didn't know if you needed something physical."

Zelda withdrew a deck of tarot cards from a drawer under the table and began shuffling them. "These cards don't really do nothing. But my clients seem to appreciate the theater of it. I've shuffled and laid these things out for so many years during readings, I just tend to do better if I'm fiddling with them."

The telephone rang.

"Excuse me," Zelda said exacerbated as she grabbed the phone from a nearby chair. "That'll be Melinda. She always calls before bed."

Beryl listened to the short exchange from Zelda's end. "Hello? Hey. I'm about to do a readin, so I can't talk…I know its late…special customer…hurry up and tell me quick then…No, that's a dumb idea…I don't care if Hanley Motors is looking for a girl to do their TV commercials; they ain't gone hire you. You ain't no girl no more…Melinda, don't nobody wanna see you selling Honda's on TV…well, go try out for it if you want to, but you ain't near young enough to breakout in television anymore…talk to you in the morning…Bye."

"You know you could try being a little more encouraging to her," Beryl remarked as Zelda returned her attention back to the reading.

"I guess," Zelda replied. "I tried back in the day. But I just never could take to her. When she was born and the doc put her in my arms, I looked at her face and thought *Crap. Nine months of back aches and vomit and this is the best I could do!*"

Zelda zoned back in for the reading. Beryl observed her taking deep breaths while closing her eyes in concentration as she tried to enter a trance—and she looked like someone trying to enter a trance--or use the bathroom. Beryl wasn't sure which might happen first. She wanted to laugh at how ridiculous the faces the old woman was making were, but she made sure not to. She respected the fact that Zelda, no matter how ridiculous she looked, held great power. Real power. Besides, Zelda's farcical mannerisms and sense of style were one of the things that endeared her to people. She was loud and boisterous, yet also genuinely kind—except when it came to her daughters.

Watching Zelda's theatrical attempt at trancing made Beryl compare her own mother's psychic abilities. Her mother never made such a show of her powers, but then again visions *happened* to Demitra; Zelda's talents lay in the fact that she could *will* her visions whenever she pleased—something Demitra could occasionally do but had yet to master.

"I see a man," Zelda began to speak. "A grim man. He walks with Fable. He is slowly seducing her."

"His intentions?" Beryl asked. "Does he care about her?"

Zelda strained her face as she searched for an answer. "I see great love in him."

Beryl's shoulders dropped slightly as she released a breath she hadn't realized she'd been holding. Perhaps everything was all right. "So, I was wrong to be worried."

"Wait!" Zelda shuddered against the chair, her hands scattering a few of the cards she'd yet to begin laying out on the table. "Mother of Hera, I see blood! He has blood on his hands."

"Blood?" Beryl cried, the tension returning. "Fable's blood?"

"Blood that nourishes. Blood that feeds. Blood is the nectar he craves."

"Is he a vampire?" Beryl asked. "Is he a werewolf?" Suddenly she thought of Lana Leighton with her clawed face and torn neck. Lana, whom she could not heal.

"There are many blanks," Zelda continued. "He has many blank spots in his field. As if he doesn't exist at moments. I need to focus harder. I see his eyes. So black, those eyes. No!" Zelda screamed. She clutched the table with both hands, her eyes still pressed firmly shut.

"Zelda, what is it?!"

"He's looking back," Zelda gasped. "He's looking at us. He knows what we're doing. He can see us too! He knows I'm in his mind." She opened her eyes frantically. She looked afraid, truly afraid. Beryl had never seen Zelda afraid of anything. "What door have we opened?"

"I don't understand!" Beryl cried.

Zelda grabbed Beryl's arms across the table and shook them. "He's coming to get us Beryl! And he's angry."

"Patric?"

"Whatever I saw is not human. And he now knows exactly where we are."

Beryl grew frightened, but reason stepped in and reminded her how impossible all this was. There was no way he could have seen Zelda reading his mind. No way he could possibly know where Zelda lived.

"We have to do something!" Zelda wailed.

"Hold on Zelda, there is no way he could possibly—"

"Beryl, I am telling you this man is not human. And he's on his way here now. He rides the night like a train, and he's coming to kill us."

Beryl was beginning to believe her. Beginning to become hysterical herself. She looked around the room. Windows all over, flimsy front door. No real place to hide.

"Can you stop him, Zelda?"

"No," the old lady grinned. "But you can. Freeze time! Give us the chance to get away before he gets here."

"I can't freeze time. That's Salem!"

"Then we're fucked."

CHAPTER THIRTY-NINE

Patric's Hasty Departure

The river was tranquil and delicate at night. It was calm enough to mistaken for a lengthy curving mirror, only tiny ripples telling otherwise. Fable always loved coming down to the river at night. In high school she and her friends would camp here. Nights full of alcohol and teenage rebellion. In college, she often studied here along the riverbanks between classes. There was something about the Black Warrior River that relaxed her. She could vaguely recall her father taking her and Beryl there when they were young. He'd told her once how the river had gotten its name. Something about why the Indian tribes that predated Alabama had named it that. She couldn't remember the story now. She wanted to because she thought Patric might enjoy the tale. She should have written it down long ago with the other memories of her father. Then again, if she really wanted to know that much, she could have pulled out her phone and Googled it. But with Patric sitting behind her with his legs twined comfortably around her own, she didn't feel much like digging for her phone. She listened to the sound of his heart against her ear as she laid against his chest. Like an excited animal.

"It's funny," she said. "I feel so comfortable with you, even though we haven't gotten to know each other that well yet."

"I know all I need to know about you," he replied. "I know you can charm the beasts and that your last name is Blanchard. I know that you are the most beautiful girl I've ever seen."

"But I want to know more about you," she said.

"Why is that important?" he asked.

"Because I like you."

He laughed, it was a kind of private laugh, like a joke he was the only one in on. "You strike me as the type to like anyone who shows you a little attention."

Fable bristled. "What does that mean?"

He licked her neck with his tongue, an odd thing to do, but she liked it a little. "Just that you remind me of a small cub that only wants to be nestled and cared for."

"Everyone craves affection," she retorted. "You do, too. Why else would you be sitting here like this with me?"

"You tell me."

Fable looked up at him and smiled, "Because you like me, too. You act gruff and brooding, but there is a heart inside there. I can feel it. It pulls at me."

"I thought it was my raw animal sexiness that drew you to me."

"That, too," she laughed. "You are sort of like a lion."

"And you'll be my lioness, I suppose," Patric replied.

"Why not?" she said. "What else would you call me?"

"A playful little appetizer," he grinned.

"Very funny. You try to act tough, but I know you care about me."

"Perhaps I do," Patric replied. "But I'm a long way from home and you are a tempting distraction."

Fable turned around so that she could see his face better in the moonlight. Through the trees the bright orb in the sky lit his face in blue and gray. "You came all this way to be with your sister," she began. "And now you've found me. I'd call that a bonus, not a distraction. Maybe Fate was leading you all this way to find *me* actually."

"Maybe so," he smirked. "Maybe Fate led me to Daihmler to find myself a Blanchard."

The way he said *a Blanchard*, instead of saying her specifically, struck a chord inside her, but she suppressed it. It was just an odd choice of words, nothing more. That was the thing about Patric, she was never quite able to tell when they were playfully joking or when he meant something altogether different. She didn't let it bother her too much. They were still in the getting-to-know-you phase of this very new relationship. Time would iron out the details and confusing parts.

"You know, I still haven't met your sister yet," she said. "Tell me about her. When can we get together?"

Patric did not respond. It took Fable a minute to realize he had grown stone still, his eyes focused off somewhere in the distance of the river water, yet also looking at nothing at all.

"Patric? You okay?"

He jerked upright rapidly.

"What's wrong?"

"I must go."

"Why?" she exclaimed. "Did I say something wrong?"

"No," he said. "I am terribly sorry, Fable. There is just something I must attend to."

He stood up from the bank, almost pushing her to the ground doing so. She got up herself and dusted off her pants. He was beginning to walk away, but she called out for him to wait.

"I'll drive you."

Patric refused. "I'll call a car. I must go now. I will see you tomorrow night, at seven. I'll pick you up at your home."

He was gone as quickly as the words left his mouth, disappearing through a cluster of trees and brambling shrubbery. She wanted to follow him but didn't. There were more important things to consider. Suddenly Fable began questioning herself. Questioning why it was that she was so attracted to this man. This wasn't the first time he'd been rude—dismissive. She dated other guys in that past that hadn't treated her well, but Patric seemed even more off-putting than they had been. And she'd reached her limit with those men and ended things. She had only known Patric a short time, so why was she putting up with his behavior and not sending him packing? She knew why. Because there was something about him that drew her in. A passion inside her no other man had ever awakened. Was this why women remain in abusive relationships? Because they are so pathetically attracted to a man that they will subject themselves to constant humiliation? Fable had always thought so little of those women. Women who would keep going back for more lies, more cheating, more abuse and allow their men to continue to exploit their love were not worth the time in feeling sorry for. They were a joke. To allow themselves one degradation after another was pathetic. But now she recognized she was becoming one of them. She understood them now. She didn't like the idea. She did not like the fact that she could find justification for demeaning herself. No man was worth that.

CHAPTER FORTY

Don't Open the Door

Fear crawled up the backs of Beryl and Zelda, clutching at their throats so hard they could not swallow from the fear. Something ferocious was coming for them, and Beryl's skeptical mind was going to have to give a little and allow her witch's instincts to prevail if she were going to survive this night.

"What do we do, Zelda?"

"My book!" Zelda cried as if salvation had sprung to mind. Rushing over to a tall bookcase, she withdrew a weathered, leather bound volume from the shelf and brought over to Beryl. "These are my mother's old spells. There's one in here to protect your home."

"We haven't time for that!" Beryl exclaimed. "We have to get out of here, now."

"I'm afraid this book is all we do have time for, Beryl. We can't go out that door. He's too fast, and we ain't got time to get anywhere."

Zelda opened the book and flung through the many pages, almost tearing some of them as she went. Moments later, she found what she was hoping for. It was a spell titled, *Home Shielding*. Holding the book open so that they could both read aloud, they simultaneously recited the words written in old handwriting on the page.

"Home of brick
Home of wood,
Evil roams
Where goodness should.
Home of love
Home of light,
Shield this house
From evil's might."

Beryl thought it seemed like such a silly spell—nothing more than a badly-worded poem. Yet it must have carried great power with it because she could have sworn the house tremored after the incantation.

"Is that it?" she asked Zelda. "That's all we do?"

"Dammit, Beryl!" Zelda exclaimed, offended. "My momma was just like your Aunt Nacaria. If she wrote a spell, it worked. Didn't need nuthin' else."

Suddenly the door shook!

Something began banging on the other side, banging violently. Beryl feared the door might bang right off its hinges. They clutched each other, both pairs of their eyes fixed, unblinking, to the front door now shaking furiously. For Beryl, it was as if the walls and furniture faded into some distant background leaving only the door in the room. Even the color of the foam green carpet melted away into nothingness as the door struggled to hold itself in place.

"It'll unhinge from the frame," Beryl said.

"No, it won't. We cast the spell. It'll hold."

"How good a witch was your mother?" Beryl asked.

"I guess we're gonna find out."

Almost paralyzed with terror, Beryl held onto Zelda's arm for assurance and denied her burning eyes a soothing blink. She thought to herself, *now I know what real fear is*. No longer was fear just something on a movie screen, or something in the faces of patients' families unsure their loved one would survive. Beryl understood now that fear is thick and blanketing and when experienced, crippling.

The door began a series of rests followed by another onslaught of bangs and shakes. The force so strong it seemed to be bending the door inward as if the wood were somehow now flexible. The women wanted to scream but didn't. Screaming wouldn't help, but that wasn't the reason. They were simply too scared to scream. At once the shaking stopped as a silence fell over the house. The soundlessness was not comforting. It did not signal victory. It signaled the anticipation of something else they were not ready for.

"It's not over, is it?" Beryl whispered.

"I'm not sure."

Beryl pulled free of the mental protection their closeness offered and walked slowly towards the front window. She knew she must look outside. She would be able to see if he were still at the door if she could just bring herself to look outside. Terror had all but crippled her. To part those drapes only to find some menacing stare glaring back at her would send her right over the edge.

"I am a witch. I fear nothing," she repeated over and over to herself as she reached out for the curtain fabric. "I fear nothing."

Slowly she watched her own shaky hand touch the fabric and begin to pull the drape aside. The very touch of the material sent chills down her spine. Her breaths were labored and her muscles tense. Her entire body felt constricted. With one brave swoop, she jerked the curtains back and peered into the blackness.

"Can you see anything?" Zelda whispered from a few feet behind her.

"Nothing. I think he's gone."

She pressed her forehead to the glass in attempts to see outside without the glare of the room's light. The cold pane against her forehead felt good. Without warning a pair of eyes rose from underneath the windowsill to meet her own. She opened her mouth to scream but screams still would not come. It felt like an eternity, standing locked eye to eye with those glaring red eyes. She couldn't move. She wanted to but couldn't. It was as though she were being held in place by her own body. Shock. She observed the creature's breath fogging the glass from the other side. It mesmerized her for a second until the beast let a slow growl emerge from behind those sharp teeth. Before Beryl had completely recognized what the sound was, it raised into a monstrous roar.

She leapt back from the window. Gleaming fangs dripped with saliva behind the glass. She saw the bristly hair along the cheekbones and forehead. She saw the pulsating snout of the monster and his eyes now ablaze like burning coals. He lifted a hairy paw to the glass. His sharp talons made the pane shriek against the razor tips.

"Go away!" Zelda yelled.

The beast roared again. His cry shook the glass and sent Beryl toppling backward into a side table. For a moment as the lamp shattered on the floor, Beryl thought he'd broken through the glass. The room was darker now without the lamp. Being unable to see into the blackness outside the window made their fear multiply. They held each other once more and moved to the center of the room. They couldn't tell if his fiendish eyes were still watching from the window until a high-pitched cry echoed from the chimney.

"He's on the roof!" Zelda shrieked as they now heard the shuffling and scraping above their heads. They sank to the floor in wait.

More wails ensued, and even more noises from above. The sounds of clawing at the shingles and the wood beneath, made them shiver. The loosening shingles sliding over the ones still attached sounded like sandpaper being rubbed over their heads. He was trying to claw his way down on top of them. But he never dropped from the ceiling. Occasionally the scraping above would cease as the front door shook again, then the window--then back to the roof. Beryl and Zelda spoke nothing as the series of attempts to infiltrate the house waged on. None met with success.

"I don't think he can get in," Beryl said eventually. "Looks like your mother was a great witch after all."

The realization provided some comfort, but not much. The clock showed that it was not even midnight yet. It would be an exceedingly long night huddled together, waiting to see if he'd find a way in and if this was going to be their last night on earth.

CHAPTER FORTY-ONE

A Friend at Home

As her car pulled in the driveway, Salem breathed a sigh of relief to have the day behind her. It had been as though it would all never end. Everyone in the firm felt the need to drop by her office to extend their deepest sympathies. She appreciated the sincerity behind it and knew it was all out of genuine affection for her and appreciation of her loss, but what she desired most was to resume normality. Salem needed to drown herself in her work but that was inevitably not possible. Travis had warned her that the office staff would probably not leave her alone very much on her first day back, but assured her "It'll be better tomorrow."

She was relieved to be pulling up in front of her house again—the place she'd been relieved to get away from that morning. Salem grabbed take-out on the way home after receiving a frantic call from Arielle that she had burned dinner again. Salem opened the front door and walked inside. She nearly dropped the take-out containers when she saw the pile of boxes stacked in the living room. Dozens of boxes all labeled either *David* or *Michael* and sealed with box tape.

"Don't get mad," Arielle begged, meeting her at the door. "I went ahead and boxed up their things. But now I'm thinking that might have been wrong. You might have wanted to do that. But I just thought it was too soon for you to deal with, but you also can't keep running into their things, which causes you pain, every time you walk into a room or open a drawer. I'm sorry. I realized after the last box was sealed that this was a huge mistake and I overstepped."

Salem was speechless. She didn't know exactly how she felt about it.

"The boxes written in red ink are things I thought you might want to keep--toys, books, clothes. The ones in blue might be things you want to give to charity--David's suits, old shoes, stuff like that. The ones in black are things I'm not sure what you want to do with. Are you mad?"

"No," Salem muttered. "Just shocked. You have been busy today. I—I'm not sure what I feel. I know I'm not ready to throw anything out yet, but I also am not strong enough to keep seeing their things all around. Thank you for packing it up for me. We'll put everything in the basement and later on, when I'm ready, I can go through the boxes."

"I was so afraid you'd be furious with me."

"No, Arielle," Salem reassured her. "Even if it was presumptuous, it was also thoughtful and well intended."

They watched television while they ate dinner. Salem felt a peace in the house with Arielle there helping to fill the emptiness. And she admitted to herself that Arielle's removal of the painful reminders did do a lot to make the house seem less depressing.

"You're good for me, Arielle," she said, gnawing a rib from the barbeque take-out. "I really think your coming here to visit was exactly what I needed. I'm enjoying getting to know you."

"I love being here," Arielle replied. "I love getting to know my big sister. Cassandra has never made it easy to be close to her. When I saw you that night at Oleander—I can't explain it. I just felt something. As if something I've been waiting for all of my life showed up. I've heard your name a few times when people didn't think I was listening. The mysterious other daughter of Xander Obreiggon. And now here I am, in your house eating out of a carton, watching TV. I'm so happy."

"When are you planning to go back to Charleston?"

"I haven't thought about it," Arielle said. "I suppose in a day or two. But if I'm in the way, or if you think you need some time alone, I can go tomorrow. I'll understand."

Salem looked at the naive girl in front of her. Salem already felt very protective of her. Arielle was so innocent, so understanding, so vulnerable. *My little sister*. She didn't like the idea of her having to live with people that were unkind to her.

"I don't want you to leave."

"Oh, good," Arielle exclaimed. "I was hoping to be able to stay with you for a few days at least. I can go back home this weekend. That'll give us more time to visit, and then I'll be out of your hair, and you can have your privacy back."

Salem gave a frustrated groan. Poor Arielle was so unable to pick up on even the simplest cues. *What must her life have been like?* Always feeling she was in the way, or a burden. Here Salem was attempting to convey that she liked having her around, and Arielle was still under the impression her company was merely being tolerated. *She's probably never in her life been made to feel wanted or important.*

"No, Arielle, I was thinking that I don't want you to leave at all," Salem explained. "I really like having you around. Of course, I know that's selfish on my part. Oleander is your home. There's your father. And surely you have friends in Charleston. But I was thinking, you have never been on your own before. Here you could come and go as you please. And you and I can keep on building a relationship. Would you like to stay with me?"

Arielle was confused. "Do you mean extend my stay? Or are you inviting me to move here permanently?"

"Live here. With me. Your sister."

The bliss on Arielle's face was answer enough, but she still shouted, "Oh, Salem! I would love to! I'll have Daddy send the rest of my clothes. I don't really have anything else. Mother decorates our rooms to her taste so I don't have anything of mine to move."

"Will he mind too much if you move here?"

"He'll be sad without me, but once he hears who I am moving in with he will love the idea!" Arielle beamed. "And I'm sure he will find a way to send me money for expenses until I find a job. Although Mother does control the finances...but he has ways of getting around her when he needs to."

"Even if he can't, don't worry," Salem assured. "I make a decent income and can take care of us both until you find something you want to do." She paused for a moment, wondering about what Arielle said. Then she asked, "How did Atheidrelle manage to get control of your father's money?"

"Oh, the money was always Mother's," Arielle explained. "Daddy owns Oleander. It's been in the Obreiggon family forever. And he has a reasonable inheritance of his own. But the real money is all D'Angelo money. My grandfather, Hugh D'Angelo, had millions. When he died, he left everything to my uncle Thaddeuss and Mother. My Aunt Blackie didn't get a thing."

"Did old Hugh not like his other daughter?" Salem asked.

"He died a few months before I was born, so I don't really know a whole lot about him. My mother and her sister haven't spoken in years. I think there was something peculiar about the way Grandfather died, but no one ever proved anything."

CHAPTER FORTY-TWO

The Coven Intervenes

The scratches and dents in the vinyl siding of Zelda's house stretched all the way around. Hedges underneath windows were trampled, and the front door was so badly damaged it would need replacing. Beryl stood with her on the lawn in the light of day surveying the damage.

"Pack up some things and stay at the house with us for a while," Beryl told her. "You aren't safe here alone. While you pack, I am going to call in sick to the hospital. We have to call an emergency coven meeting."

...

Yasmine was typing contracts when the call came through. After she hung up, she went into Howard's office. He was reading over documents a client had messengered over. She waited a few moments, waiting for that specific expression which would come over his face the moment he had finished the important, uninterruptible parts. Once he made that face, she spoke.

"I'm sorry to do this to you, Howard, but I'm afraid I have to cut out early."

"Anything the matter?"

"I don't know yet. Beryl just called me on her way home. She's calling an emergency family meeting."

"It isn't Olympia, is it?" he said, putting down the documents.

"No, nothing like that. She just said I had to come home immediately."

Howard nodded. "Nothing here that can't wait till tomorrow. But call me if something serious has happened. I'm a junior member of the Blanchards myself, you know!"

THE COVEN INTERVENES

...

By the time Beryl and Zelda reached Blanchard House everyone was assembled in the living room awaiting her explanation. Upon entering, Beryl was bombarded with questions. Zelda took a seat on the sofa beside Olympia.

"Settle down," Beryl began. "We have a lot to handle, and it's very serious. This is so serious in fact that I am asking that no one interrupt me, and I am calling for *vows*."

"Vows?" Artemis cried.

She, along with everyone else knew it had to be very serious indeed. For a witch to call for *vows* meant that only the truth could be spoken. To lie, withhold, or misdirect would mean certain consequences from the Natural Order. A vow was like a temporary verbal spell which, if broken, would rip a witch's powers from her. It was like *binding yourself* if you lied or willingly withheld pertinent information. Witches took vows very seriously.

Beryl went first. *"I vow to speak the truth in every word I speak. I will not mislead, nor will I omit. I pledge my powers stricken if I betray this trust."*

Olympia, right on cue, understanding the severity involved if Beryl made vows, took her own vow next. Glances of confusion and apprehension darted around the room as each member of the coven took their turn making vows. It was unnecessary for Yasmine to make the pledge since she held no physical ability, but she was part of the meeting all the same.

When the last vow was spoken, Seth demanded to know what was going on. Beryl waved his protest away as she said, "Let me speak uninterrupted, please."

"You have the floor," Olympia agreed.

"Mother," Beryl addressed Demitra, sitting with Fable on the second sofa. "Mother, you are currently assisting with the police investigation into the recent murders occurring in Daihmler, aren't you?"

"Yes, I am."

"Fable," Beryl addressed next. "Tell us about Patric, everything you know."

Fable was bewildered, and a little infuriated at the inclusion of her personal life into whatever Beryl was upset about. But she had taken vows and knew she had to answer anything asked of her. "I don't know very much," she said. "He came here to be with his sister. I don't know where they live. I don't really know where he came from."

"How do you know so little about this man you've been seeing?" Beryl asked.

"He doesn't say much."

"Why are you dating him?" Beryl asked.

"I like him," Fable huffed. "Why else would I be seeing him?"

"What is it that you like about him?" Beryl pressed.

Fable was incensed. "I don't know Beryl! There is just something about him I'm drawn to. I'll admit he's not always very nice, and sometimes I even think I don't want to see him anymore. But then he comes around, and I'm just all heady again."

Beryl hated asking the next question, "Have you had sex with him?"

"That is crossing a line, Sister dear!" Fable yelled angrily. It was embarrassing to be asked something so personal, especially in front of her mother, grandmother, and everyone else.

"I need an answer."

"Yes!" Fable snapped. "Yes, we have had sex! You bitch!"

Beryl stopped for a second and looked sympathetically at her younger sister. "There really is a very good reason I'm asking you these things. I'm sorry it's so awkward. But it's necessary."

"I ask for truth now," Fable demanded. "Why are you asking all this?"

Beryl walked over to her sister and knelt at her knees. She took her sister's hands in her own, looked her dead in the eyes, and replied, "Patric is the killer."

"You're wrong!" Fable shrieked as the thrust Beryl's hands away from her.

"No, I don't think she is," Demitra interjected. "I've felt something off with him from the start."

"That doesn't mean anything!" Fable scoffed. "Beryl is lying for some reason."

Olympia shook her head, "Fable you know that she isn't. Not after vows."

"Then she is mistaken," Fable cried. "Patric would never hurt anyone."

Zelda, who had been silent all this time, leaving the family to tend to their own business, couldn't be silent any longer. "He practically tore my house to shreds last night trying to get at me and Beryl! It's a wonder we're alive."

"Patric was with me last night," Fable said, discrediting the accusation.

"He was?" responded Beryl with a perplexed expression. Was there some possibility she was mistaken after all? "He was with you all night?"

"Well, no," Fable admitted. "He actually left rather suddenly when we were at the river."

"He saw me looking at his mind," Zelda informed them. "I was in a trance and got into his head. But he saw me looking, and he looked back. Then he came after me and Beryl."

"Why Beryl?" Seth asked.

"I was at Zelda's," Beryl replied. "I asked her to take a look in his head for me."

"And he saw you both looking?" Olympia inquired in amazement. "That is remarkable."

Beryl looked into her sister's eyes. She tried to be sympathetic. "When he left you last night, he came after us. I saw his face. He isn't human, Fable. Mother discovered it first. You were with her when she did. The killer is a werewolf. And the killer is Patric."

Fable was in tears now. The room fell silent. Fable didn't want it to be true, but she understood it was. It had to be. Beryl would have never made the assertion under Vows if there was any doubt at the possibility. Yasmine felt a pang of heartbreak for her cousin. She went over to the sofa and wedged down between Fable and Demitra. She put her arm around her and pulled Fable onto her shoulder.

"Fable," she said. "Maybe you don't really care for Patric at all. If all this is true, then maybe your power explains why you're so drawn to him."

"What do you mean, my power?" Fable sobbed.

"Well," Yasmine continued, "your power grants you a kinship with animals. Maybe you connected to the animal inside him."

"That doesn't make *any* sense," Seth said.

"Actually," Olympia noted, "it's the only thing that does."

"I can't believe this is happening," Fable wept.

"Wasn't last night a full moon?" Seth recalled.

"A full moon isn't actually necessary," Olympia informed them. "A werewolf cannot help but transform under a moon that is full—that doesn't mean he isn't capable of willingly transforming any other phase of the moon as well, if he likes."

Demitra and Beryl exchanged glances. "That could mean there are even more bodies in his wake I didn't account for," Demitra gasped. "I only searched for killings during the full moon cycle."

"I have a question," Artemis called out. "How did you become involved in all this, Beryl?"

Beryl answered her aunt. "I have a patient who I suspect was attacked by the werewolf. I went to Zelda for help seeing if it was Patric."

"The real question here now is," Seth started, "what are we supposed to do?"

Demitra exchanged glances with Artemis and Olympia. A knowing nod between the women let her know that they were on the same page she was. "We are going to have to kill him."

"Kill him?" Seth gasped. "We don't kill people! None of us have ever killed anybody!"

"Some of us have," Zelda snorted. "Back in the day, Lympy, Pastoria, and..." Olympia shot Zelda a look of caution. Zelda winked at her friend and continued. "In our youth, your Hecate and I had to take out a monster or two."

"Hecate, you've killed someone before?" Seth asked in utter disbelief.

Olympia sighed softly, "There are times in this world when help is needed. A minister, a police officer, a fireman, a doctor...but there are some forces that cannot be stopped by regular avenues. Witches have always had to step in where necessary for the greater good and to protect the Natural Order. It is why we exist—we protect the realm, so to speak. It is why I trained you all for all these years."

"We thought you were just trying to help us control our powers so that nothing bad happened because of us," Seth gasped.

"That was part of it," Olympia admitted. "But mostly I needed the next generation to be ready to do the things the generations before you had to do to keep this world safe. It didn't used to be this peaceful. My father, his father, all those before us did their part. And I have stepped up to the task at times in my life when I was needed."

"It appears you are going to be needed again," Artemis noted. "Sounds like we all are."

"Yep," Zelda huffed. "We got us a werewolf to kill."

"Or two?" Seth quipped.

Everyone turned to look at him. "What do you mean?" Artemis asked.

"Well, Beryl, didn't you say your patient was attacked? If your patient is still alive doesn't that mean he's a werewolf too."

"She," Beryl mumbled, mostly to herself. "My patient is a she. And I never even thought about that. What if we have two werewolves now?"

Olympia took over the meeting. As coven leader, and the most experienced member of the family, she needed to formulate a plan. "The time for conversation is over. We must prepare. Fable has a date with Patric tonight. She told us at breakfast. He will be coming here. And he is sure to know by now that Beryl has told us about last night. At all costs we must keep Fable protected. He wants her, but he'll have to come through the rest of us to get her."

CHAPTER FORTY-THREE

Witches Brew

Quintessential witches at their pot, Artemis, Demitra, and Zelda were stirring the cauldron as it rose to a smoky boil. Yasmine made several trips back and forth to the walk-in pantry, taking what she could carry of the ingredients needed for the potion. Beryl was in the vault collecting various books from Olympia's library of spells. Seth was on a ladder in the living room, mounting a security camera to each corner of the room. He'd already done the same thing in the foyer, on the front porch, and at the back entrance to the house. Fable sat in a chair in the corner of the kitchen. She had succumbed to the acceptance that Patric was a monster, but she was still stunned into silence. Yasmine, and Beryl brought their collections to the kitchen and laid them out on the table where Artemis was now placing them into the pot.

"Garlic," Artemis said, reading off her checklist.

"Garlic," Seth said, tossing it into the pot.

"Bat claws."

"Bat claws," Yasmine said, holding her nose from the putrid smell as she shook them out of the jar into the cauldron.

"Hemlock."

"Here," Demitra said, reaching across the table and dropping the plant clippings in.

"Viper venom."

"Is that this gooey stuff?" Yasmine asked, handing the jar over. "There are so many weird jars of things on the back shelves in the vault."

"Most of this stuff I've never even seen used before," Seth noted. "Where did y'all get this stuff anyway?"

"There are witches who make a living collecting these necessities and selling to fellow witches. Our vendor comes by twice a year," Olympia said. "You know her, Mrs. Waddling."

"I thought she sold you jellies, jams, and pickled okra!" Seth exclaimed.

"She also sells us bat wings, falcon hearts, spider legs, and tongue of an African tree frog as well. Among other things," Olympia laughed.

"I'll finish the brew," Artemis said. "You kids better gather the protections and charms."

Olympia lifted a pair of kitchen shears and walked over to where Fable was sitting. Without even asking first, Olympia lifted a clump of Fable's hair and snipped off. "Wrap this hair around the entry protections."

Fable looked at her in disbelief, "You cut my hair."

"Yes, I did." Olympia replied. She directed Fable to move to the table whereupon she outstretched her granddaughter's arm over the steaming concoction. Giving a quick wave to Beryl to approach, Olympia lifted a dagger from the table. Clasping Fable's arm she apologized, "I'm sorry, Baby, but this will hurt."

She sliced Fable's forearm with the blade, longways to the elbow. Fable screamed from the shock and the surge of pain. Blood gushed from the wound as Olympia held Fable's arm over the cauldron, mixing her blood into the brew. When she felt there was enough, she released Fable's arm to Beryl, who quickly laid her hands over the wound, healing it as if it had never happened.

"It's a good potion, Mother," Artemis announced, pleased with their results. "It's got everything from Wolfsbane to bat claws, all stirred together with the blood of his chosen mate. I think we stand a chance."

"The kids placed the charms at the entrances," Demitra announced to the kitchen. "They're on their way back downstairs now with the weapons."

Seth, Yasmine, and Beryl bounded down the kitchen stairs holding several objects in hand. They had to pause midway because Beryl had forgotten to close the door to the vault after she had gone into it. The last riser of stairs was now hinged upwards before them, blocking them from the kitchen.

"Why didn't you just come down the front stairs, the same way you went up?" Demitra scolded as she rushed to push the vault door closed and allow them to descend to the kitchen.

Placing their individual objects on the table beside the cauldron, they each identified what they brought as they laid it down. Seth went first, clicking open the bullet cartridge to show that the gun was loaded.

"Uncle Larry's gun."

"Great grandfather Constantinople's sword," Beryl said, laying the long sharp blade carefully on the table.

"A canister of hydrochloric acid," Yasmine announced, slipping the medium-sized tank off her back by the straps and placing it gingerly on the table's edge.

"Why do we have that?" Seth asked in the ear of his Aunt Artemis, who simply shook her head as if to say *I have no idea*.

Olympia inhaled deeply and proudly as she professed, "This is it. The Coven of the Blanchard Witches are prepared. He will be here shortly."

"Correction," Zelda said. "He's coming up the drive."

"What?" Fable gasped.

"You can see him?" Demitra asked.

"Yeah," Zelda said looking down at her feet in discouragement. "He's lettin' me know he's here. He knows what we're plannin'. He's comin' up the driveway, laughing at us."

CHAPTER FORTY-FOUR

Battle with a Werewolf

"Assume your positions," Olympia commanded. "Active powers in front. Secondaries guard Fable. Third line grab the arsenal."

Seth and Artemis took the front lines, standing in the foyer by the stairs, poised for attack. Of them all, they had the most active powers in the family, besides Olympia, but Olympia would be the last line of defense. Her age and agility were too precarious to risk at the front. Behind them stood Yasmine, taking aim at the door with a metal rod attached to the canister of acid strapped to her shoulder. Demitra and Beryl stood guard around Fable. Zelda brandished the gun, and Olympia armed herself with her father's sword.

"We should'a done a protection spell on the house," Zelda whispered as they heard the porch creak underneath Patric's footsteps.

"No," Olympia whispered back. "We have to face him and stop him. We need him to enter."

The entire house was still. Everyone stood breathless as every second felt like an hour waiting for Patric to approach the door. An army of witches standing, fight ready, for the battle of their lives against a ferocious beast. They listened as a threatening laughter penetrated the door and echoed in the foyer.

"You are all fools," he said from behind the door. His voice was deep and menacing, but it was definitely Patric's voice, not the growls of his wolf form. "Let me take the one I have come for."

"Never!" Demitra shouted back.

Before the word was out of her mouth, a hole opened where the front door previously stood--pulled from its hinges so cleanly and efficiently as if it had been merely the door of a doll house. Patric stood heaving with a strength he had never displayed before. He panted before them like the wild animal surging beneath his flesh.

"You cannot stop me!" he bellowed thunderously.

"You are not immortal," Seth cried defiantly. "You *can* be killed."

"As can you," sneered Patric.

As his words hit the air, any bravado the family had possessed was doused as they turned their horrified eyes to a pack of gray wolves lining up on the porch steps just behind him. Their teeth, razor-sharp and jagged, protruded beneath their gums as drops of saliva dripped from the points of their fangs. These beasts were on the ready, awaiting their master's command to shred anyone to bits.

"You see," Patric mocked, "I have *my* army as well." With that, he charged inside the door.

Instinctively, Seth outstretched his hand toward the living room whereupon a side window shattered with a strong current of wind sending a winged-back chair sailing across the floor to knock Patric onto his back. As Patric landed on the floor, one of the wolves leapt high over him toward Seth. Yasmine jumped forward to Seth's defense, her fingers squeezing the trigger of the canister spray, releasing streams of searing, burning acid into the face of the wolf. The animal let out an excruciating cry as he fell to his side, writhing in pitiful agony. The fur on his face, as well as the flesh itself, sizzled and deteriorated, leaving only bare bone and melting tissue. It was dead by the time Seth understood what had happened.

"Beautiful, Yasmina," Patric snarled from the floor, seemingly impressed with her achievement. "So brave, so strong, so fearless. But you have no real power. Would you like to have power? Would you like to join me? I can make you invincible."

"I'd rather die!" she shouted.

"What would be the fun in that?" Patric teased. "You could learn much from me. Watch this!" Suddenly the remaining wolves, eight in all, came rushing forward, too many to stop at once.

Artemis had only seconds to react. She envisioned the wolves being impaled on spears and instantaneously a patch of boards from the foyer's hardwood floors broke away and stabbed into three of the creatures, impaling them completely—the wide boards inserted into their bodies shattering their rib cages, practically splitting the animals in half. The remaining five wolves managed to evade the planks and were now inside the house.

One of the five made a dive at Seth. Before he had time to defend himself, the gray predator locked its razor jaws into Seth's arm, severing it so brutally that it hung now by only muscle and a bit of bone. Unable to wield his arms to unleash his power, Seth crumpled to the floor, thrashing in unbearable pain. The wolf then pounced on Artemis, throwing her backwards to the floor. She held onto the wolf as she fell in a desperate attempt to hold it arm's-length from her body as its snapping jaws inched closer and closer to her face. It was too strong for her. She was losing ground and the fierce beast was poised for the death bite. Olympia sprang forward like a medieval warrior, impaling the wolf on her sword. The wound was not mortal. The wolf sounded a shrill cry from its gullet and then snapped back into action. It was only Artemis' lightning-fast reflexes, jerking her head to the side, that saved her from the terrible bite. The wolf's snout slammed into the hard floor, but he reared up to inflict another blow. Olympia pulled the sword free from the animal's chest and with the strength her frail old body had not summoned in 30 years, she slung the blade around her body and sliced the head from the wolf's shoulders.

Artemis scurried to her feet with her mother's assistance to face the four remaining wolves. Patric stood back to observe like a General giving orders to his troops. Fable stared at him behind the wall of Beryl and Demitra's protection. It was beyond her mental capabilities to process everything that was happening before her and that it was all happening because of the man she thought she loved. She wanted to do something, to help her family. She tried with all her might to communicate with the remaining wolves now standing still, awaiting new directions from their commander. It was the first time in her life that Fable could not reach an animal. These wolves belonged to Patric, and his mental control over them was far more powerful than even Fable could compete with.

Patric's eyes gleamed red as he flicked his hand toward the pack of wolves, as if signaling the next play. The largest of the four wolves, a black beast with muscled legs and ivory white claws, locked eyes with Demitra. She seemed to understand. Patric was coming for Fable, and he was sending his most powerful champion to disarm and destroy Fable's guard. A strange, survivalist instinct surged through Demitra. Suddenly she stopped playing defense and took the offense, dashing forward to attack the beast first! The black wolf seemed almost as surprised as Demitra herself as she landed on top of him. Beast and beauty thrashed on the floor, Demitra firmly straddling his back, her arms wrapped in a vice around his torso. His jaws snapping back at her but unable to get a proper angle to reach her throat. Pinning him to the floor, Demitra released her grip around his body to take her mortal chance. She grasped the beast's head in her hands and twisted with all her might, winding his head around as hard and as far as she could until the animal met her face to face-- even then she kept twisting until his head was almost facing its original direction. She heard every bone in its neck shatter as it fell limp in her hands. Rising from the where she left the great beast dead on the floor, Demitra walked to face Patric in the entryway. He looked stunned, shaken—for the first time, unsure he could win.

"A Mother's love," she told him, staring him eye to eye. "It is the strongest power of them all. You cannot have my daughter. Nothing on earth will stop me from stopping you!"

Patric's hand shot forward like a cannon and clutched Demitra by the throat. Possessing the strength of the ages, he lifted her off the ground with almost no effort expelled. As she dangled there, suspended in air, more battles were being waged around the room.

Beryl successively dodged her way past two of the charging wolves and crouched beside Seth's profusely bleeding body. The foyer floor was a sea of blood now, and Seth it's only island. He was nearly unconscious as his severed arm had bled him out almost completely. The healer took action placing her hands on her cousin's arm. Within seconds, bone was renewing before her eyes, muscles were reattaching, pulling the hanging arm back into place at the socket. She held onto him until the wound was closed and the scar was gone. Seth was intact again. His powerful hand was restored, but vast blood loss still kept him too weak to resume the fight.

On the staircase, Artemis and Olympia were battling another wolf. They backed slowly up the treads of the stairs as it stalked, slowly creeping towards them. Olympia swung her blade forward only for the fiend to swipe his deadly paw across her frail hand, slashing it open, sending the sword flying over the railing to the floor below. Artemis tried to envision the sword rising up and stabbing into the great beast, but before she could manage the task, Zelda tramped forward to the stairs, took aim at the head of the wolf and blasted the gun. Once again, her aim was poor. The bullet entered the wolf's back and was not a fatal shot. However, the impact, and the pain, sent the wolf reeling backwards down the stairs and into the hole left in the floor from the removed boards.

Artemis saw her sister struggling for air in Patric's grip, as he slowly continued crushing her throat. Quickly she envisioned a gust of wind, summoning it instantly, which rushed through the doorless doorway, sweeping up the injured wolf and sending it crashing into Patric. The gust injured neither Patric nor the wounded wolf, but it did successfully break Patric's hold of Demitra, and Demitra crawled to safety toward the hall.

"Where are the other wolves?" Zelda cried, surveying the room. Only Patric--now getting back up from his fall--and the Blanchards were in Zelda's line of sight. The wolves were nowhere to be found. Tension filled the room as no one knew from which direction the next attack might stem. The wolves were hiding, biding their time for the perfect strike.

Suddenly, the injured wolf Zelda had shot pounced from the hole in the floor where the boards had killed his brethren. It charged forward toward the woman who had shot him. Zelda spun around just in time to see him coming and shot him dead between the eyes.

"Oh, there's one," she said.

"That leaves three more!" Yasmine shouted. She held the acid tank firmly as she jerked around in circles bracing for the next attack. A faint, sinister collection of growls came all at once, and from all directions, but no wolf was in sight. "Where are they!"

"They could be anywhere," laughed Patric. "You have such a large home. They could be around any corner. But don't worry. *They* will find *you*."

"Don't worry about it now," Olympia shouted to her family. "Get the kettle."

Artemis dashed for the kitchen where she found Demitra still trying to catch her breath. The two of them lifted the cauldron from the table and made their way into the foyer.

"Fable," Patric beckoned softly. "Fable, you will not let them harm me."

Yasmine stepped in front of Fable, blocking Patric from her. "Leave her alone!" she shouted, shaking, afraid, but determined to save her cousin. "You know you can't kill us. If you could have, it would have already happened. The Blanchard's have defeated most of *your army*. And we will also defeat you." She pointed the nozzle of her acid tank toward Patric.

"You would not hurt me, Yasmina," he said, taking an emboldened step closer towards her.

"I mean it," she said. "I will cover you in acid."

"Do it," he laughed. "Go ahead."

"Spray him Yazzy!" Beryl screamed.

"You can't," Patric smiled, holding her gaze with his own. "You are devoid of will and movement. You will obey everything I say." His glare was bordering on maniacal as his grin spread wider and wider across his face.

"Shoot him Yaz!" Seth shouted from where he lay in the foyer. He tried to stand but was too weak to manage it. "Shoot him!"

A low growl began to rise over the sound of the shouting. No one knew which direction it was coming from, but everyone braced for another wolf to pounce. Yasmine's eyes moved slowly to her right as she caught sight of a wolf poised for attack underneath the console table behind the sofa. She tried to move, tried to break free from her place on the floor, but she couldn't. Patric said she was devoid of movement, and he was right. She could not move at all. He held her still in some kind of paralyzed state.

All at once, the wolf shot out from under the table and leapt high into the air towards Yasmine. Its jaws open, its claws outstretched, ready to devour and destroy her. She knew this was how she was going to meet her end. As the wolf flew ever closer towards her, Yasmine knew this was goodbye. But suddenly Patric hurled himself forward with all his beastly dexterity, knocking the wolf from Yasmine's path with his chest.

"Not her!" he bellowed. The wolf fell to the floor and slunk backward, whimpering like a frightened dog. Patric turned to look at Yasmine. "You will join me, Yasmina."

"Get away from her!" Seth shouted, forcing his feet to support him. Yasmine, now free of the hypnotic hold Patric gripped her with, rushed to Seth's side.

"You have no power now," Patric laughed. "You may be healed of your injuries, but in your weakened condition you are unable to be a threat to me." Patric marched toward Seth and punched him, sending Seth falling backwards to the floor once again.

"Now!" Olympia screamed.

Demitra and Artemis tipped the cauldron over so that the liquid potion bubbling inside poured across the floor. As the brew rushed across Patric's feet, the sisters chanted.

"Blood of your chosen
Herbs of defeat
Power of our coven
Weaken this beast.
Creature of night
Vanquished by day
Stilled by the blood
Of the object you crave"

As the potion flowed over Patric's feet, he felt a slight tingling sensation. Olympia walked fearlessly across the room to face him. She wielded an air of victory around her as if this one final liquid weapon sealed his fate.

"It's done. You are unable to move. Your very obsession with Fable is your undoing," she said triumphantly. Her eyes sparkled and her head lifted to an angle that could only be described as arrogant. In that moment, she no longer looked like the aged woman she was. You could almost glimpse the warrior she must have been in her youth. "If I am correct in my estimation, I believe you will be unable to control your body for about two minutes. That gives us plenty of time to end you and this reign of terror you've unleashed on humanity."

"Do you really think so?" Patric laughed. He took a surprising step forward. Olympia was bewildered. The triumph in her face dissolved quickly. Patric noticed the change and chided, "You're not as powerful as you imagined, now are you?"

The family encircled him. Seth, Beryl, Fable, Yasmine, Zelda, Artemis, Demitra, Olympia. Each with their power or their weapon of choice. Patric was trapped by the coven. The remaining wolves now revealed themselves and stalked around the circle, growling at the witches encompassing their master. Instinctively Yasmine whirled around and sprayed the two wolves closest to her with the acid. Like the one that died of the same means before, they writhed and howled in agony before crumpling onto the floor. The third one pounced only to meet the end of Olympia's sword.

"Looks like that finishes off your army," Beryl smirked. "Now let's finish you."

In the blink of an eye, Patric lurched into the air and jumped against the wall. His hands, now transitioning into claws, dug into the sheetrock, holding him perched in place. His face was morphing as well, changing faster than anyone could register, into the face of a beast. He leapt across the room back into the foyer, out of range of the Blanchard circle. The Blanchards stood more mesmerized than afraid at how complete and instantaneous his transformation had been. Patric now was a grotesque amalgamation of man and wolf, too much like both but not enough of like either. He stood in the foyer, slowly backing towards the doorway.

"This was an interesting first round. An exploratory study of sorts. Now I know what I am up against. I'll be better prepared for our next battle." With that he bolted on all fours away from the house. By the time Seth reached the window to look outside, there was no trace of Patric at all.

The family stood in silence for quite a while. None of them quite knowing what to make of the events they had just been through. Beryl healed the minor injuries while the others began dragging wolf carcasses out into the yard to burn. Yasmine got out the mop and pail and began cleaning up the potion puddled on the floor.

"I don't understand why the spell didn't work," Demitra said, breaking the silence.

"Maybe it wasn't strong enough," Artemis suggested.

"No, that wasn't it," Olympia declared. "He seemed to know it wouldn't work. As if there is something we are not accounting for. He should have been frozen for two minutes. I have worked this spell before, a long time ago—not on a wolf, but something equally as devilish. The spell was not the problem. There is something we are missing."

"Well, we better figure it out fast," Beryl stated. "Because he made it very clear, he will be back."

CHAPTER FORTY-FIVE

A Fresh Morning

The smell of sizzling sausage patties and biscuits baking in the oven climbed the back stairs and tugged at the Blanchards, luring them from their beds and down to the kitchen. The back door was open in the kitchen allowing the cooler air of summer's end and autumn's beginning to drift inside now that it was free of humidity. Yasmine was standing at the stove, oven mitts on her hands, pulling the biscuits from the oven.

"Breakfast!" Beryl cried. "I am so hungry."

Seth plopped down at the table. Looking down to the floor where his bare toes grazed something gritty, he saw a sprinkling of herbs the broom had missed from the potion of a few days ago when they'd last faced Patric.

"I am so excited to have breakfast again!" Beryl told him as she took a seat herself.

"I think I've managed to master Aunt Artemis' biscuits," Yasmine proclaimed, laying the pan before them.

"Where's the sausage, where's the sausage!" Seth demanded.

"Give me a sec," Yasmine snapped. "I'm about to bring it. I'm waiting for the last few eggs to fry."

"I'm still replenishing from my injuries," her fiancé said.

Fable stomped angrily down the back stairs. She'd not been herself since the battle with Patric. Though she could blame no one but herself for becoming involved with him, the family was getting the brunt of her frustration. She settled herself with a thud into her chair and barked, "Where's my cereal?"

"We're out of cereal," Yasmine answered.

"But I always have cereal and milk. What good is the milk if I don't have the cereal to put in it?"

"Then don't have milk," Beryl quipped.

"If you want cereal," Yasmine said. "Then you have to write it down on the grocery list. I can't remember everything."

"Aunt Artemis always knew to get my cereal when she went to the store."

Olympia, overhearing the exchange, came in from the living room to join the family at the table. "Things are changing around here Fable now that your aunt has to be at the restaurant every day. A wise person learns to adapt."

Seth took a look at the plate of eggs making their debut at the table. "I feel like scrambled eggs, not fried. Can you make me some?"

"No," Yasmine said. "I can't. I made fried eggs today."

"Fine," Seth groused. "I'll make them myself."

"Can't," she replied. "We're out of eggs."

Seth's response, "We have chickens in the chicken coups," didn't supply him with a desirable outcome. Yasmine quickly pointed out that if he wanted scrambled eggs, he could walk down to the chicken house himself to retrieve a new basket of eggs to scramble.

"Why didn't you just get more eggs when you collected these this morning?" he asked.

"Because I only had time to collect the eggs from the first house. You'll have to get the others later," she told him. "I have to go to work. Then I have classes all afternoon."

"Why do I have to get the eggs?" Seth cried.

"Dear Lord, Seth Blanchard," Yasmine shouted, throwing the spatula at him--missing him and hitting the chair leg instead. "Would you like me to wash your hair for you too before I leave for work!"

"Geez," Seth sulked. "You're in a fun mood."

Yasmine shook her fist in his face, "I am only doing the cooking—I am not a hired hand. You do nothing all day but go to the gym and barely attend classes. You can get the damn eggs!"

"I'm still recovering." Seth whined. "You seem to keep forgetting I had my arm ripped off a few days ago."

"Seth, you were recovered from that by the next day," Beryl pointed out.

"Maybe you're tired for other reasons," Fable smirked. "I see Yazzy sneaking off back to her room every morning like she hadn't spent the night in your bed."

"Fable!" Yasmine exclaimed, blushing and looking at their grandmother.

"Don't be embarrassed my Dear," Olympia laughed. "I certainly do not begrudge you test driving the car before you buy it—as long as you still buy it on Halloween."

"Hecate!" Seth said turning red.

...

Much more work was going into the preparations for the grand re-opening of The Cobblestone than Artemis had expected. The kitchen needed two new Hobart dishwashing machines, the exhaust fan above the open pit grill needed replacing, not to mention the new fabrics for the chairs and tablecloths and the floors had chinks here and there requiring fresh mortar. Amid overseeing the touch ups around the place, Artemis was also familiarizing herself with her new staff and learning the already established routines and protocols in place for daily operations. She wanted the staff to know that she had no plans to upheave their way of doing things or making any big changes to a workplace which already ran smoothly.

It was a big relief to Artemis when Carol Saunders, the restaurant manager, met her with positivity and an open mind toward the new owner. Carol was going to be indispensable if Artemis had any hope of transitioning the place under new ownership without frightening off staff and customers. In the days since Artemis stepped into the place, Carol was at her side day and night helping her acclimate. Carol knew all the suppliers and made the appropriate introductions. Carol knew the restaurant's menu as to what worked and what didn't. She was also welcoming to Artemis' ideas. Carol even had a friend on the state board and was currently paving the way for a new liquor license. The two were becoming fast friends as they plowed ahead day after day readying things for the opening.

The two women were deep into a discussion on how to best incorporate Artemis' dishes into the menu when Demitra walked into the office. Carol took her cue to leave, giving the sisters a few minutes' privacy.

"How is everything going?" Demitra asked.

"Look at all these papers and you tell me?" Artemis said. "Recipes from the last ten years of this place. Some are good, some not so much. I plan to take some of these home tonight and see if there are ways I can spruce them up and introduce back onto the menu later."

"What about your own creations?" Demitra inquired.

"Oh, I've already added about ten of my things to the menu. That is enough for now. We have to slowly adjust the clientele to my cooking." Artemis changed the subject. "So, any word from Charlie about Patric's whereabouts?"

"None," Demitra said. "He's on the lookout for him, and the police have accepted Patric as the killer at large, so the mystery is solved. But Charlie isn't really going to too much trouble to find him. It's mostly perfunctory for the papers and police force. Charlie understands now what he is dealing with is supernatural. Even if they found Patric, the police can't stop him."

"That was a terrific idea you had, Dee. Having Seth mount those security cameras. I bet it was easier to convince Charlie what we are dealing with by showing him the battle footage."

"He was shocked at first," Demitra reflected. "It's scary to see, especially if you've never believed in such nightmarish creatures. But now he knows what Daihmler is dealing with, and he knows it's best to leave Patric to us."

"Yeah, well, we aren't doing a really good job finding him ourselves."

"I don't think we need to find him," Demitra pointed out. "He made it very clear that he will come to us when he's ready. Our job is to be better prepared to stop him."

"We have no idea how to do that," Artemis admitted.

"Yes, we do," Demitra contradicted. "We are much more informed now as to his strength and his outreach. He came with reinforcements last time. We weren't prepared for that, yet we managed to defeat them. Next time we will be over prepared for whatever arsenal he comes supplied with."

"Since there haven't been any murders since that battle at the house, I wonder if he's even still in town."

"I don't know," Demitra admitted. "Charlie is keeping watch on surrounding communities, but so far everything seems pretty stable. There was one questionable death in Oneonta, but police there said it was a mountain lion. There was also a witness that saw a mountain lion a few days before in the general area. So, we just can't be sure."

"Or perhaps Patric is hiding his kills a little better now," Artemis suggested. "I somehow doubt he's gone too far from Daihmler. I just wish I knew why he was waiting so long to stage his next attack."

"I'm hoping that fear is the reason," Demitra replied. "He didn't anticipate running into a coven of witches that were going to find him out. Maybe he talked a good talk but in reality has realized he can't win against us. Maybe he moved on."

"He didn't seem like the type to move on," her sister pointed out. "His infatuation with Fable seems premeditated to me. He had a plan all along. We just don't know what it is yet. But at least we stopped him from hurting Fable. She seems to be coping rather well in this aftermath. Granted I haven't been home much in the last few days, but when I've seen her, she acts like she's doing all right."

"I'm not so sure," Demitra frowned. "She's holding something in. This has troubled her more than she lets on. I think it is safe to say he held some sort of hold on her even she doesn't quite comprehend yet. And he will try again to come after her. You heard him when he said *we'd stolen* something from him. He will come back for her. That's when we stop him."

Artemis pressed her lips together tightly and shook her head. "I'm not so sure he meant Fable when he said we'd stolen something from him. If he had meant Fable, he'd have said Fable."

Demitra was perplexed. "What else could he have meant? What could the Blanchard family have stolen from him? Everything we have we've owned for generations—except this restaurant."

Artemis stared out of the windows at the Black Warrior drifting past. "None of us know anything about this Patric person. Who is he? Where does he really come from? Why is he here? Who is this sister we have no trace of? For all we know, he could be an Obreiggon."

"An Obreiggon?"

"Or a D'Angelo," Artemis added.

"I know Atheidrelle hates us, but enough to unleash a werewolf on us?"

"I'm just saying, we should be prepared for any surprises."

CHAPTER FORTY-SIX

Settling In

Salem didn't quite know what to make of the sight she caught out of the bathroom window that Sunday morning after she'd put in her contacts. A soapy sponge was pressing against the bathroom window making circular motions. It withdrew from the window just as Salem looked down, in its place came a surge of water from a floating hosepipe. She hurried downstairs to the back yard. She found Arielle sitting in an Adirondack chair reading an iPad tablet.

"Good morning!" Arielle greeted her. "Have you ever played Sudoku? It's very relaxing. Watch out for the sponge!"

Salem jumped back as the sponge soared down from her bedroom window and plopped into a foamy bucket nearby only to dart back up to the windows of Arielle's room. The hose was shifting in the air from the bathroom window to Salem's window.

"I thought it was a good day to clean the windows," Arielle explained. "This fall pollen is getting thick."

Salem began waving her hands and shaking her head at her sister, "Arielle, what if the neighbors see! You have to be careful."

"We're only cleaning a little," Arielle replied.

"Uh, no, phantom sponges are cleaning by themselves," Salem pointed out. "We can't let anyone catch on that we are witches."

"People know about witches," Arielle argued.

Salem ran her hand through her auburn hair in exacerbation, "Yes, people know there are others that practice witchcraft, but that's basically Wicca and earth magic nothingness. People do not actually know there are real witches who have the kind of powers we do. That has to remain very hush hush if we don't want the world hounding us."

"Back home we just do whatever we want," Arielle revealed.

Salem sat down beside her, trying to make the naive girl understand. "Yes, but you live on a plantation back in the marshlands. You don't have neighbors living on either side of you. In Atlanta, we have to be a little more private."

Over breakfast of toast, bacon, and hot coffee, Salem expressed her curiosity about the vastness of Arielle's abilities.

"What all can you do exactly?"

"Not so much," Arielle started. "I can move objects around as you know. That's really about it."

"That was pretty amazing to me," Salem laughed.

"Besides freezing time, what all can you do?"

"I recently discovered I can move much larger objects than I thought could—like the ground and trees." Salem answered. "I can also blow things up."

"Mother call's people with that gift *flamethrowers*. I wish I could do that one."

Salem laughed. "I'm afraid I can't teach you that one. I don't even know how I did it. I was terribly upset at the time."

"Daddy's great aunt was a flamethrower," Arielle noted. "And your freezing power comes from our grandfather Obreiggon. I can't freeze people, but I can stop objects in place. Can Seth freeze people too?"

"No, but he can control the elements," Salem said. "He can summon lightning, wind and rain, or sunshine. It's really pretty cool."

"I'd like to meet him," Arielle admitted. "I've never had a brother before."

"I was thinking you might get to meet him very soon." Salem revealed. "He's getting married in a few weeks. I thought I'd take you."

"Really? Oh, my word I would love that! When?"

"Halloween."

"Oh," Arielle sounded downtrodden. "My mother always throws an annual ball on Halloween. I know she'll expect me."

"That's all right," Salem looked disheartened. "You've been here awhile now, and I know you must miss your family."

"Not particularly," Arielle admitted. "I'd rather meet my brother. Mother has called me twice to find out where I am. Daddy told her I'm traveling with friends. She's left me messages ordering me to return home by the ball. Of course, I am not moving back. But I did plan to tell her at the ball where I'm living now."

"Then go to Oleander for Halloween," Salem said. "You can meet Seth at

Thanksgiving."

"No, I want to go to Halloween at your house. I want to meet Seth. I'll figure out a way to get out of going home."

Salem thought for a moment. "Maybe you shouldn't come home with me. There's been some trouble at Blanchard House. Apparently, my cousin has been dating a werewolf. He has tried to kill them once already, and they beat him. But they all expect another attack from him at some point. Maybe until he is captured, you shouldn't go around the family. Although if they manage to locate him, I may need to return to Daihmler to help stop him."

"Well, if you go, I'll go," Arielle said. "Werewolves are dangerous. My mother knows a few. I believe her cousin is one, but it's not something she ever talks about. I heard about him once when I was little. She was discussing it with my aunt Blackie. But I already told you they don't talk to each other anymore."

"Why not?"

"Blackie was your mother's best friend."

CHAPTER FORTY-SEVEN

Fable and her Father

The cemetery was deserted by 5 o'clock usually, which was the main reason Fable liked to go at that time. All of the day's funerals were held between 11 a.m. and 3 p.m., so by 5 o'clock mourners were usually gone. Only the occasional elderly widow placing flowers on her late husband's grave stole any of Fable's solitude.

It had been her other grandmother, Grandmother Mariner, who insisted Fable's father be buried at Memory Hills in Tuscaloosa. The Mariners didn't even live in Tuscaloosa, which made it all the more puzzling to Fable as to why her father had to be laid to rest there. Larry Mariner should have been at Blanchard House in the family plot along with Grandfather Sinclair, David Lane, and all the others. Demitra had given in on her mother-in-law's request, partly out of guilt for Larry's time being mostly monopolized in life by the Blanchard family. Demitra and Grandmother Mariner never liked each other, maybe it was the guilt from that which made Demitra acquiesce. Whatever the reason, when Fable Blanchard wanted to visit her father, she had to drive into nearby Tuscaloosa to do it. It had been almost a year since she last visited his grave, but after the Patric debacle, Fable needed to feel close to him again.

"So how are they treating you out here?" she asked his headstone as she sat down in the grass. A cool breeze blew past chilling her nose and ears. She was glad she'd worn a sweater. "It's fall now, Dad. Sorry I haven't been out here to see you for so long. I've been going through some things. I guess you know David died. And little Michael. I know you never met them, but if you run into them or their energy out there, just know they're family."

She waited for a maintenance guy to finish driving by on a tractor before she continued her talk with her father. "I met someone too," she continued. "It was this past summer. I liked him a lot, but he turned out to be an asshole. Actually, Dad, he turned out to be a deranged killer. Oh, guess what? Seth and Yazzy are getting married...to each other! Wedding is in a couple of weeks.

"But it's my life that brings me out here, Dad. I've messed it up again. I'm hurting so much." Tears streamed from her eyes. "I really thought this guy was going to be special. Not that I loved him, exactly. I didn't even like him that much. He just had a way of drawing me in. It was like being under his spell or something. He was a monster. Literally, Dad.

"I wonder what you were thinking when you married into this crazy family full of supernatural things. I guess what I'm looking for is a man who can be the way you were. Someone who will love me for me and accept my family the way you always did. Sometimes I get so lonely I think I might die from the loneliness. Beryl doesn't seem to need people the way I do. I've always had Seth and Yazzy to while away the time with. The three of us were single, usually, and didn't mind because we had each other. Now they have each other, and I'm the third wheel. I feel even more alone. Beryl says there is someone for everyone, although she shows no interest in love. I feel like whoever was out there for me, has lost his way and isn't coming anymore. Besides, I think it might be too late for me now."

Fable leaned her cheek against the cold marble headstone. Desperate for some sympathy, needy for someone to talk to, Larry Mariner's headstone was all she had. She wiped her eyes and took a deep breath inward.

"Dad, I have something to tell you. This man, this monster, he was a werewolf. He *is* a werewolf, I should say. He's still out there, and he's still going to come back for me. I'm supposed to be afraid of him, supposed to want to stop him. But, Dad, I don't know what's going to happen if and when he returns. You see, Daddy...I'm pregnant. I found out yesterday. And I don't know what to do."

Fable placed her hands on the flat of her stomach. There was no baby bump yet but she knew her child was there. There were so many thoughts racing through her mind all at once. Thoughts she never dreamed she'd ever have to consider. Most of her life had been a series of mistakes. Sneaking out to parties when she was grounded, only to be caught coming in late. Falling for the wrong guy and going way further than she should have just to prove she could get him. Using her sardonic wit as the way to garner attention in a family full of kids she never felt equal to. But this...this was a doozy mistake. A kind of mistake an apology or a shift in attitude could not fix.

"What if this is my only chance to ever be a mother? But if I have this baby, what am I a mother of? An innocent baby? A baby werewolf? This child could be the only thing to fill this hole inside my heart. But Dad, what if my baby turns out to be a killer? Will it be able to stop itself? Is there a chance it can be born human? I don't know anything about how these things work, and I can't talk to the people who do. Mother, Aunt Artemis, and even Hecate would force me to have an abortion. What if I want to have this baby? What do I do?"

CHAPTER FORTY-EIGHT

Sinclair's Request

Olympia and Zelda were out in the garden tending to the pumpkins when Yasmine drove up in the yard. The girl smiled when she saw the two old women because she knew they were lovingly tending the pumpkins so that they would be ready for her wedding.

"They are getting so big," Yasmine exclaimed walking over. "They are going to be perfect."

"They'd be a hell of a lot bigger if Lympy'd used the Miracle Grow."

Olympia rolled her eyes at the suggestion. "The concoction Artemis made for us to pour over the root system has worked just fine," she said. "I refuse to use factory chemicals in my garden."

"Ain't nothin' wrong with taking advantage of technology."

"You do your garden your way, Zelda, and leave me to do mine my way. These pumpkins are perfect."

Yasmine rolled a couple of pumpkins over and checked their undersides. They were utterly perfect. These gourds had been well tended and adjusted every day to ensure they didn't become misshapen. She looked at the two old women working so diligently to make her wedding perfect and felt gratitude.

"Did Howard send those checks off for me as I requested?" Olympia asked her granddaughter.

"Yes, ma'am," Yasmine answered, adding with a laugh, "He almost had a stroke doing it, too. He complained all morning about the amounts."

"The Wildlife Preservation Fund, Greenpeace, and ASPCA are excellent charities. They deserve large contributions. Times were hard this year for the average income earner. I'm sure their organizations had a reduction in donations. I wanted to supplement the loss."

"You know Howard," Yasmine laughed. "He thinks you're foolish to give so much away."

"Your granny may be a lot of things," Zelda said, pulling a clump of weeds from around one of the pumpkin vines. "She's old as Methuselah, stubborn as a mule pulling a square-wheeled wagon, and can't ever admit she's wrong about anything, but a fool she ain't."

"Well— thank you, Zelda," Olympia huffed. "I don't know if I want to hug you or hit you with this jug of fertilizer."

The two old friends exchanged a playful smirk as they went on with their work. They had been bantering this way all of their lives. Yasmine picked up a soft towel nearby and reached down to wipe her grandmother and Zelda's sweaty brows. They each rose up to meet her as the soft towel dabbed their foreheads.

"Zelda, did you invite Sarah and Melinda to my wedding?" Yasmine asked.

"Yes, but I hope they won't come. I'll have more fun without them," Zelda gave a hearty chuckle and gave a quick slap at Yasmine's wrist. "Wait till you hear what happened to Sarah yesterday."

"Don't tell that story again," Olympia scolded. "It's disgusting, and I've heard it three times already today."

"Shut up, you old heifer," Zelda snorted. "Yazzy ain't heard it." Zelda righted herself to a stand and began telling Yasmine the latest saga in the world of her miserable daughter. "Sarah's been constipated this week. Result of some terrible new diet she's on..."

"I'm serious, Zelda," Olympia snapped, rearing up on her knees. "I do not care to hear this story again."

"Then don't listen.' Zelda scoffed before continuing. "Anyways, Sarah had a job interview. She's trying to break into local commercials. She did that one car commercial, and so she went in to talk to a guy shooting one for a real estate office. She done pretty well through the interview. Then the guy wants to test her on camera, so he hauls her off to the production room, and they start recordin' her doin' a script they had ready. Well, she does pretty good. She's pretty sure she'll get the job, but as she's fixin' to leave, she knocks her purse over. All these suppositories fall out on the floor—which is bad enough. But while she's bent over pickin' 'em up, something cuts loose, and she shits herself right in the office building!"

Yasmine burst into laughter. "You're joking!"

SINCLAIR'S REQUEST

Zelda's weathered face, now pinched in laughter, accentuated the crags and crevices time had marked. "Naw, she just soiled herself right there in the production room—with the camera still rollin'. They got it all on digital!"

"That is a revolting story, Zelda," Olympia said sternly. "I don't think Sarah would appreciate your telling it around."

"Not my problem," Zelda snickered. "I think it's funny as hell."

Olympia heard enough. Handing the hoe over to her friend, she said, "You finish up, I have to show Yasmine something in the house."

Yasmine joined Olympia in Olympia's bedroom whereupon Olympia removed a large box from her dresser. Opening the box there was a beautiful white dress inside. She lifted its delicate lace out to show it to Yasmine in its full length.

"This dress belonged to your mother and your grandmother. Both of them wore it on their wedding day. Your grandfather asked me to give it to you to wear whenever you got married. I've had it cleaned and restored and resized to fit your small frame."

Yasmine stared at the dress. Olympia had obviously gone to great trouble to make it this lovely again. She knew she should have been overjoyed. This had been her mother's dress, but Yasmine's reaction to it fell flatter than she expected.

"It's really beautiful—it is—but I thought I would wear your wedding dress. The one Salem wore. She told me she'd bring it to me before the wedding and help me with the fitting."

"That's lovely, child," Olympia beamed. "And I'd be honored to see you wear my original wedding dress. But it meant a great deal to your grandfather that you wear this one. As I said, it was worn by your mother and your grandmother."

"You are my grandmother."

A lot was hidden in that sentence, for both of them. Olympia stared into the bright eyes of her youngest granddaughter and smiled. Those eyes—Hazel most of the time, green when she was sad, and on rare occasions blue if she were hiding something. They were a bluish green now.

"I am your grandmother, Yasmine, in every important way that matters. Nothing changes that between us. Certainly not a dress, but I have never broken a promise to Sinclair. I do not plan to begin now. I have given you the dress and told you his wish. The rest is your decision."

Yasmine shrugged her shoulders and said, "Why not? If it was that important to him, I'll wear his dress. For you."

Olympia smiled and patted her shoulder. "You know of all my husbands, I cherished your grandfather most of all. Now do not get me wrong, I loved all the men I married. John Windham was my first and father of my children. He is always special to me for that. Martin Caswell was a kind man, but he was not very well, even when I married him. Had two heart attacks before he died.

"But your grandfather, Yasmine. Oh, that man! That man gave me the deepest happiness of them all. And the most frustration."

"He was destroying some land you were fighting to persevere, right?"

Olympia's eyes lit up a little at the recollection. "Oh, how we fought over that land. He was the most egotistical, stubborn man I had ever met. I hated his guts. And I fell head over heels for him at every turn. I remember being so excited for one of our courtroom battles simply because I'd get to see him again."

"And for your wedding present he gave you the land he'd won in the court battle," Yasmine beamed.

"You know the story as well as I do."

"It is my favorite story about him," Yasmine smiled. "Then he brought me here to live with you after my family died."

"And that, my dear, gave me more happiness than I ever thought possible. Having you here made it so much easier after he was gone. You are so much like him—but thankfully you are more like me."

And you have always been my favorite. Olympia thought it, but did not speak it. That would not have been appropriate, despite how true it was.

Yasmine kissed her grandmother's cheek. "I have never once felt alone in my life. Even losing my parents and brother in the crash…then when Grandfather died. I have never felt alone or unloved in this family."

"And now, my dear, although you have always been a Blanchard, you will have the name to match!"

CHAPTER FORTY-NINE

Autumn Leaves

Every cloud was sweeping briskly across the faded blue of the sky. Winter hadn't yet cast its gray tinge to the horizon, but the autumn sky had lost the vividness of summer. The air was crisp, like kicking off a warm blanket in the night and having the cold air grab you. The shadows on the ground had already changed their positions as October was winding down and November was getting dressed and ready to start its reign. The leaves were turning gold and orange now, and everything around was bursting in warm colors to shield against the coming cold. Yasmine and Seth were walking through the woods of the Blanchard property, marveling at the beauty around.

Seth took notice of his intended as she stood beneath the branches full of fall color. "You look pretty enough to marry."

"Oh, you're not my type," she quipped.

"And just what exactly is your type?"

"Skinny. Latino. Or older, maybe. Yeah, old man. Rich enough to give me a carpet of gold to walk over."

"You want carpets of gold?" Seth smirked.

"I wouldn't turn it down."

He kissed her softly. "I love you. I love you so much, you ridiculous little idiot. And you should have carpets of gold."

Seth raised his arms to the sky and brought them down with a whoosh to his sides. Yasmine stood in bewilderment as a splendorous sight began. A gentle wind came by, loosening the leaves from the many trees above them—loosening only the leaves of yellow and gold. Slowly each leaf dwindled its way down, fluttering to gently fall upon the path before them. Above her, leaves of red and orange still clung to their limbs like a canopy of rich color. At her feet, stretching out down the path, lay her carpet of gold.

She laughed. She leaned into the chest of the man she loved as he wrapped his arms around her waist and buried his face into her neck. "I sometimes forget I'm marrying a witch. To me, you're just my stupid cousin—that I've been in love with all my life."

"I promise to stay stupid for you."

She jerked around, as if realizing something for the first time. "My children will be witches."

"Yeah," Seth nodded. "You just figuring that out?"

"I never really thought about that before," Yasmine said. "How do I discipline a child that can hurl me across the room?"

"You'll have me to whoop their ass if they do that," Seth smirked.

They walked along the golden path a while, holding hands. Yasmine stopped after a few yards and asked, "Are you sure you want to marry me? You're a full-blooded witch. I'm just a regular person. Your kids' powers will be diluted by me. What could your children be like if they had a witch for a mother?"

"My kids would probably be thoroughly unhappy because their dad would be miserably married to someone he didn't love."

Yasmine began to cry. "Seth Blanchard, you can sometimes be the sweetest man on this earth. It shocks me every time."

He took her in his arms and kissed her passionately. "Yaz, I'd do anything for you. The idea that I get to spend my entire life loving you, teasing you, making love to you—I don't know I got that damn lucky. I don't care about witches and family blood. I'd bind my powers in a second and run off with you and be just normal people working at a Waffle House, if that's what it took to get to spend my life with you."

She was definitely crying now. Crying and smiling and laughing as he held her tightly against him. "Seth," she finally said looking up into his eyes with her tear-stained face. "I'll meet you at the gazebo next week. I'll be the one in the veil shaking, because I'll be getting everything I have ever wanted in this life."

...

Walking into the kitchen after their romantic stroll, Seth and Yasmine were still lost among each other and paying very little attention to anything they were walking into. It was only when they heard the words coming out of Demitra's mouth that they pulled apart and listened to what was going on.

"There's been another murder," Demitra grimaced. "In Cottondale this time."

Yasmine's joy disintegrated and replaced upon her face was a look of concern. "That's only about twenty minutes from here."

"Patric is still around then," Seth said, now pacing the floor.

Beryl was looking out the window, but not at anything in particular, her thoughts were strictly cerebral. Then something occurred to her. The possibility of it had come before, but she'd dismissed it. Now, it seemed worth imparting. "It doesn't mean it's Patric," she said to the others.

"Not Patric?" Seth cried. "Then who?"

Turning from the window to face them, Beryl asked, "Don't you remember? You're the one who pointed it out. It could be that patient I had who was attacked. Lana Leighton. Last night the moon was full. It could have been her."

"What do we do?" Seth asked.

"I don't know," Beryl said. "Do we have the right to go after her? I am a doctor. My job is saving lives, not ending them. And we aren't the police."

"But the police can't stop a werewolf," Demitra offered. "I think it is actually our job to go after her. This could become an epidemic if left unchecked. I think it's our duty to protect the Natural Order by stopping this creature—both creatures."

Beryl knew she was right. True, she was sworn to an oath to save lives and do no harm–but that was meant for people. A werewolf was no longer people, and her obligations as a witch were just as important as her obligations as a physician.

"If we could find them," Beryl said. "I can get her address from the hospital record."

"Get it," Seth suggested. "You, Yazzy, and I will pay a little visit to your patient."

...

Acquiring Miss Leighton's address was simple. However, the moment Seth pulled the car up to the little house on Matthews Street, Yasmine recognized it immediately. She'd run from that house just a few weeks ago after sticking a fork into the leg of the man she'd been dating when he got just a little too aggressive.

"What the fuck Yaz!" Seth shouted from the driver's seat as Yasmine quickly told them the story. "Why am I only now hearing about this? Jake tried to rape you!"

"I handled it," Yasmine answered. "I got out of here and got back home."

"You handled it," Seth huffed. "You handled it. This man tried to rape you, and you stabbed him with a fork?!"

"It worked," she smiled meekly.

Seth Blanchard was livid. He wanted to kill Jake and he wanted to shake Yasmine for being so naive and endangering herself. "A man like that is crazy, Yasmine!" Seth yelled. "What makes you think he won't come after you again? Hell, he's probably really pissed now. This is shit you should have told me!"

"Could you two fight over this later?" Beryl called out from the back seat. "Yazzy is fine. She took care of herself like all women have to do at some point or another. Let's just focus on the task at hand."

"Don't you think it's a mighty big coincidence that Yaz's boyfriend lives here with your werewolf patient?"

"Let's just go knock on the door."

When Jake came to the door, Beryl opened her mouth to ask for Lana. Unfortunately, before she had an opportunity to ask anything, Seth's fist landed squarely into Jake's face, knocking him backward into the house. Seth charged in and wasted no time in targeting a barrage of blows at the man on the floor.

"Seth! Seth stop!" both Yasmine and Beryl pleaded.

Seth did not stop. Jake's bloody face looked upon them in stunned disbelief as Seth pummeled him. Finally, Yasmine flung herself onto her fiancé's arm in an attempt to prevent mortal injuries. Seth pushed her off but stopped punching Jake, who now laid covered in his own blood on the floor of his living room.

"You touch Yasmine again and I will kill you, you sorry son of a bitch!" Seth roared. He turned to Beryl and, still heaving from rage, said, "Ask him your fucking questions."

Jake said nothing. He simply laid in place, frightened–seething with a mixture of outrage and pain. He wiggled two of his now broken front teeth, pulling one out completely. Beryl stepped forward and tried to act like nothing crazy had just taken place.

"Hi, Jake," she smiled in an unfruitful way to soften the mood. "I am Dr. Blanchard. I am looking for a patient of mine who left the hospital last month. Her name is Lana Leighton. This was the address listed on her insurance information."

Jake was still in shock at the recent chain of events. After innocently opening his front door, he had been violently attacked by his ex-girlfriend's new boyfriend. He didn't respond to Beryl's question. Still wriggling his one remaining front tooth and simultaneously choking on blood in his throat, he looked up at them in disbelief.

"Answer her!" Seth screamed charging back towards him.

"Wait! Wait!" Jake stuttered. "Give me a second." His "s's" made a whistling sound now when he spoke, thanks to the missing tooth. "Lana moved out a while ago. I don't know where she lives now."

"How do you know her?" Beryl asked.

"We were together for a while. We moved here together. But she left when we broke up."

"Did you used to mistreat her, too?" Seth growled.

"Seth, stop," Yasmine said.

"I don't know where Lana is," Jake repeated. "I haven't seen her since Yasmine and I went out." He looked up at Yasmine, who was standing behind Seth, gripping his arm. "You're marrying your fucking cousin, huh?"

Seth charged forward again, pulled back by Yasmine. "Talk to her one more time! I fucking dare you. Say one more word to her!"

"Let's go," Beryl demanded.

"I'm gonna have you arrested!" Jake yelled at Seth. "This is assault."

"What you tried to do to me was assault, too," Yasmine yelled back.

"But you can't prove it," Jake shouted. "Look at my face! I can get your asshole boyfriend/cousin put in jail a long time for this. Then I'll get you, you little tease bitch!"

Suddenly Seth jumped loose of Yasmine's grip and bounded on top of Jake again. There was not a surface of the room that Seth did not either toss Jake's broken body into or punch him up against. When the fight, (if you could call one man beating another man almost to death, a fight) was over, Jake laid on the floor, bones broken, face crushed in by Seth's relentless blows. Jake was dying. Beaten and torn, his flesh split open across his face from Seth's knuckles. Seth stepped aside and allowed Beryl to come forward. She laid her healing hands upon Jake's body and within a few seconds, her power restored him to his pre-brawl condition. He lay on the floor, astounded by the events. His clothes and the carpet around the room were drenched in his own blood which had poured from wounds that were no longer there. Even his teeth were back in place in his mouth.

"There goes your evidence," Beryl grinned.

Jake lay there, unable to comprehend what was happening. Something from within reached up and gripped him. A paralyzing fear of what all had just taken place.

These people were not normal. Were they even mortal? Never at any time during his relationship with Yasmine had he any hint that her family were superhuman. Seth just nearly killed him, and then Yasmine's other cousin inexplicably wiped his injuries away. How was this possible? What kind of power had he just tangled with?

"What-what are you people?"

"You walked away without a mark this time," Seth warned. "But I think now you know what'll happen if I ever see you come near Yasmine again. Next time, my cousin won't be around to fix you."

Seth grabbed Yasmine by the arm and led her back to the car. Beryl glanced around the battlefield of the living room. A wooden chair that might have previously been a rocker, was now a broken mass of spindles, a seat, and one in-tact curved piece. A set of glass shelves lay toppled over. Broken shards sprinkled like glass snow over the knick knacks which once sat atop them. Blood dripped from furniture upholstery and a tiny section of window drapes. Beryl looked down to the man she had just healed.

"If you see Lana, will you please ask her to contact Dr. Blanchard at Daihmler County Hospital? Thank you so much." She shut the door behind her, and the Blanchard cousins pulled away from the curb.

CHAPTER FIFTY

Preparing for the Big Day

Maybe it was that Salem was due to arrive back home at any minute, or maybe it was because Halloween was only two days away and so was the wedding, or perhaps it was because Artemis only had eight days before her grand reopening of The Cobblestone, whatever the reason the Blanchard household was in chaos.

"Don't forget to pack your new swimsuits, Yaz," Fable reminded her cousin. "It may be cold here, but it'll be hot in Jamaica."

"I've already packed them," Yasmine called back behind her as she rummaged through the chest of drawers for more clothes to add to the suitcases.

Fable was helping her pack for the honeymoon now so that it would be one less thing to worry about as the wedding day approached. Everything was going smoothly. The hotel in Ocho Rios was booked. The flights were handled. The wedding was set to happen Halloween afternoon so that the family could celebrate Halloween night together. Seth and Yasmine would depart for their honeymoon the next morning and be back in time for the restaurant's opening.

Yasmine's bedroom was a mess. Clothes strewn everywhere. She could not decide what to take with her and what to leave behind. She had been ordering clothes online for two weeks and now she seemed to have way more outfits for her honeymoon than there would be days or places to wear them. Beryl interrupted the packing by tapping on the half-opened door. She motioned for Fable to step into the hall.

"Is everything ready?" Fable asked her sister.

"All set. The stripper will be here by eight tomorrow night. Mother is taking Hecate to a movie and Aunt Artemis will be at the restaurant. It will be just you, me Yazzy, and Salem. It'll be an intimate little shower, but Yaz won't forget it. Does she suspect anything?"

"Not a thing," Fable said. "Since we all went to that dinky little shower her friend Marsha gave last night, she doesn't expect a bachelorette party."

"What do we do about Seth?"

"I already called Howard. He put a bachelor party together with some of Seth's buddies. You know how rowdy they get. Seth will be gone all night." Fable thought a second and added, "Do you think this wedding will be tough for Salem?"

"Salem is strong," Beryl replied. "Besides, she can't avoid weddings forever. Plus, she loves Seth so much and Yaz is already like a sister to her. She'll be focused on them, not David."

"She says she has a surprise for us, but she wouldn't say over the phone. Do you think she's met a new guy?"

"Fable!" her sister snapped. "Her husband died four months ago. I really doubt she'd be dating again."

"Hell, I would," Fable laughed. "Four months is a long time to go without."

"I'm surprised you're taking a break now," Beryl teased. "I think it'll be a long time before our cousin is dating again."

Yasmine called out from the bedroom, cutting the secret chat short. "Fable, I don't know what shoes to take!"

Seth was pacing the front porch, counting the minutes until his sister arrived. Artemis came walking around the side of the house. When she saw her nephew, she quickly tossed something she'd been holding.

"I'm not going to tell Hecate or Demitra that you're smoking again," Seth laughed. "You don't have to toss it every time you see me and douse yourself with air freshener."

Artemis returned a grin and sat down beside him, "Good, then I can save my story of how Demitra's car really got dented for another time."

Seth jabbed her in the side with his elbow. "I want to talk with you a minute if you have time."

"This isn't going to be another parent/son talk is it? I'm still not recovered from explaining sex to you at 12 years old," Artemis chuckled.

"I don't know which of us was the most embarrassed," Seth nodded.

Artemis laughed again, "Oh, it was definitely me."

"I wanted to say a few things to you," Seth began. "I know Yaz and I are still going to live here, and not that much will be different, but I feel like it's a time for saying stuff. You know?"

"I know."

"I want to thank you," Seth said, tearing up a little as he looked his aunt in the eye. "You did everything for us—for me."

"I didn't do so much," Artemis blushed.

"No, you did. You did a lot." Seth's jaw muscles tightened a little. His face held an earnestness Artemis rarely saw from him. The sincerity he was displaying, captured her attention. "You could have had a life, but you gave everything up for me and Salem—and Yazzy, too. I don't think I ever told you how much I appreciated that. Or that I even recognized that. You were a better mother than anyone could have ever been born to."

"Stop it Seth," Artemis said crying now. "I don't like when you get gushy."

"I don't care," he smiled. "I want it said that everything you did for me did not go unnoticed. I was a handful, and I know it."

"That you were."

"You raised me. You raised Salem. You raised us all in many ways, but especially me. I love you, Artemis. I know I'm the clown of the family most of the time, but never does a day go by that I don't appreciate the sacrifices you made for me."

Artemis broke down. She tossed her arms around her nephew's neck and hugged him tightly. Giving him a kiss on the cheek she said, "I never desired children of my own, because I already had them. You have been my son since the day Nacaria left. I have never thought of you any other way. I love you so much, Seth. I wish you all the joy the world can offer. My greatest joy of life is going to be watching you be a father. I want that kind of happiness for you because you've been nothing but happiness for me."

Seth was about to say something else when he saw Salem's car pull into the driveway. Artemis perked up as well, both excited to see her again after these last few months. Seth bounded from the porch to her car. Salem rolled down her window to blow him a kiss as she parked.

"Hey Bro!" she cried, getting out to give him a hug.

Seth didn't see at first, too busy hugging his sister. Artemis noticed right away when a young woman stepped out of the passenger side of Salem's car. The woman looked quite young, younger than Yasmine. With her long, wavy red hair, she looked a little like Salem herself if Salem's hair had been more vivid.

"And who's your friend?" Seth greeted warmly as he pulled back from Salem to acknowledge her guest.

Salem's face held a tinge of worry, anticipating how Arielle would be received.

"This is the surprise I told you guys about," Salem revealed. "I wanted to say something so many times through text or our conversations, but I didn't know how you'd take it."

"What?" Seth exclaimed. "Are you gay now? Is she your girlfriend or something?"

Salem laughed and took hold of the girl's hand, "Seth, this is Arielle. Arielle Obreiggon. She is our sister."

CHAPTER FIFTY-ONE

An Obreiggon at Blanchard House

Jarring disbelief consumed the front yard of Blanchard House. Seth's mouth hung open like a garage door as he stood blank faced and speechless. Artemis was at a similar loss for words as Olympia stepped onto the porch to greet her returning granddaughter. Beside the old woman fluttered the shadow of Nacaria who hovered there a moment before dashing off to disappear around the side of the house.

"She's what?" Artemis muttered.

Salem squeezed Arielle's hand in solidarity. "She is my sister, Aunt Artemis. This is Arielle."

"You don't have a sister," Seth gruffed.

He was staring Salem down now with the angriest eyes she'd ever seen cross his face. He was almost shaking with fury. This was not the welcome Salem had expected. She knew he wouldn't be warm to the idea at first, but she had underestimated the power of their childhood resentment toward anything Obreiggon. That resentment still lurked within him deeper than she knew.

"We both have a sister," Salem reminded him with a gentle tone, hoping to douse a little of his rage. "And here she is."

"She's not welcome in this house!" Seth shrieked, charging forward closer to Salem. The intensity in eyes frightened her a moment.

"Maybe this was a bad idea, Salem," Arielle whispered, retreating back behind the car door.

Salem whipped around to look at Arielle, slinging her hair across her shoulders as she did. "You're staying!" She ordered Arielle. She turned back to her brother and asserted, "My sister is welcome here because I want her here."

The vein in Seth's neck bulged as every muscle in his body tensed. For a split-second Artemis thought he might hit Salem. She took a step forward to stand between them.

"Calm down, Seth," she cautioned.

"Salem," Seth grimaced. "If you want to associate with Obreiggon's then you aren't welcome in this house either."

Artemis should have been more worried about what Salem planned to do, because to everyone's surprise Salem Blanchard reached back and slapped her brother across the face. He charged at her until Artemis flung her arm out to stop him.

"I'll give you that one," he growled. "But the next one, I hit back. And I hit a lot harder than you."

"I guess you forget I can blow you up with the flick of a wrist," Salem huffed.

"And I can bring a bolt of lightning down on you to fry you like catfish!"

"That is enough!" Olympia shouted from the porch; her frail voice thundered with a force the Blanchard kids rarely heard. "Seth, stand down. Salem, back off."

It wasn't often that Olympia Blanchard got riled, but when she did it caught everyone's attention immediately. She left the porch and made her way down the front steps, gesturing for the frightened young guest to come forward. Arielle did so meekly.

"Arielle, we have met before. I am Olympia Blanchard."

"Yes, ma'am," she replied. "I know."

"You are welcome in this house," Olympia announced more to Seth than to Arielle Obreiggon. "If it is important to my granddaughter, then it is important to all of us."

"I don't want to cause problems," Arielle stammered. "I'm sorry Seth, if I have upset you by being here. I just wanted to meet my brother."

Seth flared his eyes. Turning on his heels he stormed off across the lawn.

"I can leave, Ms. Blanchard," Arielle told Olympia. "I don't want to cause trouble."

"Seth is a prick sometimes," Salem said, directing her sister up the porch steps with a steady hand. "Ignore him. We all do."

The two of them went inside the house leaving the screen door to slam behind them. Artemis exchanged concerning looks with her mother. Olympia raised a brow and shook her head, then she clasped her daughter's arm and they joined the others in the house.

Seth stomped around the property for a while, trying to clear his temper and make sense of his sister's stupidity. After about an hour, he had made no progress at all in accomplishing either. As he made his way back towards the house he was met by his grandmother and aunt near the pumpkin patch where they were removing the best of the garden for Halloween and wedding décor.

"Feel any better?" Artemis asked Seth, wiping her cheek where a disoriented gnat decided to rest.

"Not one bit."

"I suggest you make peace with it, son," Olympia suggested calmly. "We must have respect for Salem's wishes."

Seth kicked at the ground, loosening a clump of dirt with his feet. "Hecate, have you suddenly lost all of your marbles?"

"Watch it, boy!" Artemis scolded. "Do not speak to your grandmother like that."

"I do not trust this girl," Seth insisted. "She's one of Atheidrelle's children. That alone makes her dangerous. The Obreiggon's are evil."

Olympia rolled an almost perfectly shaped orange pumpkin to the side, cut its vine with her clippers, and gave it a friendly pat on the side. She then looked up at her grandson and clarified, "The Obreiggon's are not evil. Xander Obreiggon is a kind man. Weak, but kind."

"Excuse me, " Seth corrected sarcastically. "The D'Angelos are evil. Atheidrelle's family."

"Again, you are not necessarily correct, Seth," Artemis began, "a long time ago there was a woman who loved your mother very much—"

Artemis was cut short in mid-sentence by her mother by a stern look..

"That is not our secret to tell," Olympia warned.

"It might help him to understand," Artemis argued. "Atheidrelle's sister-"

"All Seth needs to understand is that he has a sister here. A sister he has never known. It is time that he did."

"I don't trust her," he repeated.

"Salem does," Olympia said. "That's good enough for all of us."

Upstairs, Salem and Arielle unpacked in Salem's room. Arielle ran her fingers along the quilted bedspread under the suitcase. The entire room was charming in her opinion. White plank boards covering the walls, beautiful flower arrangements placed on the nightstand and dresser. The curtains looked hand sewn in lace and frilly ruffles. Arielle felt a peace in the room she had never felt in her room back at Oleander.

"I love this house," she said. "The whole house is so crisp and clean and light. And I smell flowers everywhere."

Salem grinned. It delighted her to see her little sister appreciate the beauty of the house she had grown up in. Sometimes Salem lost sight of just how tranquil

Blanchard House could be until she saw it through a stranger's eyes. It was a vast difference from the austere coldness Arielle had been raised in.

"Hey, I'm sorry about Seth's behavior. He's normally not an ass."

"I understand," Arielle shrugged. "It was the same at Oleander. We were raised to believe the Blanchards were awful people. The enemy. Of course, I figured out early my mother was a terrible person, so I didn't buy into her version of events very much."

"I'm glad you understand," Salem said with a grateful nod.

"It's not really crazy for him to react this way," Arielle continued. "With all that happened to your mother, it was natural for you guys to think of my mom and our dad as the bad guys. You and I have had some time to get to know each other. And you even got to meet our father. But we just kinda sprung me on Seth without warning. I get it."

Salem thought about what her sister said and realized Arielle was incredibly wise for her age. She hadn't played fair with Seth. She had expected him to greet Arielle with open arms, but why? She had also been wary of Arielle at first. How could she expect Seth to so blindly trust? She and Seth spent their lives blaming Xander and Atheidrelle Obreiggon for their mother's removal from their life.

As they grew up and came to understand their mother's role in what happened, Salem and Seth came to resent Nacaria as well. Only recently had Salem learned to forgive her mother once she had met their father. Seth did not have that privilege. He did not have any closure. Salem knew now she owed her brother an apology.

She found him sitting by the pool in a lounge chair. It was getting colder out, but he had lit a fire in the firepit nearby. The crackling wood sent tiny sparks into the air every so often to mix with the wafting smoke. He saw her approach but did not leave, nor did he acknowledge her.

"I came to apologize," she said.

Seth acknowledged her presence with a grunt.

"It started at the Consort," she explained. "Arielle introduced herself to me after the cremation. Her mother and her sister Cassandra were not very kind to me. She offered me sympathy. And she took me to meet our father."

"You met him?!" Seth asked. "You actually saw him?! What was he like?"

Suddenly his anger was broken, replaced by curiosity for the man they had never known very much about. Seth found himself wanting to know about him, what her impressions of him were. That trumped any amount of anger he bore.

"I was not very kind to him at first," Salem admitted. "But I heard him out. And I have to say I believed him."

She paused to grab her brother's hand. He did not snatch it away. This was a bond they had always shared—the dream—and Salem had accomplished it. She had been in the presence of their father, and Seth wanted details.

"What did he have to say?"

"He loved her very much," Salem began. "He still does. He told me that their affair was wrong, but he'd loved her too much to end it. He was planning to leave Atheidrelle to be with our mother, and with us. But he was too late. Mother had already gone back in time and committed her crime before she knew he had chosen us. When she returned it was too late, the Consort knew what she'd done."

"How did they find out?" Seth wondered.

"He didn't say. I don't think even he knew. Mother was arrested by the Consort, and they tried her. She was going to be hanged but our father advocated for her. He made a deal with his wife that if she would intervene to punish Nacaria in a different way, he would relinquish his rights to us and share his Council seat with her. He did not know beforehand how the Council would curse our mother. Xander still believes she will be returned to us one day."

"So now you're besties with his daughter?"

"It was sweet, actually," Salem explained. "She phoned me in Atlanta, worried about how I was doing at home alone. She came to see me. We got to know each other. She actually lives with me now. She saved me. She really did."

"I would have gone back with you," Seth scoffed.

"I know you would have," Salem said, laying her head on her brother's shoulder. "But you have your own life to live. The point I am making is that Arielle has had a miserable life. She doesn't have a close, loving family like ours. We each always have someone on our side. Someone looking out for us, but she has been very alone."

Seth's eyes changed from angry to slightly sympathetic, but only *slightly*.

"I care about her a lot. I'd like you to try and know her."

"I can't promise anything."

"Just try," Salem asked. "She's been every bit as wounded as we have. All she has is her father, and he has been a shell of his former self since our mother went away. Arielle just wants to be part of a family. I like having her around."

...

Taking the night off from work, Artemis prepared an elaborate meal for the family. It was a special night with everyone home. In a few days, Seth and Yasmine would be married. And once they returned home from their honeymoon, Artemis would be at the restaurant all the time, and Yasmine would be taking over the family meals. Artemis spared no culinary expense to make the last big family meal under her watch spectacular.

"I would like to make a toast," Olympia announced, raising a glass of wine to the table.

"Oh Hecate, just eat while you can enjoy it," Fable laughed. "This is probably the last time we will have a decent meal. I don't relish the idea of Yazzy's cooking after The Cobblestone opens."

"Hey!" Yasmine whined.

Artemis chimed in at her niece's defense. "I'll have you know that Yasmine has already learned quite a bit. She will do splendidly. Besides, it is much better than Demitra taking over."

"I'll have you know that my husband loved my cooking," Demitra argued.

"No, he didn't," Artemis revealed. "I always left him a plate of whatever I cooked in the fridge, and he'd sneak down after you went to bed and eat again."

"He did not!" Demitra said.

"Oh, he did!" Seth laughed. "Uncle Larry and I used to have 10 o'clock supper together all the time."

"Mother, your food was bad," Beryl chimed in. "Fable and I used to ask Hecate for lunch money every day because we did not want to eat the leftovers you put in our lunch boxes."

"You are all worrying over nothing," Yasmine snorted. "My meals will be great."

Seth kissed her softly on the cheek, "Don't worry, baby. I will eat whatever you prepare. If I get sick, Beryl can always heal me after."

Everyone had a hearty laugh at Seth's joke. Arielle smiled too. She had never experienced anything like this. Most of her life she had taken all of her meals in her bedroom alone, until she'd reached 16 years old and was expected to sit at the formal table with her family in complete silence as meals were consumed. Sitting so casually around a table amid laughter and good-natured insults was refreshing to her. No one was dressed up. Elbows were on the table. Bowls of food were simply laying in the center for anyone to help themselves to more if they wished. This was a new experience.

Olympia cleared her throat, "Anyway, I was attempting to make a toast to the bride and groom." She raised her glass to Seth and Yasmine. "May you both have every happiness this world can provide. And may your love for one another remain its own source of power for the remainder of your lives."

Everyone sipped their wine to her words as Seth stood up himself. "Thank you, Hecate. I would also like to make a toast." He looked down at his bride-to-be. "First, I would like to toast my best friend, and soulmate—soon to be my wife. I promise to make you the happiest wife that ever lived. I promise to protect you, love you, be faithful to you, and tell you off anytime you make me mad—lovingly, of course."

The family chuckled.

"I would also like to thank Hecate, and my lovely aunts for making me the man I am today."

"Should we throw our glasses at them for that?" Fable asked her sister.

"I'm not finished," Seth continued. "I would also like to thank Fable and Beryl for being tolerant of me all these years. For being my sisters and not just cousins. I would also like to toast Salem. My big sister. Thanks for always being there for me, loving me, forgiving me, and especially for always freezing Beryl whenever she was winning one of our wrestling matches when we were kids."

"I knew it!" Beryl cried.

"He was littler than you," Salem laughed.

Arielle was smiling at the scene around her, but she was also drifting off in thought. Behind her smile lingered a twinge of sadness for having missed out on a family like this. She and Cassandra never bantered. They had never been close. Arielle hadn't realized how much she'd missed out on in life until sitting there at the Blanchard table.

"And lastly," Seth finished, reaching across the table and tapping Arielle gently on the shoulder to get her attention. "I would like to welcome my new...sister."

Arielle was not prepared for that bit of unexpected sentiment. She glanced up at him with disbelieving eyes, certain she'd misheard, but hoping that she hadn't.

"Yes, sister. My new little sister. I hope we will get to know each other. I *am* actually glad you are here."

There was no concealing the happiness Seth's words brought to Arielle. Her eyes were full of moisture and joy. She smiled and whispered a thank you. She nervously looked up at all the members of the family now staring at her with warm, welcoming smiles. Salem reached over and squeezed her hand.

"Welcome to the family."

CHAPTER FIFTY-TWO

The Bachelorette Party

Jack-o-lanterns lined the wide front porch, each carved with happy smiles. The half-moon hovered in the sky while leaves the color of Autumn paintings were gathering gently upon the porch steps. All the lights in Blanchard House were extinguished except for a few lamps and candles in the upstairs den. The bulbs were softened by rose and pumpkin-colored scarves draped over the shades. Everyone's shadow looked three times larger than their bodies as the delicate light cast them to the walls. Occasionally one shadow, Nacaria's, appeared dwarf-like among them.

Artemis was at the restaurant. Demitra had taken Olympia to a movie. Seth was meeting Howard at a local tavern. It was October 30, and Yasmine's bachelorette shower was underway. Tomorrow was the wedding. Arielle turned on the den sound system and hooked her phone's Bluetooth to the speakers. As she twirled around the floor to Fleetwood Mac's Gypsy, Salem realized her little sister had a very low alcohol tolerance. Fable and Yasmine were huddled on the floor giggling as Beryl came upstairs with two fresh pitchers in hand.

"Yay!" Arielle cried. "I'm on empty!"

"Which do you want?" Beryl asked. "Margarita or Rum Runner?'

"Lum Bunters," Arielle hiccupped.

"She's wasted," Fable laughed.

Salem refilled her sister's glass but decided before handing it to her that it was probably best to also escort her to a chair. "You've never been drunk before have you, Ari?"

"Not so much," Arielle admitted. "It's quite wonderful. I think people should drink more."

"You should see this girl try to fry chicken," Salem teased to the others. "It was by far the funniest thing I have ever seen in my life."

Salem sat back down and continued the job she had begun earlier and abandoned, of braiding Fable's hair. Her raven hair had grown some over the summer, long enough now to actually do something with, but it was still probably much too short for braiding. As she put her hands back into the job she remembered why she had abandoned it earlier. It was less braided than it was tied into knots. *Maybe I'm a little drunk, too.*

"Okay, okay, I'm ready!" Yasmine cried.

"For what?" Beryl said, a little louder than was called for, causing her to also realize she had consumed too much herself.

"What?" Yasmine replied, totally forgetting it was she who started the topic..

"You said you were ready for something," Beryl repeated, even more amplified.

"Beryl, you are awfully loud," Salem pointed out.

"Oh."

"What are you ready for, Yaz?" Salem asked.

"Presents!"

"Alright, alright," Salem said, pulling the coffee table forward toward Yasmine. It was stacked with gifts wrapped in paper of orange and black with corresponding ribbons tied around for accent. Everyone gathered around the table and watched as Yasmine tore into her wrapped treasures.

"What are these, Fable?" Yasmine asked pulling the lid off a box to reveal lacy underwear with no middle section.

"Crotchless panties," Fable grinned. "I figured they'd save time whenever you and Seth are at dinner parties and he can't control himself and decides to sneak you off to another room."

"Yes, I was wondering how to solve that particular problem at all those *dinner parties* we go to," Yasmine answered sarcastically.

"Here," said Salem, picking up another gift. "This is from Zelda. She dropped it off this afternoon."

Yasmine ripped the paper off and opened the box. The box was filled with fast food gift certificates, restaurant gift cards, movie theater gift cards, two bottles of wine, two pewter goblets, and two one-night stay certificates at two different hotels. *In case you two need some privacy in a house full of relatives.*

"Zelda is so sweet," Yasmine giggled.

"She really is," Fable added. "It's a shame my boyfriend tried to kill her."

Everyone looked at each other and then burst into laughter. It was the first time Fable had made light of the situation, proving that perhaps she was getting over it and healing from the disappointment Patric had proven to be.

Fable took another sip of her margarita and then discreetly poured a little of it out into a potted plant beside her. She wasn't sure yet what she planned to do about this pregnancy. She was pacing herself appropriately. Taking a few sips if everyone was looking was all right but the majority of her liquor was consumed by the philodendron.

"Look!" Yasmine cried. "Grandmother's silver candlesticks she bought on her honeymoon with Granddaddy!"

"Aw, she gave them to you," Salem smiled brightly. Olympia treasured those candlesticks. It was a beautiful gesture to give them now to Yasmine.

Yasmine reached for another gift which had been stacked beneath the previous two. It was not wrapped in orange or black. It was covered in shiny red paper--almost Christmas red. Unwrapping the box and lifting the lid she found only a note, *Open the door.*

"I wonder what's behind the door?" Yasmine feigned chuckling. Walking towards the door she added, "Possibly a naked man? You guys thought you were so clever! I knew the whole time."

"Cool idea," Fable whispered to Beryl. "Having the stripper waiting in the hall."

"The stripper isn't due for another hour," she replied. "And I didn't tell him to come upstairs."

"Yasmine, wait!" Fable called out, but it was too late. Yasmine pulled the door open.

Standing before all of them was Patric. His menacing eyes glowing red with victory. Yasmine screamed. She tried to close the door on him, but he ripped it from the hinges with one fierce tug. Yasmine stumbled backward and fell over the coffee table. Her cousins grabbed her by the shoulders, pulling her backwards to cower with them behind the table—as if that were somehow safer.

"Little pig, little pig, let me in," Patric sneered.

"Go away, Patric!" Fable screamed rising to her feet. "Leave us alone! I don't want you. I'm not going with you."

He cocked his head to the side, giving an incredulous look. Then he laughed. It was a sinister, guttural, echoing laugh. Fable's statement amused him for some reason they did not understand. He took a step forward into the room. Salem glanced at Arielle and instinctively reached her arm out to shield her little sister. It was almost the same way a mother outstretches an arm to the passenger seat to block her child when tapping the brake suddenly. Neither of them had ever seen this man before... this creature. The sight of him made them shudder.

"I did not come back for you, Fable," Patric growled. "Your arrogance is amusing." His eyes slowly turned back to Yasmine. "It was *always* you Yasmina. It has always been you."

The others were spellbound by the revelation, unable to physically react with their brains now processing the surprising information. Patric was not after Fable. He wanted Yasmine. But why?

Patric leapt forward with a lightning speed, the likes none of them had ever witnessed before. Salem flung her hands forward to send her freezing power forth and stop him. Simultaneously, Fable flung herself forward to block the path to Yasmine. Neither attempt made a difference. For, in the flash of an eye, Patric was gone, and so was Yasmine. Only the sound of shattered glass from the window behind them was left in their wake.

CHAPTER FIFTY-THREE

Frantic

Growing more petrified with each passing minute, the Blanchard's assembled in the living room to plan Yasmine's rescue. A minor comfort came from knowing that Olympia, the aunts, Zelda, and Seth were now home, all called instantly after Yasmine's kidnapping. But even their presence was of little relief. No one had any clues as to their beloved Yasmine's whereabouts.

Zelda was doing her utmost to connect to Patric's mind again. She strained from the effort but could produce no results. "I can't do it," she moaned.

"Keep trying!" Seth cried. "You have to. You have to find them."

"I'm trying," Zelda panted, still trying to scan the world for their location. "He's got a fortress 'round his mind. It's stronger than I am."

"You must find a way in, Zelda," Olympia urged.

"They could be anywhere." Beryl said. "We cannot just sit here waiting for Zelda to make a connection. We have to do something else."

"Arielle?" Artemis asked. "Do you have any special abilities that might help us?"

"I'm sorry, I don't."

Arielle looked disappointed in herself. With all of her abilities there was nothing in her arsenal which might be of help locating Yasmine. The Blanchards needed help. and she wished she could be the person to provide it, but there was nothing she could do.

"Demitra," Artemis said. "You are the only other psychic here. You have to try."

"I'm not even half as strong as Zelda," Demitra admitted. "If she can't do it—"

"Yes, but perhaps the reason she can't do it is simply because he knows her mind now too. He can stop her. But he hasn't been inside yours. Just try."

Demitra closed her eyes. She focused on her niece. Yasmine's soft, delicate features came into her mind. Her voice. Her laugh. Her sweet innocence. She strained to connect. Strained to find the slightest trail of her energy. Nothing would come.

...

Yasmine was groggy. Her head was pounding. She groaned as she lifted her hand to rub her sore neck, and the bump on her head. Sharp pains swept through her back and shoulders. She had been standing in the den at home. Now she was here, wherever here was. *What happened?*

"I'm sorry for the discomfort you feel," Patric said standing above her. She realized she was laying on some sort of rectangular folding table.

"What did you do to me?" she asked.

"I'm afraid it was the force of us going through the window. You got banged up a little."

"Where are we?" She fought her own dizziness for the power to speak. Her words, when they came, were slurred. Perhaps from the alcohol she had consumed or perhaps it was a concussion. "What are you going to do to me? Where have you taken me?"

"Relax, my dear," he whispered, stroking her hair. "I had to knock you out in the car so that you wouldn't try to escape."

"What car?"

"The car I took from the unfortunate man last evening. I myself do not need transportation. But I could hardly carry you across town on my back. I had a car waiting for us down the road. We drove here."

She glanced sideways to take in her surroundings. It looked to be a vacant studio loft apartment. The room was very large and judging from the dust and dirt, no one had lived there for quite a while. Candles were lit around the floor and the walls--many of which clearly stood in place of where older ones had been burned at some earlier time. There were trails of long dried wax in many colors streaming beneath them. This had to be where Patric lived. From the appearance of the candle wax, he had been staying here for some time.

"Where is this place?"

"Do you like it?" Patric asked. "I secured it a few months ago when I first arrived. We are in Tuscaloosa."

"Downtown?" she asked. "I can see the marquee of the Bama Theater."

"Very good," he grinned. "Your sight is growing clearer. We are across the street above a row of shops. I would not bother to scream. This area is rather vacant after five o'clock. Nothing is open. The nearest people are two blocks away in the restaurant district."

She sat up on the table, still wobbly. He did not try to restrain her. He assisted her in fact, quite gently even. As if he cared for her comfort. For some inexplicable reason, Yasmine wasn't afraid. Not the way she should probably have been. She had no sense of terror. She didn't fear being raped or killed. This man was a monster and she knew it, yet she felt no feeling of imminent danger from him.

"Why did you take me? Why did you bring me here? I thought it was Fable you loved. What use can I possibly be to you? Seems like an awful lot of trouble, just to eat me."

He laughed. His laugh made her feel momentarily afraid, but the fear passed. And in its place came a kind of recognition. For the first time, she felt something very familiar about him. That laugh was familiar. Not the tone, nor the richness of quality to it, but the cadence. The melody of it she had heard before.

"I assure you I won't eat you," he grinned.

"But you're a werewolf."

"After living with witches, I'd think you would be the last person to stereotype anyone, my sweet Yasmina," he said.

It was bizarre. Everything was so confusingly bizarre. Yasmine had seen him rip Seth's arm off. Seen him unleash a pack of wolves onto her family. Yet now, in the dim flickering light of the loft, she found herself almost feeling safe with him. She might have even liked him had she never known what he was capable of before. Things began to click in her mind. Little light bulbs going off. He had always been kind to her. That night at dinner, when Seth poked fun at her weight, Patric had defended her. The night of that terrible battle, when the wolf pounded towards her, ready to kill, it had been Patric who had charged forward to stop it. Patric saved her from the wolf's bite that night.

"We know each other, don't we?" she asked. "I don't know how. But your face. It's like the face of a man from a dream I don't remember."

"There is an old saying," he began. "*This is a thought I thought I'd think again, I think I thought, when I remembered that none of this happened.*"

"What does that mean?"

"To understand, you have to have remembered," Patric told her as he gently stroked her cheek.

"Remember what?"

"Your soul knows. Listen to it."

"I don't understand," she said. "Why didn't you run far away from here after the family confronted you? You know how strong they are. And yet you came back. Why? Why not get out of here as fast as you can?"

"Are you worried for me?"

"Yes," she said automatically, without thinking. Then realizing that she did actually care she corrected herself. "No. No, you're a monster. You are a werewolf. You're a killer."

"I wasn't always a wolf. I wasn't always a killer," he said. "And I came back, for you."

"Why me?"

"Because you are the very reason I came to Alabama," Patric's eyes were glowing now, not with the rage she had seen during his attacks. It glowed with some other emotion. It felt like love. "You are the reason I sought out Fable," he continued. "I knew from the moment I saw her that she was a Blanchard. And the Blanchards had you. And you belong to me."

"...you belong to me." Demitra whispered.

"What?" Seth cried, confused.

Zelda removed her arms from around Demitra's waist where they had been standing entwined together, surging their power into one larger force. Olympia's idea had worked. Combining their psychic powers amplified their strength, and they had found a trail. Backing away from each other, the two psychics shared a mutual nod and a knowing smile.

"I know where she is," Demitra informed the others. "She's alive. She's with Patric. They are in an old loft in Tuscaloosa."

"There are dozens of lofts in Tuscaloosa!" Fable exclaimed. "Which one?"

"That's where you come in, daughter. Let's get down there and you use that animal sense you have and locate Patric."

CHAPTER FIFTY-FOUR

Ties that Bind

Peering into Patric's eyes through the dimly lit room, Yasmine knew he would never lie to her. She could trust whatever he said. He was a fiend. A monster. A killer. But she also knew now that he was not going to harm her in any way.

"Are you in love with me?" she asked him.

"I do love you," he admitted.

"So, this is some kind of *reincarnation* thing? We were lovers in another life, and you've been trying to find me?" she asked.

He laughed, "You have a very romantic outlook my dear. But I'm afraid our bond isn't as complicated as all that."

Suddenly she knew. He had laughed again. The familiar cadence of that laugh and the flicker in his eyes as she stared into them. Now she recognized him. How could she have missed it before? He even looked the same, only older. Yet inside that man's face dwelled the boy she once knew. The realization shocked her. How had she never seen it before?

"Your name is not Patric," she smiled, lifting her soft hand to his cheek. "You made that name up. You're my Ollie."

Patric grabbed her in his arms and held her tight against his powerful, inhuman chest. "Yes, my dearest Yasmina. It is me. It's Oliver. Oliver Sinclair. Oh, my baby sister, how I've missed you."

Yasmine began to cry. She could not comprehend what was happening. It was too much. Too surreal. How could this be? The killer her family had been searching for, the man who had sat across from her at the dinner table that night at Blanchard House. The man who had attacked the house with his wolves, set to destroy everyone she loved. He was her brother.

"No," she said, pushing away from his embrace. "You can't be Ollie! Ollie died. He died with our parents in that crash."

"No, Yasmina," he replied. "I did not die with our parents that night. It may be difficult for you to wrap your head around, but your brother is alive. He is powerful, and he is standing in front of you now."

It was too much to process. How could it be? This monstrous nomad was her brother? Her long dead brother Oliver. Her sweet, loving big brother. How could he now be this thing she'd seen attack her family? She looked into his eyes again, studied the features of his face. He looked the way Ollie might look all these years later, but she could not be sure. She had only been six years old when the crash came that killed her parents and brother.

It all came flooding back to her—memories from a lifetime ago. She had been at home with the neighbor—Mrs. Jenkins, kind Mrs. Jenkins. Mrs. Jenkins had fed Yasmine hotdogs for dinner. Her parents were driving back from the summer camp where Ollie had been the last two weeks. She remembered how excited she was because she had not seen her brother in all that time, and they were all driving to Alabama the next day to meet her grandfather's new wife. She hadn't seen her grandfather in over a year.

Yasmine remembered how she must have sat in Mrs. Jenkins' window for hours waiting for her parents to pull up with Ollie. But they never came to get her. She'd stayed the night with Mrs. Jenkins, both of them very confused as to why her parents never showed up. The next day her grandfather appeared at Mrs. Jenkins' door. Yasmine had not understood. Grandfather sat her down in Mrs. Jenkins' living room and told her how her parents and her brother had been in an accident. While driving home from camp Yasmine's father swerved to miss a dog on the road, and lost control of the car. Her family was sent tumbling over a hill, plummeting into the Ohio River. They had all been drowned. Her mother, her father...

"They never found you," she remembered. "Everyone figured your body was swept out the back window. They didn't find you."

"Because I didn't die," Patric replied. "I didn't even hit the water. I was thrown on the hill."

"But—" Yasmine stuttered, wiping tears from her face. "You can't be him?"

"I am, Yasmina. And I have finally come to find you."

"But—"

"I've had a lot to overcome," he continued. "It took me some time to be ready. Time to learn to control the beast within me, so that I wouldn't hurt you."

"How?" she asked. "How did this happen? How did you become this thing?"

Patric began to pace the floor as he recounted the night to fill in the gaps which made no sense to Yasmine. "It wasn't a dog. The animal our father swerved to miss was a man--a wolf. I know the witnesses said it was a dog, but it wasn't." Patric grew silent, reflective, lost in his thoughts momentarily. "His name was Teague. He was a good man. He had been fleeing from a kill. Oh, how killing tortured him. Every kill was like a private hell for him." Patric walked to one of the loft windows and looked out into the night.

"He did this to you?" Yasmine asked softly.

"The wolf saved me. He dragged me by his teeth to safety. He was quick and clever and acted fast. Teague lived in the mountains of West Virginia. He nursed me and cared for me. He had every intention of returning me to whatever family I had left. You see, he felt very guilty for my orphanhood. But something happened he had not counted on. He had to wait for the next month's moon to know for sure. When he had been dragging me to safety, his teeth punctured my flesh. I inherited his curse. From that moment on he knew I could go nowhere. I remained with him in the mountains."

"He raised you?"

"He was my father in every way. He taught me the ways of the beast. I was weak at first. Only the moon could transform me. But every kill made me stronger. Hungrier. More powerful. And I tried to forget you."

"But you didn't?"

"No, I couldn't. I eventually left Teague two years ago to find you. I only knew our grandfather's name. I didn't know the ways of this world. The Internet. How to drive a car. I had to learn much before I could find you. Grandfather was dead by then and his wife did not carry his name. It took time. But I've found you at last my sister. And to find you among witches! You already knew things that exist in the world others never dream about. When I discovered you had been raised by witches, I knew you would be able to accept me. You'd join me."

"Join you?" Yasmine repeated.

He pulled her back into his arms. "You and I will go far away from here. I will turn you, teach you. I will teach you all the things Teague taught me. You will grow powerful in time. You will become the wolf the way I have. It isn't killing, Yasmina. It's nature. It's survival. It's instinct. In time you will grow to understand. You must come with me now, and we will start over the way it always should have been for us...together."

CHAPTER FIFTY-FIVE

Beauty and the Beast

It took three cars to deliver all of the Blanchard witches to the downtown streets of Tuscaloosa. Downtown, consisting of merely six streets horizontally and six streets vertically, wasn't too challenging when it came to finding the most likely lofts where Patric might have Yasmine stashed. The streets where the local restaurants and bars were located seemed an unlikely choice to hold someone against their will without being seen or heard. The family focused their attention to the avenues of shops which were already closed up for the night. The avenue of shops proved to be a pretty desolate area at this time, therefore it was likely a perfect locale for Patric's plans.

Standing on the sidewalk in front of two dress boutiques and a cigar shop, Fable focused her instincts to feel out the air around, trying to locate any possible animal scents. It did not take long for her to pick something up. She bristled and slowly reached out to grab her grandmother's wrist.

"We've walked into a trap," she said. "Look up slowly."

Shadowy figures prowled the rooftops of the buildings all around. Hunched figures, on all fours, stalking the perimeters of the three-story structures in every direction they turned. Low growls could be faintly heard over the night wind.

"They know we're here," Olympia warned the others.

"Can you freeze them Salem?" Artemis asked.

"I'm too far away from most of them," Salem said, gesturing to the buildings down the block.

"Which building is Patric in?" Demitra asked Fable.

Fable closed her eyes and concentrated. She could not locate him. She didn't expect that she'd have much success in the first place. It wasn't as if she ever really used her power to search out animals. But then she remembered her one ace in the hole which no one else knew about. *I'm pregnant. I have Patric's child inside me. A part of him.*

She tried focusing again, this time inwardly. She directed her power to hone in on the being inside her body—to *feel* it, to sense it. It was a distinctive and singularly different kind of being than she had ever felt before. Then she focused outward to the air, searching—scanning—the buildings around her for a sensation that resembled what lay inside her. She found something. A very similar feeling coming from somewhere inside a building diagonally opposite her. The building housed a small lunchtime café in the bottom, now closed. On the top floor, cast in glowing red from the lights of the Bama Theater across the street, she felt Patric. On the rooftop above paced a disturbing number of wolves.

"Salem," she whispered, pointing. "Can you reach those over there?"

"I think so," Salem said. "Maybe."

"Wait for my signal," Fable advised. "Grandmother, Aunt Artemis, Seth... get ready to use your powers. Everyone waits for my signal. I have to get some reinforcements first."

"Reinforcements?" Demitra questioned.

"I'm going to try something I've never tried from this far away before," Fable explained.

She closed her eyes and focused her brain. Her family watched, unsure what it was exactly she was doing. It all became clear when after a few seconds, the distant sound of squawks and calls drifted into earshot. Overhead in the distance, the half-moon was temporarily covered, not by clouds, but by a wave of black soaring across the sky. Birds. Hundreds of birds.

"Now!" Fable shouted.

The wolves atop the buildings jerked to attention as Salem tossed her hands to the air and froze in place the wolves standing sentry on top of Patric's building. Two blocks down the wolves which had been the furthest away began charging across the rooftops, lurching across alleys to leap onto the next roofline, gaining closer ground to the Blanchards below. The swarm of birds in flight dipped their wings to bank left and began their descent, swooping down onto the rooftop wolves, attacking, pecking, stabbing their sharp beaks into the backs of the beasts. Some tumbled off the roofs to the street below, some fell injured only to be engulfed by the winged warriors in victory. But other wolves, most wolves, escaped Fable's army and began leaping down to the streets, charging forward at the Blanchards.

"I can't go with you," Yasmine told Patric inside the loft. "I'd have to leave my family. Leave Seth."

"I am your family!" Patric shouted angrily.

"Ollie, listen to me," she pleaded. "I am a Blanchard. They have raised me. Raised me the way Teague raised you. I don't want to leave them. And Seth, he's the only man in the world for me. We're being married tomorrow."

"No, you aren't," Patric hissed. "I will not allow that. You belong with me." Suddenly he turned his attention away from his captive sister and bolted to the windows. "They are here."

He saw the attack happening below on the streets and above on the rooftops. The birds wounding and killing his soldiers. He saw injured bodies of wolves falling to the ground below. But he also saw his most persistent warriors hitting the streets on their hooves charging towards his enemies. Patric whirled around to face his sister.

"The Blanchards are here. But they will all die on these streets."

Yasmine rushed to the window herself. She saw the havoc below. Grabbing the first object she had near her, a large iron lantern with a candle inside, she hurled it through the third-floor window, sending it crashing to the sidewalk below.

"Seth!" she screamed.

Below on the street, Seth heard the cry of his beloved and looked up to see her frightened face in the window. He sprinted forward into race mode. He had to get to her. Had to save her from the clutches of the monster who held her there.

Above, Patric stood watching. He lifted his fingers to his temples and closed his eyes, focusing his intentions for his target. "Now," he said.

Suddenly as Seth darted towards the building, something crashed through the second-floor window landing sure-footed on the sidewalk below. Beryl could see from several yards back the face of her patient, Lana Leighton standing on the sidewalk, quickly transforming into her wolf form.

Salem had seen this as well. With one broad clap of her hands above her head, the sidewalk on either side of Lana rose up, as if hinged on either side, and slammed together, smashing Lana between the now exploding rubble. Seth sidestepped the onslaught of flying stone and rock from the explosion. He jumped through the door of the building and bounded up the stairs. Lana, bloodied, battered—but still alive, and now enraged, stood heaving in place, staring murderously at Salem. Salem watched Lana's face; it appeared to be deliberating. Lana's monstrous eyes wanted revenge on the witch for injuring her, but her master's command was more powerful—stop Seth. She dashed inside the building after him, leaving Salem unharmed, for now.

Salem ran forward after Lana, freezing some wolves and dodging others, as well as blowing one or two up into a fiery burst. Others, too far away to blow up or freeze, she sent tumbling down the street out of her way with the wave of an arm. Arielle followed Salem's footsteps, using the cleared path laid before her to get to, and back up her sister.

In the street, the wolves not killed by birds were coming full force at the rest of the Blanchards. Fable turned to see poor old Zelda, wolf on her back, being ripped to shreds. Fable directed what birds were still around to aid the poor woman. Down the street, Fable's next line of defense was heading her way as every free dog in the surrounding area came racing forward through the city blocks to assist in the fight. Dogs leapt onto wolves, occupying and distracting them from their murderous attempts on the Blanchards.

Olympia raced to her friend and waved her hand, sending the wolf attacking Zelda flying through the plate glass window of the cigar shop. The flight of birds darted through the dangling shards of the window frame, all after the wolf now laying on the cigar shop floor. Beryl moved quickly to Zelda and began healing her mortal wounds.

Artemis took out six wolves with two parked delivery vans which she pulled into action by envisioning them driving over every wolf in their path. Demitra now brandished the acid tank and hose she'd withdrawn from the trunk of her car. The fact that she had no active power to assist in battles did not stop her from reducing wolves to mush with the squeeze of the trigger.

Inside the loft, Yasmine was pleading with Patric to stop the attacks on her family. "Please Ollie, stop all this. They can help you. They can help you overcome this. The Blanchards can stop your suffering."

"Suffering?!" he bellowed. "I'm not suffering. Do you not comprehend the power I wield? I am one of the strongest creatures this earth has ever known!"

"But you're a killer Ollie."

"Even that is breathtaking!" he said. He was frightening her now. Gone was the safety she had felt in his presence earlier. Now her brother was the ruthless killer he had been that night at Blanchard House. "Do you know what real power is, Yasmina? To hold someone's life in your very hands. To watch them plead, scream, cry, beg for your mercy... and then not give it to them. It is ecstasy."

Yasmine started backing away from him. Backing her body against the wall, trying to place as much distance as she could between herself and the monster she saw before her. "Seth!" she screamed.

"You are mine!" Patric roared, bounding forward onto his now transforming haunches, transitioning mid leap into the ferocious creature inside. Yasmine saw the wiry fur burst forth from her brother's flesh; his nose twist and contort into a dark shiny snout; his skeletal form morphing into the broad, powerful beast he really was. The wolf grabbed her wrists, thrusting her forward into him. "You are mine! You are coming with me. But first I will make sure you will never be one of them. You will be like me!" He opened his jaws to show her his sharp, deadly fangs.

"Patric, no!" she shrieked.

His eyes changed momentarily. Their fury turned to hurt. "So, it's Patric now. Not Ollie," he snarled.

"Ollie wouldn't hurt me," she said. "Patric is evil!"

Patric swiped at her face, gashing it deep, sending her hurtling into the table she had awakened on. He pounced forward again. She dodged him, diving under the table and standing suddenly with it, knocking him back into the wall as she whipped it around to protect her body from his reach. He swiped at the table with his paw and sent it flying out of her grip. He crept closer, backing her steadily against the brick wall. He gripped her shoulders, digging his razor claws into her flesh and piercing her shoulder blades as he pinned her to the wall. His jaws inched closer to her neck. Yasmine knew it was all over now. This was the end. She screamed one final scream.

CHAPTER FIFTY-SIX

The Calvary

Seth bounded through the door, panting from the flights of stairs he had just raced up. He thrust his hand forward summoning a powerful gust of wind from the broken window to pound into Patric's back. It did nothing. It did not even budge him. Seth could see Yasmine's terrified face twisting over Patric's shoulders, trying with all her might to avoid the deadly teeth now almost at her throat. Seth sprang forward and jumped Patric, punching the monster in his back as hard as he could. Seth held tight despite Patric's thrashing around. Seth knew if he let go of the monster, Yasmine was sure to be bitten. The effort succeeded in pulling Patric away from Yasmine, but it did little to subdue him. Patric swiped his paw behind himself and grabbed Seth by the side, digging his talons into Seth's abdomen and lifting him off. With Patric's other arm he sliced Seth down the back. Yasmine screamed as Seth, flayed and bleeding profusely, stumbled backwards and fell to the floor. His sliced muscles exposed as he writhed in agony.

Lana sprang through the door and raced toward Seth's body as Seth tried, with much effort, to stand again. Salem came next, followed by Arielle. Salem froze Lana in place but watched horrified as the female wolf slowly began to twitch herself loose of the spell. Before she'd completely freed herself, Salem shouted to her sister.

"Arielle! The bricks! Like washing the windows!"

Arielle understood right away and focused her power on the walls around. Their decades old mortar was loose, and it was easy. One at a time, bricks began to loosen from their hold in the wall and flew like bullets directly into Lana Leighton's wolf form. Freed from one spell, Lana was powerless to attack Seth as she found herself preoccupied with dodging bricks or winching from the blows as dozens sailed directly at her from across the room.

Patrick turned his attention back to Yasmine. If he could just bite her, there would be nothing the witches could do to save her. She would be his again, forever. He lurched forward and grabbed his sister by the throat with his paw, dragging her across the room like a rag doll as he stood on his powerful hind legs.

Instinctively Seth, outstretched his arms and leaned back, attempting to summon something greater than he had ever summoned before. He teetered clumsily from the dizzying pain of the exposed sinew and tissue of his torn back, but he managed to stay upright. From outside a thunderous roar surged overhead, it shook the building. Without warning the six windows surrounding the room lighted in a flash of white as bolts of lightning exploded forth through them, all striking Patric's chest. Patric stumbled backward, falling to the floor, his grip on Yasmine released. Yasmine lay on the ground still flinching from the surge of electricity she'd endured.

Suddenly the street-facing wall exploded outward, sending the remaining bricks which had not been pulled out from Arielle's spell, splintering out into the street. In the void where the wall had been removed, hovered Olympia, Zelda, Demitra, and Beryl. Olympia's arms still open from where she had blown the wall out, the four of them stood atop a van. On the broken sidewalk below stood Artemis, holding them in place with her power. Fable stood nearby protecting Artemis from the few remaining wolves stalking. Fable was busy directing her army of birds and dogs, now assisted by dozens of neighborhood cats, opossums, and rats—all attacking the remaining wolves below. Try as the wolves might to reach Artemis, the siege they were under from Fable's friends proved too encompassing.

"Beryl! Heal Yaz!" Seth commanded as Beryl took a giant leap from the van into the building, racing forward to her cousin. Yasmine still lay tremoring from the violent flow of electricity that had been conducted into her by Patric's grip. Patric, not human, was already righting himself, ready to strike again.

"How do we kill him?" Zelda screamed.

"Haven't you learned by now?" Patric growled. "A werewolf is ridiculously hard to kill. Now watch Yasmina, as I rip your fake family apart. Only then can we be together, united as brother and sister again."

"United," Arielle said.

Salem turned, "What?"

Arielle's face beamed. "United!"

Salem understood her sister's meaning. "And *united together*!" Salem cried. "Seth, grab Arielle's hand!"

Seth stumbled forward and clasped hands with Arielle. Salem grabbed her brother's other hand and the three of them stood together facing Patric.

"Now!" Salem screamed.

In unison she and Arielle both lifted their free hands and directed them towards each other across Seth. An unseen power surged from each towards the other, linking, cycling through the three of them, amplified by the presence of Seth gripped between them. Arielle and Salem could feel the force intensifying and once it reached an unstoppable level both sisters instinctively swept their arms back, as if mimicking a parting motion. Instantly a torrent of energy burst from the bodies of Arielle, Seth, and Salem and pounded into Patric, tearing his body into pieces. Before all their eyes he was ripped apart at the seams. His arms broke away. His head tore off as his legs shredded from his torso, flying into the back wall. Patric lay in bloody mangled tatters on the floor. He did not move. His eyes were closed. He was dead.

Behind them came a gasp. Lana stood dumbstruck at the sight before her. The three siblings whirled around and presented her with the same end. Yasmine, wobbly and shaken, assisted by Beryl's steadying arm, stood up to see the foul sight before her. The floor of the loft was strewn in body parts, tissue, and organs drenched in oceans of blood. The werewolves were dead.

Yasmine caught her breath as the realization of everything set in. She looked over at Seth, still standing with his sisters purveying the carnage they'd inflicted. His eyes met Yasmine's and he was snapped back to reality. Her eyes were awash with anguish, relief, and shock. Slowly she reached her trembling arms out in desperate need of his strength. Seth dashed to her, sweeping her up into his embrace, burying his face into her neck where her hair tickled his nose. Yasmine went limp in his strong arms knowing that she could be weak now, and he would not let her go. Seeing Seth's exposed, tattered back, Beryl rushed to the embracing couple and began healing Seth from behind. He never let go of Yasmine. Beryl finished the job and stepped away, giving them their space. Everyone gave them their space. Their privacy. Time to breathe. Time to savor the victory their love just won. Seth Blanchard held his beloved, neither saying a word, and nothing else but the two of them existed.

CHAPTER FIFTY-SEVEN

The Light of Morning

Good vibrations were flowing through all of the twenty-three rooms of Blanchard House. Artemis was in the kitchen whipping up a breakfast to end all breakfasts. They had been through a lot the night before…a lot didn't even begin to describe it. But a new day had risen to wash away the horrors of the night before. No one had been certain they would have survived it, but they did.

There was some concern in Artemis' mind about where things stood this morning. It was supposed to be Seth and Yasmine's wedding day, but she now had her doubts as to whether that would remain the case. Yasmine had suffered greatly last night. Would she be recovered enough to go on with the plan? Then again, it was Halloween. The most special and precious day of the year for their family. Perhaps it would heal the hurts from the day before.

"Happy Halloween!" Demitra called coming down the stairs in her nightgown and bathrobe.

"Same to you. Did you sleep at all?"

"Not much," Demitra confided.

A ring sounded from Demitra's robe pocket. She withdrew her phone and made a face at her sister. Charlie Bennet was calling.

"Hi, Charlie," Demitra answered.

"Have you turned on the news this morning?" Charlie chided loudly on the other end. "Everyone is trying to understand how a tornado hit Tuscaloosa last night and only damaged one building and one other shop window. And of course, why there was such a collection of dead wolves, dogs, cats, and birds strewn around."

"I just got out of bed," Demitra told him. "I haven't seen anything yet."

"I suppose you know nothing about it?"

"Let's just say your case is closed now," Demitra assured him. "The killer has been neutralized."

"Do I need to know any details or can I trust there'll be no repercussions from whatever went on?"

"Everything is fine now Charlie. Daihmler is safe."

She ended the call and shook her head at her sister.

"Poor Charlie," Artemis said. "He always gets the job of covering up the mess."

"I'm not too worried about Charlie Bennet, right now," Demitra confided. "I'm more concerned about Yasmine. I wonder if we'll have a wedding today after all."

...

Upstairs, Yasmine sat on the edge of the bed staring down to the floor. Seth sat beside her, his arm lovingly around her shoulder. She had spent the morning crying, but now the tears were dry and she sat reflecting on what to do. The birds outside were chirping and the sun was rising. It was a new day, but it did little to dispel the events of the night before.

"I still can't believe Patric was my brother all along," she said. "And there was a moment last night when he had me in that loft...Seth, he was so gentle. For a moment, for just a moment, I loved him. He was my brother again. Then, then he just turned."

Seth took her hand in his own, "Yaz, it's okay if you love him somewhere inside. The brother you knew did exist somewhere in that guy we had to kill last night. It wasn't his fault he became what he became. I think both things are true. We killed a monster last night, and you lost your brother all over again. It's okay to mourn that."

She leaned her head on his shoulder. It was a lot to think about. Too much to process at one time. It would take her months to make heads or tails of everything she'd learned in the last twenty-four hours. Too much to worry about now. This was her wedding day.

Seeming to read her mind, Seth said, "We don't have to do this today. We can get married later. Maybe Thanksgiving?"

"Trying to back out?" she said with a brow raise.

"Never," Seth declared. "I already knew I loved you, but last night just proved beyond any doubt that I cannot live without you."

"I could tell by the way you electrocuted me," she laughed.

"Hey! I was desperate. I had to get him off you before he bit you."

"I know," she replied. "You saved me."

Seth kissed her softly. "So...wanna marry your brave hero today?"

...

Fable sat alone in her room, still shaken by the night before. She felt such sympathy for Yasmine. To discover that the killer stalking Daihmler was actually her own long-lost brother. It was devastating. Fable understood a little of what she must be feeling. It hadn't been a happy surprise to discover her boyfriend was that very same killer. Of course, now Fable realized she had never meant anything to Patric, not really. She was just a pawn in his advance towards capturing the Queen, and Daihmler had been the chess board. So many lives lost, so much damage done.

Fable put her hands to her stomach. *And I still have this thing. A piece of Patric still lives.* She knew she should say something to the family. It was irresponsible not to. Yet something inside Fable could not do it. She couldn't betray her child like that. The family would insist she abort. After all no one could have any reasonable idea what kind of monster this baby might turn out to be. But what if it wasn't a monster? Fable was human. Patric had been human once. Did anyone really know if werewolves could be born? What if a werewolf could only be made from the bite of another wolf? Her child might be human despite his paternity. There was too much to consider, and Fable needed time to consider everything. Patric was gone, and he had not loved her. She wasn't even sure if she'd even loved him. But this baby was a different story. This baby was a part of her, too. Perhaps the only chance she would ever have to be a mother. She did not know what she was going to do, but she did know now was not the time to let anyone else in on her secret.

CHAPTER FIFTY-EIGHT

The Witch Takes a Wife

A tapestry of golds and oranges clinging to the limbs of the many trees surrounded the gazebo. Two symmetrical rows of jubilantly carved jack-o'-lanterns stretched from the gazebo steps all the way to the front porch and all along the banisters of both. With the aid of Artemis's concentration, two ropes woven completely with black eyed Susan's, sunflowers, and yellow snapdragons hovered above the pumpkin lined path. This was the bride's walk, the walk she had waited her lifetime to make.

Seth stood under the wood-tiled roof of the gazebo, fidgeting nervously until Jasont'e Barstow nudged him to be still. Jason'te, member of the Council of Witches, was also a resident of nearby Birmingham and had come down to officiate the ceremony as a favor to Olympia.

Four stone benches in front of the gazebo, two on the left, two on the right, were in place to house the family of the bride and groom. Being both a part of the same family made things difficult to split, but it was decided that Olympia and the aunts would sit on the first bench of Seth's side, with Salem and Arielle on the second row. On Yasmine's side would house Howard, Zelda, Fable, Beryl, and Queen Ursula. Placed on the borders of the gazebo steps were picture frames housing photos of Sinclair, David, Michael, Larry, and Seth's biological grandfather John Windham. At the edge of the gathering sat Jason'te's daughter Brenda, playing a harp.

As the calm, cool breeze blew past, sweeping up fallen leaves here and there, the harpist began to play as Yasmine appeared on the porch steps. Howard stood beside her, beaming with pride as if she were his very own daughter. Behind them fluttered the shadow.

"This is it, Nacaria," Yasmine whispered. "You're about to be my mother-in-law."

Nacaria's silhouetted hand outstretched along the plank board wall. Yasmine pressed her own against it. For a moment it felt like a blessing from the unseen guest. Yasmine kissed the wall where the shadow's cheek might have been.

Seth took one look at his bride on the porch and told himself that he should never forget this moment. Never forget how beautiful she looked. Yasmine had always been pretty in his eyes, even when she was his irritating pest of a cousin, but this woman standing on the back porch about to walk down the aisle to marry him—this woman was exquisite. Salem had wrapped her hair in bright pastel flowers. Olympia had made a veil to match the wedding dress. The lace of the veil matched the intricate lace overlay of the silky white dress. Yasmine looked so different. He looked at her with a pride he had never felt before. It was then when Seth realized this marriage was more than a uniting of their hearts, it was also a cleansing of who they had been to one another in the past and a redefining of what they would be moving forward. This was his wife.

Yasmine made her way across the yard, guided by Howard. They reached the path flanked with jack-o-lanterns and the hovering cords of flowers. Slowly they walked the aisle as guests looked on, taking in the breathtaking sight of her. At the end of the aisle Howard declared his giving of Yasmine in marriage to Seth and took his seat up front. Seth and Yasmine faced Jason'te and took their vows.

"Yasmine, I promise to love you, cherish you, remain faithful in body and mind to you. I will stand in front of you in times of trouble and behind you in times of encouragement. I looked for love in a lot of places in my life. Imagine how surprised I was to learn that I only had to turn around to find it. It was standing beside me the whole time."

Yasmine's vows were simple, "I have loved only once, with my entire soul, for all of my life."

"May all the elements, Earth, Air, Fire, Water bond these two together for the rest of time. It is the Natural Order of things for life to flourish. Love is one of the greatest lifeforms there are. May the love these two young people share encompass them for all time."

Seth kissed his bride to the cheers of all those around.

"I present to you," Jason'te announced. "Mr. and Mrs. Seth Blanchard. Blessed be."

Guests wandered around the lawns of Blanchard House partaking of the delicious spread Artemis, and her workers from the restaurant, had prepared. It was a perfect afternoon. Olympia took solace in the knowledge that her grandson had chosen well for his mate. Salem stood watching her brother and new sister-in-law laugh together as they crammed cake into each other's mouths. David would have enjoyed seeing Seth so happy. The thought comforted her rather than making her sad. A lot of changes had come over the last several months. She had lost family, and she'd gained family. She turned to look at everyone she loved mingling before the house. It was then when she observed the shadow on the back porch. Her mother's shadow. It seemed to be waving. *Who is she waving at?*

The wind blew Salem's auburn strands over her face. She lifted a hand to swipe them away, turning out of the direction of the breeze. It was then she saw. Saw what her mother's spirit was most likely waving towards. He was standing in the field, far away from the lawn of the house. Only Salem saw him, and perhaps Nacaria. Xander Obreiggon was there, watching from the field. He had come to see the wedding. Salem felt a lump come up in her throat. A deep sadness crept up as she watched their father standing alone, uninvited but unable to miss such an important milestone. It then occurred to Salem that this might not be the only time Xander Obreiggon had done this. How many moments of importance had he witnessed from a respectful distance? Had he also seen her get married all those years ago? Had he popped into the hospital nursery to look down upon his only grandson when Michael was born? Her father possessed the ability to will himself to any destination he desired by mere thought. She smiled at the idea that perhaps her father had never been such a stranger to their lives after all.

Salem turned to signal Arielle to join her but was happy to see Arielle already walking her way, with Seth in tow, holding her hand. They had seen him too. They joined Salem at the edge of the lawn. The three siblings looked out across the field at their father. Arielle raised her hand to throw a kiss she'd blown him. Xander reached up to catch it in his hand. Lowering his arm back to his side, he simply stood there, watching his children.

Arielle laid her head on Seth's shoulder and squeezed his arm with her fingers, "He came to see his only son get married."

Seth Blanchard continued to stare ahead, watching the man in the field. His father. Their father. Seth wrapped his arms around both of his sisters and smiled Xander's way. It was much too great a distance for his father to see, but somehow Seth knew his father was smiling back. Smiling at the sight of his three children together. Seth, Salem, and Arielle remained in place, arm in arm, staring across the field until their father evaporated into the breeze, back to the world he belonged to, leaving them to theirs.

ABOUT THE AUTHOR

Micah House lives in Birmingham Alabama. He is a former columnist for two Birmingham magazines. He has written two short stories, *Thursie and The Three Mrs. Rogers*, appearing in the compilation book *It Was a Dark and Stormy Night*. *The Blanchard Witches of Daihmler County* is his debut novel and the first of an ongoing series, which to-date includes *The Blanchard Witches: Prodigal Daughters* and *The Blanchard Witches: Stitches In Time*.

BOOK 2 SYNOPSIS

THE BLANCHARD WITCHES
: PRODIGAL DAUGHTERS

Welcome back to Daihmler County, Alabama. Come sit on Blanchard House porch and visit a spell, but don't get too cozy. The Autumn leaves aren't the only things changing as more problems emerge for the Blanchard witches. One of Olympia's daughters is missing, and the family must figure out why. Another daughter has herself a new beau, but he isn't who he appears to be. And Fable continues to conceal her secret pregnancy not knowing what the family will do if they discover her baby was fathered by the werewolf they recently destroyed. While the love that fills Blanchard House may be magical, that love will be tested by secrets and new dangers in this second installment of the Blanchard Witches series.